ADVANCE PRAISE

"The sinking of the passenger liner *Athenia* is a gripping story. In *Without Warning*, Tom Sanger brings this tragedy to life and makes it personal. As a reader, you share the fear and the anxiety with the survivors. This is an amazing story about how the Second World War began."

—FRANCIS CARROLL, Professor Emeritus, Manitoba University, and author of *Athenia Torpedoed*

"*Without Warning* brings to life a little-known episode of World War II and celebrates the human capacity to endure under the most harrowing circumstances."

—ROSEMARY BURSTALL, *Athenia* survivor

"An exciting read told from actual survivors' perspectives."

—GEOFF ETHERINGTON, *Athenia* survivor

WITHOUT WARNING

THOMAS C. SANGER

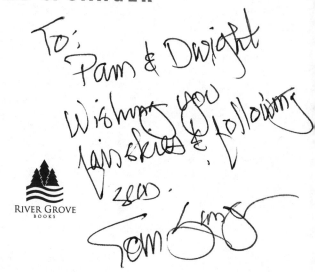

RIVER GROVE
BOOKS

This is a work of fiction. Although most of the characters, organizations, and events portrayed in this novel are based on actual historical counterparts, the dialogue and thoughts of these characters are products of the author's imagination.

Published by River Grove Books
Austin, TX
www.rivergrovebooks.com

Distributed by River Grove Books

Design and composition by Greenleaf Book Group and Kim Lance
Cover design by Greenleaf Book Group and Kim Lance
Cover design concept by Monkey C Media, www.monkeyCmedia.com

Cataloging-in-Publication data is available.

Print ISBN: 978-1-63299-141-6

eBook ISBN: 978-1-63299-142-3

First Edition

FOR RHODA, WHO inspired this story, and for Kay, who never stopped believing in it.

AUTHOR'S NOTE

MY GRANDMOTHER, RHODA THOMAS, was a passenger on the British ship *Athenia* when it was torpedoed and sunk in the opening days of World War II. She survived the attack, returned home, and wrote a vivid account of her experiences, which became my inspiration for this book.

Without Warning is a work of historical fiction. Although the story is based on actual people and events, I have imagined characters' thoughts, conversations, and motivations, as well as scenes that may or may not have taken place. In researching the book, I read dozens of eyewitness accounts, met with five *Athenia* survivors, and interviewed the descendants of four of the book's main characters. Readers should understand that my portrayal of all these characters is intended to serve the story's dramatic arc and may not reflect their actual personalities.

Where eyewitness accounts differ, I invented circumstances to explain these differing views or chose the one that best served my story's dramatic purpose. I have also taken the liberty of changing the timing of certain events, though not the events themselves.

The *Athenia* tragedy is largely unknown today, despite the fact that she was the first ship sunk in the Atlantic Ocean by a German submarine in World War II. My purpose in writing this novel is to bring these events to life and honor the quiet sacrifice and heroism displayed by the men, women, and children who unexpectedly found themselves in harm's way on September 3, 1939.

—THOMAS C. SANGER, 2017

PRINCIPAL CHARACTERS

BARBARA CASS-BEGGS is a music teacher and choir director travelling to Canada with her husband, David, and their three-year-old daughter, Rosemary. The three Britons plan to live there for a year while David lectures in electrical engineering at the University of Toronto.

BARNET COPLAND is chief officer and second-in-command of *Athenia*. The thirty-two-year-old native of Glasgow, Scotland, is unmarried and has served in the Merchant Navy for seventeen years.

RUTH ETHERINGTON is returning home with her husband, Harold, and their ten-year-old son, Geoffrey, after visiting relatives in the British Isles. All three were born in Great Britain but have lived in the United States for nine years. Harold recently became a US citizen.

JUDITH EVELYN is an actress returning home to Canada with her friend and former fiancé, Andrew Allan, a radio producer, and his father, the Reverend William Allan.

DAVIDSON "DAVID" JENNINGS is concluding a vacation in the British Isles with friends Hamilton "Tony" Cassels and John Woods. The three Canadians are returning to complete their studies at the University of Toronto.

SPIRYDON KUCHARCZUK is a farmer emigrating from eastern Poland to Canada with his wife, Ewdokia, and their five children.

FRITZ-JULIUS LEMP, at age twenty-six, is one of the youngest commanders in the German Navy's submarine fleet. An eight-year navy veteran, he is single and the son of a German army officer.

RHODA THOMAS is a grandmother traveling alone to visit friends and family in southwestern England, where she was born. She is returning to America where she and her husband, Frank, have lived for twenty-five years. Both are naturalized US citizens.

PART I

DEPARTURE

Article 22, 1930 Treaty of London

1. *In their action with regard to merchant ships, submarines must conform to the rules of international law to which surface vessels are subject.*

2. *In particular, except in the case of persistent refusal to stop on being duly summoned, or of active resistance to visit or search, a warship, whether surface vessel or submarine, may not sink or render incapable of navigation a merchant vessel without having first placed passengers, crew, and ship's papers in a place of safety. For this purpose the ship's boats are not regarded as a place of safety unless the safety of the passengers and crew is assured, in the existing sea and weather conditions, by the proximity of land, or the presence of another vessel, which is in a position to take them on board.*

—LONDON SUBMARINE PROTOCOL OF 1936

(A DISTANT ECHO of the "Prize Rules" that governed warfare in the age of sail, the 1936 protocol declared Article 22 of the 1930 treaty remained in force, and its terms were agreed to by thirty-five nations, including Germany.)

SUNDAY 7:38 P.M., SEPTEMBER 3, 1939

Oberleutnant Lemp

FRITZ-JULIUS LEMP TRACKED the approaching ship in his submarine's periscope. It had become a silhouette barely distinguishable against the darkening twilight sky, but Lemp was close enough to see the foaming white wave thrown up by its bow. He smiled when the spray arched higher, signaling the ship had begun changing course again.

"You're right on schedule," he said to the image in his eyepiece.

Lemp's pulse quickened with the knowledge that his war was about to begin. He called out the data that would guide his first salvo—the target's speed, distance, and course relative to his own. His second watch officer fed the details into the submarine's targeting device that electronically relayed a final course to the waiting torpedoes.

Lowering the scope to avoid detection, Lemp tamped down his eagerness and let a minute tick by. When he raised the scope again, the big ship was exactly where he expected it to be. He curled his fingers around the upright firing lever.

"Tube one, fire," he barked into the speaking tube and pulled back on the lever.

A muffled *whoosh* sounded through the submarine's hull, signaling the torpedo and its six hundred pounds of high explosives had left the tube on its way to the target.

Chief Officer Copland

ABOARD THE BRITISH passenger ship *Athenia*, white-jacketed stewards moved among the tables in the ornate, domed dining saloon reserved for cabin-class passengers. Seated at a round table with six other guests, the ship's chief officer, Barnet Copland, ordered the curried chicken and resumed his conversation with an older woman to his right.

"To answer your question, Mrs. Penney, we are two hundred fifty miles northwest of Ireland." Copland leaned closer and lowered his voice. "I trust you won't relay that information to the German Navy."

"My lips are sealed," Mrs. Penney said. "Seriously, do you think we are out of danger?"

"I'd say we are fairly—"

A jarring crash shook the room. Copland leaned into the table for support as passengers screamed. Dishes rattled, stemware toppled, the lights blinked and went out. In the dark, he felt the room begin to tilt.

"Are you alright, Mrs. Penney?" The flickering light of matches struck by nearby diners illuminated the woman, who remained seated next to him.

"What in God's name was that?" she said.

Copland came to his feet. He ignored the question, intent on determining the extent of damage caused by the crash. Instinct told him it had occurred toward the stern on the port side.

Moving aft, he entered the galley and heard men shouting over the hiss of escaping steam. Copland inched along the bulkhead until he found the service stairway and used the banister to haul himself up. After climbing two flights of stairs, he exited and headed down a carpeted hallway as quickly as he dared in the dark. Distant clanging bells told him *Athenia*'s watertight doors were closing.

The sickening realization washed over Copland that the ship's hull had been breached, and he broke into a run.

JUNE 1939

Chief Officer Copland

THE CROW'S NEST public house sat at the end of a row of shops across from the gray stone warehouses of Glasgow's busy waterfront. Barnet Copland entered the pub and was met by the din of shouted conversations and the mingled aroma of tobacco smoke and stale beer. He searched the crowd for his friend and fellow Merchant Navy officer, Gordon Dunbar. When he saw Gordon's rangy figure waving to him from across the room, Copland shouldered his way through the crowd to greet his friend and sit next to him on the maroon leather banquette.

"You're looking quite sleek," Gordon said, leaning in to be heard over the noonday clientele at the bar. "Ferrying passengers across the Atlantic must agree with you."

"It's the food, Gordy. We eat better than you poor donkeys hauling cargo. You should think about a transfer."

"God no," Gordon said, waving his hands. "I don't fancy working with any cargo that can talk back to me. Besides, you shouldn't be so smug about your passenger trade."

"And why is that?"

"There's some American company starting what they call 'air passenger service' from New York to London. It's only a matter of time before your passengers will fly right over your head, taking a day to cross the ocean instead of a week."

"Go on with you. The aeroplane will never replace the comfort of an ocean voyage."

"Times change, Barty. You've got to change with them."

Copland ignored the gentle jibe and went to the bar to order their drinks. When he returned, he placed a dark amber pint of Younger's Ale on the small table they shared.

"Where's yours?" Gordon asked.

"It's coming," Copland said. "Tell me, what do you hear from the Royal Navy? Will they take you up?"

Gordon shook his head. "I haven't heard a thing," he said. "The Admiralty says it's going to arm a few merchant ships as a precaution. If they do they'll likely call back officers with experience in fighting ships. I'm thinking unless Mr. Hitler does something really stupid, I won't be called."

A signal from the barman interrupted their conversation and Copland went to collect his order. He returned with a pot of tea and a china mug.

"You're not drinking?" Gordon asked.

"We sail in two days, so I've cut myself off."

"Seems a bit extreme. When did you start this routine?"

"A few years ago," Copland said, pouring himself a steaming cup of black tea. "Don't look so worried. It's only when I'm working."

"Aye, but I do worry. You're always with your head down, buried in your work. It's not healthy, Barty." Gordon took a gulp of ale and licked the foam off his upper lip.

"This is your fault, you know," Copland said. "You're the reason I became an officer. Can I help it if I love my work?"

"But do you have to be so intense about it?"

Gordon wasn't the first person to express concern about his driven work habits. In truth, Copland was unsure if his love of the sea had inspired him to work hard or his hard work had led to his love of the sea. The two elements were so intertwined in his mind he could no longer separate them.

"My intensity only makes me a better officer. What's wrong with that?" he said, taking a sip of tea.

"All I'm saying is you need to apply some of that intensity to the other parts of your life."

"Now you sound like my ma."

"Maybe you should listen to her. You travel all over the world, Barty, but do you see what's in it?"

"When did you become such a philosopher?"

Gordon fixed him with a steady gaze. "When I realized a good friend of mine was missing so much of what life has to offer."

For a moment, Copland recalled a bright summer day and the image of a young woman walking away while he sat pinned to a park bench by the words she had spoken, words that still wounded after four years: *"I'm sorry, Barty, but I can't wait any longer for you to establish your career. I truly hope you find what you're looking for."*

The intensity of the memory surprised and unsettled him. Was Gordy right? No, he would not allow himself to believe the sacrifices he'd made for his career were too costly. But this was not something Copland wanted to discuss. Clearly, he needed to end their conversation or he risked saying something regrettable. He glanced at his watch without seeing the time.

"Gordy, I have to get back to the ship. I didn't realize it was so late." He stood and started buttoning his dark-blue cardigan.

"But we haven't eaten yet," Gordon protested.

"I know. I've a busy schedule. It was a mistake to try to squeeze in this lunch."

Gordon cocked his head and sat back into the padded banquette. "You haven't heard a word I've said, have you?"

"Of course I have. I'm too wrapped up in my work. I know that, but I wouldn't know how to change even if I wanted to." Copland shook Gordon's hand. "Sorry, but I have to go."

"Mark my words, Barty. If war comes, your future may be very different from the one you have planned."

"I'll ring you when I come back next month." He turned and was out the door before his friend could say another word.

THOMAS C. SANGER

Spirydon Kucharczuk

BY TEN O'CLOCK in the morning, the sun beating down on Trosteniec's town square had become oppressive. As he walked in search of the fortune-teller's street, Spirydon felt the air's humid closeness and wondered if it held the possibility of an afternoon shower for his thirsty pasture. His dusty boots clopped along the cobblestones, adding to the clatter of horse-drawn carts, the rumble of an automobile, and the shouts of boys playing in the square. After twenty years, these were familiar sights and sounds, and he would miss them once he and his family left this little market town in eastern Poland for Canada.

"Spiro." A familiar voice interrupted his thoughts, and he looked up to see the butcher beckoning to him.

Spirydon waved and approached the short man who filled the doorway of his shop. "Good morning, Vitaly," he said. "How are you holding up in this heat?"

"Not so good, but at least I'm not going for a walk," the butcher said, wiping his hands on his apron with its rusty offal stains.

"What can I say?" Spirydon shrugged. "I told Ewdokia she shouldn't walk to town in this heat. So here I am."

"Oh Spiro," Vitaly said, shaking his head slowly, "you are too good to that woman. You make it hard for the rest of us. But as long as you're here, tell your wife if she has some eggs tomorrow, we could make a trade."

"I'll let her know." Spirydon turned to resume his errand then turned back. "Have you heard any more about Dr. Goebbels' speech in Danzig last week?"

"Not a thing. You're the one who reads the newspapers."

"Maybe you heard something from your customers?"

Vitaly frowned. "All I hear from them are questions about extending their credit. Why this concern about the Nazis? You're not Jewish. And who believes even half of the stories they tell about how Germans treat their Jews?" He cleared his throat and spit in the gutter.

"I believe them," Spirydon said. "You forget *Kristallnacht*. If they can do that to Jews, they can do it to Poles. And what makes you think the Nazis would be satisfied just with Danzig?"

"Ha," the butcher snorted. "If they come after us, maybe Mother Russia will come to our rescue and we'll all be Ukrainians again."

"I worry about that, too," Spirydon said, turning to go.

"You worry too much, Spiro," Vitaly called after him.

☆ ☆ ☆

SPIRYDON FOUND THE fortune-teller on the second floor of a dreary brick building two blocks off the square. He paused in front of the door, its chipped paint the color of harvested wheat. A practical man, he believed in the things he could see and feel—a straight furrow or the stout handle of an axe. For more abstract matters, he relied on the rituals of the church. But the church did not concern itself with the world of curses and prophecies, which is why he had come to the fortune-teller.

"Enter, please," a woman's voice responded after he finally knocked. Spirydon opened the door to a jumbled room with a pair of windows that looked out on the gray-green wall of another building. Gauzy purple curtains hung from the ceiling, dividing off a portion of the space. Books crowded the room's shelves, along with a few small mounted creatures under bell jars, an animal skull, and a few burning candles that filled the air with a flowery perfume. In the center of it all, the fortune-teller sat in a straight-back chair at a small, round wooden table. She wore a black blouse with a simple gold chain around her neck. Her pleasant, round face and dark eyes were youthful and welcoming.

"Not what you were expecting?" She seemed to read his bewilderment.

"I don't know. I thought you would be older."

"You mustn't judge by appearances alone," the woman said. Her voice was confident and reassuring. She gestured to the chair across the table from her and Spirydon sat down. "Now, what is the reason for your visit?"

"It's my wife. She wants to know if our family is cursed."

The woman shook her head. "I cannot tell you if your family is cursed. I can only tell you about the future. You must decide if it is cursed."

Spirydon thought for a moment. "We plan to travel to Canada," he said. "Can you tell me anything about that?"

"Of course." The woman picked up a well-worn deck of oversized cards from the table, handed the deck to him, and asked him to shuffle the cards. When he concluded, she took back the deck and laid out nine cards face up on the table in front of her. The pictures on the cards were a mystery to Spirydon—a jaunty fellow in a red cape, another holding a golden cup—and he watched the woman as she studied the images.

"You have a large family," she said. He nodded.

She picked up the cards, put them back in the deck, and asked him to shuffle them once more. When he finished, the woman took the deck and laid out another nine cards in the same configuration as before. This time, however, she glanced at the cards, quickly gathered them up with a frown, and stared at the empty table top. Spirydon thought he had done something wrong, but after a long pause the woman looked up at him.

"You will travel to Canada soon," she said, "but not all of your family will arrive with you."

☆ ☆ ☆

"THAT IS WHAT she said?" Ewdokia asked her husband later that evening. "'Not all of your family will arrive with you'?"

"Yes, her exact words," he said as they sat by the vegetable garden at the side of their small wooden farmhouse. Spirydon had carried the chairs outside so they could enjoy the temperate evening and gain some privacy from the children.

"But she didn't say they would never arrive," Ewdokia said. "Perhaps she meant some would come later?"

"She didn't explain," he said, thinking Ewdokia should have gone to the fortune-teller so she could have asked all the questions that hadn't occurred to him.

"Does this mean we are cursed?" she asked. If it weren't for his fear of the German Army, Spirydon would have found it amusing that his sensible wife could be so obsessed about a curse supposedly arranged by her oldest sister over a dispute involving her family's land.

"No," he said with all the conviction he could muster. "I think the fortune-teller meant that Jan will stay here with his political friends rather than come with us to Canada."

"Oh no, Spiro. He must come. He is the oldest. You will need him to help with the new farm."

"That would be nice." Spirydon's wistful tone reflected just how far apart he and Jan had drifted over the last year. "The trouble is he's a dreamer, not a farmer."

"And whose fault is that? You were too lenient with him when he was a boy."

He had to admit there was some truth to Ewdokia's observation. His childhood had been so bleak that he invariably identified with his children whenever they forgot their chores or made a mess. In the end he simply found it easier to leave the discipline to her.

"Right or wrong, I cannot change things now," he said. "I don't want to leave Jan behind any more than you, but what can I do? Every time we talk, we end up in an argument."

Ewdokia folded her arms across her chest. "I am not leaving without all of my children." Her declaration worried him. If he could not convince her to leave, he could not save his family.

"Think about what you're saying," Spirydon said. "Jan is twenty. He's not a boy anymore. He will do what is best for him, and we must do what is best for the family."

"But what happens if the Germans don't come?"

"Evka, this is madness. I tell you they are coming. Either Poland gives the Nazis what they want, or they will come and take it. Sooner or later, we will all be living under Hitler's boot. If you refuse to go, then you are putting all our lives in German hands. Is that what you want?"

"No, but maybe we could wait another month."

"If we are going, we must start planning now," he said. "It took weeks for Niko and your sister to arrange all their travel documents for Canada. And before we can go, we have to sell the farm. That won't be easy with money so scarce."

11

The practical considerations of their journey appeared to weigh on Ewdokia. When she spoke again, she seemed to be arguing with herself.

"How can we just leave Jan behind?"

"We are not leaving him. We are leaving Poland. Whether he stays here or comes with us is up to him." When Ewdokia did not respond, Spirydon offered a final observation. "Every day we put this off brings us a day closer to living under the Nazis."

She stood and turned to look down the rutted dirt road in front of their farm. The chirping of crickets filled the evening air, and he knew her silence meant Ewdokia had accepted his argument. In the fading light, he could not see the small creases that had begun to line her face or the thin strands of silver in her auburn hair that she kept pulled back in a tight bun. Spirydon preferred to see his wife as the beautiful young girl with inquisitive gray eyes who he had loved since the day he arrived in Trosteniec.

"We will tell the children tomorrow," he said. "Jan can decide to stay with his friends or to come with us. Agreed?"

Ewdokia nodded.

AUGUST 1939

Oberleutnant Lemp

THE LATE AFTERNOON sun beat down on the submarine tender *Hecht*, docked at the *Kriegsmarine* base on the Kiel Canal in northern Germany. In the ship's wardroom, Fritz-Julius Lemp waited with fifteen other U-boat captains for the arrival of *Kommodore* Karl Dönitz, the commanding officer of the German Navy's submarine fleet.

Wall-mounted fans in the room labored to provide some relief from the heat, but their droning efforts were subsumed by several animated conversations. Most of the men in the room would sail within twenty-four hours, heading to their waiting zones along the western approaches to the British Isles in anticipation of war with England. Eager to prove himself in the eyes of his older, more experienced fellow commanders, Lemp chafed at the fact that repairs to his ship, *U-30*, would prevent him from being part of this initial group.

Not long after he took command of *U-30* less than a year ago, his boat collided with *U-35* during underwater maneuvers. He had remained calm, assessed the situation, and reacted swiftly, saving his boat and all the men aboard her. Recalling the emotional rush of that emergency only made him more frustrated.

A hand shook Lemp's shoulder and he turned to see Gunther Kuhnke's schoolboy grin. They had been members of the same officer-training class, sailed together on *U-28*, and were promoted to the rank of *oberleutnant* on the same day in 1937.

"So tell me, Fritz, how long do you have to wait for your boat? Are you going to miss the war?"

Lemp shook his head and smiled, hoping to mask his disappointment. "She'll be ready in three days. So don't slow down, Gunther, or I'll be charging right up your ass."

"You're going to be so far behind us you'll be lucky to even see my ass when the shooting starts."

"You think so? How about a bottle of *Schnaps* to the first one of us who sinks a prize?" Before Kuhnke could answer, the door to the passageway swung open.

"Attention!" The order silenced all conversation and brought the men to their feet. The slender figure of Karl Dönitz entered from a side door, wearing a dark-blue navy dress uniform and a high-peaked hat with a gold-braided visor. Everything about the man was sharp edged, from his aquiline nose to the creases of his pants legs. Dönitz raised his right arm in a stiff Nazi salute as he stepped to the plain wooden table at the front of the room. The men responded in unison, raising their arms to return his salute.

"Be seated, gentlemen," Dönitz said, removing his hat and setting it on the table. A thin layer of dark hair topped his high forehead; his close-set brown eyes reminded Lemp of a hawk.

"What I am about to tell you must be kept in strictest confidence." Dönitz paused, and Lemp leaned forward in anticipation.

"The *Führer* has set August twenty-sixth as the day our army will march on Poland." A low murmur swept the room. "It is almost certain that we will be at war with the English before you return from your patrols." Lemp and his colleagues cheered. Dönitz raised his hands calling for silence, leaned against the table, and waited until the room quieted before continuing.

"I must tell you the *Führer* believes there will be a chance, once Poland falls, that the English and French will negotiate peace treaties with us. Many of our leaders think the English will not fight.

"I disagree. I believe they will fight. And if they do, we face long odds at sea. You are all volunteers; the best of the best. You and your crews are well trained, and you are as ready as you can be for this moment. You have the best equipment we can provide. But there are not enough of us to match the English Navy today. In three or four years, perhaps, but not today." The bleak assessment made Lemp even more anxious for his boat to be ready.

"You have one great opportunity," Dönitz continued, "the element of surprise. So, if it is war, you must strike quickly and hit hard." He slammed his fist on the table for emphasis. "Surprise is crucial. We must make them think we are everywhere and in great force. If you succeed, if you draw enough blood, then the English may see the wisdom of signing a treaty with us." Dönitz pushed himself away from the table, and his dark eyes seemed to take Lemp into his confidence.

"For the next few weeks, the future of the Reich may very well be in your hands. You, each of you, must do your duty to the utmost." No one moved. The sound of the droning fans filled the room as Dönitz nodded to them and snatched up his hat.

"*Sieg Heil,*" he said, with another stiff-armed salute. Along with everyone else, Lemp shot to his feet and repeated the phrase, raising his right arm. *Kommodore* Dönitz left the room, and the men let out a collective roar.

"Don't worry, Fritz," Kuhnke said. "I'll leave a few ships for you."

Lemp smiled and poked a finger into his friend's shoulder.

"I don't need your scraps, Gunther. I'll get more than my share. I'm going to show these old men how it's done."

Barbara Cass-Beggs

AT THE SOUND of the front door latch, Barbara stopped making notations on her sheet music. Moments later, her husband, David, walked into the small sitting room that doubled as a joint workspace in their tidy Oxford cottage. A concerned look in his blue eyes told her something had changed, and not for the better.

"Were you able to pick up the tickets?" Barbara asked.

"Yes, but they're not on the *Aurania.*"

"What do you mean?"

David sighed, dropped a thick envelope on the table where she had been working, and settled into the faded green wingback chair near the fireplace. "Our booking's changed to the *Athenia*, leaving from Liverpool in two weeks. The agent said the *Aurania*'s been withdrawn from service. Apparently, the Royal Navy is fitting her with guns."

Barbara set her pencil on the music score and sat back in her chair. She and David followed the news and knew Hitler had demanded that the Free City of Danzig be turned over to Germany and a corridor opened across Poland to connect with East Prussia. Two months ago, when David had accepted the invitation to lecture for a year at the University of Toronto, they had convinced themselves a resolution to this latest crisis was at least eighteen months away, more than enough time for them to go to Canada and return to England. Could the change in ships be giving her husband second thoughts?

"It seemed far worse last year before the Munich Agreement," she said. "Mr. Chamberlain settled things then. He could do it again."

"Yes, but everything feels more urgent now."

"Are you thinking we shouldn't go to Canada?" Barbara addressed her worst fear, hoping to head it off before David made up his mind.

He frowned and ran his fingers through his thick brown hair, as if contemplating the question for the first time.

"The cottage is let for the coming year," he said, "so if we stay, we either turn out our tenant or scramble to find another place to live. I'd be pulling the rug out from under the poor chap who's coming in to teach my classes. Then I'd need to cable the dean in Toronto to let him know I'm not coming. They'd have to find a replacement on short notice."

And I doubt they'd ever offer you another invitation like this, Barbara thought.

David leaned forward and fixed his gaze on Barbara. "What do you want to do, Bar? You had to make arrangements for your students and your choir obligation."

Without offering an answer, she picked up the envelope, felt its satisfying heft, and pulled out the steamship tickets with their promise of a life-changing journey. Barbara thought of their conversations with the Canadian students, Bill and Jim Gibson, who often visited the cottage during their studies at Oxford. They frequently expressed surprise at England's class consciousness, in contrast to Canada's more egalitarian society. The invitation to teach in Toronto was a chance to sample a different life.

"This may be our very best chance to live in a society where we are not defined by parents' pedigree, the school we attended, or the clubs we belong to."

"I dislike this antiquated system as much as you," David said. "But how can we live with ourselves if we go to Canada and England goes to war?"

"How can we live with ourselves if we let this opportunity slip away?" she asked. Barbara's forefinger played along the edge of the tickets' stiff card stock. "Suppose we give up these tickets and war doesn't come for another year, or ever? Mr. Hitler may seem daft at times, but he's no idiot. I can't imagine that he wants to risk a war with England, and very likely France as well."

David leaned forward in his chair. "It's possible all our troop movements and the air defense balloons will give Hitler some pause."

"Yes, put him on his back foot," she said, sensing an opening. "Buy more time for diplomacy." Before David could comment, Barbara added one more point in favor of Canada. "Besides, Rosemary is so excited about sailing on the big ship to Canada and seeing Bill and Jim. It would be a shame to disappoint her."

"I agree, but we can't make this decision based on the desires of a three-year-old."

"Of course not," she said, certain her husband's tone indicated he had resolved the question in favor of Canada.

"If we go," he added, "we ought to make sure we pack away everything from the house that's irreplaceable, just in case something happens."

"Good idea. I'll make a list."

Oberleutnant Lemp

ON THE BRIDGE atop *U-30*'s conning tower, Lemp shivered and closed the top button of his gray leather coat in the predawn air. The lights of

Wilhelmshaven, Germany, his submarine's home base, disappeared behind him an hour ago. Clouds in the east began to brighten. Splashing bow waves nearly drowned out the clatter of the submarine's twin diesel engines, but he could feel their throbbing power through the steel deck beneath his boots.

Three days earlier, fourteen other U-boats left for their waiting stations in the Atlantic waters around Great Britain. With repairs to *U-30* finally completed, Lemp was in a hurry to join them. The previous night, he had met with *Kommodore* Dönitz, who had a few final words of encouragement before Lemp's departure, including the news that Germany and Russia had concluded a non-aggression pact. The treaty would be publicly formalized in Moscow the next day, thus removing the last significant obstacle to Germany's invasion of Poland.

Oberleutnant Hans-Peter Hinsch, *U-30's* first watch officer, clambered up the ladder to the bridge. In the gray dawn, Lemp acknowledged his lanky second-in-command and asked for Hinsch's report.

"Bow and stern tubes are loaded and five eels are stowed in the forward torpedo room," Hinsch said, using the navy slang for torpedoes. "We have two hundred rounds for the deck gun and four thousand for the twenty millimeter, all safely stowed."

"Good," Lemp said. "Let's hope we have a chance to use those eels before we return."

"Do you think the English will fight?" Hinsch cupped a match with his hands to light a cigarette.

"Dönitz thinks so. If it comes, I hope it's soon. We can't stay out as long as the newer boats."

Hinsch nodded, and both men looked toward the wide gray horizon beyond *U-30's* bow. Lemp took a moment to consider the tortuous track he was to take for the next six days. To preserve the element of surprise, he would maintain radio silence as they sailed through the North Sea, up the coast of Norway, and around the Faroe Islands, almost reaching the Arctic Circle before heading to his waiting zone out of the shipping lanes northwest of Ireland. During daylight hours, *U-30* would submerge whenever the lookouts spotted a ship or a plane. The circuitous route offered the least amount of ocean traffic but would cost him precious days in transit, and he saw no way he could arrive at his waiting zone before the army marched into Poland.

"I don't think the English will fight," Hinsch said, picking up the thread of their conversation. He handed his cigarette to Lemp, who filled his lungs with the strong Turkish blend. "They've stepped back every time the *Führer* has taken a step forward. If they were going to fight, they would have done so by now. Besides, Poland will fall before the English can decide what to do."

Lemp took another deep drag off the cigarette. "Hans-Peter, I hope you are wrong."

"Sir?"

"I hope they do fight," Lemp said, exhaling a thin cloud of smoke and handing the cigarette back. "You win honor on the field, not by signing a piece of paper. Dönitz is right. We need to knock those pompous island monkeys back on their heels. Only when they taste their own blood will they deal with us as equals."

"Yes, sir." Hinsch nodded. The two men turned again to look out to sea. In the dawn's flat haze, a slate-gray ocean stretched away ahead of them, its vastness mocking Lemp's sense of urgency.

Rhoda Thomas

IN THE WANING sunshine of a long summer day, Rhoda pushed her chair away from the table in the back garden of her brother's stone house. Albert Fisher, a manager at Clark's shoe factory in the little town of Street in southwest England, had invited his neighbors to come meet his sister, who was visiting from America. As the guest of honor, Rhoda found herself exempted from any chores, so she sat with half a dozen men as they stoked their pipes, rolled up their sleeves, and eased the suspenders off their shoulders, while their wives collected the last of the dishes and serving bowls from the table.

For several weeks, she had enjoyed a series of teas, shopping excursions, and days at the seaside, reconnecting with relatives and friends from her childhood. The idyllic days had allowed Rhoda to forget the Continent's rising political tensions . . . until now. Seated with her brother and the other men, she listened with some concern as the usual social banter turned somber, reflecting on the day's news that Germany and Russia had signed a nonaggression treaty in Moscow. How sad, she thought, that this should be the topic of conversation on such a lovely summer evening.

"It's a stab in the back, by God," offered a middle-aged neighbor who worked at the shoe factory.

"That it is," Albert said. "I can't understand Hitler signing a treaty with Russia, of all countries. The Nazis hate the Reds." Albert reached for his cup of tea and took a small sip before frowning at the liquid that apparently had grown cold.

"Yes, but there it is," said a white-haired pensioner at the far end of the table. The conversation paused, and Rhoda recalled that the elderly gentleman had fought in the Great War. Everyone at the table seemed to wait for his assessment.

"If the Poles don't give Hitler what he wants now, there's nothing to stop him from bloody well marching in and taking it. Oh, sorry about the language, Mrs. Thomas," he said, nodding in her direction. "The point is, lads, we're treaty-bound to stand with the Poles. I think it means war for sure now. I don't see how Mr. Chamberlain can keep us out of this mess, without going back on our word. And how would we live with ourselves then?"

"But I can't believe anyone wants to go to war again so soon," Albert said. "Surely the Germans have the same ghastly memories of the Great War as we do."

"How can the German people continue to put up with this clown for a chancellor?" the first neighbor said. "They've got to get rid of him now. That's the only way we can all avoid a war."

"And if they don't?" asked the pensioner.

"Ah, we've been coddling that bugger for too long," spat one of the younger neighbors. "If he wants a war, I say we give it to him. We've got the greatest army and the greatest navy in the world. If we just stop backing down all the time and stand up to him, he might decide he don't need another strip of land."

"If it comes to war, what about America? Where does she stand?" someone asked. All eyes turned to Rhoda.

"Dear me, I certainly don't know the answer to that," she said. Then, hoping to sound a little more informed, she added, "We've got our own troubles, you know. Still so many people out of work and families going hungry."

"We're all in that same boat now, ain't we?" observed the younger neighbor.

"I sympathize," Rhoda said. "Really I do. You know my heart's with all of you. But a lot of people think we should just keep to ourselves and not get involved in Europe's arguments. The newspapers all say there's no sentiment for war. I do pray it doesn't come down to that again."

"Now, gentlemen, my sister-in-law's no bleedin' American diplomat."

Albert's wife, Flora, came through the kitchen door carrying a pot of hot tea. "Where does America stand?" she mimicked. "Honestly, you'd think she were having daily correspondence with Mr. Roosevelt."

The mood of the evening brightened as several of the wives trailed out of the house behind Flora.

"Did you know," Flora said, changing the subject and addressing no one in particular, "Rhoda's daughter just married a boy in America whose father come from Street?"

"Would I know the father, Flo?" asked the pensioner.

"Indeed, you would," Albert said. "He's Bert Sanger. Went off to America the same year as Frank and Rhoda."

"Charlie Sanger's son? Oh I knew Charlie when he were foreman at Clarks—"

"Hold on a minute," Albert interrupted, raising his hand. A neighbor lady had appeared at the side gate, a worried expression clouding her face. Rhoda remembered Flora saying that the woman's husband had not been feeling well.

"Oh, Flo, I'm sorry to interrupt," she said.

"What is it Mary? Is Davey all right?"

"It's nothing to do with Davey. I just come to tell your Rhoda that we heard on the wireless all American travelers in England are being told to return home as soon as possible. They say there's going to be a war."

Spirydon Kucharczuk

A PATCHWORK PANORAMA of green and brown pastures stitched together with hedgerows rolled past the train window, but Spirydon found the pastoral scene disquieting. Traveling with his family on the first leg of their journey to Canada, he was keenly aware they had entered Germany and were approaching their first stop in the Nazi Third Reich. No reason to worry, he told himself. The German authorities had checked their papers at the border and found everything in order. It would take thirty-six hours to cross Germany on the way to Antwerp—thirty-six hours during which they would be subject to the caprices of every Nazi official they met.

We must make ourselves as invisible as possible.

Spirydon turned to check the other family members seated in the rows behind him. He smiled at Ewdokia, who held Jakeb, their two-year-old son, on her lap. Their oldest daughter, Neonela, sat next to her mother. Framed by a gray head scarf, the teenager's pretty, open face was a younger version of Ewdokia, with darker eyes and a more radiant complexion. Spirydon nodded to his son and daughter in the row behind Ewdokia and Neonela. Stefan and his sister Aleksandra shared the same fine auburn hair and wide-set brown eyes, but a recent growth spurt had left the gangly teenager towering over his little eight-year-old sister.

Most surprising for Spirydon was the fact that his eldest son sat next to him at the window. Jan had chosen to come with the family because, he said, the endless talk of his political friends had made him impatient and ready to try something new. Watching Jan's dark, almost sullen expression reflected in the train's window, Spirydon knew the trip would not be easy for both of them, but he was pleased with his son's decision.

Beyond the window, green fields gave way to more houses and buildings. The train's slowing pace told Spirydon they would soon enter Dresden, where they would change trains to continue on to Antwerp. He told himself not to worry; people changed trains every day without incident. A dull ache took up residence in the pit of his stomach.

Twenty minutes later, their train crawled slowly into the Dresden terminal and came to a stop. Spirydon reminded the family to be careful and stay together while they determined where to go for the next train. After shepherding his wife and children onto the terminal platform, he saw a long-faced man in a blue linen jacket with an arm band that read "Conductor" in Polish. The man shouted the same phrase over and over in Polish, directing passengers changing for Antwerp to wait next to the gate at the end of the platform.

The huge interior of the Dresden terminal could easily swallow their hometown church, Trosteniec's largest structure. Spirydon wondered what his younger children were thinking as they gawked at the expansive scene beneath the high ceiling with its exposed iron girders. Crowds of well-dressed people hurried along the platform. The shiny deep blue cars of a passenger train sat on an adjacent track like giant toys just removed from their boxes. On an elevated track in the adjacent hall, a freight train chugged through the terminal.

His thoughts were jolted by the sight of several soldiers in green-gray uniforms, high peaked hats, and polished black boots strolling around the terminal, watching the parade of passengers. Some had rifles slung over their shoulders, while others wore pistols in holsters on their hips. He avoided eye contact with the nearest soldiers, but their presence made him feel like a turtle out of its shell. At the end of the platform, Spirydon and his family were joined by several more passengers. After ten minutes, the long-faced man approached and announced in Polish, "If you are continuing to Antwerp, follow me."

"Where's Jakeb?" Ewdokia cried. Spirydon froze. He looked around quickly and did not see his small son.

"Nela, where's Jakeb?" Ewdokia demanded.

"I don't know, Mother. I thought he was with you."

"Is something wrong?" the conductor asked in Polish.

"My boy is not here," Spirydon answered.

"You need to find him, now. I can ask the soldiers to help, but the train to Antwerp leaves in twenty-five minutes. It will not wait."

"Twenty-five minutes," Spirydon repeated, trying to translate the time frame into his native Ukrainian, but his mind seized on the word "soldiers."

"Everyone, quickly, spread out. Find Jakeb," Ewdokia told the family. "We don't have much time."

Spirydon looked around and immediately saw the long-faced man signal to a soldier. He tried to look for Jakeb, but his attention constantly snapped back to the tall man in uniform with a dark, unfriendly demeanor. His rifle was slung behind his left shoulder and its barrel held tightly against his thigh with a beefy left hand. He conferred with the conductor and glanced at Spirydon, following the long-faced man's gesture.

As the two of men approached Spirydon, he swallowed hard and gathered himself. The conductor asked Spirydon to describe the child. In his broken Polish he explained the boy's name was Jakeb, he was two years old, and indicated Jakeb's height with his hand. But he couldn't remember what Jakeb was wearing or the Polish word for "blond," finally resorting to "white hair."

The conductor shook his head and said something in German to the soldier, who laughed and strolled away, much to Spirydon's relief.

"You people," the conductor said in Polish, looking as if he had just smelled something unpleasant, "you have so many children you can't even remember what they look like."

The conductor started toward the other passengers, but Jan pushed past Spirydon and grabbed the man's shoulder. "Excuse me," he said in Polish, "what do you mean 'you people'?"

"Jan, no," Spirydon cried.

The long-faced man pulled away from Jan's grasp. "Get your hand off of me," he said. "I'll have you detained if you can't control yourself." He raised his arm to signal the soldier, and Spirydon suddenly saw his family's escape to Canada unraveling.

Not all of your family will arrive with you.

He lunged after Jan. "Please, no need of trouble," he said to the conductor, clamping Jan's bicep in his powerful right hand and pulling him away.

"Leave me alone," Jan said. He tried to break free, but Spirydon was too strong and marched his son down the platform out of earshot from the others. He stopped and fixed Jan with an angry glare.

"Don't you fuck this up," Spirydon hissed. Jan's head snapped back from the verbal slap, and he looked wide-eyed at his father. Spirydon had never before sworn at his son, and a part of him felt pleased to see the word have its intended effect. "You listen to me," he continued. "We are in Germany now. We are at the mercy of these buffoons. If you're not careful, you'll get us all arrested and we might never see Canada, so calm down. Understand?"

Jan stopped his struggle, but Spirydon could still see the anger in his eyes. All that mattered at the moment was that Jan not do something stupid to jeopardize their journey.

"Do you understand?" Spirydon repeated. Jan stared at his father and finally nodded. Spirydon relaxed his grip.

"I found him." Aleksandra's shrill announcement cut through the general commotion of the crowded terminal as she led Jakeb by the hand back to the family. The little boy's face was tearstained, and he wiped his nose with the back of his free hand. "He was standing over there." Aleksandra pointed to the platform near the track on the other side of a broad stairway. "And he was crying." Ewdokia gathered up the little boy in her arms, but there was no time to savor Jakeb's return.

"Come everyone," Spirydon called out. "Be quick. We must go." The conductor had already moved away with the other passengers in tow, and they ran to catch up.

Twenty-five minutes later the family had taken their seats on the train to Antwerp, and it began rolling out of the terminal, on schedule, past several sidings filled with freight cars and through an industrial part of Dresden. The dreary landscape mirrored Spirydon's gloomy concerns. It seemed to him that somewhere just out of sight, a wolf was loping along behind them, waiting for a moment's inattentiveness to strike at Spirydon's flock.

Chief Officer Copland

"THE PIES WERE very tasty, Ma." Copland eased back in his chair, happy for a midday break from the modifications and provisioning needed to ready *Athenia* to sail from Glasgow in three days. Scotch pies, with their spicy meat and crisp pastry crust, were his particular favorite, and he sought them out every time he returned to Scotland.

"I could've eaten a dozen. Did they come from Wallace's?" he asked his mother, who carried an armful of dishes from the small dining room into the kitchen.

"Don't you think I can make a savory pie with my own hands?" Lizzie Copland dumped the dishes into a tub of water in the kitchen sink. "Besides, you're never home long enough to eat a dozen pies."

Copland shook his head and glanced at his father seated across the table. Peter Copland rolled his eyes in silent sympathy. Lizzie never missed a chance to find some fault with her son's career choice. In spite of her criticisms, he tried to see his parents whenever he had time to travel to their little brick home in Dundee on Scotland's east coast.

"Will you stop talking about pies and come sit down, woman," Peter called to his wife. "The boy has a train to catch, you know."

"I'm coming." Lizzie returned to the room, wiping her hands on her apron. "We've told you about the rest of the family," she said, "now what're you doing to keep yourself out of trouble?" She removed her apron and settled into the chair next to her husband.

"I haven't any time for getting into trouble, Ma," Copland said. "We're too busy making changes to the ship so we can carry more passengers. There's a big demand because of all the Americans and Canadians trying to go home. The Donaldson people want us to take two hundred more passengers and forty more crew on this next crossing."

"Will you have enough lifeboats for all those extra people?" Lizzie always looked out for her son's safety. His father had worked all his life for the railroad, which she considered a more sensible career. She often noted if a train broke down, at least you could get out and walk.

"We'll have more than enough room in all our lifeboats," Copland said, "and we have life rafts we can pull out of storage to carry even more. So there's no reason for you to worry."

"But where will you put all those people?" Peter asked, reaching for his pipe on the sideboard.

"We're building dormitories in some of the public spaces. Every third-class and tourist cabin can accommodate four people. But to fit everybody on board, we'll be separating men and women."

"Will you be sharing your cabin?"

"I don't think so, Ma. At least, nobody has said anything to me."

"What're your bosses saying about a war?" His father's sober question caused Copland to take a moment to search for a reassuring response.

"If anything happens before we sail, we'd likely come under the Royal Navy's protection. If we leave and then something happens, we're protected by international maritime treaties. Unescorted merchant ships can't be attacked without warning. But we're taking some precautions. The Admiralty wants us to blackout the ship, so we're boarding up our lounge windows and painting over all the portholes."

"Oh, I don't like the sound of that, Barty," Lizzie said. "Couldn't you ask those Donaldson people for a job on land? It would be safer. You'd be more settled, maybe even get a place of your own and meet a nice young lady."

Copland's bachelor status was a particular concern for his mother. It irritated him that she couldn't accept her thirty-two-year-old son's decision to delay starting a family. Normally he deflected her entreaties with a few oblique comments, but this time he decided to ignore the voice of caution in his head and seek to put the subject to rest.

"Ma, why do you keep bringing this up? We both know my work keeps me away at sea for weeks and sometimes months at a time. I don't want to put that burden on any girl right now."

"But that's a decision you and your young lady should make together," Lizzie said.

"There is no young lady in the picture, Ma."

"I'm sure there are plenty of young women who would be willing to make that sacrifice for you. What about that nice librarian you met a few years ago? You probably never gave her a chance, did you?"

Her accusation stung more than he expected and goaded him to press on.

"I know what this is about. Why can't you accept my decision to go to sea?

It's my life, and I can't think of anything more important than taking a ship halfway around the world to deliver her cargo and everyone aboard safely into port. All my years at sea have brought me this close to getting my own ship," he said, holding his thumb and forefinger a hair's breadth apart. "I'm not going to toss away all that hard work for the sake of a job behind a desk. And certainly not so I can start a family. Maybe someday, but not now. There's nothing I'd rather be than a ship's master, and I'm sorry if you can't understand that."

"Son, we don't mean to criticize," his father said. "We just want to see you happy, that's all." Peter put his arm around Lizzie's shoulder, and Copland realized he'd sounded more strident than he intended. He didn't want to apologize for his strong feelings, but this wasn't how he wanted to end his visit.

"I know you want me to be happy," he said, adding a contrite smile. "Maybe I didn't sound like it, but I am happy. I'm doing exactly what I want to do. Please don't worry about me."

Lizzie looked out the dining room window and let the soft ticks of the clock on the sideboard fill the room. After a minute with no response, Copland knew his mother had finished their conversation.

"The train for Glasgow leaves in an hour," he said. "It's probably best if I go now."

Judith Evelyn

JUDITH REGARDED THE stone cottage bathed in the long amber rays of the setting sun. On this final day of August, she sat in the back garden of the cottage, which occupied a tranquil knoll in the central lowlands town of Alloa, Scotland. The sturdy little structure seemed the only thing in her life right now that wasn't falling down around her.

The cottage belonged to the grandmother of Andrew Allan, the man with whom she maintained a romantic relationship that recently had turned tepid. The next day, she would accompany Andrew and his father on a ship sailing back home to Canada. Could she rekindle the relationship, she wondered, and how might it be affected by the news she had yet to tell him?

"Judith, are you out here?" Andrew stuck his head out of the back door of the cottage.

"Over here," she called.

"Do you want to say goodbye to Granny?" He stepped into the garden, a slender figure whose height was emphasized by his receding blond hairline, though he was only thirty-two. "She's going to turn in shortly, and we'll be on our way in the morning before she rises."

"I'm coming," she said, but Judith did not move.

"Is everything all right?" Andrew approached her in the fading light.

"It's so peaceful here," she said. She looked away to the north, where the rolling hills were turning golden in the sunset.

"Yes, I loved coming here as a boy," he said, following her gaze. "With a sunset like that it's hard to believe they're rehearsing for another war across the channel."

"Did we do the right thing coming to England?" she asked.

"Oh, time for our final curtain soliloquy, is it?" Judith did not answer. "Well, yes," he continued. "I gained a lot more experience in radio production, and you certainly showed you could hold your own on a London stage."

"But what about us, Andrew? What happened?"

Andrew frowned and folded his arms. "I thought we both agreed we needed to focus on our careers first. The timing wasn't right."

"Will it ever be right?"

"Judith, something's amiss. What is it?"

She took a moment before responding. "I'm late." she said, unable to meet his gaze. "I should have told you sooner but I wanted to be sure."

"Late?" Andrew responded. "What do you . . . oh. How late?"

"Two weeks."

"Two weeks?" he repeated, as if having difficulty comprehending the significance of the time frame. Then again, she thought, he probably didn't want to seriously consider the implications.

"Is that enough time to be sure?"

"I've never been this late."

"Okay. If you're pregnant, do you want to keep it?" The abruptness of the question caught her by surprise.

"Oh God, Andrew, I don't know. I've hardly had time to consider it. Jesus, you got to act three pretty fast."

"All right. Please keep your voice down." He sat beside her on the stone bench, hands on his knees and looking a bit embarrassed. "You're certain it's mine?"

Judith stared at him in utter exasperation.

"Yes, you're right," he said, his voice softening. "Dumb question. I'm sorry, but this is all new to me as well." Andrew took a deep breath and stared into the setting sun.

"I suppose this adds a note of verisimilitude to our performances," he said. It took her a moment to realize Andrew was referring to their decision to maintain the fiction of a pending engagement while traveling on the ship with his father, the Reverend William Allan.

"Believe me, I could do just as well without it," she said.

"I'm sure you could." The sun finally dipped below the horizon, leaving an orange glow in the sky. Andrew put his arm around her shoulder and pulled her a little closer. "Listen, I want you to know that I'm prepared to do the right thing, if that's what you want." The note of resignation in Andrew's voice saddened her. This was not how she wanted to rekindle their relationship.

"Everything's happened so fast. I don't know what I want to do," Judith said. "When you called two days ago about sailing back to Canada, I said yes because all this damn war talk was giving our backers second thoughts and rehearsals have been totally distracted. I went home, closed up the flat, got on a train, and suddenly here I am, getting ready to board a ship to Canada. I feel absolutely disconnected."

"The whole world is disconnected right now." Andrew took his arm from her shoulder and hugged his elbows against his body. "We should talk about this later. Let's go in."

He smiled at her for the first time since entering the garden and patted her thigh.

"Come on. Let's see what a good actress you are for Granny."

Oberleutnant Lemp

"*ALARM!*"

The warning shout echoed down from the bridge and electrified everyone in *U-30*'s control room. Lemp looked up from his navigation chart and counted the three lookouts sliding down the ladder in quick succession, followed by First Watch Officer Hinsch.

"Flood the tanks," Lemp cried to begin the boat's emergency dive. "Take us down to thirty meters," he called to the chief engineer, *Leutnant* Wolfgang Meckbach. Sailors scrambled to their battle stations up and down the boat as she began to slide beneath the waves. The throb of her diesel engines stopped, and the electric motors took over. Lemp watched the needle on the depth gauge track *U-30*'s descent, and he steadied himself with a hand on the periscope housing as the dive angle steepened.

"Thirty meters," Meckbach announced as the boat leveled off.

"Stand by," Lemp said. "Mr. Hinsch, ask the lookout what he spotted." After conferring with the sailor, Hinsch reported the lookout had seen a plane coming out of the sun. Lemp nodded and turned to Meckbach.

"Chief, take us up to periscope depth."

Minutes later, with *U-30* submerged at twelve meters, Lemp leaned into the rubber eyepiece of the boat's wide-angle periscope, his white peaked captain's hat pushed back on his head. He turned slowly, scanning the horizon and sky to identify the threat, noting scattered clouds, but no signs of any aircraft. After two careful revolutions, he ordered his crew to stand down from their battle stations.

"Tell Seaman Greiner the plane he spotted was a seagull," Lemp said to Hinsch in a voice just loud enough to be overheard in the adjoining compartments. They were not far from Rockall, a seventy-foot monolith that jutted out of the sea above the Rockall Banks. It was a popular roosting spot for seabirds, and the overeager lookout had made an honest mistake. Lemp knew the laughter now circulating at the young seaman's expense would cause him some embarrassment and provide a bit of relief from the tedium of the past several days. It also would encourage the lookouts to exercise even greater care.

Lemp led Hinsch and the watch crew back through the dripping hatch onto the bridge as soon as *U-30* broke the surface. The boat's twin diesels roared back to life, and a black cloud caused by the momentary union of engine exhaust and seawater danced away on a brisk wind.

"Maintain course," Lemp said into the speaking tube to the control room below. "Both engines half ahead." The men on the bridge silently fell into their watch routine, but after ten minutes of scanning the empty seas, Lemp's concentration began to wander and he lowered his binoculars.

"It's been nine days, and not a word from Wilhelmshaven," he said to Hinsch. "I thought we'd hear something on the twenty-sixth about the army going into Poland."

"Maybe they just postponed the action," Hinsch said.

"Maybe, but it's hard to maintain an edge without knowing what's going on. We're just burning up fuel in this damned waiting zone, diving out of sight like a thief when anything appears on the horizon."

"Message coming in from headquarters," a voice called up to the bridge. Unable to wait for the message to be delivered, Lemp scrambled down the ladder and headed for the cramped officer's quarters just beyond his own alcove. He found his second watch officer, *Leutnant* Friedrich Bothe, carefully punching a coded message into the keyboard of the boat's Enigma machine. The secret cipher device resembled a typewriter, with a keyboard augmented by a series of wheels, plugs, and alphabet display. Its operation was a mystery to Lemp, but with each keystroke a letter lit up on the machine's display and the young officer copied it on a paper form. When he finished, he handed the form to Lemp, who read the brief message and smiled.

"NEGOTIATIONS FAILED. HOSTILITIES WITH POLAND."

Now we'll see what the English are made of.

FRIDAY, SEPTEMBER 1

Judith Evelyn

JUDITH FOLLOWED ANDREW Allan, stepping down from the train onto the platform of Glasgow's Central Station and into a swirling midmorning crowd. The station's huge interior, with its graceful iron girders, glass ceiling, and tile floor, amplified the sounds of the multitude, while the echo of public announcements and the shrill whistles of departing trains contributed to the din. Walking toward the front of the station, Judith became aware of another sound—the silvery high-pitched singing of children.

"Underneath the spreading chestnut tree," they sang as they approached, "there we sit both you and me . . ."

A tall boy carrying a school banner led the singing procession. The matronly figure of a teacher followed the boy, and after her came the students, the youngest ones walking in front and holding hands two by two. Judith judged them to be no more than five or six years old. Several held small shopping bags or small valises, and all carried white cardboard lunch boxes over their shoulders.

It took her a moment to recall that this was the first day of a national evacuation to move thousands of children to the countryside, away from population centers that might become targets in wartime. Only then did she realize the white boxes contained gas masks, not lunches, and it stopped Judith in her tracks.

"Did you forget something?" Andrew asked.

"No." She pulled the strap of her purse higher onto her shoulder. "Let's keep moving."

Continuing across the station with Andrew, Judith noticed more groups of children standing with their teachers. Some children laughed and jostled each other, some seemed bewildered by all the activity, and a few of the young ones cried. Just when she thought the scene couldn't become more sorrowful, she noticed the mothers standing behind a barrier, waving to their departing children and smiling broadly, their cheeks moistened with tears.

"Oh, Andrew, this is all too much," Judith said. A sense of despair closed down around her. "We have to leave before I give way completely."

"Steady there. We need to get to the taxis on George Street. I think the exit is this way." Andrew took her hand and resumed wading through the crowd when a railway worker pushing a handcart full of baggage passed in front of them.

"Excuse me," Andrew said, stopping the man. "Can you tell me if we are headed in the right direction for the taxis?"

"Indeed you are sir," the porter said, touching the bill of his soft cap. "But there ain't no taxis this morning, and not many buses either. They've all been given over to the evacuation, you see."

Andrew looked surprised, as if considering for the first time the consequences of all the activity around them. "Listen," he said, "we have to get down to the Prince's Dock. Do you have any suggestions?"

"I'm afraid not, sir. It's a fair walk from here." The man studied Andrew for a moment then asked, "Begging your pardon, but are you planning to go somewhere by ship?"

"Yes, to Canada. Why?"

"You're sure the ship is going, what with all the rumors about?"

"What rumors?"

"They're saying the Germans marched into Poland this morning."

"Oh God," Judith exclaimed.

"Sorry, miss, I thought you'd have heard."

Judith couldn't think of a thing to say. Andrew seemed taken aback as well, and the three of them stood for a moment in an awkward silence. Finally, the man offered a brave little smile, touched his cap again, and pushed on.

"What do we do now?" Judith said, recovering her voice. "Do you think he's right? Would they cancel the voyage?"

"I don't know." Andrew glanced at the clock above the crowd in the center of the station. "We're sailing at noon, so we haven't much time if we're going. Let's find a telephone and ring the Donaldson people to see if it's still on. If it is, they can get in touch with Dad to send a car after us."

"Yes, that should work," Judith said, but she was no longer sure she wanted to sail if the rumors were true.

Rhoda Thomas

DISTRESSING RUMORS OF a predawn German invasion of Poland circulated through the village of Street in southwest England and kept Rhoda and her sister-in-law, Flora Fisher, within earshot of the wireless for most of the morning. The Philco's large cherrywood console occupied a place of honor in the Fishers' front room, and they listened periodically as they went about their business—Rhoda laying out her clothes on the bed to begin packing for her trip home and Flora busying herself in the kitchen. It was 10:30 when the BBC confirmed the rumors.

"Rhoda, come quick," Flora called from the front room. Rhoda entered to hear a plummy voice on the wireless reading the news with such calm detachment that at first the significance of the words did not register with her.

". . . crossing into Poland shortly before five o'clock this morning, local Polish time. German aircraft have bombed the Polish capital of Warsaw and several other cities. German forces in the Free City of Danzig have attacked Polish military positions there. We hope to bring you further details of these events later in our broadcast. In London and elsewhere, the evacuation of—" Flora shut off the wireless, and they sat in the front room for a moment in stunned silence.

"What terrible news," Rhoda said at last. "I feel so badly for you and Albert."

"There's nothing to be done about the news." Flora said, jumping to her feet. "I'm putting the kettle on. Do you fancy a cuppa?"

"Yes, thank you." Rhoda thought about helping Flora or resuming her packing chores, but she couldn't find the energy to move. Flora continued their conversation from the kitchen.

"Under the circumstances, I'd say you're fortunate to be leaving tomorrow," she said.

"Oh, I agree," Rhoda said, "even if it means driving overnight to Liverpool."

Rhoda considered the morning's terrible news as an apt climax to a frantic week during which she had arranged her early return to America following the embassy announcement. The Cunard shipping offices changed her departure date twice before booking her on the *Athenia*, leaving September second from Liverpool. When the British government asked citizens to avoid train travel on September first to facilitate the evacuation of children, Rhoda organized a car and driver from a local garage for the trip to Liverpool. The young man who would drive her planned to sleep a few hours after work, then pick up Rhoda following supper and drive through the night to reach Liverpool in time to board the ship tomorrow.

Her thoughts were interrupted by the telephone in the front hall. It rang twice before Flora picked up the receiver.

"Yes, she's here." Flora motioned to Rhoda to come take the phone. "It's Reg," she said. Reginald Cooper owned the nearby garage and had scheduled the car and driver for Rhoda's trip to Liverpool.

"Mrs. Thomas, I'm afraid I have some bad news," he said after Rhoda took the phone. "The chap who's driving you to Liverpool learned this morning that he's being mobilized, and I haven't been able to find another driver on short notice."

"Oh dear," Rhoda said. She began contemplating another call to the Cunard offices.

"I hope you don't mind, but I took the liberty of calling the railway office," Reg continued. "They told me the Pine Express is running today, and if you can get up to Shepton Mallet, you should be able to catch the train when it comes through at noon. That would put you into Liverpool by half five this evening."

"Reggie, you're a dear. Thank you for your trouble. I'll see what I can do." She hung up the phone and called out to the kitchen, "Flo, never mind the tea."

Flora helped her quickly fold the last of her clothes into her suitcase. A small trunk containing more clothes and wedding presents for her daughter stood packed in the corner of the room. Flora rang Albert at the shoe factory, who arranged a taxi for Rhoda and walked home. A few minutes later, when the taxi arrived, Albert hustled the baggage into the car's boot as Rhoda hugged her sister-in-law and climbed into the little sedan.

"Please say goodbye to everyone for me," Rhoda called out the window to Flora. "I'll write as soon as I get home."

"I'm coming with you," Albert announced, joining Rhoda in the back seat. The last half hour had been a whirlwind, and she was grateful to spend a little more time with her brother before leaving.

"What's going to happen now?" Rhoda asked Albert as the taxi drove along the two-lane road toward Shepton Mallet.

"I expect Chamberlain will try to work something out again, but it won't be easy with German soldiers already in Poland."

"I meant what's going to happen to you and Flora. I feel so awful having to leave you like this."

"Now, don't you worry about us. If it comes to war, I don't think Germany is going to bomb our shoe factory." Albert fell silent, staring out the taxi's window. Minutes passed before he spoke again. "Hard to believe, isn't it? Only twenty years after the war to end all wars."

"It doesn't seem fair," Rhoda said. "Everyone's just getting back on their feet from this horrible Depression and now you have to face this."

"We'll face it as we always have," Albert said, "with our famously stiff upper lip."

"It's no laughing matter. I wish there was something I could do."

"Perhaps you could put in a good word with your friend, Mr. Roosevelt. Ask him to give us a hand."

"You're incorrigible," she said, slapping her brother's knee. "But now that I think of it, there is something I can do. I'll appeal to a higher authority. I'll say a prayer every night that the good Lord keeps you all safe from harm." Albert reached across the taxi seat to take hold of her hand.

"Thank you, Rho."

The taxi pulled up in front of the station at noon, with no train in sight. Rhoda rushed to the ticket window and sighed in relief when the man on the other side told her the Pine Express was running ten minutes late. Albert waited on the platform with her until the train pulled in, and they hugged one last time before she boarded. Her brother remained on the platform as the train slowly departed. At least, Rhoda thought he was still standing there. She couldn't see him clearly through the tears welling in her eyes.

Judith Evelyn

"JUDITH? YOU SEEM a million miles away."

Andrew's comment pulled Judith back from her dark thoughts as the two of them stood with Andrew's father, the Reverend William Allan, on *Athenia*'s forward promenade deck. This choice space just below the ship's bridge was reserved for cabin-class passengers, the ship's premium customers. Andrew's father had suggested this vantage point to watch their departure from Glasgow.

"I'm sorry, darling," she said. "My mind is still reeling from the past week. I've gone from rehearsals in London to standing on the deck of a ship about to depart for Canada. And it's all thanks to your kind offer, Reverend Allan." She nodded and smiled at Andrew's father, but the distractions eating at her were due to more than the rush of events. First, there had been the sight of the school children being evacuated at the train station, followed by word that Germany had invaded Poland. Making matters worse was the complication of her possible pregnancy. And all this had come before she caught sight of *Athenia*.

☆ ☆ ☆

"I THINK THAT'S the *Athenia*," Andrew noted as their car crossed the bridge over the River Clyde on the way to Glasgow's docks from the train terminal. "She's the larger ship in the center basin at the end of the dock."

Judith followed his direction and spotted the ship's long, coal-black hull. A single black funnel with a thick, white stripe around it dominated *Athenia*'s white superstructure, which rose two or three stories above the hull. Tall masts near the bow and stern supported booms busy loading nets filled with cargo into open holds. There was nothing streamlined about the ship. Her bow dropped straight down to the water like a prominent chin. *Athenia* looked as though she would shove her way through the seas, rather than slice through them. But there was something about the long, black hull that tugged at Judith.

God, it looks like a coffin.

Later, when they came aboard, signs of wear caught her eye. She noticed thin patches of carpet in *Athenia*'s passageways and worn fabric on the arms of lounge chairs. Dark curtains and blackened portholes lent a melancholy air to the ship's interior. Try as she might, she could not shake the sense of gloom that settled like a dark shawl around her shoulders.

☆ ☆ ☆

"WAS THERE ANY more news about Mother's condition when you arrived this morning?" Andrew had resumed his conversation with his father as they waited on deck for *Athenia*'s departure. Judith recalled Andrew telling her over the phone that his mother had suffered a stroke in Toronto.

"No, nothing since midweek." Reverend Allan pushed his round, black-rimmed glasses higher on the bridge of his nose with a pudgy forefinger. "I had hoped to spend more time here with your grandmother. It's so distressing to think I may never see her again. But under the circumstances, I consider it a blessing you and I are able to return home together. It'll give me a chance to become better acquainted with my future daughter-in-law."

"And me with you," Judith said, returning the elder Allan's smile. She drew closer to Andrew, careful not to overplay her role as the doting fiancé.

"What are your plans when you get back to Toronto?" the Reverend Allan asked his son.

"I hope to find something with the CBC," Andrew said. "They inquired about my availability to work on some new productions. Nothing specific, but very encouraging. Of course, I don't know what will happen if there's a war."

Before they could explore the subject any further, *Athenia*'s deep bass whistle announced her departure. Below them, they watched gangs of dock workers lift the ship's hefty ropes from the pier's squat metal bollards to free *Athenia* from Glasgow's shore. A tugboat pushed its blunt, padded nose between the big ship's bow and the dock, gently nudging her out into the basin.

"Away at last," Reverend Allan said with an air of enthusiasm Judith wished she could share.

With tugboats fore and aft, the liner slowly made her way out of the basin and into the muddy green water of the Clyde, which connected Glasgow to the Irish Sea and the world beyond. As *Athenia* approached the cranes that rose like steel skeletons above a large shipyard along the river, Judith noticed several workers on their lunch break shouting to them. Trying to affect a gaiety she did not feel, Judith waved to the men until she was able to make out what they were shouting.

"Cowards!"

"Why don't you stay and fight?"

"What're you runnin' from?"

Chief Officer Copland

THE ANGRY SHOUTS also reached Copland and a companion as they stood on *Athenia*'s aft docking bridge, a small raised deck astern of the promenade deck.

"What're they so unhappy about, Mr. Copland?" asked Jimmy Turnbull, a nineteen-year-old cadet on board for the crossing to Canada.

"If we go to war, these shipyards could be a prime target for German bombers," Copland said. "I expect they're not happy about having to stay here while we sail away."

He felt a kinship with Jimmy, an earnest young man with an unruly shock of red hair, who was completing a demanding four-year apprenticeship to become an officer in the Merchant Navy. Jimmy's devotion to hard work reminded Copland of his own approach to his duties, and he happily put the young man through his paces for the day's departure procedures.

Along the shoreline, the city's familiar skyline emerged through the gray mist lifting off the river. Moisture dampened the sooty riverside buildings and gave the entire scene a somber feeling.

"Were you in the Great War, sir?"

"Good heavens, no," Copland said with a laugh. "I was seven when the war started. So if we go to war again, it'll be a new experience for both of us."

"If war starts, do you think the Germans would attack our ship?"

"Not according to the protocol. They'd have to warn us before they could attack, and we'd be able to show them we're not carrying anything more dangerous than crates of scotch whiskey, school textbooks, and a couple of tons of bricks. The question is whether the Germans would follow the protocol." Copland paused to concentrate on the stern's clearances to port and starboard as *Athenia* entered a particularly narrow portion of the river's main channel.

"Anyway," he resumed, "we're not at war, and if it does come, with any luck we'll be halfway to Canada. Speaking of which, I need to stop bumping my gums and go over what we're doing here."

The Clyde River pilot on *Athenia's* bridge would guide the ship for the next three and a half hours through the river's many twists and turns down to the town of Gourock. But for the first few miles below Glasgow proper, Copland explained, bridges, ferry crossings, and the anchorages of shipbuilding yards crowded the river.

"We provide an extra set of eyes to make sure our stern doesn't swing from the main channel. In an emergency, we'd alert the wheelhouse and could steer from here."

"Have you ever had to do that?" Jimmy asked.

"Thankfully, no," Copland said. "You need to understand there's a bit of tension on the bridge right now. *Athenia* is still the captain's ship, but the pilot commands her trip downriver. The last thing either of them wants is a call from you saying our stern has drifted from the channel and you need to bring her back on course."

"I see what you mean."

The two men watched a ferry cut across the wake of *Athenia's* trailing tugboat, accompanied by the hoot of the ferry's steam whistle.

"How many times have you been down the river, Mr. Copland?"

"I'm a Glaswegian, born and raised," Copland said. "Been up and down this river a hundred times or more, and I can tell you what's around every bend." He pointed out the large shipyard off the portside. "We're coming up on the Fairfield works. That's where *Athenia* was launched."

"Looks like they're working on a pretty big ship right now," Jimmy observed. The ship, somewhat larger than *Athenia*, sat at a dock while workers near the stern appeared to be tearing up some of her planking.

"She's the *Caledonia*. The Admiralty commandeered her about a week ago. They're putting a heavy gun on her afterdeck. She'll be an armed merchant cruiser when they finish, helping patrol our shipping lanes."

"Will they convert *Athenia*?" Jimmy asked.

"I haven't heard anything, but I hope not. I've made twenty crossings in her. She's reliable and comfortable but not very fast compared to the newer ships. If war comes, she could carry troops all right, but the old girl wouldn't make a good fighting ship."

Copland glanced at his watch. "Almost two hours before we drop the pilot at Gourock, then we'll be really busy, starting with passenger lifeboat drills. After that, we'll check the blackout measures in the public rooms and the final touches to the new dormitory in the gymnasium. We need to accomplish all that before we take on our Belfast passengers tonight. I'm going to need you to stay close."

"Yes sir," Jimmy said.

Athenia would pick up one hundred thirty-six passengers in Belfast and nearly five hundred fifty more in Liverpool tomorrow. The manifest said they could expect eleven hundred passengers and a crew of three hundred fifteen when they finally sailed for Canada. A disquieting thought settled on Copland, which he did not share with Jimmy.

I've never left Glasgow under more uncertain circumstances.

Spirydon Kucharczuk

LIVERPOOL'S WELL-EARNED REPUTATION as a crossroads of world commerce provided a welcome distraction for Spirydon as he walked along the city's crowded streets with his family. The walks had helped to fill up the three days before they would board the ship to Canada tomorrow. But in bed at night, with the city's boisterous attractions muted and the family back in the inexpensive room they had rented, Spirydon found himself staring for hours at the faint, spidery cracks in the ceiling's plaster.

"You didn't sleep again last night," Ewdokia said as the family waited for a traffic signal on the way down to the river.

"No," he said, offering a guilty smile. "I can't stop thinking about all the details of our plans. We crossed Germany, crossed the channel to England, and crossed England to this Liverpool. Everything is done except sailing on the ship tomorrow. But I keep going over and over the details. I worry that I've missed something."

Ewdokia found Spirydon's hand and interlaced her fingers with his. "When you worked all day on the farm, you were tired at night and never had trouble sleeping. Now you are not working so hard and your body's not so tired. I think you will sleep once we are on the ship."

☆ ☆ ☆

A FEW HOURS later, on the way back to the center of the city, they stopped in a shady green park to eat a lunch of fresh fruit Ewdokia had brought along in a string bag. Spirydon was halfway through a juicy pear when he looked up to see Jan striding purposefully toward him.

"You're just in time," he said to Jan. "Have a pear. They're delicious."

"Never mind the pear, Papa. I've just heard some news about Poland."

"What news?"

"You were right. The Germans invaded."

Though he had expected it would happen, Spirydon still found the news unsettling.

"Where did you hear this?"

"At a ticket agency a kilometer from here. They had a sign in Polish in the window, so I went in. I found a man there who could speak some Ukrainian, enough to tell me what was happening. I can show you if you don't believe me."

"No, no. I believe you." Spirydon looked at Ewdokia napping on the lawn, her pewter-colored skirt, dappled by the shade of a tree, fanned out over her legs. Aleksandra played with Jakeb, and Neonela had found a quiet spot to read. Stefan sat nearby, listening to the conversation.

"Did the man say where the Germans are invading?" Spirydon inquired.

"No, but he asked me why I was in Liverpool, and I told him we were leaving tomorrow to go to Canada. He said if we had tickets to sail on *Athenia* tomorrow that people would pay a lot of money for them, a lot more than we paid."

"I'm not surprised."

"He said we could sell our tickets for at least double the price, but it might be even more than that. I was thinking, Papa, if we sold our tickets and went on a later ship, we would have more money when we arrive in Canada. Maybe you could afford to buy more land." Jan meant well, Spirydon was certain, but he often seemed drawn to such moneymaking schemes.

"Son, we didn't come all this way to England to sell our tickets."

"I know, but now our tickets could be worth a lot of money."

"You have to look at more than the price you get for the tickets," Ewdokia said without opening her eyes. "If we can't find room on another ship to sail soon, we'd have to spend the extra money just to live in England. And we would have to pay more for the tickets we buy because many people will want to go. Listen to your father."

Without a word, Jan shook his head and walked away in the direction from which he had come. As Spirydon watched him disappear around a corner, the unsettling words came to him again.

"Not all of your family will arrive with you."

David Jennings

A LARGE CROWD gathered in the late afternoon sunshine on the sidewalk opposite Number Ten Downing Street in London as news of the German invasion spread. David Jennings, a senior from Canada's University of Toronto, stood near the back of the crowd, along with his friends and fellow students Tony Cassels and John Woods. For the past month, David had traveled throughout Great Britain with Tony and John, enjoying one last fling before returning to Toronto for his final year at the university. They had tickets for the next day's early train to Liverpool, where they would arrive in time to board *Athenia*, sailing for Quebec and Montreal.

After taking some time to write letters and postcards early that afternoon, David suggested they stroll down Whitehall, where curiosity had attracted them to the crowd in front of the British prime minister's residence.

The people gathered four deep on the sidewalk appeared to be a cross section of London: women in Marks & Spencer's latest fashions, men in black bowlers and three-piece business suits, boys in school uniforms with their ties loosened, pensioners in cardigans, and even a few laborers in dusty dungarees and soft flat caps. They were mostly quiet, but judging from comments David overheard, the crowd seemed resolute.

While he studied the people, David sensed his friends growing restless. "How long do you want to stand here?" John asked him. "It's our last day in London."

"I know, but this is history in the making," David said.

"Yes, but it's being made behind closed doors."

Trying to buy a bit of time, David nodded in the direction of a black limousine parked at the curb in front of Number Ten. A black-liveried chauffeur stood at the car's rear door, and a bobby waited nearby. "Don't you two want to see who's going to get into the limo?"

"Not particularly," John said. "Just what is it about this scene that you find so fascinating?"

"It's the thought that Chamberlain and his ministers may be deciding to go to war as we stand here."

"I suppose we can make allowances because you're an engineering student," Tony said, "but if Chamberlain announces any deadline for going to war it will be in Parliament. You're standing in front of the wrong building, Davey."

"Very funny," David said.

"All this talk of war is making me hungry," John added. "There must be some place around here where we can get a cup of tea and a bite to eat."

"I give up. Neither one of you has any sense of history. What was I thinking touring England with you two philistines?"

"At least we know how to enjoy ourselves," Tony said, removing his glasses and attacking a smudge with the end of his tie. "Besides, who else would put up with your insufferable good nature?"

David shrugged in resignation. "All right. If you're ready, let's go." He took one last glance across the street just as the simple black door of the prime minister's residence opened and the crowd stirred. Two men in gray suits emerged and stepped onto the footpath to talk to the bobby. A group of newspaper photographers began moving toward the black car.

One of the men talking to the bobby turned to the open door of the residence and nodded. A slender man with light-brown hair stepped through the doorway. The people standing around David suddenly let out a cheer.

"What's going on?" David asked the man next to him, as Prime Minister Neville Chamberlain appeared on the porch.

"It's the King," the man responded. David glanced back at the slender man and recognized the long face and high cheekbones of King George VI, absent his full military regalia seen in most photographs. The king wore a dark business suit with a white handkerchief in his breast pocket and carried a homburg hat in his left hand. The photographer's flashbulbs began popping, and David felt a tightness in his throat as cheers continued rising from the onlookers.

The shouts grew louder when the two men turned and waved to the gathering. The prime minister bent slightly to say something to the king, who nodded and smiled. They shook hands, then King George stepped off the small porch, crossed the footpath, entered the rear seat of his limousine, and the car drove away. With one more wave and a toothy grin, Chamberlain stepped back inside and the black door swung shut. Only then did David think of the movie camera hanging from his shoulder and the opportunity he had missed to film England's king and prime minister together.

"I have to admit that was worth waiting for," John said. "It isn't every day you see the king."

"Or the prime minister," Tony added. "Poor fellow, I wouldn't want his job right now."

On their way to find a tea shop, the trio passed a newsstand with its posters confirming the day's troubling events in bold capital letters. "GERMANY INVADES POLAND" proclaimed one broadsheet, while a second read "I WILL TEACH POLES A LESSON—HITLER."

David unhinged the leather case from around his camera and asked his friends to pose behind the broadsheets. He focused on the iconic, honey-colored stone tower of Big Ben, then panned down Westminster Palace to his two friends in the foreground, capturing their self-conscious grins.

Ruth Etherington

THE TRAIN BRINGING the Etherington family to Liverpool, England, was an hour late, arriving at the Lime Street Station just past seven o'clock in the evening. The chaos of the evacuations that filled the station for most of the day had subsided. By the time the family collected their baggage and made the short run by taxi to their hotel, the sun had disappeared and so had the city, a result of Liverpool's first total blackout.

Ruth Etherington stood in the hotel lobby and waited for her husband, Harold, to complete the registration formalities. She watched their son, Geoffrey, thread his way around the hotel guests, tufted settees, and potted plants to examine the thick black curtains covering the lobby's front windows. Ruth considered their good fortune in scheduling this trip to see relatives on both sides of their family. Natives of Great Britain, the Etheringtons now permanently lived in the United States, and they had booked tomorrow's return voyage months before there had been any talk of an impending war. She hoped they could board the ship tomorrow and sail before anything happened.

"Is the whole city really blacked out?" Geoffrey asked his mother, returning from his inspection.

"I believe so," Ruth said. "Did you see any lights when we drove to the hotel?"

"No, but it's so silly. If the roads between the cities are lighted, then the airplanes can just follow the roads until they come to a big dark spot. They'll know that's where the city is and that's where they drop their bombs."

She wondered if all ten-year-old boys had such a fascination with war. Ruth disliked discussing the subject with Geoffrey but knew avoiding his questions would only pique his interest, so she answered in the most disinterested voice she could manage.

"Maybe the airplanes want to bomb a special place. But if there are no lights in the city, they won't be able to see it."

"Why don't they just come in the daytime when they can see?"

"I don't know, honey. Ask your father."

"Ask me what?" Harold said, returning from the registration desk.

"Why the bombers don't come in the daytime?" Geoffrey said.

"What brought this up?" Harold asked Ruth.

"All the blackout measures, I suppose."

"That reminds me. The reception clerk says we shouldn't—"

"Are we going to be bombed?" Geoffrey asked. Ruth gave her husband a wry smile and bent slightly to look her son directly in the eye.

"No, dear, we are not going to be bombed," she said, "because England is not at war. Tomorrow we will get on a ship and go home. We'll be far away from any danger, so you don't need to worry about that." Having made what she hoped was her final pronouncement on the unlikelihood of being bombed, Ruth turned to Harold, who waited to complete his sentence.

"Thank you," he said. "The receptionist suggested we stay in the hotel tonight because of the blackout. This is the first night and people aren't used to the conditions, so we're better off staying here. He says the hotel has a grill and they're serving dinner."

"Maybe they have fish and chips," Geoffrey exclaimed. Ruth smiled at his enthusiasm, knowing how fond her son had become of the same simple fare she enjoyed as a child.

"Why don't we all go find out what's on the menu?" she said, taking her husband's arm. Together they steered their son toward the grill, leaving the subject of war hanging in the lobby.

Chief Officer Copland

ATHENIA'S CHIEF OFFICER oversaw the general loading operations as additional passengers came aboard by tender while the liner sat anchored in Belfast Lough, Northern Ireland. By ten-thirty that evening, with *Athenia* on her way back across the Irish Sea to Liverpool, he began his nightly walk. Though not part of Copland's duties, his tour of the ship's six passenger decks had become a routine that helped him relax before retiring for the night. Given the informality of his ritual and the late hour, he sent Cadet Turnbull off to bed.

Copland spent nearly forty-five minutes on his rounds, starting with narrow passageways of D and C decks with their crowded third-class accommodations. Dining facilities for the three passenger classes and the large gleaming galley that supplied them also occupied C deck. Tourist-class cabins, lounges, shops, and the ship's hospital facility lined the two more spacious internal passageways on B deck, while the remaining tourist cabins and all cabin-class staterooms filled A deck. Along the way, Copland checked to assure portholes were painted over, larger windows were boarded up, blackout curtains were properly installed at all doorways leading outside, and signs forbidding passengers to smoke on deck at night were in place.

The two topmost decks were reserved for the enjoyment of cabin- and tourist-class passengers. The promenade deck, only two-thirds the length of the decks below it, contained tastefully appointed smoking rooms, card rooms, writing rooms, and lounges in a central structure, with open areas fore and aft. Covered galleries with wide wooden walkways ran down the port and starboard sides of the structure, providing a refuge for those who wanted shade with their fresh air. The rhythmic splashing of the sea sliding along *Athenia*'s hull accompanied Copland's footsteps on the pine decking. As he went, he checked the promenade deck's rooms from the outside looking for chinks of light and noted those he found. Concluding his tour, he climbed an outside stairway to the boat deck, so called because fourteen of the ship's twenty-six lifeboats were located there.

Copland was responsible for assuring all *Athenia*'s lifeboats were seaworthy, contained the necessary supplies and equipment, and had fully trained crews. If passengers had to abandon the ship, he personally would oversee launching the seven boats located on the port side of the boat deck. While the sight of lifeboats reassured passengers, he knew in an emergency, getting people into the boats and safely off the ship depended as much on luck as on the skill and training of the crew.

Each lifeboat relied on a pair of davits, small crane-like devices, to lift it off its resting place and lower it into the sea. Ropes, called falls, ran up to the davits from the lifeboat's bow and stern by way of a double block and tackle system that gave the team of seamen at the ends of the falls the mechanical advantage to raise the boat by hand. Once the boat was lifted up, each of the davits would be cranked out over the side of the ship using a hand-turned gear at its base. To lower a boat, the seamen relied on gravity. They wrapped each fall several times around a "gypsy barrel," a small flanged cylinder near the base of the davit. This provided them with sufficient friction to control the boat's descent. Keeping the boat level throughout this process was a challenge that required coordination between the seamen on the fore and aft falls. The system worked well in calm seas. But Copland knew that being able to perform all these tasks in stormy conditions or on a ship with a pronounced list could be problematic, even disastrous.

His concern at this hour, however, was not with the lifeboats but with the skylights over the lounges on the promenade deck below. In the darkness, he quickly saw a few places the work crew in Glasgow had missed when they painted over the skylights. He would make sure someone finished the job just as soon as *Athenia* dropped anchor tomorrow in Liverpool.

He took a moment to observe the broken clouds in the star-filled sky and noted that the moon had risen almost twenty degrees above the eastern horizon. It would be waning toward a half-moon during their Atlantic crossing. For Copland, few sights were as mesmerizing as moonlight dancing on the long running swells of an open sea. How unfortunate, he thought, that the ship's blackout conditions meant few passengers would have the opportunity to see it.

SATURDAY MORNING, SEPTEMBER 2

Barbara Cass-Beggs

WHILE SHE WAITED for her three-year-old daughter, Rosemary, to buckle the straps of her new shoes, Barbara scanned the parlor to make sure she hadn't missed repacking any items. She had driven from Oxford the day before with her husband, David, and Rosemary to stay the night with David's older brother, Noel Beggs, and Noel's wife, Bessie, in their modest brick row house near central Manchester. This morning they planned to drive the thirty miles to Liverpool to board *Athenia* and sail to Montreal.

"Do you want mummy to help?" Barbara asked.

"I can do it." Seated on the floor, Rosemary struggled to make the prong of the tiny silver buckle poke through a hole in a strap, while her honey-brown curls fell down around her face. A black and white toy panda bear that Rosemary called "Panthy" lay on the floor behind her. A recent birthday present from Barbara's mother, the cuddly bear never seemed to be more than an arm's length from the little girl. Her devotion to the toy reminded Barbara of the teddy bear she had loved as a companion when she was a child.

Bessie appeared in the parlor doorway holding a brown paper sack. "I've made you some sandwiches, in case they stop serving lunch by the time you board your ship."

"How sweet, Bessie. You're a dear."

"Mummy," Rosemary interrupted, "will Jim and Bill be on the boat?"

"No, darling, they're all the way across the ocean. We'll see them when we get off the boat in Canada."

"Who are Jim and Bill?" Bessie asked, handing the sandwiches to Barbara.

"They're Canadian graduate students we met at Oxford. We let our spare room out to Bill Gibson when Rosemary was a toddler. Through Bill, we met his brother, Jim. Both boys really became quite fond of Rosemary."

"They're my very best friends in Canada," Rosemary observed, shifting her attention to the buckle on her second shoe.

"Yes they are, dear." Barbara turned back to her sister-in-law. "I suppose you could say the Gibsons are the reason we're going to Canada."

"They are?"

"The boys were so enthusiastic about the opportunities Canada offered, when the chance to lecture there came up for David, we decided to go." Barbara's voice faded, her thoughts overtaken by the worrisome events of the past twenty-four hours—young men mobilizing, school children evacuating, the Nazis marching into Poland.

"Barbara, what is it?"

The question was an invitation. Should she keep her concerns private or unburden her conscience to her sister-in-law? Before she could decide, the words tumbled out of her.

"Oh Bessie, I'm really struggling with our decision to go. A few weeks ago, David had serious doubts about this trip. That's when I realized how important it was to me. I thought if we didn't go now, we'd never go. We'd be here the rest of our lives. I know he feels the same way, but he was quite concerned about leaving England and then watching the country go to war. I really argued for Canada, and he finally agreed. We didn't think there would be a chance of war coming so soon. Now I'm afraid he's going through with the trip because he knows it means so much to me."

When Bessie started to respond, Barbara held up her hand.

"Here's the worst part," she said. "I know it isn't fair that we're leaving and you're facing such a hellish situation, but I still want to go more than ever." She fixed her sister-in-law with a beseeching look.

"Do you despise me?"

Bessie sat on the sofa and reached for Barbara's hand.

"You listen to me, Barbara Cass-Beggs. Our situation isn't going to change one whit if you're here or in Canada. You should go—for Rosemary's sake if not your own—and keep your family safe over there."

Before she could respond, David appeared in the doorway. "Bar, we really should start." He seemed to notice her expression and stepped into the room. "Is everything all right?"

"Yes, dear, everything is fine," Barbara said.

"Good. Our bags are in the car, and we don't want to leave things to the last minute." David disappeared back into the hallway.

"Thank you for understanding," Barbara said, turning to Bessie. "It means so much to me."

Rosemary finished buckling her shoes and stood in triumph, while Barbara gathered herself and took one last look around the room.

"Don't forget Panthy," she said, pointing to the little bear lying on the floor. Rosemary scooped up the bear and clutched it to her chest. Barbara took her daughter's free hand, and together they followed David down the narrow hallway to the waiting car.

Spirydon Kucharczuk

A GRAY, LATE-MORNING sky hung over Liverpool's Mersey River, mirroring Spirydon's mood as he stood at a large window in Cunard's passenger departure area. He had brought his family to the waiting area well ahead of the appointed hour, still concerned he might have missed an important detail that would prevent them from boarding the ship to Canada. Along with the family's embarkation cards, Spirydon held a separate piece of paper with paragraphs printed in German, French, Italian, and Polish. He knew enough Polish to determine that they would board a separate boat to take them from the shore to the *Athenia*.

Spirydon stood next to his son, Stefan, who seemed mesmerized by all the river traffic. On the dock below them, men loaded cargo from large nets onto the deck of a broad-beamed tender. Beyond the tender, which ferried people and cargo from the shore to ships at anchor, a large ship with a black hull sat in the middle of the river.

"I think that is the ship to take us to Canada, Stefan." The boy followed his father's gaze to mid-river and nodded. "And that," Spirydon said, pointing to the craft being loaded below, "is probably the taxi boat that will take us out there."

They sat and waited while the room steadily filled with people. After nearly an hour, Spirydon heard a shrill whistle and looked up to see the tender moving away from the dock. He hadn't noticed if any passengers had boarded the boat and worried he might have missed an important announcement.

"Did you see if any passengers got on the boat?" he asked Stefan.

"No, Papa. I was watching the other boats."

Several people in the waiting area continued talking, seemingly unconcerned with the departing tender. It occurred to Spirydon they might be going on a different ship, but he needed to check.

"Pardon, pardon," he said in heavily accented English to a couple that appeared close to his age. They turned at the sound of his voice. The man, who was shorter than Spirydon, wore an expensive looking three-piece suit and held a heavy black coat over his left arm. The woman, with her dark hair in a simple finger wave, appeared similarly well dressed in a tailored navy blouse and skirt. They looked at Spirydon and smiled.

"*Athenia*? Go *Athenia*?" He pointed at the departing boat.

"Yes, the tender is going to the *Athenia*," the man said.

Unsure of the man's response, Spirydon pointed to himself, then to the tender in the river and shrugged his shoulders in a gesture he hoped would convey his uncertainty about not being on the boat. But his gesture drew a momentary blank stare from the couple.

"Howard," the woman said, "perhaps he thinks the tender is the *Athenia* and it has left without him." The man indicated Spirydon should stand next to him. When Spirydon complied, the man turned him to face out the window and pointed to the large ship near the middle of the river.

"*Athenia*," the man said. Spirydon nodded. He understood the big ship was *Athenia*, but the man apparently missed his question about being on the taxi boat. He began to despair that his poor language skills might prove to be their undoing. Stefan, who witnessed his father's concern, approached to find out what was the matter.

"I don't understand why the taxi boat goes without us," he said, speaking Ukrainian to his son. "Perhaps I made a mistake. Maybe we should have been standing somewhere else to go aboard the taxi boat."

"Are they going on the *Athenia*?" Stefan nodded in the direction of the couple who were watching their conversation.

"Of course, Stefan. How stupid of me." Spirydon turned to the couple and pointed to them. "*Athenia?*"

"Yes," they answered in unison.

"No you boat?" Spirydon pointed again to the tender, which was nearly halfway to *Athenia*. He wanted to be sure the couple was unconcerned about not being on the tender.

"U-boat?" the man said. "No, you needn't worry about U-boats here."

Their response puzzled Spirydon until he realized his poor mastery of the language had made it appear he was concerned about submarines. He shook his head in frustration.

"What is it, Papa?"

"They think I want to know about U-boats."

"I have some English from school. Do you want me to talk to them?"

"Not now," Spirydon said, waving toward the window. "You watch that taxi boat." He turned again to the couple and sought to rephrase his question.

"No you *go* boat?"

The couple appeared confused by the question, turning to each other and repeating Spirydon's words. "What do you think he means, Howard?" the woman said.

"*Athenia*," the man declared to Spirydon, pointing to himself and his wife. With a grand sweep of his arm, the man appeared to indicate the entire room and repeated, "*Athenia.*" Spirydon nodded and thanked the man.

"Perhaps we are in the correct place after all," he told Stefan. "Tell me when the taxi boat comes back." Spirydon started to return to his seat, then turned back to his son. "And from now on, you will speak to the English. It is too confusing a language."

Chief Officer Copland

CAPTAIN JAMES COOK'S spacious quarters were directly below *Athenia's* bridge. In response to Cook's summons, Copland entered the captain's quarters to find him preparing to go ashore for a meeting and luncheon at the Admiralty offices. Copland watched *Athenia's* master, wearing his smartest dress blues, check the mirror, smooth down his gray hair, and place his white peaked hat squarely on his head.

"You'll need to keep things moving with the new passengers coming aboard," Cook said. "I should be back in about three hours, and I want us ready to sail by four o'clock."

"Yes, sir. Before you go, Captain, several of the crew have picked up rumors that German U-boats are off the north Irish coast. I wonder if you could mention that during your meeting." *Athenia's* normal course out of Liverpool took her up the Irish Sea and around the north of Ireland, exactly where the U-boats were rumored to be waiting.

"I'm not surprised," Cook said. "If they are there, it's probably to shadow our Home Fleet." With one last look in the mirror, he ran his thumb and forefinger along the edge of his hat's visor and its golden oak leaf border. "I'll see what the Admiralty knows about any U-boat activity in the area. If there's going to be trouble, let's hope it starts well after we've sailed." The two men stepped outside and shook hands. Cook started down the stairway headed for his motor launch, while Copland watched him from the railing.

As *Athenia's* second-in-command, Copland assumed responsibility for the ship while her captain remained ashore. During these periods, he exercised authority with some restraint, mindful of its temporary nature. Each episode whetted his desire for command, and he wondered how near his opportunity might be, before a second, more troubling thought occurred to him.

How might war affect my opportunities?

He had no answer for that question. *Better to take things one step at a time*, he thought as he climbed to the bridge and greeted First Officer John Emery, whose watch continued for another hour.

Athenia's bridge stood four stories above her main deck. Aside from the crow's nest, the bridge deck and its wheelhouse provided the highest vantage point on the ship. The windows fronting the wheelhouse provided a sweeping view of the harbor. The morning sunlight poured in through the windows and glinted off of every polished surface.

"Is the old man on his way?" Emery asked.

"He is."

"And you asked him about the U-boats?"

"He's going to see what the Admiralty knows about the rumors. Said he wants to sail by four o'clock."

"Looks like the tender is on its way." Emery nodded toward the shoreline where the broad-beamed boat, her decks laden with cargo, headed toward them. "That reminds me, the radio room just heard from the head office. There's a train running late with fifty of our passengers on it. They're mostly Jewish immigrants from the Continent and we're supposed to wait for them."

"Did they say how late?"

Emery shook his head. "They didn't say."

"I'll let Mr. Harvey know," Copland said. "He's going to have his hands full clearing all the cargo in time." The chief officer excused himself and headed down to oversee unloading operations from the tender.

On his way, he noticed several passengers taking pictures of the big, gray, sausage-like barrage balloons floating on long tethers above the city skyline. It occurred to Copland that having photographs of Liverpool's air defenses circulating in Canada and the United States probably was not a good idea. On the other hand, the people weren't violating any restrictions with their photos.

"I'd be careful who I show those pictures to, if I were you," he said to no one in particular. His cautionary remark prompted several passengers to put down their cameras, while others continued taking their snapshots.

"Thank you," Copland said to the obliging passengers. "We can't be too cautious."

He found Bosun William Harvey on A deck by the number two cargo hatch near the ship's bow. A short fireplug of a man, Harvey began his career in sailing ships near the turn of the century, and aside from the captain, there was no other crewmember whose seamanship Copland respected more. He told the bosun of the captain's desire to sail by four o'clock and of the late-running train.

The bosun lifted his cap and ran his stubby fingers over a barren scalp. "Sure would be easier doing this operation dockside."

"That it would, but the captain wants to be out here when the tide turns, not sitting at a dock. Let's see if we can accommodate him and be ready to sail by four."

"Aye, Mr. Copland. I'll do my best."

"You always do, Mr. Harvey." Copland gave him a quick nod and headed off to check the cargo placement in the ship's forward hold. There would be very little turnaround time to oversee arrangements for the five hundred forty-six new passengers who would board in a few hours, doubling the passenger manifest. He checked his watch and realized they would need a minor miracle to be ready to sail by four.

SATURDAY AFTERNOON, SEPTEMBER 2

Rhoda Thomas

A SENSE OF disorder greeted Rhoda as she boarded *Athenia* in Liverpool. Passengers crowded the ship's B deck entrance, waiting for overworked men in blue uniforms to direct them to their accommodations. Crew members pushed handcarts piled high with luggage down the adjacent long passageway, adding to the general turmoil.

She noticed what appeared to be several large refugee families from Eastern Europe, judging from the bearded men carrying odd-shaped bundles and the women in heavy skirts, head scarves, and shawls. While the children gawked in wonder at all the activity, their parents' faces betrayed a general wariness. When she looked closer, Rhoda was struck by the presence of so many mothers with small children and babies.

It took nearly thirty minutes to reach the front of her line, where she found a man peering at her over a clipboard filled with dog-eared papers. She handed her embarkation card to the man, who seemed calm in spite of all the activity around him.

"Sorry about all the fuss, ma'am," he said. "Appreciate your patience."

"It's a wonder you have space for everyone."

"Ah, yes," he said, consulting his clipboard without looking up. "We're asking everyone to share a cabin, and we've turned some of our public rooms into dormitories. Quite a demand, you know."

"So I see."

"There will be three other women with you in your cabin, D230. That's two decks below us." The man turned to wave his hand toward the bow. "You'll need to go forward to the last set of stairs. They'll take you down to your cabin." He handed the card back to Rhoda.

"Thank you. And my suitcase?" she asked.

"It should be in the corridor outside your cabin. If it's not there now, it'll be along directly. And ma'am," he said as Rhoda turned to leave, "because of all the people, we will have three seatings at every meal. May I suggest that as soon as you are settled, you check with the dining steward to determine your seating preference. The third-class dining saloon is on C deck just astern of amidships."

She thanked the man again and joined a meandering stream of passengers moving down the corridor in search of cabins or stairways, eddying around stacks of luggage in the passageway. Passing isolated knots of people, she overheard conversations in a variety of languages. Some English-speaking passengers voiced disappointment with their accommodations, while others seemed to consider the discomforts a price worth paying in order to escape the threat of war. The more she heard, the more Rhoda began to think a sense of disorder would underlie the entire voyage.

She took a few wrong turns on D deck, which seemed even more crowded because of its narrow corridors. When she finally entered cabin D230 Rhoda found a stout middle-aged woman leaning over an open suitcase placed on a lower bunk. She turned to introduce herself as Mary Townley from Toronto.

"We're practically neighbors," Rhoda said. "I'm from the other side of the lake, Rochester, New York." Mary greeted the news with a wan smile that Rhoda overlooked in her relief at finding a surprisingly spacious cabin with four bunks, two upper and two lower.

"Judging from all the comments I heard on my way down here, I'd say we've done rather well for ourselves."

"It is an interior cabin," Mary said, "but they say all the portholes have been painted over, so we wouldn't have sunlight anyway."

Rhoda chose to ignore the melancholy tone in Mary's voice. She retrieved her suitcase from the passageway and put it on the other lower bunk. After hanging a robe and a couple of dresses in the cabin's only wardrobe, she noticed Mary was simply staring into her open suitcase.

"Is something wrong, dear?" Rhoda asked.

"No, not really. I can't decide what to unpack. I'm still thinking about leaving England so soon."

"Were you visiting relatives?"

"It's been twenty-five years since we moved to Canada, and in all that time I never came back to see my mother and two sisters until now." Mary shook her head. "My husband couldn't get away from work, but he bought a ticket for me to come anyway. It was a surprise for my birthday."

"My husband, Frank, couldn't get away either," Rhoda said, sitting on the bed next to Mary. "The state employment office where he works would only give him a week off. It's such a pity because all his relatives are here. We grew up in the same town."

"We didn't think anything about a war," Mary said, ignoring Rhoda's remarks. "There was a cable from my husband waiting for me when I arrived in England. He said there was going to be a war and he wanted me to come home right away. I was only able to spend four days here. It's just so unfair. After all these years, they decide to have a war now. Why couldn't they have waited another month at least?"

"I'm so sorry. I know just how you feel. I had to leave my brother and sister-in-law." Rhoda recalled her own rushed departure with no time to say goodbye to other relatives and friends, but she felt grateful to have spent nearly a month in their company instead of just four days.

"You know, I don't really feel much like unpacking now, either," Rhoda said. "Why don't we go up to the dining saloon and see about our seating assignments. Maybe they'll be serving tea."

"With all these people," Mary sighed, "they're probably out of tea by now."

David Jennings

DAVID AND HIS friends, John Woods and Tony Cassels, squeezed past the luggage stacked along D deck's forward passageways as they searched for their cabin. They had been up early to catch the first train from London to

Liverpool and arrived with an hour to spare before boarding the tender that brought them out to *Athenia*. Along the hallway, a few white-coated stewards knocked on cabin doors to reunite the occupants with their baggage.

"David, why don't you ask that fellow if he knows anything about the rumor you heard?" Tony nodded toward a steward who was collecting empty suit-cases for storage.

"Excuse me, sir," David said. The steward straightened up to face him.

"Looking for your cabin, are you?" he said with a helpful smile.

"Yes, but I was wondering if you could answer a question," David said. "I heard that our captain has gone ashore to ask for a Royal Navy destroyer to escort us to Canada. Do you know anything about that?"

"'Fraid not, gov'nor. But it sounds like a good idea to me. Now, where are you chaps headed?" The steward reached to see the embarkation card in David's hand. After a glance, he told them to take the first corridor on the right and go to the end.

Cabin D245 was located on the starboard side of the ship where the hull began to taper toward the bow. David and his friends entered a cramped, irregular-shaped room to find two sets of bunks and a short, wiry man seated on one of the lower beds.

"Hello there." The man popped to his feet. "You must be my new roommates."

"Looks like it," David said.

"Name's Alfie Snow," the man said. "They call me the 'Mad Miner from Timmins.' Pleased to meet you."

David noticed that, despite Alfie's agility, he was an older man with thin-ning, sandy hair and a ruddy complexion. Alfie's left sleeve was empty, its cuff pinned to the shoulder of his shirt.

"Don't mind this, lads," Alfie said, shrugging his left shoulder. "Lost my arm in a mining accident a few years back, but it don't slow me down much. Only takes one hand to lift a pint."

"Now, there's an excellent idea," John said, glancing at David and Tony. "Why don't you join us, Mr. Snow, and we'll head to the lounge and lift a glass or two?" A broad grin lit up the Mad Miner's face.

"You lads are all right," he said as they headed for the door.

First the King of England and now a one-armed miner, David thought. *How many more surprises will there be before we get to Canada?*

Ruth Etherington

WITH THEIR TEN-YEAR-OLD son Geoffrey in tow, Ruth and her husband, Harold, descended into the bowels of *Athenia*. They were a long way from an open deck and fresh air, and Ruth began to worry about Harold.

"Do you think you'll be alright down here?" she asked him when they reached the small D deck foyer.

"Of course, why not?" Harold responded absently, consulting their embarkation cards and searching the cabin numbers.

"You're the one who told me you were so sick whenever you went to sea during the war. Perhaps a cabin is available on a higher deck." They flattened themselves against the wall to make way for a crewman wheeling a pushcart full of luggage down the narrow passageway.

"That was twenty years ago," he said, resuming his search. "And I'd be very surprised if there's an empty bed or cot anywhere on this ship. They probably could have thrown a mattress on deck and sold it for passage to Canada."

"I'd be happy to check with the purser. You never know. Something could turn up."

"Here we are," Harold announced, ignoring Ruth's offer. "D98 is for Geoff and me. And you're right next door in D100." He handed her embarkation card back to her. "I'll be fine, Ruth. Who knows where we'd be scattered if we tried to change things now. Come on, Geoff."

Harold and Geoffrey entered their cabin, leaving Ruth standing in the corridor. She was pleased to see her suitcases had been delivered, but her mood changed when she entered D100 to find three women and a cabin that felt like a closet. Noting the room's lack of ventilation, its darkened porthole, and recalling that *Athenia*'s third-class cabins did not include running water, she began to think a mattress on deck might not be so bad.

THOMAS C. SANGER

Barbara Cass-Beggs

AN AFTERNOON BREEZE blowing down the Mersey River ruffled her hair as Barbara stood in the third-class promenade area at *Athenia*'s stern. She began to doubt her decision to leave her cardigan behind, but the crowded ship discouraged any thought of returning to retrieve it from her cabin two decks below. At least Rosemary seemed happy enough, kneeling next to the ship's railing and telling her toy panda about all the boats moving up and down the river. Barbara glanced up to see her husband, David, approaching through the sea of passengers. He did not look happy.

"There are no deck chairs left to be reserved," he told Barbara. "I suppose we're too late. This certainly isn't shaping up well, is it?" She wondered if David might be taking the trip's discomforts too personally.

"Rosemary seems content," she said. "We could spread a blanket here on the deck, and it will be fine." They paused to watch their daughter, who appeared perfectly content in her own world with Panthy. The breeze stiffened, and Barbara snuggled close to David and the warmth of his tweed coat.

"Have you noticed all the children on board?" she said.

"I doubt all of them could have been vacationing here," David said. "I expect some are being sent off as a precaution."

"Yes, sort of like being in the middle of our own evacuation." Barbara thought of a photograph in yesterday's evening paper, of children lined up at a train station waiting to be sent to the countryside. The thought made her shiver, and David put his arm around her shoulders.

"Do you want my coat?" he asked.

"No. I just thought about all those schoolchildren being evacuated. How does a mother send her child away like that?"

"At least that's a choice we won't have to face, now that we're leaving England in the lurch," David said. Barbara needed to move their conversation off the threat of war.

"Have you met your roommates yet?" she asked. David's D deck cabin was on the opposite side of the ship from Barbara and Rosemary.

"No, how about you?"

"Yes, actually. An American woman and her son, who is about two, I think. They seem nice enough. But the cabin is so small."

"You saw the note?" he asked. Barbara nodded. The Donaldson Atlantic Line had placed a stenciled letter on every bed, acknowledging the crowded conditions due to the "present emergency" and asking everyone's indulgence in overlooking "any difficulties that might occur."

"I wonder," David said, "what have I got us into?"

Barbara reached for her husband's hand and squeezed it. "I don't know about you, but I'm looking forward to a relaxing sea voyage to a new country, where we're going to spend the coming year exploring all it has to offer," she said, smiling up at her husband.

Chief Officer Copland

THE THREE *ATHENIA* officers seated in Captain Cook's quarters below the bridge waited in silence for him to unbutton his dress-blue uniform coat and hang it in his wardrobe. Judging from Cook's dour expression, Copland thought the news would not be good. First Officer Emrey and Chief Engineer John Carnegie sat with Copland at a rectangular table that occupied a corner of the tidy room. Cook sat at the table, shuffled through several papers in a portfolio he had brought back with him, and cleared his throat.

"Thank you for being so prompt. I'll come right to the point. Most of the officers I spoke with think we will be at war with Germany in a day or two." He paused, seeming to let the gravity of the words settle.

"Naval Control did not confirm any U-boat sightings in the western approaches, but we should assume the subs are there. So, gentlemen, we will double the watches on a twenty-four-hour basis once we leave the Irish Sea . . . or sooner if events dictate."

"There's a rumor among the passengers that we've requested a destroyer escort," Copland said.

"There'll be no escort," Cook said. "I asked and was told there are none available. For now, it appears our best defense is the wide open sea. The

Admiralty has given us a course thirty miles north of our usual run to the St. Lawrence." Cook pulled a thick naval chart from his portfolio and the three men leaned forward as he spread it out on the table. The new course, marked in red, followed a Great Circle arc over the thin lines that delineated shallower depths of the Atlantic Ocean. It would take them closer to Greenland than normal, but Copland knew in late summer there should be no worry about ice.

"I think it's best to refrain from posting any information for passengers about our course or position," Cook continued. A chart showing the ship's progress usually occupied a prominent space in the corridor outside the purser's office.

"The chart's very popular with passengers," Copland said. "We're likely to be asked about its absence."

"Yes, of course. I think most passengers will understand. But if you get a question, you can say we're just being cautious. Assure them we know where we are and so does the Admiralty. It really isn't necessary for anyone else to know our exact location and course.

"Obviously, it is very important that all our blackout measures are in place and effective. Mr. Copland, you'll do another check tonight on your walk, and please be sure all public notices prohibiting smoking on deck at night are in place and clearly visible. The only lights we'll be showing at night are the side running lights."

"Sir, what if we get questions about German subs?" Emrey asked. Cook thought for a moment before responding.

"Don't lie to passengers, but don't emphasize the danger either," he said. "A lot depends on your demeanor. Be confident. Reassure them we're taking all precautions.

"Quite frankly, if war is declared and Germany abides by the international treaties, we shouldn't be in any danger. We're sailing unescorted, so they would have to warn us if they wanted to attack. I'd even invite the bastards aboard if it were necessary to prove we're not carrying any war materiel." The captain stood to signal the meeting was at an end.

"Gentlemen, the very best measure we can take is to put as many miles as possible between us and the subs. Mr. Carnegie," Cook said, nodding at the chief engineer, "for the next forty-eight hours, I want to maintain fifteen knots day and night."

"Aye, sir," Carnegie said.

"Two hundred miles beyond Ireland should do it." The men rose from their chairs but hesitated when it was clear Cook had something else on his mind.

"One last thing," he said. "The fate of eleven hundred souls is in our hands. Let's make sure we deliver them home safely. Now, are we ready to weigh anchor, Mr. Copland?"

"Within the half hour," Copland said. "The tender was late arriving with passengers. Something about a refugee train coming in behind schedule from London."

"No later than four-thirty, Mr. Copland."

"Aye, Captain."

SATURDAY LATE AFTERNOON &

EVENING, SEPTEMBER 2

Rhoda Thomas

TWENTY MINUTES AFTER weighing anchor, *Athenia* entered the Irish Sea, heading north on long rolling swells toward the Isle of Man. Standing in the ship's open portside gallery on the promenade deck, Rhoda felt the chill of a stiff breeze on her face and noticed the slanting shadows of rain beneath distant dark clouds to the southwest.

"Glad we thought to wear our heavy coats," Rhoda said to her roommate, Mary Townley. They stood with several other newly arrived passengers waiting for their lifeboat drill to begin.

"I should have brought my scarf," Mary said. "My ears are freezing." Rhoda began to wonder if Mary's forlorn disposition would be a permanent fixture of their crossing.

Like everyone else, Rhoda carried a beige canvas lifejacket, a vest-like garment with four brick-sized pieces of cork, two in front and two in back, sewn into vertical pockets. A jumble of cloth ties hung down from the jacket like strings of spaghetti.

"Not wasting any time, are they?" said a young woman standing to the other side of Rhoda. "I could practically swim ashore from here." She guessed the girl to be about twenty, the same age as her youngest daughter.

"I doubt I could swim that far," Rhoda said. "Perhaps you could give me a lift."

The young woman smiled at Rhoda, then waved to two other girls her age who rushed up to join her. Rhoda's acquaintance was the shortest of the three young women, but the most animated. Judging from their easy banter, the three were good friends, and Rhoda tried to think of a time when she had been so carefree.

"Are you girls all from the same town?" she asked at a pause in their conversation.

"We're all Delta Gammas at the University of Michigan," said the tallest of the three. "We toured Europe together, but our return booking was scrambled because of all the war talk. We were lucky to all get on the *Athenia*. What about you?"

"Oh, I'm in the same boat as you," Rhoda said.

"So I see," the tall girl said with a laugh, before resuming the conversation with her friends.

Assuming she and Mary would share the same lifeboat with the people gathered around her, Rhoda began to take stock of her likely companions. In addition to the college girls, she noticed several mothers with children and several more women her age.

"All my friends in Louisville will be so envious when I show off the latest fashion from Europe." The shortest of the university girls had put on her lifejacket and took a few flouncing steps with one hand on her hip, to the amusement of her friends.

"Makes you look like a big waffle, dearie," a man said near the back of the crowd. Everyone laughed, including the "model" and her classmates.

"All right, ladies and gentlemen, give me your attention." A short, balding man wearing a lifejacket over his dark-blue uniform coat walked to the front of the group. "Name's William Harvey. I'm the ship's bosun and what I'm about to tell you will come in very handy if we have an emergency during our crossing." His commanding voice soared over the babble of conversations, which quickly subsided.

"That's better," Harvey said as the voices quieted. "First of all, this is your muster station. In the event of a signal to abandon ship, this is where you will gather and be directed to board your lifeboat. I suggest you become familiar with this location and how to find your way here from anywhere on the ship." Harvey paused. Two of the college girls who had been talking softly stopped their conversation and looked up. They smiled at the bosun, but he did not appear amused.

"If we have to abandon the ship, the signal is eight short blasts followed by one long blast on the ship's whistle. If you hear that signal, stop whatever you're doing and go to your cabin to collect your lifejacket and a warm coat or blanket, even if it's the middle of the day. Then proceed here immediately. The lifeboats have some blankets aboard, but not enough for everyone. Believe me, if you have to spend the night in an open boat on the ocean, you will want something to keep you warm.

"Now, if we have to load the boats, we will load women and children first. Please, gentlemen, don't make us have to enforce this rule, because we will. Let the missus and the kiddies go first. Don't worry, gents. Even with all the people we have aboard, there's room for everyone, so I guarantee you will get a seat."

Harvey explained that their group's lifeboat was actually located on the boat deck above. A smaller boat stowed on top of their boat would be loaded with passengers from the boat deck and lowered into the water. After the smaller boat moved away, their boat would be lowered into the water with just a few of the ship's crew in it. When everything was ready below, they would be directed by crew members here at their muster station to climb down rope ladders over the side of the ship to enter their lifeboat.

"Why can't we get into our boat when it's on the deck, like the people above us?" asked one of the older men.

"Yeah, why do we have to climb down a rope ladder?" asked a woman holding a restless toddler.

"Because we're in better shape than the geezers in cabin class," Rhoda's short acquaintance answered. Several people laughed, but Rhoda thought it was a good question. She wasn't sure she could climb down a ladder into a boat.

Bosun Harvey raised his hand to regain the group's attention.

"Your boat is bigger than the top boat. It holds eighty-six people. It would be quite a strain for the crew to lower away one of those big boats filled to capacity. That's why we put it in the water first. We'd hate to drop you.

"The last topic I want to cover is the thingamajig you folks are carrying." Harvey held up his lifejacket with its dangling straps. "This is your lifejacket, and it can save your life if you put it on properly. If you jump or fall into the water and your straps aren't tight, your lifejacket could slide up and break your neck."

"That would ruin your day," someone in the crowd said. A smattering of laughter was cut short by Harvey's scowl.

"Truly, ladies and gentlemen, this is no laughing matter." Harvey demonstrated how to put on a lifejacket and to tie it securely, then invited all the passengers to do the same. "I want everyone to tie on your lifejacket, and no one's to leave until I've checked you. Now, while you're tying, can anyone tell me the signal to abandon ship?"

Several people called out the sequence of eight short and one long blast on the ship's whistle.

"Very good. If you hear that signal, grab something warm and your lifejacket, and come here straightaway. Are there any questions?"

"Are you going to be in our lifeboat?" one of the university girls asked.

"Much as I would like to accompany you all, if we get the signal, I will be moving from station to station to make sure my men are doing everything they're supposed to do to assist you safely off this ship. I will be one of the last ones to leave."

Following the last question, Bosun Harvey took his time inspecting the lifejackets and adjusted the ties for several of the passengers. As she waited for the bosun to check her straps, Rhoda wondered how many of her fellow passengers had taken his remarks seriously.

"I wonder, Mary, how many people will remem—" Rhoda stopped, surprised by the smile on Mary's face. "Is something funny?"

"You really do look like a big waffle," Mary said.

Spirydon Kucharczuk

THE THIRD-CLASS DINING saloon began emptying as the early dinner seating came to an end. Spirydon anxiously scanned the large room, with its dark wooden pillars, gray walls, and maroon velvet curtains covering the blacked-out portholes. He hoped to find someone able to substantiate Stefan's interpretation of the English sailor's remarks at that afternoon's lifeboat exercise. Some elements of the boy's translation hadn't made sense to Spirydon, so he eagerly sought a third party to confirm the procedures. He also wanted to ask why Ewdokia and the younger children had been directed to a different muster station. The challenge was finding someone likely to speak Polish or, better still, Ukrainian.

As he shuffled toward the exit with his family, Spirydon spotted a stout man going up a nearby stairway and wearing a cloth cap and woolen jacket similar to his own. He told Jan and Stefan he would meet them in their cabin shortly and bounded up the stairs to approach the stranger in the corridor.

"Pardon," he said in Polish. "May I speak with you?"

The man turned to reveal a wary expression framed by a neatly trimmed black beard showing flecks of gray. He was shorter and appeared to be older than Spirydon. The man nodded, and they continued along the hallway while Spirydon introduced himself and explained his dilemma.

"I will be happy to help a fellow Pole," the man said, adding that his name was Chaim Mazur. "We should go to the lounge where we can talk."

Minutes later, they found seats at an empty table amid several card games, loud conversations, and a mahjong tournament. They spoke quietly, Chaim saying it was better that they not draw attention to themselves as "foreigners." Spirydon did not understand the man's caution, but was pleased to confirm much of what Stefan had translated.

"The English sailor did say something about women and children being first," Chaim said in response to Spirydon's question. "I am not sure why that should be, but he made it clear they would enforce the rule."

Spirydon shook his head slowly, recalling the German soldiers with their rifles in the train station.

"There is one other thing that troubles me, Chaim. I must go to a different lifeboat than my wife."

Chaim explained that the muster stations appeared to be tied to the location of passenger cabins. The fact that Spirydon's wife and children were given a cabin on the opposite side of the ship was the likely reason for their different assignments.

"The sailor did not have a list of the passengers reporting to his station," Chaim said. "I think if we had to go to the lifeboats, you could go with your wife. Nobody would know the difference."

"My friend," Spirydon said with a smile, "you have been a very big help to me and my family. I wish to buy you a beer."

A few minutes later, the two men sat back down at their table, hunched toward each other over a pair of amber ales while they lamented the German invasion of their homeland. They exchanged stories of how they came to be on *Athenia*, and Spirydon learned Chaim was Jewish. He had known a few Jewish merchants in Trosteniec, but had never talked to them about the Nazis' harsh treatment of the Jews. He asked Chaim if the stories were exaggerated.

"I have a cousin in Czechoslovakia that I used to hear from every month," Chaim said. "But after the Nazis began taking over the country last year, my cousin started to write to me almost weekly. He told me they were being treated the same as Jews in Germany. He wrote to me about seeing synagogues burned, about Jewish property being taken by Nazis, and about Jews being thrown out of businesses they had started and built up over many years. Jews could not own property. Jewish artists could only perform in certain places. It was as if we'd been erased from all forms of public life." Chaim paused to take a sip of beer.

"And what about your cousin?" Spirydon asked.

"I am coming to that. About six months ago, he wrote to say the Nazis went to some villages in his area and separated most of the Jewish men and older boys and marched them away to train depots. The Nazis told the women that their men were going to work camps, but they did not say where these camps were, and the women did not receive any letters from their husbands or sons. My cousin said he was very depressed and was moving his family to Hungary. That's when his letters stopped coming. At first, I thought he was relocating and I would hear from him when he got to Hungary. But there has been no word from him since April. I tell you, more than anything, that silence convinced me I had to leave Poland."

By the time they finished their drinks and said their goodbyes, Spirydon was more certain than ever he had made the right choice to move his family to Canada, far beyond the reach of the Nazis.

Chief Officer Copland

SEATED AT ONE of several round tables beneath the domed ceiling of the cabin-class dining saloon, Chief Officer Copland felt a slight increase in *Athenia's* roll. The motion told him that the squalls expected just after sunset had arrived. He took the last few sips of his tea, stood, and excused himself. Before he could leave the room, however, the young cadet, Jimmy Turnbull, approached him anxiously and asked to have a word.

"A woman has fallen on the stairs, and the stewards haven't been able to revive her," Jimmy said in a low voice. "I thought you'd want to know."

"Has anyone alerted Doctor Sharman?"

"I don't know. It happened a few minutes ago."

"Where?"

"The third-class dining saloon. She was going down to D deck."

"Let's go," Copland said. He led Jimmy through the galley that separated the cabin and tourist dining facilities from the third-class saloon. They entered the large room, with its heavy maroon curtains, and stepped around the tightly packed tables to come upon a small knot of people at the head of the stairs leading down to D deck. Copland moved through the onlookers and saw a woman lying facedown at the bottom of the stairs. A stewardess knelt beside her, and two stewards held back a group of passengers that had gathered at the base of the stairway.

Copland came down the stairs quickly, asking people to please step back and give the woman some air. He knelt next to the stewardess.

"She's still unconsciousness, Mr. Copland," the stewardess said. He noted a small pool of blood on the carpet beneath the woman's head. Her pulse was weak but steady.

"We need to get her up to sick bay," Copland said. Glancing up, he nodded to the nearest steward. "Get a stretcher from the aid station. Jimmy, find Doctor Sharman and tell him to meet us in sick bay as quickly as possible."

☆ ☆ ☆

THE SHIP'S HOSPITAL facilities were located on the port side of B deck near the stern. Copland and two stewards arrived with the stretcher just ahead of Jimmy and Dr. Albert Sharman, a middle-aged Glasgow physician serving as the ship's doctor for the voyage. The doctor directed them to place their patient on the examination table and wait in the corridor. Copland dismissed the two stewards, but Jimmy asked if he might stay on a bit. As the minutes ticked by while they waited, it became increasingly apparent to Copland that the cadet had something on his mind.

"Something troubling you, Jimmy?"

"It's silly, I know. But . . ."

"Go on."

"Sir, do you think I might be, ah . . . a Jonah?"

"A Jonah? Good heavens, man, has someone been filling your head with old superstitions?"

"No, sir. But since I've come aboard for this voyage, there's been talk of war and German submarines, there were those men at the shipyards calling us cowards and such, and now this woman's been injured. Am I bad luck?"

For a moment, Copland wavered between a response filled with laughter at the ridiculous notion or a stern rebuke for even considering the idea. He decided on a little of both.

"It seems to me, just about everyone aboard meets the criteria you just laid out."

"Aye, but I'm the youngest and newest member of the crew."

"Jimmy, look at me," Copland said, placing a hand on the young man's shoulder and turning to face him directly. "I don't subscribe to such nonsense and neither should you. Have bad things happened with every ship you've sailed on?"

"No."

"How about your shipmates? Are they shunning you, refusing to talk to you?"

"No."

"I didn't think so," Copland said, training a stern eye on the cadet. "You're a sober, smart, capable lad, and you'll make a fine officer someday, I've no doubt. So you're to put all thoughts of being a Jonah out of your head."

"Aye, sir. Thank you, Mr. Copland."

☆ ☆ ☆

IT TOOK ANOTHER twenty minutes before Dr. Sharman opened the examination room door and invited them to join him. They entered to find the woman still unconscious and lying under a gray wool blanket. White bandages turbaned her head, and the blood had been cleaned from her face, revealing a badly swollen lip, a deep purple bruise on her left cheek, and two black eyes.

"I've sedated her, so she should remain unconscious for the next twenty-four hours," the doctor said. "She apparently landed very hard on her face. I've stitched up the cut on her lip, but the poor woman also has a broken nose. We'll have a better idea of her injuries when the swelling goes down."

"Is there anything else we should do, doctor?" Copland asked. "Do you think she needs a proper hospital?"

"No, I don't think that's necessary at the moment. She'll rest for the next day or so. Nurse Weir and I will keep a close watch on her condition."

Minutes later, Copland stood in the passageway outside the sick bay with Jimmy. "I need you to help identify this unfortunate woman. She was headed down to D deck, so you should start with the stewards and stewardesses working the cabins toward the stern."

"Yes, sir." The cadet turned toward the stairway.

"And Jimmy," Copland called, "remember what I said about that nonsense we discussed earlier."

"Yes, sir. I will." As the cadet turned again for the stairs, Copland thought he detected a faint smile on Jimmy's lips.

Oberleutnant Lemp

THE COOK STOOD before Lemp, who sat on his bunk and quietly fumed at the news he had just received.

A trivial mistake, but it comes at such a bad time. If we don't see some action soon, a little thing like this can destroy morale.

"You've checked all the boxes?" Lemp asked.

"Yes, sir, they're all mislabeled. Every one contains condensed milk."

Lemp shook his head. *U-30*'s crew had eaten the last of the fresh bread, picking away the flecks of mold that appeared on the loaves in the last few days. Normally, at this point in a patrol, they would begin consuming the supplies of canned brown bread. But when the cook opened the first box labeled "Brown Bread," he found it filled with cans of condensed milk instead.

"What do we do now?" he asked the cook.

"I'll have to serve the men rice or noodles at breakfast. I don't think they'll be very happy about that."

"No, they won't. Do the best you can, Cookie." With a half-hearted salute, the cook retreated unsteadily through the rocking boat's control room to his small galley.

More than twenty-four hours had passed since the German Naval High Command transmitted news of the Fatherland's invasion of Poland; twenty-four hours and still no word of any reaction by England or France. Could Hinsch be right? Were the English backing down? The idle hours of waiting and not knowing grated on him, and he sensed a similar growing frustration in his crew.

To take his mind off the present circumstances, Lemp checked again with the radio operator, who confirmed there were no new messages from high command, and then he stepped into the control room and climbed the ladder to *U-30*'s bridge atop the conning tower.

Leutnant Bothe, the boat's second watch officer, saluted his captain. "Any word from Naval Command?" he asked.

"Nothing new." Lemp blinked in the late afternoon sun and raised his binoculars to scan the horizon ahead. "Keep a sharp lookout now," he cautioned the men on the bridge, before silently rebuking himself for stating the obvious. The lookouts were well aware that the half-light of dawn and dusk were the most difficult times to spot a gray airplane fuselage against a gray sky.

It's bad enough I drive myself crazy with all this waiting. I don't need to get on the crew's nerves, too.

After a few minutes of sweeping the horizon with his binoculars, Lemp lost his concentration and returned to his quarters. He pulled the curtain across his alcove and lay back on his bunk, mulling over his general orders once again. Upon a declaration of war, he would be ordered into his combat zone and advised when to engage the enemy. His primary targets would be merchant ships. The *Führer* wanted to avoid embarrassing the English or French by sinking one of their warships while there might be a chance of reaching a peace accord with either country. Attacking enemy merchant ships meant abiding by the submarine protocol: giving warning, stopping, and searching a ship for war contraband.

But the protocol was unworkable. Like every U-boat commander, Lemp knew the increasing range of aircraft, the presence of aircraft carriers far out to sea, and the development of radio made his boat vulnerable to attack under these rules. Dönitz understood this. He had personally warned Lemp the night before *U-30* sailed that he should not risk his boat and his crew by surfacing unless he was certain his target was unarmed. He could still recall his commander's warning.

"We know the English are mounting guns on merchant ships to use as auxiliary cruisers," Dönitz had told him. "The English newspapers claim several are already at sea. If you surface to challenge one of these ships by mistake, a good gun crew will have you in range before you even step onto your bridge."

Lying on his bunk, swaying in the middle of a churning sea, Lemp turned Dönitz's words over and over in his mind.

Did he tell me in so many words to ignore the protocol?

He made up his mind he would consider every enemy merchant ship to be armed unless he could be sure it had no place to conceal such weapons. Of course, the matter would be far simpler if he spotted a passenger liner. Under his general orders, attacking these ships was absolutely forbidden.

Chief Officer Copland

AN HOUR AFTER leaving the ship's hospital, Copland sat across the table from Captain Cook, who was finishing his evening meal in his quarters. The captain had asked his chief officer to join him to review new communications signals to be employed in the event of war. While Cook sipped his tea, Copland briefed him about the woman's accident and her condition.

"Bad luck," Cook said, "and even worse timing. If it's serious, we'll need to find an eastbound ship to take her off."

"Dr. Sharman doesn't think that's necessary, for the time being."

"Well, keep me informed." Cook placed his empty dinner plate on a tray, took it to the sideboard, and rang for his steward. At his corner desk, the captain withdrew the ship's Admiralty books and brought them to the table along with an envelope containing the new procedures he had received in Liverpool. The two men pored over the new code signals to be used in wireless transmissions as well as changes in *Athenia*'s usual operations in the event of war.

"They want us to zigzag as a precaution no matter how far we might be from England."

Copland nodded but wondered if such precautions were really necessary. Cook seemed to read his concern.

"I think it's a bit much. I'd rather just make a run for it, but we'll comply if it's war."

"Yes, sir."

"I don't mind telling you, this is a bad business." Cook slumped back in his chair. "I've been taking meals in my cabin because I'm afraid I can't keep my worries off my face. Too distracted to make small talk. It wouldn't do for passengers to see their captain so concerned."

"Well, sir," Copland said, "by this time tomorrow night you should be free of your worst concerns."

Cook nodded and began collecting the papers on the table. "Do you know what happened to our namesake?" he said.

"Our namesake? I'm afraid not, sir."

"The last *Athenia* was about half our tonnage and went into service in '04. Just like us, she carried passengers and cargo between Britain and Canada. In 1917, on her way to Montreal, she was sunk by a German U-boat in the Great War. Happened just north of Inishtrahull. We sail right past her resting place later tonight."

"Well, sir, let's hope lightning doesn't strike in the same place twice." For the first time since coming aboard in Glasgow, Copland saw a smile cross Cook's face.

"I don't believe in omens either, Mr. Copland." The smile disappeared as Cook shook his head. "Still, with all the women and children on board, I shouldn't like to see us have to abandon this ship."

☆ ☆ ☆

AFTER LEAVING THE captain's quarters, Copland conducted his usual walk, beginning in the forward section of third-class cabins on D deck. Once again, he methodically checked the ship's blackout precautions. Stepping outside on the promenade deck, he turned up the collar of his heavy wool peacoat and settled his peaked hat more firmly on his head to face the night's blustery squalls. As the rain let up, he climbed to the boat deck and was pleased to see that the day's work crew had painted over all the streaks he had noted the night before.

Copland turned toward the railing and looked out on a dark ocean. Whitecaps, barely visible in the night, caught the wind, tore apart, and settled like lace on the backs of the waves. The faint throbbing of *Athenia*'s steam turbines, the seas crashing on her bow, and the wind sighing in her rigging told him the ship was moving smartly on her way. Yet something about these familiar surroundings unsettled him. Perhaps it was the darkness that was so complete, the deck devoid of people despite the ship's crowded conditions, or the lurking threat of U-boats.

Copland thought of the coming war and of the warning his friend, Gordon Dunbar, had issued about all of Copland's careful planning. That memory triggered an unpleasant recollection of his heated comments to his mother before he sailed. What had possessed him to be so strident? He decided to make it up to her by finding a nice gift in Montreal. But as he began to consider an appropriate present, he wondered about *Athenia*'s return trip under probable wartime conditions.

Will there be enough passengers bound for England for Athenia*'s return crossing? If not, what will happen to this tough old girl?*

And what will that future hold for me?

The raindrops from a new squall began softly drumming on the tarpaulins covering the deck's swaying lifeboats, and Copland retreated back to his cabin without any further thought of the future.

SUNDAY MORNING, SEPTEMBER 3

Ruth Etherington

THE FAINT SOUNDS of creaking wood and rushing water awakened Ruth, and for a moment she was completely disoriented. Total darkness enveloped her. Warm, heavy air pressed down on her face and somewhere nearby a person snored softly. Coming fully awake, Ruth felt her body gently swaying and remembered she was aboard a passenger ship.

The warm darkness, still air, and rocking corkscrew movement converged in her stomach, which began to churn uncomfortably. Ruth sat up and threw off her bed covers. She scooted to the foot of her bunk, searched for the wooden ladder with her toes, and climbed down.

She found the door handle in the dark and opened it just enough for the light in the corridor to fall on her watch: six thirty-five. Not wanting to turn on the cabin light and wake her roommates, Ruth dressed in the clothes she had worn the night before, felt around for her handbag, and stepped out into the corridor. She tapped on the door of cabin D98 and called her husband's name in a hoarse whisper.

After several moments, Harold cracked open the door, blinked into the light, and frowned when he recognized his wife.

"What time is it?" he said.

"Six thirty. I'm feeling a little sick. I wanted you to know I'm going up on deck."

"Oh. You'd better go. I'll find you in a few minutes."

☆ ☆ ☆

STANDING AT THE railing with the early morning breeze in her face and a view of the horizon, Ruth felt her stomach settle. Thinning patches of clouds to the west seemed to promise blue skies at some point during the coming day. Swells on the wide, steely blue ocean marched in endless rows toward the ship, striking *Athenia*'s hull at an oblique angle that produced the rolling pitch Ruth had felt in her bunk. After several deep breaths, her queasiness disappeared.

"Feeling any better?" Harold approached along the gently rolling deck, dressed in a dark tweed jacket and gray flannel pants.

"Yes, a bit. The room is so stuffy I just had to get out. What about you?"

"No problems . . . touch wood," he said, rapping his knuckles on the railing. "Do you want my jacket?"

"No, the breeze feels good," Ruth said, "but I will take an arm." She slipped her arm under his and pulled tight against him. They gazed at the horizon as the sky continued to brighten.

"No sign of land," she said.

"We probably left Ireland behind early this morning," he said. "Nothing between us and Canada now but the open sea." They stood at the railing for several minutes, watching the restless vista of the rolling swells until Ruth broke the silence.

"It's so hard to think of everyone in England facing another war. A part of me feels like we're running away."

"Don't be silly," Harold said, his gaze still fixed on the horizon. "We've lived in America for a decade, and I'm an American citizen now. We're not running away from anything."

"Of course, but my heart feels divided."

"I can't help you with that."

"If only there was something I could do."

"Like what?" he said, looking down at her with a bemused expression that seemed to mock her concerns.

"Oh I don't know. I'd like to take Mr. Hitler by the scruff of his neck, sit him down, and talk some sense into that horrid little man. He's causing so much pain and suffering."

"Whoa, you don't usually get so worked up," Harold said. "Where did that come from?"

It was a good question, and she took a moment to consider her answer. "Because so many people we love are being driven down the road to war by his ambitions. How can that be?"

"I have no idea," he said with a note of admiration. "But if you and Mr. Hitler came together in a room right now, my money would be on you."

Harold's comment caught her by surprise. Ruth didn't doubt her husband's support, but he so rarely complimented her that she had come to accept such expressions were mostly beyond the lexicon of his well-ordered, engineering mind. She took a deep breath and rested her head against his chest.

"Even if I sometimes feel that I'm running away," she said, "I'm glad to be going home to America. No matter what happens, I know you and Geoff will be safe. Nothing is more important to me than that."

"Speaking of Geoff," Harold said, "I told him to wait in the cabin for me to take him to breakfast. Do you feel up to it?"

"Let's get Geoff and I'll see how I feel." They started for the stairs, and sunshine broke through the morning clouds with the promise of a pleasant day. Ruth began to feel she might have a bite of breakfast after all.

Judith Evelyn

THE CLINK OF cutlery on china punctuated quiet conversations in the cabin dining saloon. Judith noted the sparse attendance at the second breakfast seating as she, Andrew, and Andrew's father followed the maître d' to their seats at a table for six with three empty place settings.

"Looks like quite a few people are feeling the ship's motion this morning," Andrew said. The maître d' draped a white napkin across Judith's lap and wished them all a pleasant meal.

"Can't say I blame them," Judith said, adjusting her beige angora sweater over her shoulders. "I'm thinking of just having the porridge."

Within a few minutes, the waiter took their orders and Andrew excused himself to go wash his hands. Judith watched him go and wondered how long she would have to parry his father's inquiries before Andrew returned.

"May I ask you something?" Reverend Allan leaned across Andrew's empty chair.

"Yes, of course," Judith said, putting her well-honed performance skills on alert.

"How is Andrew's health?"

"He's fine, Reverend Allan . . ."

"Please, my dear, call me William."

"Yes, well, he's in good health. Why do you ask?"

"He's so involved with his work at times I wonder if he forgets to eat. He's so skinny, almost frail. I know his mother worries about him, too."

"Believe me, Andrew is not frail. I've never met anyone with a stronger will or greater intensity."

"Intensity is the perfect word. He's an artist, like you. It seems to me your profession demands so much."

"What do you mean?" Judith wasn't certain where the conversation was headed, but she doubted the subject was Andrew's health.

"I sometimes wonder if people in the theater spend so much time and effort portraying human relationships, they don't have much energy left to engage in the real thing."

"You really should ask Andrew about this."

"Oh, I've had this conversation with him. I thought it might be a good idea to get a second opinion, as it were."

Judith thought of brushing off William's concerns, but she doubted he would be put off. "Well, yes," she said, warming to her subject, "portraying a character requires a good deal of emotional investment, but there are other demands. All the travel and auditions. And even when you succeed, it's only a matter of time before you're back searching for the next opportunity." She met William's gaze.

"I'm speaking as an actress, but it isn't very different for writers or directors, or even ministers, for that matter. Andrew's told me about all the countries you've been to and the congregations you've served."

"You draw an interesting parallel, Miss Evelyn."

"Please, call me Judith."

"What you say is quite true, Judith. But ministers have one great advantage. They travel with their families wherever they go." He stirred his tea and carefully laid the spoon on the saucer. "I wonder at times if it isn't asking too much of either of you to try to fit another person into your lives."

There it was. William Allan had posed the same question she asked herself many times over the last two months. Had she and Andrew really tried hard enough to find space in their lives for each other?

And how much more would a baby complicate our situation?

Before she could steer the conversation away from her troubling thought, Andrew's father continued on the subject of marriage. "Truly, I think both of you would be the better for it. Loving another person expands one's horizons beyond personal concerns and provides an ally to cope with life's inevitable problems."

"But you don't think we're right for each other, do you, William?" Judith was surprised how easily she had expressed her most private concern.

"Oh, my dear, it is not for me to say. Marriage is a dynamic between two people. It requires sacrifices from both husband and wife—even more from the wife if the couple is blessed with children." He smiled and looked at her over his round, black-rimmed glasses.

"You're a lovely woman, Judith, and I would be proud to call you my daughter-in-law. But you must be certain . . . you and Andrew. If you have any doubts, look to your heart for the answers."

And when your heart doesn't provide an answer, what then, William?

With Andrew heading back toward their table, Judith sought to end their conversation on neutral ground. "You've given me a great deal to think about, William, and we haven't even had breakfast yet."

Chief Officer Copland

THE URGENT SUMMONS had come from Captain Cook. It was nearly eleven-thirty when Copland rapped on the door of Cook's quarters and was told to enter. Inside, he found Cook seated at his desk and *Athenia*'s chief purser, Alexander Wotherspoon, a silver-haired veteran of nearly four decades at sea, seated on the nearby sofa.

"Sit down, please, Mr. Copland." The captain's grim tone put Copland on alert as he took a seat next to Wotherspoon. Cook turned his chair to face the two men.

"As of eleven o'clock, London time today, we are at war with Germany." Though not unexpected, the news pushed Copland back into the sofa. "We picked up the broadcast a few minutes ago. Chamberlain made the announcement. There is no word about what the French are doing." Cook shook his head as if he couldn't believe the inevitable had finally arrived.

"The radio room has the new wireless codes," he continued, returning to the business at hand. "As of now, we will send no transmissions unless they bear on our security or the security of the shipping lanes, and there will be no dispatches sent on behalf of passengers. I've also told the wheelhouse to commence our zigzag course. Mr. Copland, I want you to see that all lifeboats are made ready as soon as possible. Canvas stowed, drain plugs in, provisions and supplies checked. Also make sure someone sees to all the ship's firefighting apparatus, and inspect the watertight doors as well."

"Yes, sir."

"Now," Cook sighed, "we must break the news to our passengers without alarming them, if possible. They will see our preparations, of course, but we must make sure they understand our actions are purely precautionary."

"We can print an announcement and deliver a copy to every stateroom and cabin, or just post an announcement on the board outside my office," Wotherspoon said. "Many passengers check that regularly."

"Do the latter," Cook said. "Rumors will fly through this ship soon enough, if they haven't started already. I'd rather have something official posted right away than have to wait an hour or more to print up and deliver all those announcements."

"Has the crew been notified?" Copland asked.

"Nothing from me," Cook said. "Though I'm sure any crew member who's had occasion to visit the radio room or wheelhouse in the last ten minutes knows of the situation. Make sure you inform your subordinates immediately, and let's post that announcement for passengers as soon as possible."

Judith Evelyn

THE MIDDAY SUN shone through a gallery of clouds, providing welcome warmth to those passengers taking a turn on deck to ward off the effects of the ship's motion or simply to exercise their legs. Judith was among the cabin-class strollers on the boat deck, enjoying the fresh salt air before meeting Andrew to go to the second seating for lunch. She had not been able to find time alone with him to discuss her morning breakfast conversation with his father and was hoping to have a few minutes before they went down.

Without any word, someone tugged on her sleeve. She turned, expecting to find Andrew, but instead found herself face to face with a complete stranger, a gaunt middle-aged woman in a light-green cardigan.

"Have you heard?" she asked Judith. "War has been declared."

"No, I hadn't heard . . ." Before Judith could ask for any details, the woman had moved on. Judith stood rooted to the deck, turning over the woman's revelation in her mind. She was surprised the news had not shocked her. Indeed, she felt a sense of relief that the worst had happened. What more was there to be feared?

As if in answer to her unspoken question, Judith saw several members of *Athenia*'s crew arrive on the boat deck, approach the lifeboats, and begin removing their heavy tarpaulins. A man climbed into the first boat, took a few boxes from another crewman, and put them somewhere inside the boat along with the folded tarpaulin. Was this a normal procedure now that they were well out to sea, she wondered, or was it prompted by war?

Realizing she hadn't heard anyone confirm the woman's grim announcement, Judith began looking for Andrew, anxious to ask if he had heard the news. When she found him a few minutes later, his observation made her question unnecessary.

"It must be true," he said, noticing the men working in the lifeboats. "They're getting ready for any eventuality."

A new revelation crystallized in Judith's mind as clearly as if someone had spoken the words.

We will not complete this voyage without being in those lifeboats.

Barbara Cass-Beggs

"MUMMY, ARE YOU sick?" Rosemary rushed up to the lower bunk where Barbara lay quietly, trying to reason away the queasiness she felt. Clearly, her daughter was concerned to find Barbara still in bed after lunch.

"No, darling, mummy's not sick. I just need to lie here for a while longer." She managed a smile for her daughter, in spite of the heavy lead weight that occupied her stomach. To make matters worse, Barbara knew her husband, David, was similarly indisposed in his cabin on the other side of the ship.

At least Rosemary seemed unaffected by *Athenia*'s rolling motion. Barbara had been most grateful to send her off to the noonday meal in the company of their roommates, Alice MacIntyre and her son. Along with Rosemary, Alice had brought back from lunch the unhappy news that England and Germany were now at war. The announcement had done nothing to soothe Barbara's stomach.

"We're going up on deck to get a little sunshine while we can," Alice said. "Do you want us to take Rosemary, too?"

"I want to stay here with you and tell stories," Rosemary said to her mother.

"But darling," Barbara said, "don't you want to go and play with the other children? I'm sure Panthy would enjoy the sunshine."

"Panthy wants to rest, and I want to stay here, too," Rosemary said. With little in the way of reserves, Barbara decided on the path of least resistance.

"I guess we'll stay here. Thanks anyway, Alice. And thank you for lunch."

"Let me know if there is anything we can do," Alice said as she closed the door behind her.

Barbara edged closer to the wall to make room for Rosemary, who lay down next to her and placed Panthy at the edge of the bunk.

"Now then, what story shall we start with?" Barbara asked.

"The story about the robins."

"Oh, that's a good one." Barbara often made up stories for her daughter, which she told at bedtime to get Rosemary to fall asleep. "Let's see. You remember the trees behind our cottage in Oxford? Well, a young lady robin lived in one of those trees, and one day a daddy robin came to see her. He liked the lady robin, and she liked him." Barbara added all the details of their courtship and how the two robins loved to sing together.

"The daddy robin built her a great big nest and asked her to marry him, and they could live together in the nest. And so they were married. They loved each other very much. After a while, do you know what happened?"

When Rosemary didn't say anything about the eggs in the nest, Barbara looked at her daughter and discovered she had fallen asleep. She continued the story so as not to interrupt the sound of her voice. By the time she reached the end and the baby birds flew off to start families of their own, Rosemary's deep, even breathing told Barbara her daughter was sound asleep. With the warmth of Rosemary's body cuddled next to her in the narrow bed, Barbara laid her head on the pillow, closed her eyes, and slipped into a pleasant dream.

SUNDAY AFTERNOON, SEPTEMBER 3

Oberleutnant Lemp

U-30 SLICED THROUGH moderate seas heading south toward her combat zone. A blue sky filled with broken clouds allowed ample visibility for the boat's four lookouts and Lemp, all standing on the bridge. For Lemp, the routine and frustrations of the last few days had washed away with the announcement from Naval Command an hour earlier that England and Germany were at war.

The news had run through the boat like an electric current and sent Lemp to his quarters to open his safe and take out a sealed envelope to be opened only in the event of war. Inside he found the coordinates of his combat zone—5,600 square miles of ocean northwest of Ireland, at the northern edge of the shipping lanes into and out of the British Isles.

He squinted at the empty horizon, his senses heightened by the changed circumstances. The notice from headquarters did not authorize him to attack, but it served as a warning that he could expect to be fired upon if spotted by a British warship or airplane. His thoughts were interrupted when a sailor climbed through the hatch onto the bridge.

"Sir, another message from Naval High Command," he said. Lemp snatched the dispatch and devoured its contents.

U-BOATS TO MAKE WAR ON MERCHANT SHIPPING IN ACCORDANCE WITH OPERATIONS ORDER.

The message was clear enough about his status to attack merchant ships, but there was no word about the status of the French, and why did it reference his operations order? He read the message again and concluded that his commanders were referencing the damned submarine protocol.

Why do that? Do they really want me to follow these unworkable procedures, or are they observing a formality? Is this how a great nation goes to war?

A cry from one of the lookouts cut through his conjectures.

"Smoke bearing zero two five," shouted a sailor watching the quadrant of sea and sky forward and to starboard. Lemp saw a long smudge just above the horizon and lifted his binoculars. The dark smoke lay in a flat streak just above the water, signaling the presence of another ship. The prospect of a hunt raised the hair on the back of his neck, and he smiled at the sensation.

"Both engines ahead full," he shouted into the speaking tube. "Helmsman, maintain present course."

Half an hour later, Lemp could see three masts jutting just above the horizon like naked treetops. Ten minutes later, a single funnel came into view belching black smoke. As he watched, the ship's superstructure slowly rose above the horizon. *U-30* closed rapidly on the slow-moving ship, which appeared to be on a south-southwesterly course. Its speed, multiple masts, and configuration told Lemp she was a merchant ship.

"Keep an eye out for guns," he said to the sailor standing to his right. The ship's silvery gray hull crept into view, and Lemp could see a flag.

Plenty of red showing. It could be a British ensign.

But after several more minutes, he clearly saw a blue cross outlined in white on the red field. The ship was from Norway, a neutral country, and his orders did not allow an attack on neutral shipping.

"Hold course and reduce both engines to two-thirds," he ordered. They would run well astern of the freighter so he saw no need to submerge.

With the chase over, *U-30* fell back into its patrol routine. The men on watch changed shifts on the bridge, but Lemp remained up top, eager to glimpse his first target of the war. A few minutes into the new watch, another sailor climbed to the bridge with a message from the radio room, this one from fleet headquarters in Wilhelmshaven.

BEGIN HOSTILITIES AGAINST ENGLAND IMMEDIATELY. DO NOT WAIT TO BE ATTACKED.

He smiled at *Kommodore* Dönitz's directness and pocketed the paper in his gray leather coat. Dönitz did not mention any operations order. Lemp raised his binoculars once again, ready to attack the target he was certain waited for him just over the horizon.

Spirydon Kucharczuk

"DOWN, DADDY." TWO-YEAR-OLD Jakeb Kucharczuk squirmed in his father's arms, pushing away from Spirydon's chest and leaning his little blond head backward. The toddler seemed intent on walking like his parents as they strolled A deck's forward promenade and enjoyed the patchy afternoon sunshine.

"You know he will head for the railing if you put him down," Ewdokia said.

"It's all right," Spirydon said. "I'll watch him."

Jakeb's sturdy little legs carried him with surprising speed to the ship's railing, but his father caught the child's hand before he could climb the railing's horizontal bars. The little boy seemed content to stand and hold Spirydon's hand and watch the ocean rush past them.

"Should we be worried about this war between the English and Germany?" Ewdokia asked.

"We are on an English ship so, yes, we should have concern. But mostly, I think the war is behind us."

"I would still like to make a decision about the lifeboats," she said. When Spirydon relayed Chaim Mazur's confirmation that their different cabins meant the family would report to two different muster stations, the news seemed particularly troubling to Ewdokia.

"You're right. We should leave the ship as a family," he said. "If something happens and the whistle blows the signal, we can meet at the top of the main stairway nearest to your cabin. When we are all together, we can follow others and find a lifeboat to take all of us. That should work."

"Yes," she said. "It is like all of your planning." She peered up at him and placed her hand on top of his as it rested on the railing. "Now that we're on our way to Canada, I must tell you I'm proud of you and all you've done. I'm glad we are not in Trosteniec now and dealing with the Nazis."

"But you made this possible," he answered. "Without the farmland you kept together, we wouldn't have had the money for this trip or to buy the land we will need in Canada."

"Up, Daddy." Jakeb, apparently tired of standing, turned to his father with arms raised. Spirydon hoisted the boy up to his shoulder, much to Jakeb's delight.

"Oh, Spiro, not so close." Ewdokia pulled her husband and son back from the ship's railing. "Really, I tell you how proud I am of you and you do something foolish like that." Though Ewdokia sounded exasperated, she could not hide her smile.

They began walking again and he thought of all that remained to be done when they arrived in Canada. In Montreal, they would meet Ewdokia's middle sister, Julianna, and her husband, Nicola Zachary. The Zacharys owned a farm in a place called Whitemouth, where the Kucharczuks would live and work for a while until he found good land to buy to begin his own farm. This would not be easy. He would need to understand the differences between Polish and Canadian crops and markets, which he hoped to learn from Nicola. They all had to learn English, and the children would need to go to school in this new country as well as help on the farm. He had no idea what Jan would do, although Spirydon thought his oldest son would not be a farmer.

"You're very quiet," Ewdokia said.

"I was thinking about all we still have to do."

"Yes, but think about all you've done. Whatever is left to do cannot be as difficult. And we are a big family with many hands to help finish the job."

Ewdokia's words eased his mind and Jakeb seemed somehow lighter on his shoulders. For the first time since leaving Poland, Spirydon relaxed, no longer concerned about the wolf he had imagined earlier. In a few more days they would be in Canada.

Judith Evelyn

WITH THE MIDAFTERNOON sunshine intermittently blocked by gathering clouds, Judith and Andrew silently strolled along *Athenia*'s boat deck, where tea service was underway. Stewards in their starched white coats poured tea from silver urns perched on trollies and offered passengers fresh baked pastries. The show of elegance on such a utilitarian ship surprised Judith, but she could not work up any enthusiasm for the English afternoon ritual.

They found a place to stand at the stern railing and watch the people walking, talking, and napping on the open decks below. Beyond the stern, *Athenia*'s frothy wake ribboned away through the blue-green ocean, until it disappeared midway to the horizon.

"I take it there has been no change in your condition," Andrew said quietly as they stood at the railing.

"No change," Judith confirmed. "Do you think your father suspects anything?"

"Hard to say. Dad gives the impression of being like a comfortable old shoe, but he's pretty observant, and he doesn't give anything away. For what it's worth, he told me after breakfast that he thought you were insightful."

"Insightful or not, I'm sure he thinks we shouldn't get married, and especially not have children." Judith sighed and shook her head. "I'm beginning to think this was a bad idea."

"It's a little late for that," Andrew said. "Don't let Dad's musings upset you. I'm sure we can make this work if it comes down to marriage."

"It's more than just that," Judith said, ignoring Andrew's perception of marriage as a last resort. "I've had a sense of doom ever since we boarded this ship. The declaration of war, the blackout precautions, the crew getting lifeboats ready for God knows what. And then there was that officer's comment at lunch today."

"What comment?"

"I asked him when we might catch our first glimpse of Canada, and he said if all goes well, we should see Canada by Thursday. I can't get his words, 'if all goes well,' out of my mind."

"It's a ship," a voice shouted behind them. Judith turned to see several passengers rushing toward the starboard railing, pointing toward the distant silhouette of a ship. All around her, she overheard anxious comments.

"Can you see what it is?"

"Do you think it's German?"

"Which way is it headed?"

If they're German, Judith wondered, *would they attack us simply because we fly the Union Jack? How long until they are close enough to fire on us?*

"Poor souls," Andrew said, gazing at the mystery vessel. "I imagine they're just as afraid of us as we are of them."

Oberleutnant Lemp

AN EMPTY OCEAN rolled away in every direction from atop *U-30*'s conning tower. Since spotting the Norwegian ship several hours earlier, not a single vessel of any kind had presented itself to the lookouts standing on the bridge with Lemp. Having reached the northern boundary of his combat zone almost an hour ago, he had expected to see one or two possible targets by now. Even accounting for the declaration of war, it was hard to believe all English captains would be so cautious as to turn back to port in midcourse, especially those approaching after a long voyage from the west.

Are the other commanders finding these same conditions, or is it because my zone is so far north?

Lemp took solace from the fact that no other captains had reported any action so far. He told himself to be patient; his opportunity would come soon enough. He noted with some concern that only about two and a half hours remained before sunset. Clouds were building in the east, and he felt a freshening breeze in the russet stubble of his beard.

"Message from the radio room." A sailor handed him the latest communication from headquarters. Lemp took the paper and discovered that France had declared war on Germany. It was not a surprise, but he wondered if the *Führer* still hoped to negotiate a separate peace agreement with the French? Should he attack French shipping? U-boat command school hadn't prepared him for such open-ended questions.

"Ship bearing two one zero." Lemp swung around to his left and raised his binoculars. He could barely make out the top of a funnel and tips of two masts against the clouds forming in the northeast. After several more minutes, the white superstructure of a ship rose up over the horizon on a westerly course, but well north of the normal shipping lanes. He calculated that if the large ship maintained her general course and *U-30* took a northwesterly course on the surface at full speed, he could intersect her track.

"Helmsman, steer course three one zero," he called down to the control room. "Both engines ahead full." *U-30*'s bow responded immediately, coming around to starboard.

Moments ago, he worried that other U-boats might be fishing in richer waters. Now, with the hunt once again renewed, Lemp's concerns vanished in a rush of adrenaline.

SUNDAY LATE AFTERNOON, SEPTEMBER 3

David Jennings

DAVID AND HIS friend, John Woods, enjoyed the latest break in the clouds that had showered sunshine on *Athenia's* number three cargo hatch. The hatch cover provided a knee-high, canvas-covered platform on A deck, sheltered from the wind by the structure protecting the entrance to the forward stairway in front of them. David and John lay on the hatch with shirtsleeves rolled up, each with one arm crooked behind his head and the other arm balancing a book on his abdomen.

Looking forward to a solid hour of reading, David cracked open his copy of *Northwest Passage*. With all the interruptions of travel, he was only starting the novel's third chapter and had just reacquainted himself with the adventures of young Mr. Towne, the book's protagonist. Before he could finish a page, John interrupted.

"David, this could be our lucky day."

David followed John's glance and saw three young women emerging from the stairway in front of them. The three brunettes appeared to be in their late teens or early twenties. The first girl to catch David's eye was tall and slender. As the trio moved into the sunlight, he noticed the appealing smile of the second girl who was nearly as tall as the first, while the third was shorter and appeared to be the most animated of the group.

"Three of them," David observed. "Too bad Tony's not here." Their friend, Tony Cassels, had felt a little queasy after lunch and decided to remain in their cabin for the afternoon. John sat up, waved to the girls, and made a sweeping arm movement toward the empty space next to David on the hatch cover. After a brief consultation of nods and smiles, the three girls approached, and David and John stood to greet them.

"We've been saving this space for you," John said. "A lovely spot out of the wind. Won't you join us?"

"Thank you," said the shortest of the three girls. "It would be a shame to waste this sunshine."

John introduced David and himself and said they were seniors at the University of Toronto. David happily let John handle the introductions, a vestige of the awkwardness he'd felt with girls in his early teens before overcoming a childhood stutter.

The girls explained they were Americans, Delta Gamma sorority sisters at the University of Michigan. Joan Outhwaite, whose pretty blue eyes and feline grace both intimidated and captivated David, said she was from Bennington, Vermont. The tallest of the trio, Barbara Bradfield, brushed her hand across the canvas hatch cover before sitting down in her cream-colored slacks. Barbara came from Grand Rapids in western Michigan. Their shorter companion hopped onto the hatch cover next to David, arranged her lime-green skirt over her tanned knees, and announced she was Alberta Wood from Louisville, Kentucky.

With introductions out of the way, David eased into the ensuing conversation, and the hour passed quickly as they all exchanged information about their universities, study interests, hometowns, and the highlights of the trips they were completing. Joan, in particular, seemed interested that David and John were Canadians. Growing up in Vermont, she had visited Canada several times and was very fond of Quebec City. David tried out his rudimentary French, but gave up when it became clear that both Joan and Barbara enjoyed much greater facility with the language.

"Are you boys worried about the war?" Barbara asked.

"I don't think we've given it much thought since this morning," John said.

"Now that England's in it, I'm sure Canada will follow suit," David said. "When the time comes, we'll do our part, won't we John?"

"Absolutely," John said. "And what do you ladies think? Will America do its part?"

"I'm afraid that's not a very popular sentiment right now," Alberta said. "Don't get me wrong. I think Hitler's a jerk. But like my daddy says, we got very little to show for our efforts in the last war."

"That's not a question for us," John observed. "We're part of the commonwealth, so we'll be coming to England's aid soon enough, I expect. You folks can hold everyone's coat and watch the donnybrook from a safe distance."

"Doesn't sound fair, does it?" Barbara said.

"Ours not to reason why; ours but to do and die," John answered, paraphrasing Tennyson's lines with exaggerated solemnity.

"Ignore him, ladies," David said. "He's just playing on your sympathies."

"What do you think about our ship?" Joan asked, turning to David. "Are we in any danger?"

"I don't think so," he said, wanting to sound reassuring. "We left England almost twenty-four hours before war was declared, and that wouldn't give Germany much time to get its navy in place."

"If there was any real danger," John added, "I think we'd have sailed with an escort. Besides, it'd be very bad form to sink a passenger ship."

"Why do you say that?" Joan asked.

"Sinking a ship full of innocent civilians, including women and children? The Germans would look like the world's biggest bullies," John said.

"Joanie," Alberta chimed in, "don't you remember the *Lusitania* from the last war? The whole world condemned Germany for that. Some people said it was why we got into the war."

"I should know better than to travel with history majors," Joan said. She glanced at her wristwatch. "Oh, it's almost six. Come on, girls. We need to get ready for our dinner seating." They stood to go, and Joan turned to David. "It was a pleasure meeting you boys."

"Wait a minute," John said as the girls headed for the stairway. "What's your cabin number?"

"Don't worry," Alberta responded. "I'm sure we'll see each other again before we get to Montreal." All three girls turned to wave before they started down the stairs.

"I think that went pretty well. What do you think?" John said.

"I think our crossing just got a lot more interesting." David collected his book from the hatch cover, hardly thinking about young Mr. Towne.

On their way down to D deck, John returned to the subject of the threat posed by the German Navy. "So do you really think we're out of danger, or was that just for your girlfriend's consumption?"

"What girlfriend?" David asked, stopping in the middle of the stairs.

"Hey, I saw the way you looked at that girl from Vermont. Joan, wasn't it? And in case you didn't notice, she seemed pretty interested in you."

"You think so?" David felt his cheeks starting to flush.

"I know so," John said, seeming to enjoy David's reaction. "But my question was about the Germans. You seemed pretty convinced there's nothing to worry about."

David continued down the stairs with John at his shoulder. "I figure we're probably a couple of hundred miles past Ireland, maybe more," David said. "So I'd say we've outrun any danger. Just clear sailing home from here."

"I hope you're right. Anyway, I can't wait to get back to the cabin and see the look on Tony's face when we tell him what he missed."

Barbara Cass-Beggs

AFTER SPENDING A quiet afternoon dozing with her daughter, Rosemary, and as the hour approached for the first dinner seating, Barbara began to think a little food might help her feel better. She dressed Rosemary and had just changed her own clothes when there was a light rapping at the cabin door. Barbara answered the knock to find David, still looking a bit green, standing in the passageway.

"Darling," she said, managing a smile. "Do come in. How are you feeling?"

"A bit off, actually," he said, "but I decided to go to dinner, and I'll be happy to take Rosemary if you're still out of sorts."

"I was thinking about dinner as well. Just a little something to settle the stomach." Turning to her daughter, Barbara held out her hand. "Come on, Rosemary, we're going to dinner with Daddy."

"I want to bring Panthy." Rosemary clutched her little toy bear by its arm.

"All right," Barbara said, "but you'll have to keep an eye on him and make sure he doesn't wander off."

When they finally took their seats in the third-class dining saloon, Barbara felt less enthusiastic about food. She noticed David was picking around the edges of his pork roast, avoiding the onions and green beans in favor of a few forkfuls of the boiled potatoes. Rosemary showed no symptoms of sea sickness and managed to eat her meal as well as the dinner roll from David's plate. They left before dessert was served and returned to Barbara's cabin.

"Perhaps a good night's sleep will help settle things," David said.

"We're headed straight for bed," Barbara agreed. She kissed her husband in the hallway, and he promised to wake them for breakfast in the morning.

Oberleutnant Lemp

"FIRST WATCH OFFICER to the bridge." Lemp called the order down to *U-30*'s control room as he stood on the bridge atop the conning tower. *U-30* had closed to within four miles of the large ship, approaching it from the south. Lemp knew he risked detection by continuing to sail on the surface, but it was the only way *U-30* could have maintained enough speed to converge on his possible prize. He hoped the big ship's lookouts were enjoying the colorful display of clouds in the western sky and not searching for U-boats on the horizon.

The sun had set a few minutes earlier, but more than enough twilight remained for him to be seen, especially with rising winds pushing six-foot swells into the U-boat's conning tower and creating a heavy spray. Beyond the approaching ship, the cloudy northeastern sky grew darker, and Lemp still had not identified the vessel's nationality. *Oberleutnant* Hinsch scrambled up the ladder onto the bridge and reported to his commander.

"What do you make of her?" Lemp nodded at the ship and handed his binoculars to his second-in-command.

Hinsch focused on the mystery vessel. "No markings I can see," Hinsch said after a quick study. "She's probably moving close to her top speed."

"Yes, and she's zigzagging, sailing alone and running up here well north of the commercial sea lanes," Lemp added.

"A troop ship?" Hinsch offered.

"I don't think so. There's no escort. I think she might be an armed merchant cruiser out on early patrol." Lemp estimated her size at almost fifteen thousand tons.

"I can't just let her go on her way. She's a big prize. We're going to move in for a closer look," Lemp said. "Clear the bridge. Battle stations!"

Chief Officer Copland

SUNSET PAINTED THE thin, high clouds on the western horizon a brilliant salmon color that deepened to coppery hues above *Athenia* as she headed toward nightfall.

"Quite a peaceful sight, Mr. Copland," Captain Cook said. Copland stood next to *Athenia*'s captain in the ship's wheelhouse. "Makes it hard to believe we are at war again."

"Yes, sir. Have you given any thought to going back into the navy?" Copland knew Cook had served as a lieutenant on Royal Navy destroyers and minesweepers during the last war.

"It's been twenty years, so I don't think they'd have much interest in me. Still, if they called, I would do whatever they asked. What about you?"

"I agree. I'd answer any call. But I truly believe I'm most useful to king and country right where I am. It's not as glamorous as a service career, but I feel it's every bit as necessary."

"Well put," Cook said, nodding. They both fell silent, watching the horizon darken to a deep orange in the fading light. Copland's past conversations with the captain had rarely ventured into such personal areas, and he sought a new topic to avoid inadvertently intruding on Cook's private thoughts.

"Will you be dining in your cabin again tonight, sir?"

"No, tonight I'm going to dine with our passengers," Cook said. He glanced at the clock. "Just about time for the second seating in cabin class. Will I see you down there?"

"Yes, sir. I'll be down as soon as Mr. Porteous returns to the bridge."

Cook's decision to dine with passengers told Copland his captain thought any danger of a German attack had passed. It should have put Copland's mind at ease, yet his thoughts remained troubled, filled with concerns about their return trip and his future as his countrymen headed off to war.

Rhoda Thomas

THE FADING ORANGE hue of the clouds on the western horizon greeted Rhoda and Mary Townley, her roommate, as they stepped outside near the stern of B deck.

"Oh no. I think we just missed the sunset," Mary said.

"We may as well sit for a minute until it gets dark," Rhoda said. "Maybe we'll see the moon come up." She had taken her navy-blue crocheted woolen cap and heavy wool fleece coat to dinner so she could come up on deck directly after the meal, prepared for the twilight's chilly winds.

The two women walked to an empty bench on the starboard side of the ship, just under the shelter of the deck above. Overhead, the first bright stars already hung in a cobalt-blue sky. Looking east past the stern, dark clouds crowded up from the horizon.

"The stars are so bright out on the ocean," Mary observed. "Pity there aren't more people out here to enjoy them." They watched the sky slowly darken as a few more stars winked to life.

"God gives us so much beauty to appreciate," Rhoda sighed, "and yet all we can see are the differences that divide us. You'd think we could find a better way than war to resolve our differences."

"It's a wonder He hasn't lost patience with us," Mary said.

"I suppose that's the wonder of infinite patience." Rhoda gathered her coat tighter together at her throat against the shifting wind.

"I do hope this war doesn't last very long," she said. "When I was coming to Liverpool by train, we passed through several cities, and I saw the kiddies lined up on the platforms with their knapsacks and gas masks and name tags. They were being sent away from their families to live with strangers. I keep thinking about those children. What kind of a world do we live in when children are the targets of bombs and the like? For their sake and everyone else involved in this business, I pray it's over quickly."

"You're a lovely person, Mrs. Thomas," Mary said. "And I for one hope your prayers are answered."

Oberleutnant Lemp

WITH U-30 RUNNING at periscope depth on a course now nearly parallel to the approaching ship, Lemp could make only eight knots with his electric motors. He calculated he would have less than thirty minutes before the big ship passed him. If he decided to attack, it would be a quick maneuver to round his boat to starboard and bring her bow into firing position, but he didn't have much time.

Seated in the conning tower's small combat center directly above the U-boat's control room, Lemp raised the attack periscope. The scope's slimmer profile carved a smaller wake that made it harder to detect. Through the eyepiece, he quickly spotted the ship, which continued on her general westerly course. One quick look and he lowered the scope, still unable to make a positive identification.

He continued to track his unsuspecting prey for twenty more minutes, periodically raising and lowering the scope to follow her movements. Time was growing short, and he had to decide. In the scope's eyepiece, the ship was now a little more than a mile away, a black silhouette against a darkening sky. Something was different. It took him a moment to realize the ship had extinguished all lights except for the port side running light, an act that heightened his suspicions. Through the attack scope, he saw what could be a cargo boom, or could it be the barrel of a deck gun?

In an instant, the anomalies fell into place like the tumblers of a combination lock—blacked out, zigzagging, sailing out of normal shipping lanes. He did not question his conclusion. This was an armed merchant cruiser.

"Control room, steer course three five zero," he said into the speaking tube as he lowered the scope. "Torpedo room, ready tubes one and two." In his mind's eye, Lemp saw *U-30* coming to starboard, swinging toward her target.

Be calm. Clear your mind.

He raised the attack scope again, half expecting his target to have disappeared. But he found her right away, still holding her westerly course and apparently unaware of his presence. Only minutes now remained before he would fire his first torpedo at a live target. It would be a moment to remember for the rest of his life.

"Open tube doors one and two." He would wait for the ship to change her heading again on her zigzag course. Lemp felt an odd connection with the big ship, a sense of gratitude for presenting him with this opportunity.

"And now, my friend," he said under his breath, "your next move will be your last."

PART II

RESCUE

... It is to this high purpose that I now call my people at home and my peoples across the seas, who will make our cause their own. I ask them to stand calm, firm, and united in this time of trial. The task will be hard. There may be dark days ahead, and war can no longer be confined to the battlefield. But we can only do the right as we see the right, and reverently commit our cause to God. If one and all we keep resolutely faithful to it, ready for whatever service or sacrifice it may demand, then, with God's help, we shall prevail.

May He bless and keep us all.

—BROADCAST TO THE BRITISH EMPIRE BY
KING GEORGE VI, 6:00 P.M., SEPTEMBER 3, 1939

SUNDAY 7:39 P.M., SEPTEMBER 3

Oberleutnant Lemp

"TORPEDO RUNNING." FROM his listening post just forward of the U-boat's control room, the radio technician confirmed *U-30*'s first shot was on its way. First Watch Officer Hinsch started his stopwatch to time the torpedo's run to its target.

"Tube two, fire," Lemp called into the speaking tube and pulled the firing lever a second time.

It took only a few seconds for *U-30*'s commander and nearly everyone else in the sub to realize something was terribly wrong.

Spirydon Kucharczuk

STANDING AT THE portside railing near *Athenia*'s bow, Spirydon faced his oldest son, Jan, hoping to avoid what he feared might be an awkward conversation.

"Is this going to take long?" Jan asked his father, turning up his jacket collar as a stiff breeze ruffled his hair.

"I hope not." Spirydon had told Jan he wanted to talk to him as they were leaving the dining saloon, and they had come to this spot in the fading twilight to find some privacy.

"I know we've had our differences lately. I want you to know I understand you're not a boy anymore. You want to go your own way, and you don't want me to tell you what to do."

"But you're going to tell me what to do, aren't you?"

"No. I'm going to ask you for a favor, just like I would ask any man."

"I'm listening."

"When we arrive in Canada, I would like your help to get the family established. Once I have purchased the land, can you give me a year of your labor? Just a year to help us start out, then you can—"

A cry caused Spirydon to look up and see a man in a small structure near the top of the forward mast yelling and pointing out to sea. Spirydon followed the man's gesture but saw nothing unusual. He turned back to Jan.

An earsplitting thunderclap swallowed up all other sound.

The ship seemed to jump, and Spirydon grabbed the railing to keep from falling. Just beyond the middle of the ship, he saw a thick fountain of white water shoot into the air up the side of the hull. The deck reeled beneath him. *Athenia* slowed, her engines silenced.

As the realization of what had just happened washed over Spirydon, an unspeakable anger welled up inside him and burst forth in a spasm of noise—a long, loud, senseless scream. The wolf had chosen this moment to eviscerate all his careful planning.

Watching the column of water fall lazily back into the sea, he fought to overcome his blind rage and respond to the calamity unfolding in front of him.

"Go to our cabin and get Stefan," Spirydon cried, recovering his voice. "I'll get Mother and the girls and we'll meet by the stairs the way we planned." But Jan continued to gape in the direction of the explosion until Spirydon shoved him toward the stairway. "Go!"

Jan hurried off with Spirydon at his heels. They plunged down the stairs, and Jan disappeared into a shouting, seething confusion of people. There were no lights in the corridor. It was filling with a musty, bitter smell, as though the ship's vital organs had been pierced. Spirydon began to fear he might not see any members of his family again.

David Jennings

A HOLLOW BOOMING sound, like a huge door slamming shut somewhere in the direction of *Athenia*'s stern, interrupted the discussion in David's D deck cabin near the bow. The ship shuddered and began leaning to port as the lights went out in the cabin.

"Hello, what's this?" Tony said in the dark.

"Maybe the generator's blown," David said, "or a boiler."

"Give it a moment, lads," Alfie Snow, the former miner, advised. "Your eyes will adjust."

The cabin continued to lean to port rather than roll back toward starboard in the ship's usual leisurely gait. David sat on his bunk to keep from falling in the dark.

"What the hell is going on?" he said. The room had taken on a permanent dip toward the port side, which he found disorienting without any visual reference. David reached for his suitcase under the bed, slid it out, and found his flashlight. A flat circle of white light caught Alfie and John.

"Point that somewhere else," John said, shielding his eyes.

"Quiet," Tony said.

David held his breath. A series of short blasts on the ship's whistle was audible over the muffled voices of people in the corridor outside their room. The last short blast was followed by a long, mournful note on the whistle.

"Was anybody counting?" Tony asked.

"I think that was the emergency signal," David said. "We should get out of here."

He put on his coat, collected his lifejacket, and remembered to pull the wool blanket off his bunk. As they headed out the door, David wondered how long it would take the crew to fix the lights.

Judith Evelyn

IN THE DARKENED cabin dining saloon, Judith felt the room tilt toward the port side bulkhead and heard the shatter of breaking glass and porcelain. Sitting on the floor, she braced herself and wondered if *Athenia* was about to roll all the way over.

"This is it," she said calmly to herself, amid cries from the people around her. To her amazement, Judith realized she wasn't panicked. The sense of doom that had weighed upon her for the past several days was gone. The tilting slowed, and she struggled to her feet. An acrid smell hung in the air.

"Andrew," she said into the darkness.

"I'm over here. Are you hurt?"

"No, I'm fine. Is your father okay?"

"Yes," the Reverend Allan responded, "except for the water tumbler in my lap."

Judith could see both men now as they helped each other up in the dim light flickering from matches and lighters fellow diners began holding up.

"This way," a steward called from the dining saloon entrance. "Keep calm, everyone. Please retrieve your lifejackets and report to your muster stations."

The cries of the other passengers subsided with the makeshift lighting, and Judith saw them beginning to form a queue through the room's debris as they made their way to the stairs. She sensed no panic in the crowd and wondered if everyone else felt as calm as she did.

Rhoda Thomas

DEAFENED BY THE roar that had filled her consciousness moments earlier, Rhoda found herself on her hands and knees staring dumbly at the blond wood of the pine deck in front of her. Her confusion subsided when she noticed her friend, Mary, sprawled on the deck beside her. She remembered sitting with Mary and watching the stars come out when there was a horrific crash and something rudely pushed them toward the ship's railing. The open deck nearby was speckled with dark water spots, and there was a new, faintly pungent odor in the air.

"Are you hurt?" she asked as Mary stirred.

"It's my hip," Mary groaned. She lay on her right side in obvious pain, holding her left hip.

"Let me find some help." Rhoda leveraged herself up using the nearby bench. Shouts from adults and cries from children filled the air. The deck had tilted under her, leaning to port and making it difficult to stand. She put a hand on the wall for support and peered around the corner in the direction the ship was leaning. In the evening twilight beyond the portside railing she saw black smoke curling around a long, dark, evil-looking object sitting on the water perhaps a half mile away. In an instant, Rhoda knew what had happened.

"Oh Mary, we've been torpedoed."

Oberleutnant Lemp

FROM HIS POST in *U-30*'s combat center, Lemp heard an unfamiliar grating sound coming through the boat's hull.

"Number two torpedo is running, but it's stuck in the tube," a sailor shouted from below. Lemp assessed the situation as he straddled the ladder and slid down to the control room.

"Get that damned eel out of the tube," Lemp shouted. "Now!"

First Watch Officer Hinsch bolted forward toward the din of scraping metal. Lemp was painfully aware he had ordered the torpedoes to be armed with magnetic detonators. As a safety precaution, the detonator was armed only after a small propeller on the nose of the torpedo turned a pre-set number of revolutions on its way to the target. But the torpedo was stuck in its tube. If the arming propeller was turning as *U-30* moved through the water, it would soon activate the detonator, which would detect the U-boat's magnetic field and blow the bow of the submarine wide open. *U-30* would sink quickly with everyone aboard.

"Blow all tanks," Lemp shouted to his chief engineer, who stood only a few feet from him. "Left full rudder. All ahead full. Prepare to surface."

He would take a chance with the arming propeller turning and get the boat on or near the surface so at least some of his crew might have a chance to escape if the eel exploded. It seemed like an eternity before Chief Meckbach reported the sub was on the surface, and Lemp felt the familiar rocking motion of the ocean's waves. At almost the same instant, the awful noise coming from the bow stopped.

"Number two's away," someone shouted from the forward compartment. Lemp held his breath. How soon would the eel arm itself? As he waited, *U-30*'s diesels rumbled to life.

An explosion jolted the boat moments later. Lemp reeled but stayed on his feet.

He assumed the detonation came from the misfiring torpedo before a more worrisome thought occurred to him.

Could the enemy cruiser still have the capacity to fire on us?

"Prepare to dive." Lemp's order echoed through the boat. "Take us down to sixty meters."

U-30 gathered speed and began to push herself under the Atlantic's rolling swells. The diesels shut down as he felt the boat stop rocking and begin its descent. Lemp heaved a sigh and smiled at Hinsch, returning from the bow and looking shaken and very wet.

"It's a steam bath in there," Hinsch reported. "We kept pumping compressed air into number two tube, and it was coming back through the relief valve with seawater, but we got the damned thing away." Lemp saw the exhaustion on his first watch officer's face.

"The poor bastards up front will be sleeping in a swamp for the rest of the cruise," Hinsch said. Lemp began to laugh, and Hinsch joined him, but the commander knew their laughter had nothing to do with sleeping conditions in the forward torpedo room. They had narrowly avoided a catastrophe and felt hysterically happy to be alive.

Regaining his composure, Lemp said, "We'll wait until it's completely dark and surface to take a look at what's left of the cruiser." He put a hand on Hinsch's shoulder.

"You did well, Hans-Peter."

Chief Officer Copland

RUNNING DOWN A deck's dark portside hallway, Copland wondered if *Athenia* had been torpedoed or struck a mine. If it was a U-boat attack, would there be a second torpedo?

As the thought crossed his mind, a second explosion rattled the ship, though it seemed less powerful than the first. He stepped out into the twilight and quickly noted the stern was low in the water. The deck was listing several degrees to port.

Glancing out to sea off the port side of the ship, Copland recognized the distant cigar shape of a submarine hull, its conning tower partially obscured by a swirling black cloud. What seemed a remote possibility an hour ago had happened: The Germans had torpedoed his ship, a ship filled with women and children. Anger, deep and raw, welled up inside of him.

"Bloody bastards," he bellowed at the obscene shape moving slowly away to the west. Unable to take any action toward the submarine, Copland seethed at his powerlessness. In his fury, he climbed the stairs two at a time to the promenade deck. There he took a deep breath and realized he needed to regain his composure. The shouts and screams of passengers brought him back to the moment.

In the fading light, Copland noticed the hatch cover for the number five cargo hold was missing. Bits of debris and burned piles of rags littered the deck around the open hold. Approaching the devastation, he saw that the rags were the blackened bodies of people caught in the explosion, and he had to look away from the carnage to steady himself.

Ignoring the bodies for the moment, Copland moved to the open hatch. If the force of the detonation had come up the trunk of the hold, he thought there might be a chance the ship's engine room, immediately forward, had escaped serious damage. But when he looked into the scorched hold his hopes for *Athenia*'s survival were shaken.

Ten feet below him, a pale reflection of the sky danced on the surface of water that filled the hold. With so much water, Copland feared the bulkheads were seriously stressed if not already breached. For now, however, *Athenia*'s list seemed to have slackened. Perhaps the watertight doors had done their job.

We'll have time to get everyone off if the bastards don't hit us again.

He climbed one last flight of stairs to his emergency station on the boat deck. There he was stopped by the stout figure of the ship's nurse, Nannie Ware.

"Mr. Copland, thank God. I need help with my patient. I can't handle her all by myself."

He had forgotten about the woman who fell on the stairs the night before.

"Yes, of course," he answered. "I'll make sure she's taken care of. You go see if you can help those poor souls on the promenade deck around number five hold."

Nurse Ware hurried toward the stairs. Copland stopped the first two seamen he saw and told them to go down to sick bay on B deck and make sure they put the woman patient there safely into a lifeboat.

"She may still be unconscious," he alerted them.

Ruth Etherington

IN THE DARKENED corridor on *Athenia*'s B deck, Ruth struggled to her feet and tried to make sense of what just happened. An explosion had rocked the ship and pushed her into the wall and down to her knees. A foul-smelling gas filled the darkness and made her eyes water. She recalled being with her husband and their son in the corridor before the explosion.

Oh my God, where are they? Are they all right?

"Hal!" she called, aware of other frightened voices in the dark.

"I think it stopped listing, but they've sounded the alarm," Harold said. Ruth was relieved her husband was nearby and seemed in control of the situation.

"Geoff, where are you?"

"I'm here, Mom." Geoffrey also sounded calm.

"Dad, was that a torpedo?"

"I don't know," Harold answered, "but we better head for our muster station."

"What about getting our lifejackets?" Ruth asked, coughing to clear the smoke from her lungs.

"Not a chance. It's too far down in the dark, and people will be coming up to get to the lifeboats," Harold said. "Come on. Grab hands and let's move." Ruth waved her arms and brushed a sleeve. Harold caught her hand and, with Geoffrey in tow, they began moving toward the stern. In the dark, she struggled to keep her balance. The passageway sloped annoyingly in a persistent incline, and the floor buckled in places, slowing their progress until they could make out the twilight beyond end of the passageway.

Outside, Ruth filled her lungs with fresh air and looked at the alarming sight in front of her. Lifeboats on either side of the stern were filling with passengers. *Athenia* was not moving, and its stern sat so low in the water that the ocean's swells were approaching C deck below them. The ship's frothy wake appeared to have slewed to starboard, and a wispy column of black smoke hung over the sea at the start of the wake's semicircle.

Ruth wondered how many minutes they had left before *Athenia* sank and realized she had no sense of whether she would live or die. Instead, she was seized by a single, overriding thought.

Stay calm. I mustn't give Hal or Geoff any reason to be concerned about me.

Spirydon Kucharczuk

IN *ATHENIA*'S DARKENED interior, Spirydon heard the clamor of his fellow passengers as they crowded past him in their efforts to reach the lifeboats. After nearly falling and fearing he would be trampled, Spirydon paused next to the wall of the corridor and recreated his steps in his mind to determine his present location. He and Jan had been on A deck when they entered the stairway after the explosion. He came down one flight of stairs to B deck and worked his way along the interior passageway toward the stern. In the dark, it was difficult to tell how far he had come. He took a deep breath and pushed on until he heard what sounded like people coming up a stairway. This was the place they had all agreed to meet, and he began calling for Ewdokia. There were many cries in the dark, but he did not hear his name being shouted.

How long should I wait? What if Ewdokia needs my help? And where are Jan and Stefan?

Spirydon's anxiety rose. After shouting their names again with no response, he crossed to the stairway and pulled himself down by the bannister a step at a time through the thinning crowd. He negotiated some missing stairs to reach D deck and was grateful for the passengers holding lighted matches as they climbed past him.

When he stepped into ankle-deep water on D deck, Spirydon fought a sense of panic and an urge to race in the direction of Ewdokia's cabin. The air in the corridor was thick and unpleasant, like the acrid smell of animal waste in a stable.

Oh God, please let them be alive.

Feeling along the passage wall, Spirydon counted the cabin doors until he came to what he believed was his wife's doorway. He tried the handle, but the door did not budge.

"Is someone there?" a voice shouted in Ukrainian from behind the door. "Help us. Please help!" Spirydon's heart leaped at the sound of Ewdokia's voice.

"It's me," he called, fighting back tears. "I'm here, and I won't leave you."

"Spiro! Thank God," Ewdokia cried. "The door is jammed. We've tried everything, but it won't move."

"Stand back."

"Hurry, please. The water is everywhere in here."

Spirydon felt around near the doorway, hoping to find a piece of wood or metal that he might use to break down the door, but there was nothing. He rammed his shoulder against the door again and again in a growing panic until it began to move inward. Water pushed past his ankles through the opening, and Ewdokia screamed at the sound of the door giving way. Spirydon found her in the dark, held her tightly, and covered her face with kisses.

"I thought I had lost you," he cried. Aleksandra and Neonela, who held Jakeb, joined them, and Spirydon tried to gather all of them in his arms. "Dear ones," he said through his tears, "I love you so much."

Barbara Cass-Beggs

DISTANT VOICES INTRUDED on Barbara's dream, becoming increasingly insistent until she awoke. Rousing herself, she realized people were shouting in the corridor outside her cabin. She sat up and wondered what could be going on.

"The lights are out," Alice said. Her roommate's comment brought Barbara fully awake. She felt her daughter stirring beside her and forced herself into action.

"Stay right here, darling," she said to Rosemary. "Mummy's going to put on her shoes." She found her shoes and pulled them on, then took her coat from the foot of the bed and put it on over her nightgown, intending to check on the commotion in the corridor. Before she could reach the door, she heard it open.

"Barbara, are you here?" David's voice sounded concerned.

"Right here, darling. What's happened?"

"Put on your lifejacket, grab Rosy, and come up on deck. Leave everything else."

They found each other in the darkness, and David helped her put on her lifejacket as he explained there had been some sort of explosion and the whistle had blown the signal to abandon ship. Moving more quickly, Barbara wrapped a lifejacket around Rosemary while David helped Alice and her son with their lifejackets.

"Come on. We've got to go," David said. He took Rosemary in his arms.

Hurrying to keep up, Barbara grabbed a blanket for Rosemary and headed out into the corridor. Behind her, a little toy panda lay on the floor in the dark.

SUNDAY 7:50–8:15 P.M., SEPTEMBER 3

David Jennings

IN THE NARROW, crowded corridor near the bow of *Athenia*'s D deck, David and his friends Tony and John, along with their one-armed roommate, all pushed toward the stairway leading to the upper decks. David's flashlight beam played with the flickering glow of matches held up by others moving through the darkened passageway. Despite the emergency, he retained his general sense of well-being. The crowd around him didn't appear to be panicked, so he assumed *Athenia* was not in any real danger.

Three familiar faces appeared unexpectedly in front of him. The University of Michigan women he and John had met that afternoon entered the corridor, looking confused.

"Hello there, ladies," David said. "Going our way?"

"David," Joan Outhwaite exclaimed, shading her pale blue eyes from the flashlight's beam. She seemed genuinely pleased to see him. "Can you help us?"

"We don't remember how to put these things on." Alberta Wood held up her lifejacket with its tangle of cloth ties.

"We'll be glad to help, won't we, fellas?" David said.

They retreated to the girls' tiny cabin, where David introduced Tony as the three young men bumped elbows and backed into each other, laboring to help the girls into their lifejackets. Although each girl wore a heavy coat, David savored the delicious proximity of their bodies. All too soon, he tied the last two tethers of Joan's lifejacket in a tight bow at the base of her throat, lamenting the circumstances that precluded any playful flirting.

"Such a lovely place you have here," David said. "What a shame we can't stay."

"You don't seem very concerned," Joan said.

"You mean about this drill? I think it's an exercise to see if we can remember our muster stations while they get the generator back in service."

"It doesn't feel like an exercise to me."

"Wait and see."

The group joined the thinning crowd in the corridor and followed David's flashlight beam to the base of the stairway. When they emerged on A deck's forward open space, David began to doubt his earlier assurances. Emergency lighting bathed the deck in a blue-white glow that washed out most other colors. Deep shadows shifted back and forth as *Athenia* rolled on the ocean's swells. The vivid scene included deckhands straining to lower two fully loaded lifeboats into the water on either side of the bow.

"Looks awfully serious for just an exercise," Joan chided.

"Sure does," David said. "I'll take my humble pie with a dash of salt."

"Never mind, you two," Tony said. "We need to get up there before those second boats start loading."

They climbed the stairs to the number two muster station and watched the sailors recover the falls from the boat in the water and attach them to the bow and stern of the remaining boat. While they waited, David noticed the ship had a definite list to one side and heard snatches of conversations about a torpedo from a submarine. He felt chagrined by his earlier assurances that they were out of danger and watched in silence as the crewmen brought the boat level with the deck.

"Women and children first!" shouted an officer as people began to climb aboard lifeboat 2A. David and his friends ushered the young women forward and watched them climb into the boat. When they were seated, David turned to the officer and asked if his roommate could join the ladies.

"He's only got one arm. If we have to climb down a ladder to get into a lifeboat, I don't know how he would manage. Can't you take him now?"

"Where is he?"

"Over there, talking to those two young guys. He probably won't want to go if he thinks he's being treated as a charity case."

The officer nodded, walked over to the three men, and addressed Alfie directly.

"We need someone responsible to help with the tiller. How about you sir? Can you help us?"

Alfie seemed to weigh the officer's request and looked at the boat filled with women and children. "I reckon so," he said at last. The officer helped him into the stern of the lifeboat.

"Alright, she's full. Lower away," the officer ordered. The boat started down toward the water, and Joan, who had taken a seat on the nearside bench, turned to look over her shoulder at David.

"Thank you," she said. Her tone suggested a deeper gratitude than the simple words. "I hope you don't have too long to wait."

David smiled and waved, but the lifeboat disappeared over the side of the ship before he could say anything. Once it was gone, he wondered if he would ever see Joan or her friends again, and felt a pang of regret that he hadn't said a proper goodbye. Perhaps it was for the best. He thought briefly about how he might have managed a cross-border relationship before rejecting the idea altogether.

All four lifeboats had been launched from the forward muster stations and the knot of passengers left standing there began moving toward the boat deck above. As the crowd thinned, David became aware of a discussion between his friends.

"So what do you think?" John asked Tony.

"About what?"

"About the girls."

"Good Lord, John, don't you ever think of anything else?"

"Hey," David interrupted. "We should go up to the boat deck and see if we can help." John and Tony looked at him then seemed to notice they were standing alone on the abandoned foredeck.

"Maybe we should think about getting ourselves into a lifeboat," John said.

"The sooner we help the women and children off, the sooner we'll get off ourselves," David noted.

"Makes sense to me," Tony said. Turning up their coat collars to ward off the wind, they headed for the boat deck. Starting up the stairway, Tony offered an observation.

"Say, David, about your theory that this is all an exercise—"

"Don't start."

Barbara Cass-Beggs

A SEETHING CRUSH of passengers carried Barbara and her husband, David, up two flights of stairs and onto the open space at the aft end of A deck. A faint gray glow on the western horizon was all that remained of the sunset. David held Rosemary, who was dwarfed by the canvas lifejacket bundled around her. They pushed their way onto the stairs to the promenade deck, trying to reach the muster station assigned to Barbara and Rosemary. In the harsh glare of *Athenia*'s emergency lighting, Barbara was startled to see David wore only thin cotton pajamas under his lifejacket.

"Where's your coat? You're going to freeze out here."

"I didn't stop to get it. I was desperate to find you and Rosemary after the explosion. We don't have much time before this ship sinks." His observation filled Barbara with dread. She had no idea how they were going to save themselves.

David surveyed the large crowd on the promenade deck gathered around the nearest muster station.

"This looks hopeless," he said.

"How about back there?" Barbara pointed to a smaller crowd around two muster stations at *Athenia*'s stern.

"That's better. Let's go," David said. They headed back down the stairs in the direction of the ship's last two muster stations. Barbara glanced over the portside railing and was alarmed to see the ocean rising to within a few feet of the deck below them. David followed her glance.

"We've got to get Rosy off this ship," he said.

Now fearing for her daughter's life, Barbara forced herself to concentrate on staying with David as he moved toward the stern. They reached the lifeboat stations and again found themselves at the back of a crowd of people. When a barrel-chested sailor hurried by, David turned to stop him.

"Here," he said to the man. "Take this child and get her into a lifeboat, please."

For an agonizing moment, Barbara thought the sailor would turn and continue on his way, but he took Rosemary and pushed his way through the crowd toward the lifeboat. Rosemary looked back at them over the sailor's shoulder, her eyes widening in alarm.

"Mummy," she screamed, throwing her arms out for her mother. "*Mummeeee!*" Barbara's throat tightened and she put her hand over her mouth, hoping to hide her distress from her daughter.

"We're coming for you in another boat, sweetheart," she called. Then she remembered the blanket on her arm.

"Wait, please." She held out the blanket. "Get this blanket to my daughter. She's only wearing her pajamas." Someone took the blanket and passed it forward just as Barbara saw Rosemary lifted high over the crowd and into the lifeboat. She and David ran to the portside railing to see the lifeboat safely lowered into the water. Rosemary's tear-stained face caught their gaze as she looked up at them, still crying and reaching out. The lifeboat's oars dipped into the oncoming swells, and it pulled away into the darkness until its white hull was barely visible.

"Oh, David, what have we done?" Barbara's sense of regret overwhelmed her. One deck below them the ocean swells started washing over the base of the ship's railing.

"It was the only thing we could do, Bar," he said. "At least we know she'll survive."

Oberleutnant Lemp

ON HIS WAY to *U-30*'s forward torpedo room, Lemp ducked his head into the radio room to check with his young operator, Georg Högel. "Any radio traffic from other ships?" he asked.

"No, sir," Högel responded. "Our prize is signaling in some code, but nobody's responded so far."

"I want to know the moment you pick up anything."

Moments later, Lemp stepped into the forward torpedo room. The men quickly grew quiet when they recognized their captain. He noticed signs of the recent emergency in the humid air, damp mattresses, and wet work shirts clinging to the sailors' backs.

"I want you all to know you did well to get that eel out of its tube. Nobody panicked . . . and you saved the boat." He looked each man in the eye as he spoke and saw pride in their expressions. "I promise each of you, that when we have the chance later in this patrol, you'll get some time topside to see the sun and breathe some fresh air." The men greeted news of the rare opportunity with smiles and nods.

"Now," he continued, "you may not have noticed because of our little emergency, but we hit a big merchant cruiser with our first shot." The men cheered and several raised their fists in triumph. Lemp smiled and waited for them to quiet down again. "As soon as it's dark up top, we're going to surface and have a look at our prize." He paused to wait for everyone's attention.

"I think there's a good chance we have sent the first English ship of this war to the bottom." Another cheer erupted as Lemp saluted the men and left the compartment.

Ruth Etherington

THE LIFEBOATS HAD all departed from Ruth's muster station on the promenade deck by the time she, Harold, and Geoffrey arrived. Harold hurried them up one more level to the boat deck. As soon as they arrived, Ruth heard an officer calling for women or children to fill a departing boat.

"There," Harold said. "Quick. Get in." He pushed Ruth and Geoffrey in the direction of the boat.

"But it's so crowded," Ruth objected.

"Never mind that. We could sink at any moment. This may be the best chance for you and Geoff."

"But what about you?"

"Believe me, I'll get off as soon as I can." Harold had maneuvered the two of them to the front of a crowd of mostly men. "Two more here!" he shouted.

"I'm not going without you," Ruth insisted.

Harold shook his head. "What about Geoff? Do you want him to go off with a bunch of strangers, while you stay here? Or do you want him to stay here with us?"

"Dad!" Geoffrey sounded upset, and Ruth worried he was about to plead to stay with them.

"Not now, Geoff," Harold said, holding up his hand. "Ruth, be reasonable. This may be his best chance to get off the ship. You both need to go now." With time running out, Ruth made her painful decision.

"He's right, Geoff," she said. "We should go."

Ruth and Geoffrey were the last ones into the boat, which was swung out over *Athenia*'s port side. Sailors began to let out the falls attached to the boat's bow and stern. The pulleys on the davits squeaked under its weight, and the boat swayed as it descended. Ruth picked out Harold standing at the railing and waved as the lifeboat lowered smoothly into the water.

Riding on the ocean, the wooden boat dipped and climbed on waves that now seemed larger and more ominous than when Ruth had seen them from the deck above. She looked up at the crippled liner and was shaken by the sight of *Athenia*'s hull looming over them—a long black wall that would swamp their boat if it rolled over. Ruth's stomach dropped as she considered their situation, but she could not let the contagion of her fear infect Geoffrey.

"Well now, that wasn't so bad, was it?" she said, smiling at her son.

The bosun's mate in charge of the lifeboat urged the men at the oars to row away, but the heavy boat seemed to wallow in *Athenia*'s shadow, making very little headway. The mate ordered the men to stop rowing, and Ruth looked around to see another lifeboat approaching.

"I have room in my boat," called a sailor in the second boat. "Do you want to transfer some of your passengers?" The approaching lifeboat glided up next to them, and the people on the adjoining sides of each boat reached across to hold the gunwales of the two boats together.

"What about it, folks," the mate asked. "Anyone want to go over to Mr. Macintosh's boat?" As the last ones into their lifeboat, Ruth and Geoffrey had to stand. She weighed the prospect of being able to sit in the new boat against the risks of a mid-ocean transfer. The two heavy boats rose and fell independently on the waves, making it difficult to keep them together.

"Geoff, it looks awfully dangerous. We're not wearing lifejackets."

"We can make it, Mom. Let's go."

"Wait—"

Geoffrey scrambled over the side bench and hopped into the second boat before Ruth could stop him. Now she had no choice but to follow her son. As she started to step across, the space between the two boats began to widen. Ruth stifled a scream and leaped. Passengers in the second boat reached out to grab her arms and her momentum carried across. She dropped onto the side bench next to Geoffrey and hugged him.

"That's my girl!" She heard the shout from above and looked up to see Harold waving and smiling. She waved back, basking in the exhilaration of her accomplishment and her husband's show of encouragement, his second outpouring that day. Ruth said a silent prayer that they might all be together again before the night ended.

Rhoda Thomas

IN THE COVERED gallery along the port side of *Athenia*'s promenade deck, Rhoda waited with several other women for her turn to enter a lifeboat. She did not look forward to the experience, which would require her to climb down a rope ladder into a small boat bobbing on the ocean's swells. It was exactly the scenario she had dreaded when Bosun Harvey explained it during yesterday's lifeboat drill.

At age fifty-four, she wasn't sure she was agile enough to get onto the ladder or strong enough to climb all the way down. One by one, she watched the women and children in front of her receive instruction from a seaman standing by the railing, then climb over the side and disappear. When it was nearly her turn, Rhoda made her peace with God. She would do the best she could. The rest would be up to Him.

Finally, the woman in front of her climbed over the side, and Rhoda stepped up next to the railing. She felt a cold, damp breeze on her cheeks and was grateful she had worn her heavy coat to watch the sunset with Mary. She remembered Mary's injury, and she worried for a moment how her roommate would get off the ship in such a condition. A quick glance over *Athenia*'s side brought Rhoda back to the present. The woman who had been on the ladder had apparently boarded the lifeboat, which rode up and down on the waves. Every occupant's face was turned up toward her.

Oh no. The last thing I need is an audience.

The stout seaman standing at the railing followed her glance to the boat below. "I'm afraid she's a bit crowded," he said. "Several people boarded on deck before they could lower her." Rhoda took a deep breath and focused on the seaman. His bright yellow lifejacket emphasized his bulk and reminded Rhoda that she hadn't been able to gather her own lifejacket.

"Now listen to me carefully, ma'am. You're going to climb down this ladder. When you get to the bottom, stop and do exactly what the chap in the boat tells you." Rhoda glanced over the railing once again.

"A word of advice, ma'am. It's probably best if you don't look down once you're on the ladder. Remember, dear, do exactly as you're told when you reach the bottom. Do you understand?"

Rhoda nodded.

"Right. Off you go, then," he said, as if dispatching a child down a playground slide.

She negotiated the steps over the railing and onto the ladder with the seaman's help. As soon as she started down, however, Rhoda discovered the wooden steps between the ropes were slippery and the ropes that formed the sides of the ladder were rough and wet in her soft hands. Step by careful step, she descended on shaking legs, hoping her pace wasn't holding up those coming after her. Her progress was slowed even more by the fact that the ladder swayed uncomfortably as she neared the bottom because it hung over *Athenia*'s port side and dangled away from the slanting hull. Forgetting the sailor's advice, Rhoda glanced down and saw clearly that the ladder ended several feet short of the water. She refocused her efforts and continued a few more steps until a loud voice called out from behind and below her.

"Stop right there, luv." Rhoda froze, fighting back her fears and listening intently for the next instruction. From the corner of her eye she saw the boat's white hull surprisingly near as it rose on a large swell.

"Jump back *now*," the voice commanded. Rhoda did exactly that. Instead of falling into the water, she fell into the arms of a burly seaman, whose breath smelled of mint and tobacco.

"What? No lifejacket?" he said, and for a moment Rhoda thought the man was going to send her back up the ladder. "Step over this bench toward the tiller there, luv. I'm afraid you'll have to stand for a while. But don't you worry. We'll take turns sitting."

She climbed over the crossbench with the help of other passengers who gave her a hand and steadied her until she found a small place to stand in the well between the third and fourth crossbenches. On the fourth bench, she noticed a woman tending to a little girl who looked to be about ten years old, the age of her own granddaughter. The child had a bandage on her head and the woman looked concerned.

Rhoda took stock of her surroundings. Benches for seating ran along both sides of the lifeboat, and five more benches were spaced at even intervals between the sides. Every seat was taken and six to eight passengers stood in every well between the benches. The boat appeared overloaded, and Rhoda noticed the wooden gunwales that capped both sides of the hull stood no more than six inches above the waterline. Her shoes were wet. She wondered if this might be normal under the circumstances or if the boat had a leak. Regardless of the conditions, the boat would have to be her salvation, and she said a silent prayer to keep them all safe.

The barrel-chested seaman who had caught her appeared to be in charge. He took his position at the tiller, detached the aft fall, and called to the people in the bow to detach their fall.

"You folks on the oars pull away now," he directed.

"My mother's on the ladder," a boy near the bow of the lifeboat called out.

"Please wait for mother," a little girl next to the boy cried. Rhoda saw the woman clinging to the ladder, looking over her shoulder at the departing boat.

"Sorry, sonny, but we're overloaded as it is," the seaman said. "Don't worry. Another boat will be along for her directly."

The two children were not consoled by the seaman's remark. Rhoda's heart ached to hear their sobs at the sight of their mother growing smaller and smaller as their boat gradually moved away.

Ruth Etherington

LOOKING AROUND AT the other occupants in her new lifeboat, Ruth was surprised to see several men, particularly because she assumed it had been one of the first boats to be launched. No sooner had she and the other transfers from the first boat found seating than the oarsmen began pulling away from *Athenia*.

"Backwater, damn ye." The order came from the lean, weathered crewman in charge of lifeboat 8. A few men reversed their oars but most simply stopped rowing, as if uncertain what they had been asked to do. The boat, which still had a few empty seats on its benches, drifted up and down the large swells near *Athenia*'s huge steel hull.

"For God's sake, man, pull away. Pull away," a male passenger called from the bow.

"We're staying right here," the crewman said. "There're plenty of people still aboard *Athenia*, and many may need saving before we're done."

"But it's dangerous," the man protested. "If the ship rolls over we'll be sucked right under. You're jeopardizing the lives of everyone on this boat."

"Now you listen to me," the crewman said, standing up from his spot at the tiller in the boat's stern. "I'm Able Seaman William Macintosh, and I'm in charge of this boat. You are all now under martial law. So you'll do what I say. We're staying right here until I say we leave. Is that clear?" Macintosh remained standing and Ruth, along with several other passengers, looked to the bow of the boat to see how the man would respond to Macintosh's challenge. After a long pause, she saw the man's shoulders slump.

"Have it your way then," he said.

Despite the tension caused by the confrontation, Ruth felt reassured.

There could be no doubt who was in charge of lifeboat 8. Seaman Macintosh was committed to saving lives, and one of them might be her husband, who remained onboard *Athenia*.

Chief Officer Copland

ON THE PORT side of *Athenia*'s boat deck, Copland supervised the loading and launching of seven lifeboats. He paced up and down the deck, helping maintain order among the passengers waiting their turn to board, calling out encouragement to the sailors on the ropes, and offering a hand wherever needed. Operations had gone so smoothly, in spite of *Athenia*'s list to port, that twenty minutes after the evacuation signal sounded, Copland's crews had dispatched all but one of their boats.

His remaining concern was lifeboat 10A. It lay sideways like a giant open mouth, probably blown off its chocks by the force of the torpedo's explosion. Before he could help the three sailors trying to right the heavy boat, Copland heard the angry shouts of several men on the starboard side of the ship. He hurried to the scene and discovered two members of *Athenia*'s crew pushing back several men trying to climb into a partially filled lifeboat.

"I told you, mac, women and children first," Able Seaman Harry Dillon shouted as he held off a stout middle-aged man who wore a wool coat under his bulging lifejacket. A crowd of mostly male passengers formed a semicircle around the two men, and Copland thought they might overwhelm the two crewmen at any moment. Drawing closer, he realized the men were shouting in Polish or German and likely did not understand Seaman Dillon's directions. Both sides were clearly agitated.

"Hold on there," Copland shouted.

Whether it was the sound of his voice or the sight of his uniform, he was grateful that the angry man at the center of things stopped shouting and looked at him. The chief officer took that opportunity to learn from Seaman Dillon the men were insisting on getting into the lifeboat when clearly more women and children had yet to board.

"Yes, but I don't think they speak much English," Copland said.

"Oh no, sir, I think he understands well enough," the perturbed Dillon responded.

"Sprechen sie Deutsch?" Copland asked the angry man.

"Ja, ja," the man answered eagerly. Copland nodded to the man and silently chided his own shortsightedness. He had just exhausted his German language skills.

"Does anyone here understand English?" Copland asked the gathered crowd.

"I speak a little." A tall, slender boy, who looked to be in his mid-teens, stepped forward. "I speak mostly Ukraine and some Polish."

"That'll have to do." Copland put a hand on the boy's shoulder. "You speak to them in Ukrainian, and ask someone else to translate into Polish or German. Understand?"

"Yes," the boy nodded. Copland took a deep breath.

"Tell everyone we are loading women and children into the boats first. There are enough boats for everyone, but the women and children must go first, to assure their safety."

The boy addressed the older man and several others crowded in to hear. Some turned to speak to others in the crowd. It quickly became apparent to Copland that his words were not having the calming effect he desired. The older man shook his head and leaned in to talk to the young translator while several others began speaking insistently. Copland wondered if the translations were becoming garbled until the boy turned to him and explained the men's concerns in halting English.

"They say this is Nazi trick. Nazis separate men. Take them away. Men do not come back. They do not want to be separate of families."

Copland thought to explain that he and his men were not Nazis and to remind the passengers the ship was sinking, but the worried expressions on their faces told him they likely were aware of these facts. He pulled Seaman Dillon and the other crewman in close so they could hear what he was about to propose to the crowd. Copland turned back to the boy.

"Tell them I understand their concern." He waited for the boy to speak and the words to be translated to others. Then he continued, pausing after each phrase. "If they want to leave as a family group, they can wait here together. Women and children who want to go now should get into the lifeboat. After they are away, we will load the family groups and everyone else. There are enough boats for everyone."

When the boy finished translating the last phrase, the men looked at each other and spoke. The low murmur of their conversation led Copland to hope that the situation had been defused. Finally, the boy turned to Copland and said the men understood. They would wait with their families.

"Good," Copland said. He turned to the two crewmen. "You understand what we're doing?"

"Yes, sir," Dillon said. "Women and children, then families."

"Right, but don't force any of the women or children into the boat if they want to stay with the men. Our young friend here can help you." He nodded in the direction of boy. "And make sure he gets off safely."

Spirydon Kucharczuk

"THE MAN SAID we can stay together as a family," Stefan told his father.

"Good. That is good," Spirydon said. But his words were spoken with little conviction. His oldest son, Jan, was missing.

☆ ☆ ☆

AFTER SPIRYDON RESCUED his wife and children from their cabin, they all had waited at the place where the family agreed they would meet in an emergency. They repeatedly called out for Jan and Stefan, but the boys were not there. After ten minutes, he knew that he could wait no longer to put the remainder of his family in a lifeboat. Once they were out on deck, he told Ewdokia they should board a lifeboat before it was too late. He would continue to search for the boys.

"No, I will not go without you," she insisted.

"Papa, we cannot leave you." Neonela said. "We'll stay here until you find them."

"No, no," Spirydon insisted. "You see how the ship is leaning. You must go now, before anything happens."

"What about you?" Ewdokia objected.

"I will not leave without the boys," he said. Ewdokia fixed him with an exasperated stare. He knew she was angry with him, but he didn't know what else to do. How could he leave his two eldest sons on board a sinking ship?

"I will make you a deal," Ewdokia finally said. "You go back to search for the boys one last time, and I will stay here with Jakeb and the girls. You can search as long as you want, but we will not leave without you. When you come back, with or without the boys, we all go to the lifeboat together." Spirydon had no doubt his wife would remain on board until the ship sank unless he agreed to go with her. He stared at her, not sure whether to laugh at her audacity or cry at her stubbornness.

"Wait here," he said, and rushed back into the ship, believing he had very little time if he wanted to save his family. Smaller groups of people continued to come up the stairs, illuminating the darkness with lighted matches. Spirydon began calling for Jan and Stefan.

"Papa, I'm here," a voice shouted immediately in response.

"Who is it?" Spirydon cried. "Who's here?"

"It's me, Stefan." They found each other in the dimness and Spirydon pulled his son to him.

"How did we miss you before?" he asked at last, blinking back his tears. "Didn't you hear us?"

"I was confused. I went to the top of the stairway near our cabin on the other side of the ship. I waited and waited and called for you. When you didn't come, I thought maybe I was confused and I came here. I'm sorry."

Spirydon had reassured his son that they were together and that was what mattered. They called Jan's name for nearly five more minutes, but there was no response. Finally, thinking he had pushed his luck as far as it would go, Spirydon gave up the search and returned with Stefan to the remainder of the family.

After a quick, tearful reunion with Stefan, they went in search of a lifeboat and ended up on the boat deck with several other refugee families and single men. Spirydon waited with his family and the others, their concerns growing as the ship's crewmen continued to insist on separating the men from the women and children. When several of the men began objecting, the officer had appeared and asked Stefan to help him. Now they would be able to stay together as a family, but the family was missing one member.

☆ ☆ ☆

"I WISH I knew where he's gone," Spirydon said to Stefan. "You are sure you didn't see him?"

"I told you, Papa, I left the cabin right after the explosion and the lights went out. I took our lifejackets and tried to find the place by the stairs to wait for everyone. But I never saw Jan."

The big sailor in charge of the lifeboat came to ask Stefan for help. Spirydon turned to Ewdokia, who held two-year-old Jakeb on her hip, balancing him with difficulty because of the bulky lifejacket she wore over her dress and coat.

"Where could he be? What if we have to go without him?"

"Then we must go," she answered. "Remember what you said in Trosteniec."

"That was before he agreed to come with us. I found Stefan. I could stay behind and find Jan."

"No, Spiro. You agreed to come with us. Even if you stay behind, you may not find him. And how would we all get back together again? It's better for all of us to stay together now. Jan may already be in a lifeboat. He's a smart boy. If he couldn't find us, he would take care of himself."

Ewdokia's arguments made sense.

"Papa." Stefan approached his father. "The man in charge of the lifeboat says we should go now. He wants you to help with the oars."

Judith Evelyn

JUDITH VOWED SHE would not leave *Athenia* until she was certain Andrew and his father were both safely away in a lifeboat, with or without her. Andrew called her stance pigheaded, but he didn't try to talk her out of it. The three had been waiting more than a half hour in the promenade deck's starboard covered gallery as lifeboats filled with women and children descended past them from the deck above. The operations seemed to be going slowly, and Judith wondered if the delays had to do with the ship's list. Because *Athenia* leaned to its port side, all the lifeboats on their side of the ship bumped and scraped down the hull as they were lowered into the water.

The wait had given Judith a chance to return to her cabin on A deck and retrieve her heavy fur coat. Andrew had helped her retie her lifejacket over her coat, carefully securing the ties tightly at Judith's insistence so as to prevent a broken neck, a danger she vividly recalled from the first day's boat drill.

"There can't be more than one or two boats left above us," Andrew said to the seaman standing with them by the railing in the covered gallery. "We need to board a lifeboat now."

"We'll make sure you get off, sir. Don't worry." The seaman appeared to be in his late teens, and Judith wondered how much stock to put in his assurances. Andrew seemed to share her thoughts as he drew close to his father.

"I don't know what to do, Dad. Can we trust this boy to put us in a boat?"

"You've made your point with the lad; let's see what he can do for us," Reverend Allan advised. "After all, he probably can't leave the ship until we've gone, so he has an interest in seeing us off."

With a grating sound, the keel of another lifeboat came bumping down toward them. As it gradually came into view, there appeared to be seating available. The young seaman took hold of a grab line along the gunwale to steady the boat.

"Make room, ladies and gents," he announced to the boat's occupants. "Three more coming aboard." He motioned to Judith, Andrew, and William that they should step into the boat as it continued its slow descent.

They climbed aboard quickly and found space to sit on its starboard side.

The boat seemed to bump over every rivet on its way down the hull until it came to an abrupt stop a few feet above the water. The seas appeared to Judith to come within a foot of the bottom of the boat, but fell away to a drop of six or eight feet before rising again on the next swell. Able Seaman Dillon, the man in charge of the boat, called to the crewmen on *Athenia*'s boat deck to determine why they had stopped. Judith understood, after hearing an exchange of several choice words, that the problem was on their lifeboat. Something had snagged and could not be freed because of the weight of the boat.

"Stand by," someone shouted from above. Judith looked up to see a man with his legs wrapped around the stern fall sliding down, hand under hand, toward them like a scene out of a pirate movie. He dropped into the boat and took a hatchet from his belt. The man conferred with Seaman Dillon, who then gave a signal to the crew on deck to stand by as he waited for the next ocean swell to begin rising.

"Hold tight, everyone," Dillon told the passengers. The only thing Judith could hold onto was the bench, which she grabbed with both hands and doubled over. She heard Dillon shout and the axe blade chop twice before their heavy lifeboat hit the ocean with a loud smack. The splash didn't swamp them, and no one fell out. The men at the boat's oars began to dip them in the water when another shout drew Judith's attention back up to the *Athenia*.

She saw two men sliding down different lines dangling from the boat deck. Near the bottom of the ropes the men pushed off the hull and dropped into the water. Both wore white coats and she assumed they were stewards who had decided it was time to leave the ship. The two men swam up to their boat, and one caught hold of a grab line next to Judith.

"Give us a hand here," he said, after spitting out a stream of seawater. With Andrew and William's help, Judith wrestled the steward into the boat. She felt the man's wet clothes and realized the ocean must be very cold. She wondered how the two men would ever get warm during the night and made a mental note to take extra care not to fall overboard. Even with her lifejacket, Judith knew the last place she wanted to be was in the water.

SUNDAY 8:15–9:10 P.M., SEPTEMBER 3

Oberleutnant Lemp

TWILIGHT HAD FADED into night when *U-30* broke the surface of the water. Lemp led the watch crew onto the submarine's bridge atop its conning tower and was greeted by a cold wind and misty rain. Just above the eastern horizon, a half-moon's pale ocher light shone beneath a layer of dark clouds and sparkled on the crests of the ocean's inky swells.

Eager to assess the damage done by his torpedo, Lemp had surfaced nearly two miles from his victim on the opposite side of the ship from the moon. First Watch Officer Hinsch joined his commander on the bridge, and both men raised their binoculars to focus on the big ship lying still in the water.

Emergency lights illuminated men on deck lowering lifeboats into the water. Lemp saw the ocean's swells splash over the ship's stern, and he detected her pronounced list to port. There was no question the ship was in distress and being abandoned, but she was still afloat more than a half hour after being hit. With Ireland only two hundred fifty miles away, Lemp worried that auxiliary pumps might keep the ship afloat long enough to be towed to port for repairs.

"Do you want to finish her off with the deck gun?" Hinsch asked.

Lemp considered the question and shook his head. "Let's see how fast she's settling. We'll use another eel if we have to." After watching operations aboard the stricken ship for several minutes, a new thought occurred to *U-30*'s commander.

"Mr. Hinsch, as long as we're waiting here, go below and organize a viewing party for the men in the forward torpedo room." The torpedo room crew rarely had an opportunity to come to the bridge while on patrol, much less to see an actual victim of their attack. Certainly they had earned the privilege.

With Hinsch headed down the ladder to make the arrangements, Lemp again raised his binoculars to check the progress of his target's demise. Strike quickly and hit hard, Dönitz had told him. The war was off to a glorious start.

☆ ☆ ☆

NEARLY TWENTY MEN climbed to the top of the conning tower two or three at a time to see the brightly lit ship in the distance, its stern riding low in the water and listing to port. But as each man took his turn to look through the binoculars, Lemp grew more impatient. By the time the last man departed the bridge, he had decided his prize was not sinking fast enough. He would fire one more torpedo in a surface attack.

"Battle stations," he called down to the control center. "Mr. Hinsch, you may finish her off," Lemp told his first watch officer.

"Yes, sir," Hinsch responded. He stepped to the targeting binoculars mounted on the front of the bridge.

"Ready tube three for firing," Hinsch ordered. He eased *U-30* to within 1,500 yards of the target and received word that the torpedo doors were open and tube three was ready to fire. The big ship sat motionless in the water so this would be an easy shot, but Hinsch took his time reading out the bearing, range, and bow angle data for the U-boat's fire control system, being sure the target's speed was set at zero.

"You may fire when ready, Mr. Hinsch," Lemp said.

"Tube three, fire."

Ruth Etherington

LIFEBOAT 8, WITH Ruth and her son Geoffrey aboard, pulled away from *Athenia* after waiting another ten minutes and picking up two oil-soaked women who had fallen from their ladders. As several men and a few women labored at the oars, Seaman Macintosh gave Ruth and her fellow passengers an idea of what they could expect while aboard the boat.

"Ladies and gents," he called out from his position at the tiller, "this is how we're going to survive out here until the rescue ship comes. Forget etiquette. There's no parlor manners here. If you need anything, you yell for it. If you have to relieve yourself, men, do it over the side. For the ladies, we have a bucket. I'm warning you, if you think you'll avoid embarrassment by holding it in, the pain'll kill you." There were a few chuckles from the lifeboat's occupants, but Ruth thought for the most part they seemed subdued.

"We have rations aboard. I'll hand 'em out later. You'll go easy on 'em, because we don't know how long we'll be out here. But don't you worry, I'll make sure nobody starves. For now, we're going to keep *Athenia* in sight because the rescue ship will be coming to her location. Any questions?"

There were none.

Ruth sat on the starboard side bench near Macintosh, wearing only her black dinner dress and high-heeled dancing slippers. She felt the cold wind and wondered if the lifejacket she had been unable to retrieve would have provided her with any more warmth. Ruth put her arm around Geoffrey and huddled close to keep them both a bit warmer as a light rain began to fall.

The lifeboat was not crowded. Everyone had a seat, and the bottom of the boat was dry. Even so, it was riding low in the water, and each new approaching swell looked big enough to swamp them. Working the tiller and giving orders for one side then the other to row, Macintosh kept the boat's bow pointed toward the oncoming sea so that their little craft rode up and over the endless procession of waves. Ruth kept an eye on *Athenia* and was reassured that it remained afloat, increasing the chances that Harold would make it safely off the ship.

A faint, high-pitched whine, barely audible at first, sounded to Ruth as if it was coming through the lifeboat's wooden hull. It quickly grew to an alarming intensity then just as quickly diminished in a minor key. Tiny bubbles appeared alongside the boat in a line heading for *Athenia*.

"Another torpedo," Macintosh announced. "It's all over now."

Passengers seated near her gasped and Ruth doubled over, covering her face, not wanting to see the devastation another torpedo would cause or acknowledge the threat it posed to her husband. In her crouched position she heard Macintosh yell to the people on the oars.

"Pull away! Put your backs into it. Take us out of the line of fire."

She waited, holding her breath. Nearly a minute had gone by when she finally exhaled. Still she waited for the terrible explosion. But there was no sound except the frantic slaps of the oars hitting the water. When Ruth finally looked up she saw *Athenia* still afloat in the harsh glow of her emergency lights. Somehow, the torpedo had missed its target. She hugged Geoffrey closer to her side and said a silent prayer of thanks.

Oberleutnant Lemp

ON *U-30*'S BRIDGE, Lemp grew anxious about the long running time on this latest shot.

"What's the time on number three eel?" he called down to the U-boat's control room.

"Two minutes, twenty seconds," came the answer.

"Too long," Hinsch said. "I double-checked everything. It's got to be a misfire."

"Yes, damn it." Lemp shook his head. "Every damn one has been a misfire. Even the eel that put a hole in her hull was supposed to explode under her keel and break her back." While he pondered whether to expend yet another torpedo on his crippled target, a sailor climbed onto the bridge with information from the radio room.

"Sir, Högel is picking up radio transmissions he says are coming from the ship we hit," the man said, handing Lemp a slip of paper from the radio operator. "They're not even coding their messages now."

"Any signals from rescue ships?"

"No, sir."

Lemp dismissed the sailor and turned back to Hinsch. "We're running out of time," he said, fingering the slip of paper. "Call out the gun crew." Lemp reasoned that using the eighty-eight millimeter deck cannon would give Hinsch, the boat's weapons officer, a second chance to erase the disappointment of the misfire. While the crewmen began scrambling to come up on deck, he took a moment to unfold the piece of paper the sailor had given to him and hold it close to the dim red light on the bridge.

ATHENIA TORPEDOED 56.43 NORTH, 14.05 WEST

"Take the bridge. I'm going down to check this out," he told Hinsch. "You may fire when ready."

Lemp hurried down the ladder and quickly covered the two dozen steps from the control room to the radio room opposite his quarters. He asked the operator, Georg Högel, for the boat's copy of *Lloyd's Register,* with its listing of the world's merchant ships. Opening the hefty volume, he found the pages for British merchant ship names starting with the letter "A" and began scanning the column, eager to confirm the tonnage of his victim. When his finger stopped on *"Athenia,"* Lemp froze.

No, there must be a mistake.

But there was no mistake. The ship was the right size, and it matched the silhouette of the ship he had tracked in his periscope. The entry told him he had attacked a passenger ship, exactly the type of prize all U-boat commanders had been told to avoid. Lemp shivered. The sense of accomplishment that had lifted his spirits for the past hour vanished in an instant.

"What a mess," he said to no one in particular. Noticing the worried look on Högel's face, Lemp straightened and clapped the big volume closed without saying another word. Realizing he had called out the gun crew, Lemp bolted for the conning tower ladder and cried, "Do not fire! Repeat, do not fire!"

"Hold your fire!" Hinsch ordered, as Lemp climbed onto the bridge.

"Secure the deck gun," Lemp ordered. "Gun crew return to your stations." The sailors on deck retrieved a shell from the breech and began securing the gun. Lemp saw the confusion on his first watch officer's face.

"It's a passenger ship," he hissed in a low voice.

"We torpedoed a passenger ship?" Hinsch said.

"Yes, damn it. But why was she blacked out? God, this is a mess, a horrible mess. How could this be?"

"You're sure it's a passenger ship? There's no mistake?"

"No mistake. She carries a thousand passengers fully loaded, which she no doubt was."

"But how could you have known? She was sailing evasively and out of the normal shipping lanes."

"Goddamn it, Hinsch, it's my responsibility to know." Lemp shook his head, trying to push the terrible reality of his mistake to the back of his mind. Should he try to render assistance, perhaps offer food or water to people in the lifeboats as the international regulations required? But there would be far too many passengers for his provisions to satisfy. Should he stand by until he was assured the passengers would be rescued? What if the weather turned foul and the rising sea threatened to swamp the boats? He couldn't possibly take even fifty passengers aboard *U-30*, let alone one thousand.

"Clear the bridge," he announced. He'd made his decision. *U-30* would resume patrolling her combat zone, and he would not break radio silence to report his attack to headquarters. That would have to wait until he could speak to Dönitz in private. He would have time before then to consider how to deal with the crew, half of whom had seen the passenger ship dead in the water.

Barbara Cass-Beggs

ON *ATHENIA*'S BOAT deck, Barbara watched crewmen working to put lifeboat 10A upright. The force of the explosion had apparently knocked the boat off its blocks, and it could not be lifted by the falls. After several minutes of effort, the crew members and a few passengers managed to rock 10A back onto its keel. A ship's officer inspected the boat and directed the crew to attach the falls from the davits to its bow and stern. The men at each end pulled on the ropes to lift the boat off the deck and crewmen cranked it out over *Athenia*'s side. When they brought it level with the deck, the officer told them to stop.

"She's ready to board," the officer announced. "Please be careful and take your time. Mr. McDonald, she's all yours." A tall, weathered sailor with freckled cheeks and wisps of blond hair trailing from under his dark woolen watch cap climbed in and took the tiller in the stern.

The knot of people surged forward, carrying Barbara and her husband, David, with them. They stepped over the gunwale and into the lifeboat near its bow, with Barbara finding room on the starboard side bench and David standing next to her. Less than an hour earlier, she thought they would not escape *Athenia* before the ship sank. But it had stayed afloat long enough for them to board this last lifeboat on the port side. As the boat slowly descended toward the ocean she allowed herself to hope they might survive after all and be reunited with Rosemary.

When they were a few feet from the water something went wrong. The lifeboat's stern suddenly fell. Passengers screamed as the stern hit the water. The steep downward angle threw David onto Barbara's shoulder and toward the ocean beyond. She grabbed the waist cord of his pajamas in time to keep him from falling out of the boat just as the bow splashed into the water.

"Is anyone hurt?" Seaman McDonald called out.

A good six inches of water filled the bottom of the boat as it came level on the sea. Two passengers who had fallen in the water were helped back into the boat, and Barbara noticed they were streaked black with oil.

"Are you all right?" she asked David.

"I think so. Just cold." The splash from the drop had soaked him from his head to his knees. With his wet, brown hair clinging to his forehead, David hugged his arms and crouched down out of the wind.

"Thank you for saving my dignity," he said, kissing Barbara's cheek. His lips felt like ice against her skin and she worried how she was going to keep her husband warm during the night.

Chief Officer Copland

WITH NEARLY A full complement of passengers, lifeboat 10A presented a heavy load for the seamen slowly paying out the falls to lower it into the ocean. Copland jumped in to help the crew on the stern fall. It was a last-minute decision on his part, and he wasn't wearing gloves when the man behind him lost his grip. The line burned as it flew through Copland's fingers.

"Let go of the bow line," he yelled. Screams from the lifeboat below accompanied its entry into the water with a loud splash.

Copland looked over the railing to make sure the boat hadn't capsized. He blew on his left hand, trying to ease the pain in his raw palm, and dug a handkerchief out of his back pocket to wrap around his hand. While finishing up his makeshift bandage, he heard his name being called.

"Mr. Copland!" He turned to see Cadet Turnbull running toward him. "Glad I found you, sir. The captain wants to see you."

☆ ☆ ☆

HIS FACE SHINY with sweat and smudged with soot, Copland reported somewhat self-consciously to a scowling Captain Cook in *Athenia*'s wheelhouse.

"There you are, Copland," Cook bellowed. "Can you believe this? Nothing is beneath these Nazi apes." He paused, seeming to take in his chief officer's expression. "What is it, man? What are you looking at?"

Copland was surprised to see Cook wearing a dark brown business suit instead of his uniform.

"Oh, the suit?" Cook said. "This is just a precaution. In the last war, the Germans took captains prisoner. Damned if I'll let those bastards do that to me."

"Yes, sir." Somewhere in the back of Copland's mind it occurred to him the Germans might transfer their interest to the chief officer if the captain wasn't available.

"What happened to your hand?"

"It's a rope burn, sir. Nothing serious."

"Well, have it looked after as soon as you get a chance," Cook said. "Are all the lifeboats away?"

"No, sir. We have two left on the starboard side. Our list to port is complicating the launches, but they should be away in a few minutes."

"Very good." Cook glanced at his watch and Copland noticed it had been an hour since the torpedo had struck. "Right now, I need you to find out if we can save this ship. How I'd love to take *Athenia* to Ireland and disappoint those German bastards."

"Yes, sir." Copland turned to leave.

"And Mr. Copland . . . don't take any chances."

"No, sir. I'll be careful."

With a flashlight from the wheelhouse, Copland headed toward the stern and number five hold, which he believed had taken the full force of the torpedo's explosion. Over the years, he had become adept at arranging cargo in holds to maximize a ship's efficient passage through the water. A quick glance aft as he descended from the bridge told him another ten degrees of list could cause *Athenia*'s cargo to shift and possibly capsize the ship. He had to determine if the list could be stopped before it reached that last fatal degree.

Approaching number five hold again, Copland noticed the bodies he had seen earlier were gone. He also saw a slight buckling in some of the ship's decking and realized a few of the watertight doors might have been damaged in the blast. He entered the hold from the higher starboard side, climbing down an interior ladder into the darkness. The water had receded from an hour ago, telling him it probably had begun leaking through the hold's strained bulkheads. The smell of smoke and decay remained strong. Stopping a few feet above the water, he was struck by an eerie silence, except for his own heavy breathing and a low bubbling murmur that indicated somewhere water was moving into or out of the hold. Copland played his flashlight across the water's pea-green surface. His beam picked out floating debris and three blackened and bruised bodies in the water. From the bits of burned clothing, he couldn't tell whether they were shipmates or passengers, but there was no question they were dead.

He climbed back up the ladder, mindful of the pain in his left hand. On the promenade deck again, he went forward and descended two sets of stairs to B deck. Copland wanted to check the valves that automatically shut the outlets for the ship's toilets after they were flushed, a prosaic detail that could be critical to *Athenia*'s survival. He tried turning the wheels that manually shut the valves, but they didn't budge. The explosion had damaged the mechanism, and seawater was slowly entering the ship through its many toilets. Even if the watertight doors had done their job by sealing off the forward sections of the ship, Copland knew the water couldn't be stopped from coming in through the toilets. *Athenia* was doomed, although her end was probably several hours away.

The stewards in charge of clearing accommodations had told Copland all living passengers vacated the lower decks. There was nothing left to do now but confirm no one had been left behind, including the woman in sick bay. Cadet Turnbull had told him her name was Rose Griffin and that she was traveling alone. Copland headed aft toward the medical facilities, checking all the open rooms with his flashlight and calling out as he moved down the corridor.

The sick bay had two small wards, one each for men and women. He tried the first door and found it locked; most likely the men's ward that had not been in use. The door to the second ward stood open, and he shone his light on an empty bed. Satisfied Mrs. Griffin had been evacuated by the two seamen he had assigned to the task, Copland continued his search.

Starting down the stern stairway, he discovered the water had risen nearly to the ceiling of C deck. There would be no survivors in the aft cabins on C and D decks. An occasional metallic groan echoed throughout the hull, signaling stress on *Athenia*'s steel framework or shifting cargo. Though the ship's moans unnerved him, Copland pushed himself onward, driven to make as thorough an inspection as possible.

Back on B deck, he retraced his steps forward and descended the stairs all the way to D deck, and worked his way aft until he found the water had reached almost amidships. On C deck, Copland began moving aft again to see how far the water had advanced on the next higher deck. In the cabin-class dining saloon, the room he vacated a little more than an hour earlier, his flashlight beam caught overturned chairs and broken plates and glasses on the now soiled carpet. Oddly enough, a few tables and their place settings appeared untouched, waiting for diners who would never come. In the galley, which was approximately amidships on C deck, he picked his way through the shiny debris of pots and pans, the treacly sweet smell of pudding mingling with the pungent spices of cooked meats.

He found the water had advanced halfway across the third-class dining saloon and nearly submerged the jumble of overturned chairs and tables accumulated along the portside bulkhead. Copland called out, but no one answered, and he lingered long enough to satisfy himself that no bodies lay in the tangle of broken furniture.

Seeing the residue of destruction and evidence of *Athenia*'s distress saddened him. They had been together several years, and he had come to appreciate her as an old friend, one who had seen him through rough seas, had housed and fed him, and had never failed to deliver her passengers and cargo to safe harbors. *Athenia* wasn't the newest ship, nor did she possess the most stylish lines, but she was comfortable and reliable. She deserved a much better fate than the one she was about to suffer, a fate he was powerless to prevent.

He had seen all he needed to see. With a downcast heart, Copland started back for the bridge to deliver his report.

Rhoda Thomas

STANDING ANKLE DEEP in a mixture of water, oil, and regurgitated dinners, Rhoda watched the broad shoulders of the next ocean swell move steadily toward her lifeboat. For an hour, she had worked to maintain her balance with each wave, leaning forward as the boat rode up one side, straightening as it went over the top, and leaning slightly backward as they slid down the back of the wave. The fast-running clouds that blocked the rising moon earlier and brought light showers had broken for the moment, allowing faint moonlight to illuminate the oncoming swells. The thirty-second intervals between waves offered her little respite, and she was growing weary.

The women and the few male passengers working the oars did not seem particularly proficient as they tried to keep their craft pointed into the oncoming seas. Two or three times a big swell caught the boat sideways, prompting cries from the passengers. The first time it happened, Rhoda was certain the boat would capsize, but somehow they managed to stay afloat.

The mixture in the bottom of the boat was a result of seasickness and persistent leaks. After an hour, those suffering from the boat's bobbing motion had little left to contribute, but the leaks were another matter. Rhoda watched as seated passengers took turns with the bailing bucket, which was in constant use to keep the water from advancing any higher. Some men donated their shirts, and women used scarves or fabric torn from their clothing to wedge into the hull's small cracks in an effort to stop the leaks.

Meanwhile, Rhoda noticed the cold wind had grown steadily stronger as the evening wore on, which didn't bode well for those passengers dressed in their nightclothes or thin evening dresses.

"Ma'am, could you take this baby under your coat?" A young woman seated in front of Rhoda wore only a nightgown under her lifejacket and was holding a sleeping baby. "I'm afraid I can't keep it warm enough."

"Of course, dear. What's your baby's name?"

"Oh, it's not mine. One of the sailors handed it to me after I sat down. I don't know where the mother is."

Rhoda took the baby, which was clad only in diapers and a thin shirt, and tucked it under her coat. As she did so, the moon disappeared again and a thin veil of rain began to fall.

Spirydon Kucharczuk

THE CROWDED CONDITIONS in lifeboat 5A made it difficult for Spirydon and others working the oars to lean forward and pull back, following Able Seaman Harry Dillon's directions. Seated at the forward oar on the starboard side of the boat, Spirydon's limited language skills made it hard for him to understand the sailor's orders. Fortunately, he was partnered with Stefan, who knew enough English to keep them synchronized with the other rowers. It also helped that he and Stefan were experienced oarsmen, having rowed many times on the Horyn River near their farm in eastern Poland. Though he grew tired and the wind and sporadic rain showers chilled him, Spirydon didn't want to relinquish his position and leave his family's safety to a stranger. But he was worried about Ewdokia.

Normally a tower of strength for the family, his wife had succumbed to seasickness and was slumped down somewhere near the middle of the boat. Though he couldn't see her, he knew where she was because of the cries from two-year-old Jakeb, who remained with her. While he wished he could comfort them, he believed he would do more good rowing the boat and ending its nauseating gyrations as soon as possible.

Spirydon could see his older daughter, Neonela, seated on the side bench not far from him. She held her younger sister Aleksandra on her lap, her arms wrapped protectively around the little girl. Several times, Neonela leaned closer to her sister to speak in her ear, and more than once he saw Leksi turn and smile at her big sister. How wonderful, he thought, that even in these miserable surroundings the two girls could find something to smile about.

He began to reconsider the family's situation. All their money, documents, and possessions would be lost if the big ship sank. Jan was missing, but the rest of the family was together with him in the boat. They could start over and find a new way to Canada. Ewdokia was right; they were a big family with many hands to help. But in that moment, Spirydon recalled the fortuneteller's prophecy.

Not all of your family will arrive with you.

The prophecy's meaning now painfully clear to him, Spirydon pulled on his oar and silently mourned the loss of his oldest son.

David Jennings

ON *ATHENIA*'S EMPTY boat deck, David watched the ship's last lifeboat move off into the night. For the previous hour, he, Tony, and John had helped passengers locate lifejackets, put them on, and find their muster stations. They even assisted in launching a few lifeboats. Despite the cool, damp weather, David's sweaty shirt clung to his back under his overcoat and lifejacket, but he felt more energized than exhausted.

"Looks like we just marooned ourselves on a sinking ship," John said. "I thought the idea was to make sure we were on one of those boats."

"Don't worry, Johnny," David said. "There's still crew aboard, and I'm sure they're planning to get off somehow."

David and his friends found a dozen crew members, including all the ship's officers and two more passengers, on A deck. They took a seat on the same hatch cover where David and John had entertained the three University of Michigan girls a few hours earlier. The harsh emergency lighting and shifting shadows washed back and forth over the men, who stood or sat in small groups, recovering from the night's work. An older man in a brown business suit finally broke the silence.

"Gentlemen, first let me say, well done." David wasn't sure who the man was, but sensed all the crewmen and officers knew him.

"With all the women and children and refugees on board," the man continued, "the evacuations could have been chaotic, but I think we put everyone off in good order. Mr. Copland, what about your hospital case?"

"She was taken off," said a dark-haired officer with a handkerchief wrapped around his hand. "I found no one left below decks. All surviving passengers are off the ship, except for present company, of course."

"Of course. Thank you, gentlemen, for your assistance." The man in the suit nodded to David and the other passengers before addressing the crew. "I'm sorry to say that *Athenia* cannot be saved. But there is good news. We've been contacted by a Norwegian freighter, *Knute Nelson*, and she expects to arrive here sometime after midnight. Right now, we ought to give some thought to our own safety, just in case we start taking on a lot more water."

As if to punctuate the man's observation, a low metallic moan reverberated from deep in the hold beneath them. One of the officers stood.

"We need to get those Gradwells in the water," he said. A few crewmen rose in response.

"Can we help?" David stood, followed stiffly by Tony and John.

"Sure. Glad to have you," said the officer.

They all moved off toward the stern. David learned the officer's name was Colin Porteous, *Athenia*'s third officer, and that the man addressing the crew was the ship's captain.

"But why is he wearing a suit?" David asked.

"Something about Germans' taking captains prisoner in the last war," Porteous said.

"Did you see the submarine?"

"No, but our chief officer and one of our quartermasters saw her. She came up right after we were hit. No doubt about it. Some passengers say they took a shot at us with their deck gun. I didn't see that either, but I wouldn't put it past them. The bloody cowards are probably far away by now."

☆ ☆ ☆

DAVID DISCOVERED THE Gradwells were inflated life rafts that could hold twenty people each. From a small hold near the aft docking bridge, they unpacked and launched four of the rafts. He helped to tow them around to the starboard side, where Porteous tied them off as a misty rain began to fall. When they returned to the rest of the group, the captain had more good news. The radio officer had raised two more ships. A Swedish yacht, *Southern Cross,* would arrive around 3:00 a.m., and *City of Flint,* an American freighter, was expected after sunrise.

His confidence renewed by the captain's announcement, David volunteered to join an expedition led by the ship's chief steward to enter *Athenia* and gather any items from below decks that might prove useful, including extra blankets and lifejackets. Tony and John didn't seem as keen on the idea, but joined David anyway.

Flashlights in hand, the boys entered the cabin and tourist-class dining saloons on C deck to see tables, chairs, food, and crockery in jumbled piles leaning against the port side of the hull. Here and there, a few tables remained upright, and the food looked remarkably appetizing. Moving carefully through the overturned furniture, they plucked bread from baskets, pieces of fresh fruit from bowls, and even a whole chicken from an undisturbed table. All the items went into pillowcases the Steward had given them.

Back on deck, they shared their bounty with the two other passengers—a university professor and a Protestant minister—and crew members, several of whom had missed dinner and were grateful for the food. When everyone had eaten their fill, another crew member shared a large cache of tobacco and matches he had found below decks. David pulled his pipe out of his inside coat pocket, filled it with the tobacco, and cupped a match to the bowl. The smoke tasted sweet as he puffed away.

It seemed odd to feel so content in the middle of the night on a sinking ship in the Atlantic Ocean, hundreds of miles from land. But to David's surprise, he wasn't particularly concerned about surviving. For reasons he didn't understand, it simply felt right to be here, among these men at this moment.

The chief steward emerged again from below decks, triumphantly holding a bottle of scotch whiskey. He took a seat on the hatch cover and invited everyone to join him. The men sat in a large circle, and each one took a welcome swig from the bottle before passing it on. The minister declined his turn but obligingly kept the bottle moving. It made nearly two circuits before being emptied.

"I was thinking," Tony said, "we never got a chance to wear those new dinner jackets we had made in London."

"I could've put that jacket to such good use," John said.

"Guess the fish will be opening a hire service for formal dress," David added.

Warmed by the glow of the scotch, David gazed out to sea. The moon had climbed halfway up the eastern sky. When not obscured by the scudding clouds, it shone brightly enough to illuminate the ship's lifeboats, arrayed like white cockleshells in a great circle around *Athenia*.

Barbara Cass-Beggs

HUDDLED DOWN IN lifeboat 10A, Barbara used her body to keep her husband warm and protected from the intermittent rain. David began to shiver shortly after he and Barbara were splashed during the lifeboat's launch. Under their lifejackets, Barbara wore a cloth coat over her nightdress, but David had only his thin cotton pajamas for protection against the cold, damp night.

"Quartermaster McDonald says we'll be picked up soon," she told her husband. It was a remark she had overheard and thought it might help to keep David's spirits up.

David nodded. "If you locate the lounge on this boat," he said through chattering teeth, "tell the waiter I'll have a hot cup of tea, thank you."

Barbara wished she could share her husband's sense of humor, but she did not feel upbeat. She had been hopeful about their chances of survival and reuniting with Rosemary when they climbed into the lifeboat. But after the mishap launching their boat and spending an hour bobbing on the ocean, their situation now seemed bleak. How far would they drift before help arrived? The ocean was so expansive she feared they might never be found.

Her thoughts strayed to Rosemary. Was anyone comforting her little girl?

She could close her eyes and still see the tears on Rosemary's cheeks as her lifeboat pulled away. The vision tore at her, and she questioned again her decision to give up her daughter. Barbara knew her troubling thoughts were not helping her situation and, worse, might threaten to depress David as well. But how was she to change her frame of mind?

Music.

She often lost herself in the music when playing piano back home. If she could get others to sing with her it might lift everyone's mood in the boat. The first song to come to mind was "Speed Bonnie Boat" because of its familiar melody. She began to sing without giving much thought to the lyrics.

"Speed, bonnie boat, like a bird on the wing . . ." A few people joined Barbara in singing the chorus. But when she got to the part about winds howling and waves roaring, the other voices died away. She tried a few more songs, "My Bonnie Lies Over the Ocean" and "Early One Morning," but her fellow passengers didn't seem very interested and her heart wasn't in it. Every song reminded her of Rosemary, who loved singing with her mummy.

Her efforts brought Barbara full circle, back to her worries about survival and rescue. The dark ocean swells continually rolled toward them, each one seemingly large enough to swallow their boat. How long could they ride over the waves before some mishap tipped them into the ocean? When she and David had first come up on deck after the explosion, she thought *Athenia* might sink at any moment and take them all with it. Did getting off in a lifeboat simply prolong their ordeal by delaying the inevitable? She didn't like the thought of drowning, but it would end the crushing anxiety she felt. This might not be a bad time to die, she rationalized. They had just said goodbye to their families and friends and the trip had forced them to put their lives in order.

If there is a God, he would know everything about my life so there's no point in asking for forgiveness or further help. When the time comes, I'll try to concentrate on something pleasant so I won't notice the drowning. At least David and I are together and Rosemary will be well cared for. I only hope she will remember how much we loved her.

Judith Evelyn

NEAR THE BOW of lifeboat 5A, Judith and the Reverend William Allan made room on the bench for Andrew, who had worked for nearly an hour helping to pull one of the boat's oars. Seaman Dillon, the sailor in charge of their boat, had halted the rowing and called for volunteers to spell those on the oars who needed rest. Andrew appeared exhausted; his hands were red and chafed from his efforts.

"I've never done anything so difficult in my life," he said.

Tired of sitting and anxious to take some role in her rescue, Judith gave Andrew her seat on the starboard side bench. "I'm going to take your place," she said.

"Judith, for God's sake." Andrew sounded peeved at her decision. "Not in your . . . I mean, it's hard work. You have no idea."

"If I only row for ten minutes, I'll give someone an extra ten minutes to rest."

Before Andrew could protest further, she joined the shuffle of people changing places in the boat. Climbing over a crossbench, she sat where Andrew had been rowing near the middle of the boat.

"Hello there, miss." The big man seated by the gunwale greeted Judith as she sat down next to him. "You're not much bigger around than the oar."

"I'm stronger than I look. Just ask my fiancé."

"Name's John McGyro. I'm the ship's printer." He offered her a beefy hand, which she shook with as firm a grip as she could manage.

"I'm Judith Evelyn."

Before they could exchange further pleasantries, Seaman Dillon directed the people on the oars to pull on starboard and backwater to port. Judith had no idea what the terms meant, but John explained the maneuver, and she was able to follow. After an initial adjustment, the task quickly settled into a routine, though not without some frustrations. Judith and John leaned down on the handle to lift their oar out of the water, pushed the handle forward so that the flat end of the oar swept behind them, then dipped it into the water and pulled the handle back towards them. Every so often, the oar found no resistance when they began pulling because they hadn't dipped it far enough to reach the water. Before they could recover, a wave would catch the oar and push it forward to become twisted with the oar in front of them. Judith began to marvel that Andrew had lasted for an hour at this task.

A whimpering toddler seated at the bottom of the boat near her feet complicated matters. She was afraid of accidentally stepping on the child whenever she needed to make a sudden maneuver with the oar and thought he would be safer on her lap. When she tried to pick him up, a woman lying next to the child became hysterical. The woman, who seemed ill, appeared to be the child's mother, and she spoke a language Judith could not understand. The mother's desperate efforts to keep her child by her side convinced Judith to abandon any attempt to move the toddler. She was forced to wrestle the oar without moving her feet, and the awkward posture soon gave her a backache.

After nearly twenty minutes, Judith began experiencing cramps, a discomfort very much like the onset of her period. She feared she had hurt herself or possibly even endangered her pregnancy, and she decided to stop rowing.

"I must give it up," she said to her partner. "I'm sorry, Mr. McGyro."

When she rejoined Andrew and his father, Judith was exhausted physically and emotionally, uncertain about what her insistence on rowing might have cost her.

"Is everything all right?" Andrew asked as he stood to give her his seat. At a loss for words, Judith simply nodded as she sat on the bench and closed her eyes to shut out the world.

Rhoda Thomas

ON THE WIDE, dark ocean, only the rising half-moon gave Rhoda any sense of the passing time. It had climbed nearly halfway up the eastern sky when she thought she had reached the limit of her endurance. Rhoda continued to stand in ankle-deep water, cradling the sleeping baby under her coat. The infant was a lead weight in her arms, but she didn't want to return the child to the woman who had given it to her. The woman wore only a lifejacket over her nightgown and had no means to shelter the infant from the biting wind.

"Ladies and gents," the burly sailor in charge of the lifeboat announced, "I need some volunteers to give our rowers a rest." No one in the boat stirred in response to his announcement. "Come on now, we've been at it for two hours, and our rowers need a break. Everyone needs to do his bit if we're going to be rescued."

Three women in the center of the boat began moving toward the people on the oars closest to them. Their initiative seemed to inspire others to move up and down the boat to relieve the rowers fore and aft.

"That's the spirit," the sailor said. "I also need someone with a warm coat or blanket who can take a baby for a while. A lady here has been standing all this time with the child."

"I'll take the baby." A woman in a heavy coat seated near the bow raised her hand, and Rhoda gratefully passed the infant forward.

"Here, ma'am, take my seat." A young woman on the side bench behind Rhoda stood to exchange places with her.

"Thank you, dear," Rhoda said. They carefully moved around each other until Rhoda could take her seat. "I just need a few minutes off my feet." But once she was seated, a profound fatigue washed over her. Too tired to sleep, she gazed at the tableau before her, at once both threatening and darkly beautiful. The moon's silvery light brightened the wispy ends of clouds passing in front of it. On the ocean below, the light danced along sparkling furrows between the sea's mounding swells. When clouds blocked the moon's glow, Rhoda saw a host of brilliant blue-white stars in the black velvet sky. Around her on the water, red flares periodically erupted like Roman candles from the scattered lifeboats, as if to say, "We're still here."

She became aware of a soft whimpering sound coming from the cross-bench immediately adjacent to her. Rhoda noticed a woman comforting a girl who lay across her lap and realized she had seen them earlier when she entered the lifeboat.

"Is your daughter seasick?" Rhoda asked the woman, whose deep-set eyes looked tired and troubled.

"No," the woman said without further explanation. Rhoda thought she wasn't going to say anything else and felt embarrassed for having intruded. Before she could apologize, the woman began speaking again.

"We were sitting on deck when the explosion happened. Jacqueline was on my left and Margaret on my right. The hatch cover blew off and the people sitting on it were thrown into the air like rag dolls. Pieces of wood and metal flew out of that open hatchway. It was awful." The mother shook her head at the memory, but she kept talking, as if suddenly recalling the events for the first time.

"I grabbed little Jackie's hand and jumped up to get to our lifeboat. I told Margaret to follow me, but she didn't move. She was unconscious and had a deep cut on her forehead. I wrapped a handkerchief around her head and had to carry her. Jackie held on to my skirt the entire time. When we reached our muster station, the first lifeboat had gone. People were climbing into the second boat while the sailors were trying to lift it off the deck.

"I called out and asked them not to leave me because my daughter was hurt, and one of the sailors took Margaret and put her in the boat. Then he told me to get in and I sat next to her. The boat wasn't full, but they started to lower it down anyway. I asked the sailor to hand Jackie to me." Rhoda saw tears welling in the woman's eyes and felt badly that her question triggered such painful memories.

"He picked up a little girl and put her in our boat, but it wasn't Jackie. Everything was chaos. People were yelling, children crying. The boat was moving down. I shouted to the sailor, but he picked up another girl. I could see Jackie standing on the deck, crying. I had to decide. If I jumped out of the boat to be with Jackie, who would care for Margaret? So I stayed here, and now I don't know what's happened to my other little girl. Jackie's only three years old." The woman fell silent again, as if exhausted by recalling the traumas of the past few hours.

"I'm so sorry," Rhoda said. "I'm certain someone is looking after your Jackie. There are so many mothers and families aboard the ship that someone is bound to have taken her in."

"I hope you're right," the woman said, sounding more resigned than reassured.

"You shouldn't trouble yourself about your choice, dear. You may not know why, but I believe you're here for a reason." She reached out and gave the woman a reassuring pat on her knee. For the first time, the woman looked directly at Rhoda.

"Thank you," she said.

David Jennings

ON BOARD *ATHENIA*, the sporadic shifting of cargo in the holds reminded David of their precarious position. It was nearing eleven o'clock, and he wondered how long everyone planned to remain on board. Without saying a word, the captain rose and walked to the portside railing where he began to call in the direction of the nearest lifeboats. Several crewmen began moving toward the railing, and David sensed a shift in their mood. They had worked hard and enjoyed a breather, now it was time to get back to business.

"Looks like we're leaving," David said.

He stood, and Tony and John followed. They joined everyone else at the portside railing as the cough of a small engine grew louder in the darkness. Moments later, a motorized lifeboat pulled up alongside the ship. The captain told the young crewman in charge of the boat to transfer enough of his passengers to other lifeboats so he could return and take off everyone remaining aboard the ship. The launch chugged off into the night, but returned in less than half an hour looking just as crowded as before.

"I'm sorry, sir," the young crewman called out over the idling engine. "I went to four other boats but they all said they were too crowded to take any more passengers."

"Bloody hell," the captain snorted. He turned and signaled to one of the officers. "Mr. Porteous, I want you to take charge of lifeboat 4. We have people to get off this ship, and like it or not, the boats out there are going to take on additional passengers."

"Aye, sir." Before Porteous could leave, the captain had one more instruction.

"These five are going with you." He pointed to David, his two friends, the professor, and the minister.

"Very good," Porteous answered. "Gentlemen, if you will follow me." He stepped over the railing, took hold of a line that ran from the rail down to the launch, and slid down into the boat. "Who's next?" he called up.

David and the others followed in quick succession, and soon they were chugging into the night. The wind on the ocean's surface felt stronger and colder to David than it had onboard *Athenia*. Proceeding on its way, the launch rode up over the large swells and down into the long troughs between them, giving David some concern about transferring to another boat under such conditions. He had ample time to consider the situation as the first two boats they approached had been among the last to leave *Athenia* and were indeed overloaded. By the time they reached the third boat, it seemed to David that Porteous had run out of patience.

"We're coming alongside to transfer passengers," Porteous announced as the launch slowed to approach the next boat.

"We haven't room," the steward in charge of the boat replied.

"There are still people aboard *Athenia*," Porteous said, his voice growing hard. "You're going to take some of my passengers. Captain's orders."

The launch maneuvered next to the lifeboat and Porteous directed his crewmen to grab the other boat's oars and hold fast to lock the two boats together. Even as the steward continued his objections, Porteous ordered six of his passengers, including John, into the other boat.

"This must be my stop," John said, then climbed over the gunwales into the second boat.

With six fewer passengers aboard, the launch chugged on into the night. At the next boat Porteous approached, he was again told there was no room for more passengers.

"It's no good arguing," he said. "The captain wants me to transfer passengers to your boat."

"Bugger off," came the combative answer from the seaman in charge of the other lifeboat.

"Bugger yourself," Porteous shouted. "We're running out of time. You're taking on passengers, like it or not."

The launch came alongside the lifeboat, and its crew grabbed the oars as before. Porteous directed six more of his passengers to depart. David was the first one into the new boat, and he fell onto a woman passenger who had no time to move out of the way. He apologized and moved forward, as Tony followed behind him. It wasn't elegant, but David was thankful he hadn't fallen into the ocean.

Chief Officer Copland

COPLAND STOOD WITH the small knot of crewmen and officers left aboard *Athenia*, waiting for the motor launch to return. His injured left hand continued to throb, but the pain was tolerable. As the group waited, David Don, the ship's chief radio officer, arrived with his final report for Captain Cook.

"I wasn't able to raise any more ships than the three that are coming. *Knute Nelson* still expects to be here in an hour or two."

"They know our situation?"

"Yes, sir. I told them we're abandoning ship, and I screwed down the key contact to help them locate us."

"Very good, Mr. Don." Cook turned to his chief electrician. "Mr. Bennett, what's the status of our power supply?"

"I've set everything to run until the petrol gives out." A middle-aged man, Bennett looked weary and old with the dust and sweat of his efforts clinging to the creases in his face. "We'll have a few hours before that happens."

"All right," Cook said. "I think that'll do."

Copland noticed a polished wooden box tucked under the captain's arm. He knew it contained Cook's sextant, a navigational tool from a bygone era that had been with him since he earned his Master Mariner's Certificate more than thirty years ago. Up to now, Copland had been too involved with launching lifeboats and assessing the damage to the ship to consider the enormity of the tragedy playing out around him. But the sight of the sextant somehow brought it all home. Copland realized he was leaving *Athenia* with no tangible reminder of the ship or of shipmates whose lives had been snuffed out in an instant.

Such a high price paid, and this war is less than a day old. Damn the Germans.

From out of the night, lifeboat 4 approached *Athenia*'s portside and idled at the foot of the lifeline. Cook looked down at the boat and straightened.

"Though it pains me to say it, gentlemen, we must abandon ship."

Copland took his turn with the others, sliding down the line into the launch. The captain was the last one to leave. He tossed the sextant to Porteous, took one last look at the empty windows of the bridge four decks above him, stepped over the railing, and slid down the line.

MONDAY 0:15–3:00 A.M., SEPTEMBER 4

David Jennings

AS A PASSENGER in lifeboat 8A, David felt the awful power of the sea with each rolling swell that lifted the boat up and over its broad shoulders. Less than a foot of freeboard separated him from the Atlantic Ocean. While the rain had let up, the wind drove a fine mist off the waves and into the boat, adding to the miserably cold conditions. To keep warm, he took a turn at the forward starboard oar and saw Tony slide into the port stern oar position.

The physical effort helped him stave off the cold, but after a while the boat's irregular motion began to take a toll on his stomach. David had sailed count- less times on lakes near his home in Toronto and never suffered any motion sickness, so he was caught by surprise when the retching nausea overtook him. For the next half hour, he fell into a routine of rowing, leaning over the gunwale to cough up the dwindling contents of his stomach, and returning to the oar.

The lights of *Knute Nelson* approaching from the southwest gave David and his fellow rowers renewed purpose. In response to Murdoch's orders, they began pulling in the direction of the large ship. With the promise of rescue and the vigorous effort it required, David forgot his queasiness and hardly noticed his stomach when Murdoch called a halt to give a breather for the people rowing. Sitting at his oar, David looked over his shoulder to see the ship with its silver-gray hull sitting still in the water less than a quarter mile away. From his vantage point low on the water the *Knute Nelson* looked gigantic.

"It's the *Bremen*," a woman said. David recalled the name of the German passenger liner had been in the news the previous week as the Polish crisis came to a head. Germany ordered the ship to return to her home port, and she had left New York City four days ago without taking on any passengers.

"We'll never get away a second time." David overheard the frightened comment and turned to see a man seated nearby fumbling through the pockets of his dinner jacket. The gentleman withdrew two passports and tossed them overboard.

"What's going on?" David asked. The man looked around and leaned in toward David.

"We are German Jews," the man said in accented English and pointed to a woman and little girl seated next to him. "This is terrible for us to be rescued by a German ship. I throw our passports out so I can say we are Swiss, not German." He raised a finger to his lips indicating David should keep this information secret.

"I don't think you need to worry," David said. "Before I left the *Athenia*, the captain said a Norwegian freighter was on its way to rescue us. She was supposed to arrive about now. I'll bet you anything that's the freighter, not the *Bremen*."

The man looked at David in surprise then glanced in the direction he had thrown the passports. When he looked back, he had a smile on his face and began laughing. His wife and daughter joined in. It was such a joyous sound that David began laughing as well, which lightened his task of rowing the last quarter mile to reach *Knute Nelson*.

Chief Officer Copland

A LITTLE MORE than half an hour after leaving *Athenia* in the motor launch, Copland climbed into lifeboat 14A, placed there by Captain Cook to take command of the dangerously overloaded boat. A quick assessment told Copland there had to be at least a hundred people aboard a boat intended to carry eighty-six. The heavy load left the lifeboat with only a few inches of freeboard.

Before Copland could take control, a large swell began lifting the boat sideways. He crouched low to keep his balance as shrieks from startled passengers split the air. Water splashed in over the gunwale at the leading edge of the swell.

For a moment, he was unsure if they would bull their way through the wave or capsize, but the boat came through without tipping.

We can't take much more of this, he thought, as he positioned himself near the middle of the boat and began calling directions to the people at the oars and the seaman on the tiller, coordinating their efforts to bring the bow pointed into the approaching seas. He took note of the boat's slow response, which resulted in one more perilous transit over an oncoming wave before they were properly aligned. Once this was accomplished, he repositioned a few passengers to improve the lifeboat's balance.

Everything went smoothly until *Knute Nelson*'s lights appeared on the southwest horizon. The passengers in lifeboat 14A cheered at the prospect of rescue. They watched the big Norwegian freighter approach until she came to a stop more than a mile away, surrounded by a small constellation of lifeboats that had begun lighting flares to mark their presence. Without any direction, several passengers seated at the oars straightened their backs, dipped their oars in the water, and tried to turn the boat's bow toward the lights of the big ship. Copland had to act quickly to keep their enthusiasm from causing a disaster.

"Stop," he shouted. "You people on the oars stop rowing."

"But the ship's over there," a woman cried. "How will we get to the ship without rowing?" Copland did not miss the note desperation in her voice.

"Listen to me, everyone," he said. "I want to be rescued as much as each of you. But we are all better off staying where we are."

"Where we are is a helluva long way from where we need to be, if you ask me," a man protested. Copland could not identify the man in the dark, but the voice came from near the bow.

"Let's take a vote," another man said.

"We are not taking a vote!" Copland yelled. "This is a lifeboat, not Parliament. I'm the officer in charge, and I'm telling you the safest thing we can do is stay put."

"But what if they rescue the others and leave us here?" a woman complained.

"That's not going to happen, ma'am," Copland said. "Another ship is on its way, and I'm sure several more will be here by morning."

"But aren't we better off to save ourselves if we can?" the woman asked.

"No, we are not." Copland realized he was running out of time to stanch a sense of desperation he felt in the crowded boat. "We're overloaded. That makes our boat sluggish and hard to steer. We'd exhaust ourselves before we made it half the way there. The rising seas could easily capsize us. And even if we somehow made it that far, unloading a crowded boat at night, even in moderate seas, is dangerous. Too many things can go wrong." Copland paused, wondering if he was getting through to them. All he could see were several bowed heads.

"I know you're disappointed, but we are in good shape right now and not in any danger," he continued, "so we're staying here until the sun comes up. Is that understood?" He held his breath.

The silence that followed told Copland he had taken command.

David Jennings

THE NORWEGIAN FREIGHTER *Knute Nelson* sat in a pool of orange-white light that cast a warm glow over the ship and surrounding ocean, reminding David of an evening lakeside gala back home in Toronto. But there was nothing gay about the scene he watched while waiting to be rescued from lifeboat 8A. The *Nelson*'s crew had lowered rope ladders, resembling cargo nets, for *Athenia* survivors to climb aboard.

It seemed to David that the ship rode very high in the water, making it a long climb to the deck. He flexed his cold fingers, unsure if he could grasp the rope and make the climb after rowing the heavy lifeboat for the past hour. Seaman Murdoch, the man in charge of their boat, said the *Nelson*'s crew appeared to be deploying a gangway and asked if anyone wanted to wait for the stairway to be put in place.

David thought taking the stairs sounded like a good idea, but many of his fellow seasick passengers were adamant about not waiting around any longer, so Murdoch maneuvered the boat alongside the nearest rope ladder when it was their turn. After securing the lifeboat with a line from *Knute Nelson*'s deck, he explained how they would mount the ladder.

"When we get to the top of the swell, reach as high as you can and grab the ladder," Murdoch said. "Get your feet on the ropes quickly and climb a couple of rungs so you aren't caught by our boat when she rides up on the next swell. There's no safety harness to keep you from falling, so be careful. You don't want to fall in the water between that steel hull and our heavy wooden boat." Murdoch's directions didn't ease David's concerns.

How ironic would it be for me to fall and drown after all this? He tried to banish the thought, but Tony didn't help matters.

"Nothing to it, Dave," Tony said, standing behind him.

"Would you like to go ahead of me?" David was only half joking.

"No thanks. I want to watch your technique."

"Watch and learn from the master, my friend." If only David felt as confident as he hoped he sounded.

Three people scrambled up the netting before it was his turn to stand on the side bench waiting for the next wave to lift the lifeboat. At the crest of the swell, he reached out, grabbed the cargo net with both hands, and felt the boat drop away. He had made the transfer to the ladder but unexpectedly struggled to get his feet onto the ropes. Cursing his clumsiness, David wondered how long he had before the boat rose on the next swell. In a panic, he found his footing and pulled hard, managing to climb a few rungs before pausing to take a deep breath. The problem, he decided, was his hard-soled shoes, but it was too late now to do anything about them.

He continued up, but after gaining several more rungs, his left foot slipped off the rope, and his heart jumped as he found himself dangling from the ladder. With all his strength focused in his hands, David willed himself to regain his footing and resume climbing.

Don't think. Just keep moving.

He continued up, his shoulders now burning with exertion. Near the top of the ladder, he heard a shout and looked up to see John Woods smiling down at him over the railing. After climbing two more rungs, David felt hands grab his lifejacket at the shoulders, lift him up, and pull him over the railing. He stood unsteadily in the bright lights that washed the deck, blinking at two very tall, blond sailors.

"Welcome aboard," John said. "Man, you look like something the cat dragged in."

"Jeez, I'm tired," David responded before his knees started to buckle. He felt John's arms around his chest and staggered forward, trying to get his legs back under him. Moments later, with Tony on one side and John on the other, David stood with his arms over his friends' shoulders, feeling a bit steadier.

"Thanks, fellas," he said. "I hope I never have to do that again."

"Come on," John said. "I know where we can get some hot coffee."

Barbara Cass-Beggs

"THERE'S A SHIP on the horizon, darling." Barbara's spirits lifted as she relayed the news to David, who remained huddled down out of the wind in his thin pajamas. Quartermaster McDonald directed the passengers working the boat's oars to begin rowing toward the rescue ship, while someone lit a flare and held it up to signal their presence. In the flare's red glow Barbara saw a tight smile on David's face as he struggled up to catch a glimpse of their savior.

"What a beautiful sight," he said.

When lifeboat 10A finally approached *Knute Nelson*'s starboard side, Barbara thought the freighter looked huge. She marveled at the strength of the people climbing up a rope ladder toward the deck some twenty feet above the waterline. Fearing David wouldn't be able to complete such a climb, she was relieved to see sailors had set up an external stairway near the middle of the ship. In addition to the stairs, a contraption resembling a child's swing lifted passengers one at a time out of a lifeboat alongside the big ship and carried them up to the main deck. The process appeared to be effortless for the passenger.

Barbara noticed three lifeboats tied off along *Knute Nelson*'s hull, with the lead boat discharging passengers up the stairway. Several other boats were maneuvering to get in line behind them near the stern, but up on deck crewmen were waving them away. Barbara feared the ship was already full with *Athenia* survivors until McDonald explained the crewmen didn't want the line of boats to reach too close to the stern. Because the *Nelson* was riding high in the water, he said, her propellers were close enough to the surface they could rip out the bottom of a lifeboat.

Forty minutes later, lifeboat 10A slipped into position and received a line from *Knute Nelson* to tie off at its bow. Barbara observed the rescue operations of the boat ahead of theirs and realized passengers had to hop from the lifeboat to the platform at the bottom of the stairway, timing their jump for the moment when a wave brought the boat level with the platform at the base of the stairway. Two sailors tethered to the platform grabbed the passengers after their jump and directed them up the stairway before another wave came along. Though the jump didn't look difficult, Barbara wasn't sure David had enough strength to make it or to climb the stairs. The swing-like contraption, she now saw, was a board strung between two ropes that carried its occupant up to the deck, but required the person to hold on tightly and occasionally push off from the hull if the seat swung in too far as it was ascending.

"Do you want to try the lift?" she suggested, thinking it looked less strenuous.

David shook his head. "I'm going to take the stairs, thank you."

"Are you sure you can make the jump?"

"If I didn't think I could make the jump, I wouldn't try it."

"But the lift looks so much easier."

"It looks a hell of a lot more risky to me than jumping onto that platform. "

"What if you fall?"

"This is silly, Bar. I've decided. Don't stand here and try to talk me out of it. People are waiting. Let's get on with it."

Barbara recognized the irritation in David's voice and was angry that he had become so stubborn at such a critical moment.

It would serve him right if he fell. She quickly buried that thought, hoping he hadn't detected her pique.

"All right," she said. "Yes, let's get on with it."

She watched David climb onto the bench, steadied by McDonald, and wait for the approaching wave. He looked so frail in his bare feet and wet pajamas, she thought. As the boat rode up and over the swell her heart was in her throat.

"Now!" McDonald shouted and David jumped, landing lightly with both feet on the open mesh platform. She watched him start up the stairway as McDonald helped her onto the boat's bench to wait for the next wave. Barbara was so intent on her husband that she missed the order to jump and started her leap as the lifeboat dropped below the platform.

"Whoa. Too late, miss," McDonald said, grabbing her around the waist and holding her steady on the bench. "Let's give that another try on the next wave."

"Sorry," Barbara said. With the lifeboat now several feet below the platform, she saw her jump would have been well short and swallowed hard at the realization that the quartermaster might have just saved her life. She gathered her wits and waited. As the boat rode up and over the next crest, she concentrated on McDonald's instruction, made the jump, and went up the stairs after her husband.

"Well, now, that wasn't so hard, was it?" David said as she stepped onto *Knute Nelson*'s brightly lit main deck.

"Easy as pie," she said, knowing he hadn't seen her awkward performance and not wanting to dispel his impression.

A heavy gray blanket adorned David's shoulders, and the warmth it provided seemed to have crept into his voice. A young steward standing next to David handed a woolen blanket to Barbara, and she pulled it around her, grateful for the prickly feel of its weight on her bare neck. They both stood for a moment in exhausted silence before Barbara broke their reverie.

"Let's go find Rosemary."

Spirydon Kucharczuk

AFTER MORE THAN an hour of exhausting effort, lifeboat 5A at last approached *Knute Nelson*. Seated at the forward starboard oar, Spirydon felt every muscle in his body ache. His son, Stefan, sat next to him working the same oar and had pulled valiantly through the night, but Spirydon had felt the boy's strength flagging in the last half hour. It would take all of Spirydon's remaining stamina to bring them the last few hundred yards alongside the big ship.

Their progress had been complicated by the fact that only five of the boat's eight oars were deployed: three on the starboard side and two on the port side. Spirydon could see the handles of the three unused oars lying under the benches in the middle of the boat, but there must have been twenty or more passengers standing or sitting on them. Every time the sailor in charge tried to recover the oars he had been met with screams from the women and children afraid to move. The sailor finally gave up and steered the boat as best he could, given the uneven distribution of oars. The resulting journey had taken longer than it should have.

Spirydon welcomed the brief respite called by the sailor. Looking over his shoulder, he noticed the big ship had deployed a set of stairs leading up its side from the waterline to the deck. A lifeboat bobbed up and down as it unloaded passengers onto the platform, and there were three more boats waiting alongside the hull. As he rested, Spirydon heard several people in their boat begin to plead with the sailor in charge, a man named Dillon. Now they had stopped rowing, their boat was drifting slowly away from the big rescue ship.

"What are they saying?" he asked Stefan.

"I think they want to get at the end of the line of boats beside the ship."

It seemed to Spirydon that the sailor in charge of their boat wasn't eager to get in line, but the passengers' pleading continued and the sailor finally nodded.

"Ready on the oars," he called.

"Here we go, Papa," Stefan said, and they raised their oar out of the water.

"All pull forward," the sailor commanded from the back of the boat, and they put their backs into it with renewed vigor. Spirydon's spirits lifted with the knowledge their ordeal was nearly over and by the sight of Ewdokia, now standing in the middle of the boat, holding little Jakeb and smiling at her husband.

Judith Evelyn

WITH THE PROSPECT of rescue seemingly minutes away, Judith continued to fret as lifeboat 5A approached *Knute Nelson*. The cramps in her abdomen had not subsided, and she wasn't heartened by the prospect of a long climb up the gangway stairs. The shouts of sailors on the *Nelson*'s deck momentarily distracted her.

"What do you suppose that is all about?" she asked Andrew's father, who sat next to her on the starboard side bench near the bow of their lifeboat.

"I haven't the vaguest idea," Reverend William Allan said. "It looks as if they want us to go away."

"That's ridiculous," Judith said. "Everyone's exhausted, especially the poor people rowing. They can't refuse us, can they?"

"I don't think so."

Several passengers seemed to share Judith's resentment and began calling for the sailor in charge, Seaman Dillon, to let them join the boats lined up along *Knute Nelson*'s hull. After several minutes, he finally gave the order, and they maneuvered into place at the end of the row of boats waiting to unload their passengers up the gangway.

"Looks like we've been accepted," William said when a line uncoiled down to them from the deck above. Seaman Dillon secured the line to the bow of their lifeboat. As they settled in near the ship's stern, Judith heard a low, rhythmic rumbling.

"What's that noise?"

"I'm not sure," William said, rising up to get a better view. "Sounds like the ship's engines."

Judith turned to look for Andrew, who had taken a place at the oar near the stern on the starboard side, where he had been rowing for the last twenty minutes. He sat holding his oar at an angle into the water and gave her a smile and a little wave when he saw her. Now they were secured to the rescue ship, tension drained from her body. She would worry about her soreness later.

The sound of rushing water told Judith something was wrong. She saw the line at the bow of their boat grow taut and snap. The huge ship next to them was moving forward. Someone shouted to the people up on deck to stop the propellers, but the ship kept moving and the noise grew louder. *Knute Nelson*'s stern drew past them and the ship's churning wake drew their boat into its vortex.

"Jump! JUMP!" Seaman Dillon shouted.

Before Judith could react, the lifeboat shuddered with the crunch of splintering wood. Passengers screamed. A fine spray of red-flecked sea foam caught the light. Bodies flailed in the air. Something lifted her bench and threw Judith out of the boat.

Cold, dark water closed over her head, but her lifejacket brought her back to the surface. Her eyes and nostrils burned with the sting of saltwater.

What happened? How did I get in the ocean?

Her fur coat was drenched, and its weight pulled Judith underwater again. Hands brushed past her. The sea boiled all around her. In the dark, the water parted; she felt air on her face again and heard people shouting. Judith drew a deep breath just before the ocean splashed over her a third time. She kicked and swam up to regain the surface, where she was able to grab someone's arm.

"Please help me," she cried out, before discovering the arm was attached to a severed torso that wore a slashed lifejacket. Judith screamed and pushed the torso away, but the lifejacket kept it afloat and it drifted back toward her. She kicked and splashed in a panic until the torso came free of its lifejacket and slipped from view.

Feeling overwhelmed, she considered giving in to the chaos around her.

Drowning is an easy death. Only a few swallows and it will be all over.

She thought of her parents, of Andrew, and the possibility of a life unborn, and realized she could not to let herself drown.

"Hang on to the boat." Seaman Dillon's voice rose over the sounds of thrashing water and panicked cries. Judith swam toward the voice but quickly became disoriented. Her lifejacket kept her head up, but she felt sluggish. Alternately swimming and treading water, she rode up and over the ocean's swells until she found a large wooden object floating like a raft in the water.

With her strength draining away, Judith fought against the dead weight of her sodden coat to reach across the raft until her fingers found some purchase. She pulled herself onto its clapboard surface until her stomach was flat against it and out of the water. Stunned, she rested and tried to gather her wits. Gradually, Judith became aware of a warm, sticky sensation between her legs. She was bleeding. A moment's panic that she might be injured gave way to the realization she was experiencing the onset of her menstrual cycle.

"Oh, Andrew," she said, recalling the stress she had caused him, believing she was pregnant.

"Judith." She startled at the sound of Andrew's voice calling her name. *Am I losing my mind? Focus, damn it. This is no time to be delirious.* But she heard his voice again.

"Can you move up any further?"

"Andrew, is that you?"

"Yes, can you try to pull yourself higher?"

"But how can you be here?"

"For God's sakes, Judith, stop questioning and see if you can get yourself out of the cold water." It had to be Andrew, she thought. Who else would be so perturbed with her at such a moment?

"Yes, I'll try." Judith sought to make sense of her situation. The raft appeared to be an overturned section of their lifeboat. She reached further and found the upturned keel and used to pull herself all the way out of the water. Fingers closed over her hand from the other side of the hull and she saw Andrew's face in the moonlight.

"I can't believe it's you," she said.

They helped each other until they were able to sit on either side of overturned hull, which rocked precariously with their efforts. Judith glanced around and realized they were alone.

"Where's your father?"

"I've called his name but . . ." Andrew shook his head. "Maybe if we both try. Dad!" he shouted into the night.

"William!" Judith cried. "William, can you hear me?"

They continued calling for William, pausing only to see if he was among the bodies that floated past them in life jackets. After several more minutes, they stopped calling.

"He could be on another piece of wreckage, floating like us," Judith offered.

Andrew didn't respond, and they grew silent as their makeshift raft drifted away from *Knute Nelson*'s lights. Judith realized they had no way to signal the ship. While she contemplated their predicament, she heard splashing nearby. She and Andrew called out again for the Reverend Allan until she saw Seaman Dillon's face bobbing up and down.

"Anyone else with you?" he called out and grabbed a line trailing in the water from the overturned hull. When they told him they were alone, he nodded and hauled himself onto the hull. He caught his breath and looked further up where the keel projected a foot or two above the water.

"More will be coming," he said. "We need to keep the air trapped under the hull to support all of us." On his hands and knees, Dillon crawled up and straddled the keel.

"Hello!" he yelled. "Is anybody there? Hello!"

Judith thought how lucky they were to be clinging to a large piece of their lifeboat in the middle of the ocean. She wondered how many more people might come. Their raft could be swamped.

Good Christ, what am I thinking? Andrew's father is still missing and others will need saving like me.

"Hello!" she called, joining Andrew and Seaman Dillon in hopes of rescuing more swimmers. "Over here! We're over here."

Rhoda Thomas

AFTER MORE THAN an hour of strenuous effort by the people at the oars, Rhoda's lifeboat approached the big silver-gray rescue ship that had appeared shortly after midnight. It seemed to her that the wind and sea currents had been responsible for their painfully slow progress. As they drew near, the burly *Athenia* seaman in charge of their boat stopped rowing to light a flare and hand it to Rhoda.

"Hold it high, luv," he said. "Make sure they see us coming."

The flare hissed and popped as she stood and held it aloft in the night, bathing the boat in its red circus glare. As the flare burned down, small embers began falling around her so she held it out over the gunwale to avoid burning anyone in the boat. A few sparks fell on her hand, and she tried to shake them off, but that caused small pieces of the flare to fly off into the boat. She decided to hold still, let the sparks fall where they may, and ignore the pain.

The flare burned out as they neared the lee side of the rescue ship's stern, where several lifeboats lined its hull. They were a hundred yards from the last of these boats when the big ship began moving forward. Rhoda feared they were about to be left behind when she saw a lifeboat drawn into the ship's wake, fold up on itself, and disappear in a spray of foam and flying bodies. A moment later, the screams and awful rattle of splintering wood reached her from across the water.

"Oh my God!" one of Rhoda's fellow passengers cried. Rhoda closed her eyes to shut out the terrible sight and pressed her hands to her ears to muffle the screams.

When she finally looked back, the rescue ship had slowed, but the damage was done. Pieces of the lifeboat and dozens of people floated on the water, their khaki-colored lifejackets visible in the yellow-ocher glow of the freighter's deck lights. Many people splashed in the water and called for help. Several others were motionless, receding with the debris being driven up and over the ocean's swells by stiffening winds.

"We can't go over there," the seaman in charge of their boat declared. "They'll pull us over trying to get into our boat."

Rhoda remembered she wasn't wearing a lifejacket and noticed several other passengers in their boat didn't have one either. Without any direction to do so, the people at the oars began pushing away from the tragic scene. After several minutes' effort, they stopped rowing, and the boat drifted in silence up and over the long swells. Unable to respond to the emergency in any way, Rhoda felt empty and helpless. She began to quietly sob and bowed her head. She couldn't stop crying and didn't care to try.

When she finally cried herself out, Rhoda tried to make sense of what had happened. She had accepted the fact that she might not survive this night, and while she did not want to die, the thought of death did not scare her.

I've lived a full life, but why have so many children died when they had so much of their lives still to live? What could be God's purpose in that? Was I wrong to tell people to trust in God?

Rhoda stared into the water sloshing over her ankles in the bottom of the boat and wondered if it would do any good to pray for answers to her questions.

Spirydon Kucharczuk

FILLED WITH A sense of dread, Spirydon swam to the surface of the ocean, blew the salty water from his nose and mouth, and gasped for air. All around him was darkness and voices shouting in the night. The cold of the ocean penetrated his body. Treading water with the help of his lifejacket, Spirydon shook his head trying to clear his mind of the nightmare that engulfed him moments ago: the awful crunch of metal shearing through wood, screaming people disappearing in a spray of foam and debris, and the terrified look on his daughter Neonela's face.

"Ewdokia," he bellowed then coughed as a small wave smacked his face. "Ewdokia!"

He couldn't remember seeing what happened to his wife and youngest son when the terrible noise erupted from the center of the boat where she had been standing. All he could bring up was the haunting expression of his oldest daughter—wild-eyed with fear and anguish. There were shouts from other people in the water, but he didn't hear anyone calling his name.

"Ewdokia!" he cried again. "Can you hear me?"

"Papa?" Spirydon heard Neonela's gasping voice and swam toward it. He found her barely able to keep her head above water.

"Are you hurt?"

"I don't know," she said.

"Leksi," he said, asking about his youngest daughter, who had been sitting on Neonela's lap. "Have you seen her? Have you seen any of the others?"

"I don't think so." His daughter sounded delirious, and he feared she might be injured.

"Don't worry, Nela, I'm here now." Spirydon tried to sound calm and reassuring. He turned in the water so that his back was to Neonela and told her to put her arms over his shoulders. Spirydon called his wife's name again, but there was no response. He saw something white floating in the water and swam to it with Neonela clinging to him. It appeared to be a section of the lifeboat's hull with a piece of bench still attached. He helped Neonela climb onto the bobbing piece of wood then called the names of his other children.

"Stefan!" he shouted. "Leksi!" He waited in the water next to Neonela. No one responded, but Spirydon heard splashing coming toward them, and his hopes rose with the thought that his wife and children might be swimming to him. The first person to reach him, however, was an older man. When Spirydon saw the whites of the panicked man's eyes he feared the stranger's desperation might pull him under.

"No, go back," he yelled at the man. "I can't help you."

But the man kept coming and grabbed Spirydon's lifejacket, gasping for air. The man dragged Spirydon underwater and tried to climb on top of him. Spirydon seized the man's arm and pulled him under. With a violent shove, he pushed the man off and came up for air. The man said something Spirydon couldn't understand. He shook his head at the man, who ignored the gesture and began splashing toward Spirydon again. Others were approaching.

Should he wait to see if Ewdokia and his children were among the people swimming toward him? Should he try to swim away to save Neonela and himself? Even if he waited, there was no chance that the lifeboat's wreckage would support all of them. But how could he swim away without the rest of his family?

"EWDOKIA!" he screamed again. "STEFAN!" Still no answer. Six or seven swimmers were nearly on top of him. His family was not among them. The people began reaching out for Spirydon. Neonela screamed, and he turned to see the older man he had fought off now trying to push his daughter aside and climb onto the wreckage. In that instant, Spirydon knew he must save his daughter.

He shoved the old man aside, placed his hands on the wooden hull fragment supporting Neonela, and began to kick violently, pushing his daughter to safety. He kicked like a madman until he could kick no longer. When he finally turned around, no one was in sight, but the combination of his kicking and the ocean current had pushed them a long way from the rescue ship.

What have I done? We'll never get back to the ship from here.

Spirydon was tired and cold. He would consider the consequences of his actions later. First they had to survive the night.

MONDAY, 3:30–5:00 A.M., SEPTEMBER 4

Barbara Cass-Beggs

MORE THAN THREE hundred rescued passengers crowded *Knute Nelson*'s main deck, complicating the Cass-Beggs' search for their three-year-old daughter Rosemary. Bathed in the freighter's yellow deck lights, the tangle of humanity seemed in constant motion, searching for loved ones, for food and drink, or simply for a place to lie down. Dressed in heavy coats, in khaki life jackets worn over dinner attire or pajamas, or draped like Barbara and David in blankets thrown over their shoulders, the survivors presented a shifting landscape.

The many children on deck made matters more hopeful and more frustrating. Each time she saw a child of Rosemary's approximate size and hair color, Barbara's hopes lifted. But time after time she was deflated when she caught a glimpse of the child's face. After searching the main deck for more than a half hour, she began to lose faith that Rosemary was on board. She and David began to approach strangers, hoping to glean a clue to their daughter's whereabouts.

"Have you seen a little girl anywhere? She's three years old, has curly, light-brown hair, and is about this tall," Barbara would ask, holding her hand waist-high. "She's dressed in her pajamas."

Most of the time the answer was simply a headshake, as if the respondent was too tired to talk. A few expressed sympathy and promised to keep their eyes open. A Norwegian sailor told them at least one other ship nearby was rescuing people from lifeboats. When they convinced themselves they had searched every corner of the ship and looked at every child on the main deck, David turned to his wife.

"I think we've done all we can for now, Bar."

Barbara was emotionally exhausted. She had been certain they would reconstitute their family aboard the rescue ship.

"If only I could be sure she was safe," she said.

"At least we know another ship is rescuing passengers," David said. "If we're safe, odds are that Rosemary is also being rescued." He put his arm over her shoulder. "We'd better lie down before we fall down."

It took them several minutes to find space enough on deck to stretch out together up against the rear wall of *Nelson*'s crew quarters. Barbara fell asleep almost immediately, but her dreams were filled with the frustrations of locked doors and endless hallways in which she searched for something she couldn't name.

Rhoda Thomas

AFTER A RESPITE, the seaman in charge of Rhoda's lifeboat called to the people at the oars to row again in order to keep the boat pointed toward the oncoming seas. To shake her dismal frame of mind, Rhoda tried to row for a while, but the heavy oar was difficult for her to manage, even with another woman's help, and she was happy to give up her place to a teenage boy.

Seated again on a side bench, she tried to sleep, but each time she closed her eyes she saw the shattered lifeboat and flailing bodies. Unable to expel the images, Rhoda felt a deep sadness congeal inside her and began to wonder if the calamity had withered part of her soul.

A bright light swept across their boat, prompting cheers from other passengers. Rhoda looked up to see the searchlight of another rescue ship holding their lifeboat in its beam.

"Ahoy there," the seaman in her boat bellowed. Several passengers shouted and waved their arms. The seaman lit another flare and handed it to Rhoda. Grateful for something to do, she held the flare high out over the water, certain that its light would not allow their little boat to be lost in the ocean's nighttime expanse.

It took nearly fifteen minutes for the ship to draw up alongside their lifeboat. Rhoda thought she had never seen a more beautiful sight. The ship was long, sleek, and white. It seemed every light aboard blazed in an effort to push back the night. On the ship's fantail, she noticed the blue and yellow flag of Sweden.

For the second time that night, Rhoda negotiated a rope ladder. This time, however, the distance between the water and the ship's railing was much shorter, so that after climbing a few rungs, she was helped onto the polished teak deck by two sailors. She felt a little light-headed and was grateful when an older man in a double-breasted blue blazer and white canvas trousers took her arm.

"You are safe on a private yacht," he told her, and led Rhoda to a portion of the deck covered with canvas and several cushions. The scene resembled a battlefield from the Great War. Perhaps a hundred people lay on the ship's deck; some sat staring fixedly out to sea; one or two seemed crazed with fright; several were cut and bruised; a surprising number wore only a nightgown or pajamas, and some of the children wore even less. Most startling to Rhoda was the number of people streaked with blood, until she realized they were actually covered with rivulets of black oil. Sailors from the yacht walked among the survivors, distributing articles of clothing and blankets to those most in need.

The man in the blazer helped Rhoda onto the cushions before leaving. As a profound sense of fatigue washed over her, she saw a woman from her lifeboat holding the baby Rhoda had cradled in her arms earlier in the night. She thought of offering to take the infant for a while, but before she could say anything a young woman rushed up to claim the baby as hers, and Rhoda overheard her tearfully explain she had been taken off *Athenia* in a different lifeboat.

At least there's a happy ending for one child.

Ruth Etherington

THE NIGHT STRETCHED on endlessly for Ruth in lifeboat 8. Wrapped in a blanket, her son Geoffrey slept soundly with his head resting on her lap. She envied his slumber, something she had been unable to do except for a few quick catnaps. The cold, damp conditions in the boat, bitter winds, and the thin dress she wore combined to keep sleep at bay. If she could just manage to doze for a solid half hour, Ruth was sure she could rid herself of the weariness pressing down on her. At least she had avoided the seasickness she experienced the previous morning.

The first rescue ship had appeared past midnight. It stopped a mile or more west of their position, and Seaman Macintosh, the sailor in charge, decided against trying to reach it because he said the wind and the seas were running against them. The second ship appeared an hour later, brightly lit and coming up from the south. But it, too, came to a stop a long way from their boat. This time, however, Macintosh said they were drifting in the right direction.

Now, as they drew closer, Ruth woke Geoffrey with the good news that they were about to be rescued. Together, they watched the distance steadily close between them, and the bright ship that sat like a huge white seabird rising and falling on the ocean's swells.

"Mom, we're going to drift past them," Geoffrey said. At that moment, Macintosh ordered the people working the oars to row with all their strength and close the final gap between them and the rescue ship. They began pulling but their heavy boat barely responded.

"Miss," Macintosh said to Ruth, "do you know how to work a tiller?"

"Yes, I've sailed with my husband on Lake Michigan."

"Very good," Macintosh said. "I'm going to help us row. Just keep us heading straight for that ship. Can you do that?"

"I think so." Happy to participate in her rescue, Ruth took Macintosh's place at the tiller, and Geoffrey moved next to her. Macintosh stepped to the nearby starboard oar.

Even with the seaman's help, it took another ten minutes of exhausting effort to close on the sleek white ship. Macintosh explained they would need to get to the yacht's lee side, out of the wind. He directed Ruth to steer them around the stern, which he said was the easiest approach, given the wind and everyone's fatigue.

"Make sure you steer us well out and around," he told Ruth. "We don't want to be caught under her stern."

In spite of her efforts with the tiller, Ruth could not prevent lifeboat 8 from drifting closer to the yacht's long, graceful stern that cantilevered out over the water. A Swedish flag snapped in the breeze on a small standard at the ship's fantail. As they came around to the lee side, Ruth heard calls for help and noticed a second lifeboat riding low in the water under the stern.

"We're sinking," a woman in the second boat shouted. "We've lost our oars. Please help us."

"Oh, Christ," Ruth heard Macintosh mutter under his breath. He extended his oar across the water to the stranded passengers. "Grab the oar," he shouted. "We'll pull you over to our boat. Hurry!"

The two boats came alongside each other, and the remaining passengers from the sinking lifeboat scrambled into lifeboat 8. Without anyone rowing, Ruth could not steer, and their boat began to drift under the yacht's stern. Macintosh ordered everyone on the oars to pull away from the ship. But at that moment, Ruth saw a man seated in the bow of their boat grab a rope that hung from the ship's stern and try to climb aboard.

"No, no, let go of that line," Macintosh yelled. The man ignored the order, but he wasn't strong enough to pull himself out of the boat. As he dangled from the line, his feet remained in the bow and lifeboat 8 pirouetted back under the stern.

"Fend off!" Macintosh shouted to his fellow rowers. He raised his oar to try to push away from the ship's hull, but it slipped off the stern's smooth curved surface. "Get that man off the line *now.*"

Ruth saw the danger they were in when a large swell raised their boat sideways so close she could have reached up and touched the Swedish ship's stern. Several people grabbed the man holding the line, and the scuffle caused their boat to rock. Another wave drove them up even higher. For a moment, Ruth thought their lifeboat might hit the stern. Passengers in the bow finally wrestled the man down off the rope. Macintosh ordered the people on the oars to pull away, even as the boat began rising on a third large wave.

"Mom, we've gotta swim for it," Geoffrey said, throwing the blanket off his shoulders.

"Geoff, no," Ruth cried, but he dived over the side just as their boat slammed up against the unyielding stern and rolled over.

The passengers' screams were suddenly muffled by the water closing in over

Ruth's head. Her weariness vanished in an instant. She felt the arms and legs of her panicked fellow passengers brushing against her. Without a lifejacket, Ruth fought her way back to the surface. She came up coughing and spitting seawater. The splashing and cries of other swimmers sounded strangely distant in the darkness. It took her a moment to realize she had come up in the air pocket trapped under their capsized boat.

After a few deep breaths she dived down to swim free of the boat. When she surfaced in the same hollow blackness, Ruth realized she had misjudged the direction. Desperate to find Geoffrey, she tried to calm herself. A few more deep breaths and she dived again, deeper this time. As she rose toward the surface, she swam into a tangle of ropes. She struggled with the underwater snarl, pushing the ropes away. Yet they continued to float around her, blocking her escape.

Just as she felt her lungs about to burst, Ruth came free. She shot to the surface. The stars overhead told her she had escaped the lifeboat, and she gratefully gulped the fresh air.

Clinging to the side of the overturned boat, Ruth cleared her head amid the panicked cries and desperate thrashing of the people in the water around her. She knew Geoffrey could swim, but he wasn't terribly strong. The longer she waited to gather her strength, the less energy he would have to sustain himself.

Exhausted by her bout with the ropes but unable to wait any longer, Ruth swam off through the confusion in the direction she thought Geoffrey had gone.

"Geoff!" she called, again and again as she swam. After several minutes, she thought she heard a response and headed in that direction. She paused and called again.

"Hold on, sweetie," she cried. "Where are you? Can you hear me?" There was no answer.

"Oh, God," Ruth pleaded, swimming up and over the large swells. "Help me find him. Don't let him drown." She paused again to tread water and called to Geoffrey. All she heard in response were the distant cries of others in the water. The cold water punished her body. She came across a bright-orange life ring bearing the name *Southern Cross*. Ruth grabbed the ring and fought back anguished tears. She was physically spent and hadn't found her son. Now she doubted she could swim back to the rescue ship and save herself.

From behind, a beam of light settled on her. "We are coming," a voice called out. "Do not give up." Moments later, a lifeboat with the name *Southern Cross* stenciled on its bow came alongside, and two men pulled her to safety.

"My son," Ruth sobbed. "He's out there somewhere. Please help me find him."

"Yes, yes. We will help," said a stout little man. He wore a bright-yellow lifejacket that strained against his ample belly. Ruth saw three other people in the boat, all soaking wet, wearing lifejackets, and huddled out of the wind in the bottom of the boat.

"Please sit out of the wind. You will be warm," the little man said.

Ruth had no intention of crouching down in the boat where she would be unable to see her son. Instead, she sat on a crossbench, shivering and hugging her arms to try to keep warm. She noticed there must have been oil in the water because her black dress was soaked with a sticky sheen and her bare arms and lower legs were covered with inky streaks.

The crew in the lifeboat played their spotlight across the water and rowed slowly, looking for more survivors, while Ruth continued to call Geoffrey's name and listen for a response. Each time she called out, the stout little crewman shook his head, but he did not try to discourage her.

They rescued three more passengers, including an infant who was floating miraculously in the middle of his billowing blue nightclothes. The short crewman handed the baby to Ruth to care for while they continued their search. She cradled the child in her lap, but it was her own son she desperately wanted to be comforting. Ruth felt certain he was alive, but each passing minute made her more anxious.

The lifeboat crew rescued another passenger, a young woman wearing a lifejacket over her nightgown. Ruth thought she looked cold and miserable, but when their eyes met, the woman's expression abruptly brightened.

"My baby!" she shouted. "That's my baby." Ruth handed the infant to the woman, who held the child close to her, tears of joy mingling with the seawater dripping from her dark hair.

If one mother can be reunited with her son, why not me?

At that moment, she heard Geoffrey's voice in the distance.

"Help! Please help. I'm over here."

"Hold on, Geoff! I'm coming." Ruth stood and dived into the ocean, leaving behind the startled cries of the crewmen. She swam with renewed strength in the direction of his voice. When she stopped to tread water, she heard his trembling voice.

"Over here, Mom." Geoffrey was only a few feet from her. She cried with joy when she recognized his face with his brown hair plastered to his forehead. His arms were draped over a long oar that kept him afloat, but his worried expression told her all was not well. She longed to embrace her son but feared she might upset his balance.

"I'm cold," he said through chattering teeth. "I don't think I can swim anymore."

"That's all right, sweetie. I'm here. I'll help you." Treading water and keeping her voice calm, Ruth tried to pull Geoffrey with his long oar back in the direction of the lifeboat. She turned to search for the boat and was relieved to see it coming toward them.

"Just a few minutes more," she told Geoffrey. "The boat is almost here."

It took all of her strength to help her son into the lifeboat, and then the two crewmen pulled Ruth out of the water.

"Please, Miss, do not do that again," the short sailor said. Ruth simply smiled at the man. She held Geoff close to her to try to stop his shivering, while tears silently rolled down her cheeks.

When they drew up alongside *Southern Cross*, Geoffrey was too weak to climb the rope ladder. The two crewmen in the lifeboat lifted him up to two sailors aboard the yacht who took his upstretched arms and pulled him up on deck. Ruth marshalled all her reserves to slowly climb the ladder, but when she reached the deck Geoffrey was nowhere in sight. A crewman told her he had been taken to the engine room to warm up. Before she could ask to join him, she was startled to see her husband walking past her.

"Hal," she cried. He stopped and stared at her, his puzzled expression turning to astonishment.

"Is that you?" Harold said. Ruth realized she must look bedraggled, with her dark hair hanging in strings and arms and legs streaked with black oil.

"Yes, it's me," she said. "I know I look a fright, but our boat capsized and Geoff and I ended up in the water."

Harold folded her in his arms and held her tightly. Ruth worried momentarily about her oil-covered dress soiling his clothes but instead melted into her husband's embrace.

"Where's Geoff?" he asked.

"He was taken to the engine room," she said. "We should find him. He'll be thrilled to see you."

While they followed a sailor down a stairway and through several narrow passageways toward the engine room, Ruth filled in the details of their capsizing.

"I'm so proud of him, Hal. He never complained once while we were being tossed about in the lifeboat and everyone was sick. He was the first one to see we were in danger under the stern. He jumped out of the boat before it capsized. He was quite the little soldier."

They entered the engine room's tropical environs and were met by the pulsing din of steam turbines. Geoffrey sat on a bench with his back to them and a blanket over his shoulders. Ruth watched Harold walk over, sit next to Geoffrey, and put his arm over the boy's shoulder. She could not recall the last time she had seen her husband hug their son.

Judith Evelyn

ALMOST TWENTY SURVIVORS had joined Judith, Andrew, and Seaman Dillon on the wreckage of lifeboat 5A's bow section. The first three to arrive—a young woman Judith had met briefly their first day at sea; *Athenia*'s engineer, Thomas Hastie; and the ship's printer, John McGyro—had found space on the hull. Judith could see more than a dozen others floating with them in the water, holding on to the wrecked bow or clinging to one of the lines trailing from it. A biting wind chilled Judith as she sat on the bow, but judging from the grim expressions of the people in the water, she believed the ocean was colder.

The wind seemed to push the seas higher and felt stiff and raw on her face whenever she looked up to scan the horizon. She shivered beneath her wet fur coat, realizing it had become a liability, one she could not shed because it was tied tightly to her by her lifejacket.

Drifting on their hulk, Judith and the others twice had seen another lifeboat in the distance and desperately called for help. But no one in the other boats had responded, and she concluded their voices must have been lost in the wind.

"There's another rescue ship," Seaman Dillon said. Judith saw distant bright lights on the water but could not calculate the likelihood of it reaching them. Each time they topped a new wave, however, the blaze of lights seemed to come a bit closer.

"I think we're going to drift close by them," Dillon said.

Soon she was able to make out the low-slung hull of a sleek white ship with a rakish bowsprit. Closer still, Judith could see people moving on the ship's deck.

"Ahoy, ahoy there!" Dillon began shouting. "Lower a boat. We need help."

"Over here!" Judith cried and waved her arm. "Please help us."

Andrew and several people in the water began shouting as well. Judith saw crewmen on the ship pause to look over the bow in their direction. A brilliant white searchlight on the ship began to sweep the sea in front of them. For a few seconds, the beam of light found them on the crest of a wave, and Judith's hopes soared. Then their hulk slid down the back of the swell, and when they began rising on the next wave, she saw the searchlight had moved on.

"No, no!" she shouted. "We're back here." Several others called out as well, but the light couldn't find them again, and the distance between their floating wreckage and the rescue ship began to widen.

"It's no good," Dillon said as they drifted away. "We're just too low in the water." The night closed down around them again and Judith's hopes fell.

☆ ☆ ☆

SHE LOST TRACK of the time. The wind continued and the ocean's swells grew, threatening to throw her off her perch. At one point in the night, the moon emerged from the clouds, and Judith realized she couldn't see any lifejackets in the water around them. The survivors who had been drifting with them were gone.

"Where did everyone go?" Judith asked.

"Most of them probably gave up after we lost our chance to be rescued," Dillon said. "The odds were against them surviving the night in the ocean."

She was shocked by Dillon's matter-of-fact observation. *People don't just give up*, she thought. Maybe the rough seas had pushed them away. But then she remembered her own brief contemplation of drowning earlier that night.

Is that how it will end for me? Will I just give up?

Out of the dark, something massive slammed into her back and swept Judith off the side of the hull before she could react. Struggling to stay afloat in the rough water, she was unsure what had happened.

Where's the hull? Is it still afloat?

Judith's lifejacket barely kept her head above water as the weight of her coat threatened to pull her under.

"Help!" she gasped. "Someone please help me."

"Over here," a voice called out nearby. Judith splashed frantically toward the sound, fighting to stay up. She coughed and spit out saltwater until she felt fingers close around her hand.

"I've got ya." John McGyro, the man who had been crouched next to her on the side of the hull, held her hand. The bow section was still afloat. *Thank God for that*, she thought. He pulled her in, and Judith reached her free arm across the wooden surface. Her heavy, wet coat worked against her, but with John's help she struggled back onto the bow.

"Dear God," Andrew said, his face looking ashen in the moonlight. "I thought you were gone."

"So did I. What happened?"

"It was a big wave—"

"Help!" A cry from the ocean interrupted Andrew. Judith recognized the voice of the young woman who had been riding on the hull with them.

"Hang on!" Judith yelled, straining for breath against the cold wind. "Over here. Swim to my voice."

"Careful of the boat," Dillon warned. "We don't want to lose our bubble."

He lay along the opposite side of the keel to counterbalance the rescue effort as Judith and John joined hands to recover the woman. McGyro held the keel with his other hand, and Judith stretched her free arm toward the woman. With agonizing slowness the woman splashed toward Judith. At last, their fingers closed around each other's hands, and Judith pulled her to safety.

"Thank you," the young woman said breathlessly.

Too exhausted to reply, Judith nodded. Her encounter with the wave steeled her determination to do whatever she needed to survive.

I will hold onto this bow and live from one minute to the next.

David Jennings

ON BOARD *KNUTE Nelson*, David savored the hot mug of coffee handed to him by one of the ship's crew. He closed his eyes and let the warmth of the liquid revive his tired body. Standing with Tony and John, he felt incredibly lucky. They were together, having survived a torpedo attack, mid-ocean transfers into lifeboats, and a long, dangerous climb up a rope ladder to safety.

David's luck seemed to redouble when he looked up to see the three young women from the University of Michigan coming toward them. The last time he'd seen Joan Outhwaite, Alberta Wood, and Barbara Bradfield, they were departing *Athenia* in a lifeboat. That seemed like days ago to him.

"Well, girls," Alberta said as they approached, "it looks like they'll let anybody on this rescue ship." With their relaxed smiles and dry, unsullied clothes, it was hard for David to believe the three of them had spent any time in a lifeboat. But there they were, like a welcome mirage, and a renewed sense of well-being surged through him.

"Can't get enough of us, can you?" he responded, and the six of them hugged each other like long-lost friends.

They headed down a passageway in search of a warm place to talk and found an open door to an empty cabin. It was a Spartan room, with an upper and lower bunk each sporting a brown wool blanket stretched over a thin mattress.

A small writing desk with a straight-backed chair stood next to the bulkhead, and the entire scene was lit by a single light bulb swaying on a cord overhead. They sat on the floor, not wanting to disturb the neatly made up bottom bunk.

For nearly a half hour, David, Tony, and John regaled the girls with stories of their exploits on the sinking *Athenia*—helping the crew launch lifeboats, deploying the rafts, going down into the ship to look for food and other supplies, before finally sliding down a line into the motor launch that took them off.

"What about your time in the lifeboat?" David asked the three girls. "What happened to you?"

"Oh, nothing as exciting as your adventures," Alberta said. "The officer in charge of our boat was very organized. There weren't many men in our boat, so we each took a turn at the oars."

"Alberta even got everyone singing 'Who's Afraid of the Big Bad Wolf,'" Barbara added. "But someone said the submarine might still be around and the Germans could hear us. It got pretty quiet for a while after that."

"There was one thing kind of funny," Alberta said. "Someone found a tin of biscuits and asked if anybody wanted one. Your friend, the man with one arm, he was at the tiller and said right away he wanted one. But when he was handed the biscuit, he said, 'What's this?' Somebody said, 'It's a biscuit.' Your friend was real disappointed and said, 'Oh, I thought you said who wants a whiskey?' We all had a good laugh at that."

"That sounds like Alfie," David said.

He noticed Joan had been quiet through most of the conversation. Had he disappointed her last night by failing to say anything when the girls' lifeboat left *Athenia*? He hardly knew her, yet it troubled him that he might have somehow fallen short of her expectations. But during a lull in the conversation, Joan broke her silence.

"How close do you think we came?"

"To sinking?" David asked.

"To dying," she said.

Her question stunned him, and he struggled for an appropriate a response. "I don't really know," he admitted. "I heard some of the crew say there were bodies on deck where the torpedo hit, but I didn't see any. We were lucky to be far away from the explosion."

"We saw someone die," Joan said, her voice almost a whisper.

"Joanie, we don't know that for sure," Barbara said.

"It was an older woman from a lifeboat in front of us," Joan continued. "She was trying to get aboard this ship and fell into the water. She didn't have a lifejacket. Some people in our boat tried to reach her but the ocean swept her too far out. We saw her for a few more seconds and then she just disappeared. There was nothing we could do. No boats were behind us, nobody to save her. It was horrible."

Before David could think of anything to say, the door to the cabin opened and a *Knute Nelson* sailor helped a bedraggled man into their room. The man was dripping wet, wore a heavy coat over his pajamas, and he carried a little boy.

"You help this man," the sailor directed. The disheveled man looked to be only a few years older than David. He and the boy shivered and looked dazed, as if they had no idea where they were.

David jumped to his feet with the others, and the girls insisted that the man and boy lie down together in the lower bunk. They wrapped the blanket around both of them, but the man was agitated and kept moaning, "*Mein frau, mein kinder. Mein frau, mein kinder.*"

"What's he saying?" John asked.

"He's asking about his wife and his children," Joan said. "I don't think he knows what happened to them."

For several minutes, Joan and Alberta sat on the side of the bunk and tried to calm the man, telling him he and his son were safe and patting him on the shoulder. David doubted the man understood a word they said, but their soothing voices seemed to reassure him. When the man and boy finally fell into an exhausted sleep, all six quietly left the cabin. Joan and her friends decided to find the ship's doctor and volunteer their help.

They all promised to meet in the morning as David, Tony, and John went in search of a place to sleep.

Oberleutnant Lemp

THE COMMANDER OF *U-30* was the only man on the boat who had access to any privacy. The curtain drawn across Lemp's small alcove opposite the radio room helped shut out the boat's subdued internal lighting, but it could not block the constant chatter of the diesel engines or dampen the rocking motion as *U-30* sailed south on the surface of the ocean. The noise and movement weren't the only factors contributing to his restless attempt to get some sleep. He kept turning over in his mind the events of a few hours ago, wondering what he might have done differently before sending that first eel on its way to the English passenger ship.

She was sailing evasively, zigzagging and blacked out. But why? Why try to avoid detection if the ship could not be attacked under the damn protocol? The stupid English brought this on themselves.

The more he considered the consequences of his attack, the more he despaired. Would his actions preclude any chance of reaching a treaty with the English, as the *Führer* intended? If Americans died in his attack, would America enter the war against Germany? Was his naval career over? Would the Nazi government send him to prison, or even worse, hang him, to reassure the world's neutral countries such an attack would not happen again?

I should take my pistol and end it all right now. No, death in battle is better than suicide or dying at the end of a rope. But how? Surface to attack an armed merchant cruiser and become the victim? But that would sacrifice the boat and the crew. I could let myself be swept off the boat in heavy seas . . .

What am I doing?

Lemp threw the curtain back and sat on the side of his bunk. He could not lie there with his morbid thoughts any longer. Sunrise was still more than an hour away, and he knew his first watch officer would be on the bridge with the lookouts. He needed to talk to someone and clear his head.

"Not much going on up here," *Oberleutnant* Hinsch reported when Lemp climbed onto the bridge. He felt the bitter cold night air and the wet spray from the ocean swells hitting the conning tower. "No ships, not even neutrals with all their lights showing," Hinsch said. "Do you think everyone picked up the distress signals from *Athenia* and were scared away?"

Lemp ignored the question and pulled the collar of his coat up around his neck.

"We need to talk about something, Hinsch," he said, lowering his voice so the first watch officer had to stand closer to him.

"I think it would be best if you and I don't mention the fact that the ship we attacked was a passenger liner."

Hinsch shrugged. "Of course. But a lot of the men saw the ship from the bridge."

"But they couldn't be certain what kind of ship they were looking at. Besides, we will tell them at some point. I just want to give this some more thought before we do."

The spray from a large wave caused the two men to duck away for a moment. When they straightened, Hinsch raised the same issue that had troubled Lemp for the past several hours.

"How were you supposed to know she was a passenger ship if she was blacked out? No one can blame you for the action you took." Although Lemp had told himself the same thing for the past few hours, hearing the words from someone else made him realize how hollow and self-serving the argument sounded.

"Oh, but they will blame me," Lemp said, "They could even hang me if they wanted to make an example. I attacked a passenger ship. There is no excuse for that."

"But that makes no sense," Hinsch protested. "To remove a proven commander like you? *Kommodore* Dönitz would never let that happen."

"I'm not so sure of that." But as Lemp spoke, a new thought began to take shape.

"Mr. Hinsch, you've given me an idea."

"I have?"

"My naval career may end when we return home, but until then, I'm still commander of this boat. I can't change what's happened, but I can do something about these next three weeks."

"Yes, sir."

"Dönitz told us to hit hard and draw blood. That is what we'll do, and we will follow the damn protocol to the letter. My war may only last three more weeks, but I'll make them the most important three weeks of my life."

He vowed not to think of the *Athenia* affair again until *U-30* was on its way to Wilhelmshaven.

PART III

REUNION

The German news agency publishes this morning the following statement by the high command of the German Navy.

"One. The German fleet including every single unit thereof is in possession of orders to abide by the international obligations in every instance during the conduct of sea warfare."

"Two. In the area in question in which the steamer ATHENIA sank, there were no German naval units."

"Three. It is therefore absolutely out of the question for the German sea force to be connected in any way with the loss of the steamer ATHENIA."

"Four. The attempt to charge the German fleet with the sinking of the steamer ATHENIA—continued and repeated despite official German refutation—represents a typical product of atrocity agitation."

Accompanying editorials declare that this statement serves finally to absolve Germany from all guilt in the sinking of the ATHENIA and it is openly charged that "none other than Churchill himself had the ATHENIA sunk" as a desperate utterly unscrupulous device to arouse the American public against Germany . . .

—CABLE FROM ALEXANDER C. KIRK,
US CHARGÉ D'AFFAIRES, BERLIN, TO CORDELL HULL,
US SECRETARY OF STATE, SEPTEMBER 6, 1939

MONDAY, DAWN, SEPTEMBER 4

Judith Evelyn

COLD, WET, AND semiconscious, Judith focused entirely on the task of remaining attached to the wooden hull of the wrecked lifeboat on which she drifted. She had been locked in the same cramped position for nearly two hours when she noticed a dull-gray light stretching across the distant horizon. Had she ever seen the moon emit such a strange light before, she wondered?

Shouts intruded on her thoughts. She turned to see the side of a ship looming near.

Have I drifted back to the Athenia? *Am I too close if the ship sinks?*

With effort, Judith pushed herself to a seated position on the overturned hull. Others on the hull with her continued to shout as a searchlight beam danced across the water in their direction. She glimpsed the characters *H 66* on the ship now moving slowly past them. Even in her hazy state of mind, she realized the vessel wasn't *Athenia.*

"What if it's the Germans?" The voice belonged to a young woman whom Judith thought she knew but couldn't quite place.

"They could be Chinese for all I care, just so long as they stop," Andrew said from somewhere behind Judith.

That's right. Andrew's here with me . . . and some others. I need to tell Andrew something important. What is it?

Sounds of the splashing bow wave drew her attention to the ship, and for an agonizing moment Judith thought *H 66* might not stop. But the spotlight had locked onto their floating wreck and never wavered as the ship maneuvered to bring them along its lee side. She recalled the accident that chopped their lifeboat into pieces and felt she needed to tell the people aboard the ship about their predicament.

"We have no oars," she called out. "What do you want us to do?"

"Jes 'old tight, miss," came the reply from the deck above. "We'll 'ave you up 'ere in no time."

Still battling a fog in her head, Judith didn't understand exactly what the voice was telling her to do, but she recognized the cockney accent and thought it was the sweetest sound she had ever heard. Moments later, she saw sailors on deck unfurl a rope ladder over the side of the ship and drop the ends of several ropes to her and her companions. She grabbed one of the ropes and stared at the loop in its end.

"Stick it under your arms," the sailor shouted from above.

Arms, I know that word. But what are they? How do I find them?

While trying to reason out the meaning of the words, she heard a cry and turned to see a man in the water between their raft and the ship's hull. He looked familiar and for some reason she thought his name was John.

"What are you doing in the water, John?" Judith asked.

"Help! Help me," John shouted as he fought to keep his head above water.

"Push off," yelled a second sailor, scrambling down the ladder.

Push off what? Am I supposed to push something off?

Before Judith could take any action, the sea shoved the derelict raft into the side of the ship with a heavy thud, and John's cries stopped.

"Don't move," a voice shouted, and the scene around Judith became frantic. Two sailors on rope tethers descended from the deck and braced themselves with their backs against the ship and with their legs pushed off the overturned lifeboat hull. A sailor on the rope ladder climbed onto their bow section and wrestled the loop of a safety line under John's arms. The sailor made a signal, and Judith saw the rope draw taut and pull John's limp, dripping body out of the water and up onto the ship. She was distressed at the sight of the man dangling motionless from the rope, his chin resting on his chest. In spite of her confusion, she had the distinct impression that he had been helpful to her in some way and she hoped he would recover.

"Give me your hand, miss." The sailor who had put the line around John now extended his hand toward Judith. Still seated on the side of the upturned hull, she tried to raise her arm but it wouldn't move. With a second effort, she managed to grab the sailor's hand. He pulled her up, put the safety line loop under her arms, and placed her on the ladder.

"Try to climb up, miss. The crew up there will help you." She thought to thank him, but the sailor turned to help one of her companions. On the bottom rung of the ladder, Judith felt the full weight of her waterlogged coat and understood why it had been so difficult to raise her arm. Mustering all her strength, she began climbing the ladder's flat wooden steps. She couldn't find a trustworthy grip on the ropes up each side of the ladder, so she grabbed the rung above her, pulling with her arms and pushing with her legs to gain each new step. On the third rung, her foot slipped off and she feared she would fall, but the loop under her arms held fast and strong hands from above seized her lifejacket and pulled her up onto the deck.

"Welcome aboard His Majesty's Ship *Escort*, miss." A young, clean-shaven officer in a heavy wool coat reached out to steady Judith. She teetered on her stiff legs and felt awkward standing up. "We have a warm place for you down below," the officer said, and Judith nodded her thanks.

"Hawkins, take care of this woman." A big sailor with dark, curly hair, a full beard, and pale blue eyes stepped forward to take her arm and pat her hand.

"It's all over now, girlie," he said. His words cut through her confusion, and she understood for the first time that she was safe at last. She noticed several sailors nearby crouching over John as he lay on the deck. Judith wanted to say something to John, but the big sailor holding her arm steered her away from all the activity.

"You've no need to see this," he said. "Let's get you below into something warm."

In the *Escort*'s steamy boiler room Judith sat on a small wooden bench while Hawkins disappeared for a few minutes. He returned with a heavy wool blanket and a hot toddy in a thick china mug. She took a few sips of the toddy and welcomed the drowsiness produced by its combination of warmth, sweetness, and alcohol. Hawkins used a pocketknife to cut the strings of her lifejacket before helping her out of her heavy coat.

"Get yourself out of them wet clothes or you'll never warm up," he said. "When you're in the blanket let me know, and I'll take you to your cabin."

She emerged fifteen minutes later, engulfed in the blanket's warmth and the glow of the toddy. Hawkins lifted her up and gently carried her toward the stairs.

"We've a lovely spot picked out for you, girlie. Best on the ship, excepting captain's quarters." Feeling safe and warm, Judith was sound asleep in his arms before Hawkins mounted the first step.

Spirydon Kucharczuk

IN THE GRAY light of dawn, Spirydon began to assess his situation. For the past few hours, he had worked tirelessly to keep his daughter, Neonela, atop the floating piece of their wrecked lifeboat as they rode over the waves. Spirydon managed to haul himself onto the wreckage as far as his waist, but he was concerned about too much weight swamping their little raft, so he kept his legs in the water. Time and the cold sea were beginning to take a toll on him. He had difficulty kicking his legs with any kind of coordination, and he felt a painful, almost burning sensation throughout his lower body.

As the skies brightened, Spirydon became more aware of the terrifying expanse that surrounded him. The ocean stretched away to the horizon, with no sign of another lifeboat or the *Athenia*. How would anyone find them in all this vastness? He had no flare to light, no shiny object to reflect the sun, and nothing longer than his arm to wave. To make matters worse, Spirydon was growing increasingly concerned about Neonela, who had not responded to him for the past hour. He held her cold hand and talked to her, hoping that somehow she understood he was still there.

"The sun is coming up, Nela. Maybe a ship will find us soon." He watched her face for any sign of recognition, but her eyes remained closed and her expression impassive, though he could see she was breathing. To keep himself company, Spirydon told his daughter once again about how he had come to

Trosteniec and fallen in love with her mother, Ewdokia, the very first time he saw her.

"She was pretty, like you, Nela. What I noticed first was her eyes. They told me she was strong and smart, and no matter what, she would not fail. I knew if I could marry her, she would not let me fail either. I couldn't believe how lucky I was the day we married.

"She must be wondering where we are. She was probably picked up right away by the big ship. I think she's having porridge right now with the boys and Aleksandra and wondering where we are. We'll have quite a story to tell them, eh, Nela."

Spirydon looked again but saw no response in his daughter's face. He shivered and tried to feel his legs in the water. How much longer could he hold on? Immediately, he sensed Ewdokia's eyes watching him and banished the thought. He would not give up.

"We've had our share of hard times, haven't we? Don't you worry, we'll get through this."

He sensed a vibration and wondered if it meant sharks might be approaching. Spirydon looked around but saw no sign of anything in the water. To focus on something more pleasant, he launched into another story.

"Do you remember when you and Jan and Stefan stole the egg from the chicken house and tried to bake it in the oven? I suppose it was Jan's idea. You were just children and always hungry. You didn't understand we traded those eggs when the money was so worthless. When your mother came in the house, you tried and tried to get her to leave. She knew the three of you were up to something. Then the egg exploded in the oven, and she found out what you did. She was so angry with you, but when she told me about it later she laughed at all your excuses to try to get her to leave the house. 'Thank God, they only took one egg,' she told me."

Spirydon smiled at the thought of the children trying to outsmart Ewdokia. He felt the vibration again, but now it was accompanied by a throbbing noise that he could not locate. On the horizon beyond Neonela, he saw a gray funnel belching dark brown smoke. Could it be headed toward them? They rose to the crest of the wave and Spirydon saw a long, gray ship coming in their general direction, perhaps a half mile away.

"Here . . . here. We are here!" He shouted and waved his arm, hoping the day was now light enough for them to be seen. How close would the ship come? Each time they rose to the top of a swell, he repeated his calls for help and waved. *On the next rise*, he thought, *it will be our best chance to be rescued.*

Up they rode, and the ship was now so close he thought he could count the rivets in its hull. He pushed himself up higher onto the makeshift raft and tried to rise up on his knees, screaming at the top of his lungs, waving both arms. His added weight caused a corner of the raft to dip. Spirydon lost his balance and slipped under the water, but he fought his way back to the surface and managed to get a hand on the raft. He hung off its side, spitting saltwater and coughing. He was relieved Neonela hadn't fallen in the ocean, but the ship had moved past them and begun to recede from view. How he could have done such a stupid thing and wasted their best chance to be saved? Spirydon rescued his daughter, but to what end? Had his actions condemned them both to a long slow death?

"Oh, Nela, I'm sorry. I'm so sorry," he said to his daughter, who remained immobile on the raft. Spirydon could not hold back his tears. "This is all my fault," he sobbed. "We should have left Poland sooner. Please, please forgive me."

When he looked again at Neonela, Spirydon was startled to see her eyes open and staring over his shoulder. Instinctively, he turned to follow her gaze.

The gray ship had turned and was moving slowly in their direction. On its bow, he saw a sailor waving his arms.

MONDAY, SEPTEMBER 4, 1939

Chief Officer Copland

ONE BY ONE, Copland watched each survivor in lifeboat 14A wait for the crest of the next rolling swell to climb onto a rope ladder to board the Royal Navy destroyer, H.M.S. *Electra*. As each person departed the lifeboat, it rode slightly higher in the water, and as the boat rose, so did Copland's sense of relief.

When he boarded the crowded lifeboat the night before, only a few inches of freeboard separated her gunwales from the sea. By balancing the boat and keeping her pointed into the waves, Copland had survived the night without taking on significant water. Following sunrise, *Electra* managed to come along-side their sluggish craft in eight-foot seas. When his turn finally came as the last person to exit the boat, Copland took pride that the rescue had been completed without a single mishap.

Standing on *Electra*'s main deck, he heard a familiar voice call his name. Copland turned to see Dr. Albert Sharman smiling at him through the steam from a mug of tea cupped between his hands.

"Good to see you safe and sound, doctor."

"And you as well. I see our ship is still afloat." Dr. Sharman lifted his cup in the direction of the crippled liner almost a mile away. *Athenia*'s stern had disappeared beneath the waves, and she was leaning even more to her port side, but there was no damage visible to her snowy-white superstructure, and her bow remained defiantly pointed westward, as if she might try to resume her journey at any moment.

"She's a tough old girl, but I'm afraid she won't last much longer," Copland said. Almost as an afterthought he remembered the woman who had fallen on the stairs. "My apologies, doctor. I should have asked how your patient is doing."

"I don't know." Dr. Sharman looked surprised. "She's not on board this ship. I assume she's being treated by doctors on one of the other rescue ships. Have you heard anything?"

"No, but I'll find out. Excuse me." Copland began elbowing his way through the survivors on *Electra*'s crowded deck in search of a sailor who could tell him where to find the ship's radio room.

☆ ☆ ☆

TWENTY MINUTES LATER, he left the radio room with answers from each of the other three rescue vessels. The woman, Mrs. Griffin, was not aboard any of them. Copland headed back onto the destroyer's crowded deck, searching for *Athenia* crewmen to return with him to their ship.

How could such a mistake have been made? When he checked the hospital wards, one room had been locked and the other was empty. Now, recalling his actions, Copland wondered if the first door might have been jammed shut by the force of the explosion. If that was the case, the two men he sent down to help move Mrs. Griffin would have come to the same conclusion he reached.

"Mr. Harvey," he called as he caught sight of the bosun's bald head and stout figure.

"Aye, Mr. Copland." Harvey turned to greet the chief officer, but his smile disappeared the moment he saw Copland's expression.

"Find two volunteers from our crew to come with me back to *Athenia*."

"Back on board, sir?"

"We've left a woman in sick bay, and I've got to get her off. There isn't much time. Have the men meet me here in ten minutes." Without waiting for a response, Copland turned and headed for *Electra*'s bridge to meet with her captain and secure a boat to take him across to *Athenia*.

☆ ☆ ☆

"YOU WANT TO do what?" Lieutenant-Commander Stuart Buss, *Electra*'s captain, looked incredulously at *Athenia*'s chief officer. The two men stood on the destroyer's busy bridge as the ship continued to move around *Athenia* in increasingly wider circles, searching for survivors. Seeing *Electra*'s captain dressed in a crisp white shirt, black tie, and sharply creased dark pants made Copland painfully aware of his own soiled clothes, sweat-smudged face, and the dirty handkerchief wrapped around his left hand.

"I know it sounds crazy," Copland said, "but there's a woman still aboard in the ship's sick bay. She may be unconscious."

"I've just sent our third destroyer to answer a distress signal, so neither we nor *Escort* are running antisub maneuvers. I'm a sitting duck for any U-boat in the area if I come to dead slow long enough for you to get off this ship. And we've just taken on two hundred of your passengers and crew. Do I risk their lives and the lives of my crew to save one woman?"

"I understand, sir, but that woman is my responsibility. I can't leave her aboard a sinking ship." Copland mustered all his resolve. He *had* to get back onboard *Athenia*. "If you don't want to launch one of your boats, will you at least swing by one of our empty lifeboats and allow me to get aboard?"

"Have you spoken to your captain about this?"

"No, sir. The time it would take to locate him and discuss my plan might mean the difference between life and death for this woman. I take full responsibility for my actions."

The captain's steady gaze made it hard for Copland to know if his words were having any impact.

"And you're certain this woman is still on board *Athenia*?"

"Yes, sir, I am. If I have to, I'll swim across to get her." Copland regretted his exaggeration until he saw a faint smile on Buss's lips.

"I believe you would, Mr., uh . . ."

"Copland, sir."

"All right, Mr. Copland, you won't have to swim." Buss turned to his executive officer. "Number One, make the motor launch ready for Mr. Copland right away."

Rhoda Thomas

THE HAZY SUN greeted Rhoda as she cracked open an eyelid to confirm morning had arrived. Still feeling tired after only three hours of sleep, it took her a few moments to recall she lay among a crowd of slumbering survivors on the foredeck of *Southern Cross*. Hoping to fall back asleep, she closed her eyes, but the vivid memories of last night's tragedy immediately assaulted her.

Rhoda sat up and noticed other passengers were awake, sitting on the deck and conversing quietly in small groups. She thought maybe a hundred passengers might be sprawled on the deck around her, and their number surprised her.

When she dug her wire-rimmed glasses out of the pocket of her coat, Rhoda saw the gentleman who had helped her the previous night. He still wore his blue blazer, and she wondered if he had been up all night assisting passengers. His long face betrayed no emotion as he walked among the survivors, followed by a smaller man in a cream-colored jacket who held a large thermos in one hand and a stack of paper cups in the other.

"Thank you for your help last night," Rhoda said as the gentleman approached. His silver hair was cut short and curled up in a small wave on the right side of his forehead.

"You are quite welcome." The man's glance darted to the burns on Rhoda's hand. "You are injured?"

"Oh, no, it's not serious. Just from the flares I was holding last night."

"We have a nurse on board. I will send her to you."

"Thank you, but I'm sure she's already quite busy. Please don't go to any trouble on my account."

"It is no trouble." The man smiled and walked back in the direction of the yacht's cabins amidships. A minute later, the second man approached Rhoda with the thermos.

"Coffee, madam?"

"Yes, thank you." She took a cup from the man, who poured out the dark-brown liquid, and Rhoda felt her appetite stir when she caught a whiff of its nutty aroma.

"I don't suppose you have any sugar or cream?"

"No, madam."

She took a sip and felt the bitter, warm liquid begin to revive her. "Can you tell me who I was talking to just now?"

"Yes, that is Mr. Wenner-Gren, and this is his yacht. You have heard of him, perhaps?"

The name sounded vaguely familiar to Rhoda, but it carried a negative connotation, a feeling she did not share with the man.

"I'm not sure I know who he is."

"He is a Swedish businessman. He owns the Electrolux Company."

"Oh, yes, the vacuum cleaner. Please thank him for me." Her simple expression of thanks sounded woefully inadequate for the profound gratitude Rhoda felt, so she sought to augment it before the man moved on. "And would you also tell him I plan to buy one of his vacuums the minute I return home."

"I will tell him." The man smiled and moved off to find others in need of a morning cup of coffee.

"I mean no offense, but you know the man's a Nazi?"

Rhoda turned to see a pretty young woman with bare feet, wrapped in a striped gray blanket, pushing herself into a seated position next to her.

"No," Rhoda scoffed. "Really? He seems like such a nice man."

"All I know is he's been in the news these last few months." The young woman ran her hand through her matted brunette curls. "He's supposed to be real close with some Nazi bigwigs, and he offered to help England sign a peace treaty or something with Germany. But some people say he's really a spy. I think he also owns some kind of weapons factory, too."

"My goodness, you're well informed."

"I work for a radio station in Alberta. It's what I've heard from one of my friends in the news room."

"Whoever he is, dear, it looks like he saved a lot of people."

"Yeah. Maybe he's changed his mind about the Nazis."

Rhoda nodded and withdrew to her own thoughts.

They can say what they like, but by God, I will buy an Electrolux when I get home.

Chief Officer Copland

AS *ELECTRA*'S MOTOR launch approached the sinking *Athenia*, Copland noticed her increased list and considered how little time remained to rescue the woman in sick bay. Two other *Athenia* crew members, Bosun Harvey and a deck hand, rode in the launch with him, along with the Royal Navy coxswain driving the boat.

It was one thing to risk his own life, but now two others were gambling their lives to help undo his mistake. Copland questioned whether his pride might be too invested in this rescue. Yet to turn back now was unthinkable. He could not leave Mrs. Griffin to die, and he could not rescue her alone. He saw no other choice, but that did not relieve his churning stomach.

"I appreciate your coming, Mr. Harvey," he said to the bosun. "You didn't have to risk boarding a sinking ship."

"Yes, sir, but I couldn't ask Seaman McLeod to volunteer for something I wouldn't do myself."

"I'm indebted to you, Mr. McLeod," Copland said to the third member of their boarding party.

"Pleased to do it, sir," the sailor said. He leaned closer so the coxswain wouldn't hear him. "This way I don't have to listen to those Royal Navy blokes going on about the bloody 'fighting service.' Seems to me we've seen more action than they have."

The launch slowed as it maneuvered toward *Athenia*'s canted hull, moving through floating pieces of furniture, cushions, and other items recently fallen from the deck and drifting in an opalescent sheen of oil. Ropes dangled from empty lifeboat davits, their free ends lying on the water's surface. Copland directed the coxswain to a rope ladder hanging from the promenade deck near the bridge. He led Harvey and McLeod up the ladder and onto the ship's once familiar deck, now angled so sharply Copland felt as if he stood on the side of a pitched roof.

He entered the ship and started down the forward stairway, with the others right behind him. Their flashlight beams pierced the darkness. A low metallic moan from *Athenia* added to Copland's unease. When they reached B deck, he was relieved to find the water had not come as far forward as the stairway. They started down the portside passageway heading aft, but within several paces, they began splashing through a few inches of water and fighting to maintain their balance on the slick carpet.

The farther down the passageway they went, the higher the water level rose, until it was nearly to their knees when they reached the sick bay doors. Copland traced the "locked" doorjamb with his flashlight and immediately saw the slight misalignment he'd missed last night. He signaled Harvey, and the two of them put their shoulders to the stuck door. After three tries, the door swung inward enough for them to squeeze into the women's ward. McLeod's flashlight quickly picked out Mrs. Griffin, her head wrapped in a bandage and her upper lip still discolored and swollen. She lay unconscious on a white iron bed against the bulkhead. The dark water lapped inches below the mattress.

"Good Christ, let's move," Copland said. Mrs. Griffin did not stir when they lifted her off the bed, using a wool blanket as a sling. With Copland lighting the way, Harvey and McLeod carried the woman back up the passageway. The three of them took turns helping to get her up the forward stairway as gently as possible. At the top of the stairs, Copland felt compelled to make one last quick inspection.

"Can you and McLeod get her into the launch without me?" Copland asked the bosun.

"We should be able to get her down the ladder."

"Good. I'm taking one more look around. If I'm not back in five minutes, leave without me."

"Aye, sir. Be careful, Mr. Copland."

The chief officer acknowledged Harvey with a wave as he turned and ran down the promenade deck toward the stern. He wanted to look down number 5 hatch in daylight. If the bulkheads were holding and she wasn't taking on too much water through the plumbing, *Athenia* might still be towed to port and saved before she sank. But as soon as Copland reached the hatch, he knew there would be no reprieve for the ship. The water had risen to within a foot of the top of the hold. Indeed, they were lucky to still be afloat.

Copland raced back to the ladder just as the men settled Mrs. Griffin into the back of the idling launch. He quickly climbed down the ladder to join them.

"Well done, Mr. Harvey," he said.

"Mr. Copland," Harvey said, "I left my gold watch in the drawer by my bunk, and I know Mr. Porteous left his watch behind, too. Do you think I could go get the watches?"

"I'm afraid not. We're on borrowed time as it is." Copland turned to the coxswain. "Let's go." As the launch roared away from *Athenia*, he looked back over his shoulder and said a silent thank you to the ship's fighting spirit that had kept her afloat long enough to rescue one last passenger.

☆ ☆ ☆

BACK ON BOARD *Electra*, Copland found Dr. Sharman waiting for them. Word of the chief officer's mission must have spread among *Athenia*'s crewmen because a number of them welcomed the small party aboard with applause and a loud "hip-hooray." After seeing Mrs. Griffin safely lifted out of the launch and taken on a stretcher to *Electra*'s sick bay, Copland returned to the destroyer's bridge to thank Captain Buss for the use of his launch.

"I thought I should have my head examined when I agreed to your crazy scheme," Buss said. "But you pulled it off. When word of this gets out, I expect you'll have a hard time paying for a drink in any Glasgow pub."

"Well, now, that would be an embarrassment, sir," Copland said, "seeing as how it was my oversight that left the poor woman on the ship in the first place." He held his hands tightly together behind his back to keep them from shaking.

"Don't be too hard on yourself, son." *Electra* had pulled to a safer distance from *Athenia* since the launch returned, with the stricken liner now nearly a mile off the destroyer's starboard beam.

"You know, I can't just let her sit there," Buss said. "She's a hazard to navigation. I'm sorry, but we're going to have to sink her with our guns."

"I don't think that will be necessary, Captain. I did a quick inspection while we were over there. She can't last much longer. Do you think you could give her fifteen more minutes to go on her own?"

"I'm afraid I can't—" Buss cut himself off. "I don't believe it." He nodded in *Athenia*'s direction, and Copland turned to see the liner roll slowly over onto her back, her crimson, barnacle-encrusted bottom pointing to the sky. Like the head of a huge whale, *Athenia*'s bow lifted out of the water, paused momentarily as her stern settled, and then began to slide into the sea with increasing speed until she disappeared beneath a roiling cauldron of bubbles.

Such a graceful exit, Copland thought. He swallowed hard against a knot in the back of his throat and let out a long sigh.

Ruth Etherington

THE STARTLED CRIES of people standing near Ruth on the deck of *Southern Cross* curdled her stomach.

Another torpedo? In broad daylight?

She followed the gestures of her fellow passengers on the yacht's fantail in time to see *Athenia*'s bow slip beneath the ocean. With *Athenia* gone, she saw with perfect clarity how fortunate she was to be alive and standing with the two people in the world she held most dear—her husband and her son. She hugged them both close to her and they stood locked in silent embrace before she relaxed and smiled at them through misty eyes. Chagrined by her emotional reaction, she sought to regain her composure.

"Now, where were we?" Ruth said, clearing her throat.

"Inventory," Harold responded.

"My watch is smashed, and I've lost the amber stone from the ring you gave me when we lived in Russia," Ruth lamented. "My engagement ring is fine, though." She smiled at her husband, feeling a bit self-conscious dressed in the sailor's trousers and middy blouse given to her from the ship's slop chest to replace her oil-stained dress. She had rolled up the pant legs and sleeves to achieve a reasonable fit but thought the result made her look childish.

"My watches went down with the ship," Harold said, "but we have Geoff's watch. He put it in my pocket last night when he washed his hands before dinner. Our passports are gone, though, and all our money. All I have is one pound, three shillings."

"I've got a pound note." Geoffrey pulled the crumpled note from a pocket of the damp gray English schoolboy outfit he wore under the blanket thrown over his shoulders. "And I still have the mole's foot and tail," he added, pulling them out of another pocket. Geoffrey had helped to trap and kill the mole after it dug up his grandmother's lawn, and Ruth knew her son prized the little trophies.

"There you have the sum total of our worldly possessions until we return to Milwaukee," Harold said.

"Yes, but we're together and unhurt," Ruth said. "That's what matters most."

"*Athenia* passengers, I wish your attention, please." The yacht's public address system interrupted their discussion with a disembodied male voice. "I can report that we have three hundred seventy-six of your fellow passengers aboard." Ruth was surprised at the large number, as were several others, judging from a low murmur of the crowd on deck.

"*Southern Cross* is bound for the Bahamas," the announcement continued, "and we do not have food or water supplies for you for such a long journey. I am informed an American freighter, the *City of Flint*, will arrive here shortly and take any passengers who wish to continue their voyage to North America. If you wish to return to England you will be transferred to a Royal Navy ship. Please make your wishes known to the crew members who will come among you with a roster for each ship. Thank you." The public address system clicked off.

"What do you think?" Harold asked.

"Let's go home . . . to Milwaukee," Ruth said.

Judith Evelyn

"PLEASE COME IN," Judith responded to the gentle knock on the cabin door. A steward entered the cabin Judith and three other women now occupied aboard H.M.S. *Escort*.

"I located your fiancé," he said. "He's recovering from exposure and cannot climb the stairs to see you. If you feel up to the task, I can take you to see him."

"Yes, thank you," Judith said. After sleeping for several hours and eating a noonday meal of bully beef and toast, she felt strong enough to undertake the visit. "Were you able to find Reverend William Allan as well?"

"I'm sorry, miss, there's no record of a William Allan on board," the steward said. She accepted the news with resignation. When their lifeboat was chopped to pieces by the rescue ship, Judith considered it miraculous that she had found the boat's bow section to cling to. Andrew's presence on the bow seemed like a second miracle. Could they reasonably expect a third miracle to have saved Andrew's father?

"Perhaps he was picked up by one of the other ships," the steward offered.

"I hope so," Judith said. "May I see Andrew now?"

A biting wind and the sound of rushing water greeted her when she stepped on deck under a sunny afternoon sky. Her first impression was one of speed as flecks of foam from the bow wave flew past *Escort*'s railing. The destroyer seemed impossibly narrow, heeling back and forth as it sliced through the ocean's blue swells. Judith grabbed every handhold and railing to maintain her balance as she followed the steward down a series of gray passageways and ladders until they entered a surprisingly spacious room. People occupied nearly every square foot of space, sitting on chairs and stools and sprawling on tables. She found Andrew lying on a dark-blue blanket on the floor. An ashtray filled with cigarette stubs sat on the deck near his shoulder. He greeted her with a thin smile as she sat beside him.

"Any word of your father?" Judith asked.

"Nothing," he said, his smile melting away. "I heard several ships picked up survivors, but there's no complete list yet."

"I'm so sorry," she said, offering her own brave little smile. They both fell silent, and Judith wondered if Andrew felt as she did about his father's chances of survival.

"You're looking well," she said, changing the subject. "There's good color in your cheeks."

"Feeling better, too," he said. "I plan to walk off the ship when we get to Glasgow tomorrow." Another pause in their conversation gave Judith the opportunity to quietly tell Andrew there was no longer any question of her being pregnant.

"It happened in the water right after we were thrown from the lifeboat," she told him.

"And you're certain?"

"Yes, there's no question."

"Well, that's a relief."

Judith hesitated, realizing she felt more empty than relieved. "I suppose it is," she said.

Andrew propped himself up on one elbow, sounding concerned with her answer. "Of course it's a relief," he said. "Otherwise, you would be giving up the serious pursuit of your career, just as you're ready to take off. And now with a war on, it's certainly not any time to bring a child into this world." She noted he left himself out of the dismal picture he had painted.

"You are all right, aren't you?" he asked.

"Yes, I'm fine," she said.

☆ ☆ ☆

THAT NIGHT, JUDITH lay awake in the dark of her cabin, pondering her sense of emptiness. Certainly, Andrew was correct that a baby would have interrupted her career. Why didn't she feel relieved now that she knew she was not pregnant? Had she really wanted a child? Or was it the way Andrew treated her condition like an obligation? She knew him to be a sensitive and intelligent companion, yet these traits were nowhere in evidence when she thought she was pregnant. Reverend Allan might be a skeptical father-in-law, but at least he possessed compassion.

I'm still searching my heart, William.

Ruth Etherington

THE CABIN BELONGING to Third Assistant Engineer Edward Dodge aboard *City of Flint* was a spare, ten- by twelve-foot room. It was to be the temporary refuge for the Etherington family and a few other *Athenia* survivors spending their first night on the little American freighter until temporary quarters could be completed on the ship's shelter deck. The voyage to Canada was expected to take about a week.

"It isn't much, I'm afraid." Engineer Dodge apologized as he opened the door to his cabin for the Etheringtons. "The bed will sleep two, if necessary, and there's a small couch. You can use the extra blankets for anyone sleeping on the deck," he said, indicating the cabin's limited floor space.

Ruth thanked the young man, who said he had to return to his duties. She made a quick assessment of the room, which appeared tidy and clean in the light of the single overhead bulb. "This should be more than adequate, don't you think?" she said to her husband.

"It'll have to do," Harold said. "We'd be hard-pressed to find an empty square foot anywhere else on the ship."

When the Etheringtons transferred to *City of Flint* earlier that afternoon, they learned conditions on the ship were more crowded than they had been aboard *Athenia*. The tiny dining facilities would require eight seatings to feed everyone at each meal, and water was to be rationed for drinking only. Despite Harold's cynicism, Ruth thought most of her fellow passengers were upbeat and happy to be going home.

"What's that?" Geoffrey asked, pointing to an eight-inch brass pendulum on the wall next to the bed. Two small brass skulls mounted to the left and right appeared to mark the ends of an arc traced by the pendulum.

"It's an inclinometer," Harold said. "It measures how far the ship is leaning to port or starboard."

"What are the skulls for?"

"Ah, you would ask that, wouldn't you," his father sighed. "They probably mark how far the ship can lean and still right itself."

"What if it can't right itself?"

"Then it tips over and we all go for a swim," Harold said. "But you shouldn't worry about that, Geoff. I'm guessing this old bucket has been at sea for a long time and she probably never has come close to her limit."

Ruth could have happily done without the curious device. She guessed Engineer Dodge never anticipated hosting a ten-year-old boy when he fixed the inclinometer to his cabin wall.

☆ ☆ ☆

FOLLOWING THE FINAL dinner seating that night, the weather turned foul as *City of Flint* sailed into a violent storm that lashed the ship with high winds, rain, and heavy seas. *Flint* shuddered and creaked as the shrieking wind slammed wave after wave into her hull. They watched the inclinometer's pendulum swing left and right within an inch of the brass skulls. Ruth thought her husband's description of the ship as an "old bucket" was far less reassuring than it had sounded that afternoon in calmer seas.

The roar of the winds entered the cabin when the door swung open and a man and a woman were ushered into the room by Engineer Dodge in a yellow, rain-drenched slicker.

"Begging your pardon, folks," Dodge said, "but the captain wants these two to share the cabin for tonight." Without waiting for a response, Dodge backed out of the doorway. "Sorry about the weather," he shouted over the wind before closing the door.

The couple appeared to be refugees, a few years older than Ruth. They seemed distant and withdrawn. The man wore a long woolen overcoat and sported a dark moustache and goatee, while the woman wore a head scarf and a heavy blanket over her shoulders. The couple put on the only two life jackets in the room and sat on the bed.

In heavily accented English and in Polish, which Harold was able to partially translate, the man told them the captain said they should have the life jackets and the bed. In any case, Ruth noted they had taken possession of all three items and she felt too exhausted to argue. Harold determined the couple's names were Isaac and Emma and that they were immigrants from Danzig, Poland, on their way to live with relatives in Chicago.

Concerned about the wife's dazed expression, Ruth asked if she was going to be all right. Harold translated the question and the man answered in broken English.

"Emma is strong, but she have bad shock. Lifeboat turn over when we come to rescue ship."

"Oh," Ruth exclaimed, "you must have been in the lifeboat with Geoff and me."

"We have children with us in lifeboat," Isaac continued, without acknowledging her remark. "In water, I swim to find my boy and my girl. I find other children and take to boat, but not *my* children. I cannot save . . . my children . . ." His voice trailed away, and he stared at the floor of the cabin. Emma began to cry, her sobs barely audible over the storm winds outside.

"Right," Harold said, breaking the stunned silence. "We can sleep on the floor tonight. It's a lot better than being in a lifeboat on a night like this, right, dear?"

Ruth nodded, unable to think of anything to say. She considered her own efforts swimming in search of Geoff and felt again the desperation that seized her when she had been unable to find him. She looked at her son lying with a book on the small couch, watched his eyes move back and forth across the page, saw his chest rise and fall with each breath, and realized with an ache how close she had come to losing him forever.

She took a blanket from Harold and leaned over to say goodnight to her son. "I love you so much," she said as she tucked the blanket around Geoffrey and kissed his cheek.

TUESDAY, SEPTEMBER 5, 1939

Judith Evelyn

A GAUZY MORNING mist swirled around the gray superstructure of H.M.S. *Escort* as Judith slowly shuffled along in a line of *Athenia* survivors waiting to disembark from the ship. She noted the sign on a warehouse welcomed visitors to the Port of Greenock. Upriver beyond the warehouse, fog hung like a dense curtain across the River Clyde, presumably the reason why *Escort* and her sister ship had stopped short of their Glasgow destination.

Waiting in line, Judith heard cheering from men working on an adjacent dock. Unlike the angry catcalls and curses she had heard from dock workers when *Athenia* left Glasgow, these were clearly shouts of encouragement. Word must have spread that the people coming ashore were *Athenia* survivors.

When she finally reached the head of the line, Judith gave her name, age, nationality, and place of birth to a young officer seated at a table by the ship's gangway. The officer took down her information and gave her a card to serve as a temporary identification document.

"Buses are on their way from Glasgow," the officer told her. "They'll take you back to the city where they've set up accommodations for you."

"How long before they arrive?" she asked.

"Perhaps an hour, but please remain in the immediate dock area. Conditions are a bit primitive, I'm afraid. They weren't expecting us to land here." Judith glanced over the man's shoulder at the milling group of passengers filling up the dock below. The scene looked cold and damp.

"Sorry for the inconvenience," the officer said. "Next."

She walked down the gangway to join the rest of the disembarking passengers. *Primitive indeed*, she thought. The few benches in sight were occupied, and there appeared to be no place to get a cup of tea or coffee. The morning mist shrouded the sun, and the dampness in the air seeped into her bones, prompting her to draw the blanket she wore more tightly around her shoulders.

The dark-blue blanket had replaced Judith's fur coat, which remained uncomfortably damp even after twenty-four hours in *Escort*'s sweltering engine room. She realized the canvas-topped shoes she wore were all that remained of the possessions she brought aboard *Athenia* when the ship sailed four days ago. Beneath her blanket, she wore a petty officer's old dress-blue uniform scrounged from a member of *Escort*'s crew. Even her soft woolen underwear had come from one of the ship's younger officers who had been concerned that the uniform might prove a bit scratchy next to her skin.

Judith searched the crowd for Andrew, unsure if he would be leaving the ship on a stretcher or under his own power. Instead, she spotted the burly sailor who had helped her when she boarded the *Escort*. Seaman Hawkins stood bouncing a tiny baby wrapped in a light-gray blanket. When he recognized Judith, he winked and smiled.

"A bit lighter than you, miss," he called, cradling the baby higher for her to see. Judith smiled and waved back, but the sight of the baby drew her thoughts back to her restless night and unresolved feelings regarding motherhood and her future with Andrew.

To take her mind off these thoughts, Judith walked along the dock amidst the growing crowd of disembarking survivors. She realized they presented a sorry sight for onlookers. Several women still wore thin evening dresses smudged with oil, their disheveled hair hanging in lank strands. Many people remained in their nightclothes. Others, like her, were draped in blankets or wore makeshift outfits put together from items of clothing the sailors could spare. Some were bandaged or held their arms in slings, their faces fixed in slack expressions.

We look like a gathering of war refugees, which is precisely what we are.

"Miss, it ain't much, but you look like you could use a bite." A dockworker approached Judith with a crust of bread protruding from the gingham napkin in his hand.

"How kind. Thank you." She took the bread and smiled at the man. The brittle crust and its soft center tasted sweet and awakened her hunger. She savored each small bite, seeking to make the crust last as long as possible. As she did so, Judith noticed other dockworkers with open lunch buckets, giving away food likely intended for their midday meals.

More activity drew her attention to the large iron gates at the dock's main entrance, where dozens of women were arriving with their arms filled with clothing. It looked to Judith as if the women had gone through their homes gathering up anything that might be of use and offering the articles to the poor souls who had survived a tragedy at sea.

She recognized these men and women—their careworn faces reflecting a life of limited means. They were working people, the kind she had known as a young girl in Canada's prairie provinces. In their simple acts of charity, Judith saw a demonstration of human decency that transcended the brutality of war, and she thought about how much Reverend Allan would appreciate their generosity of spirit.

Standing on the dock, Judith smiled at the scene as tears rolled down her cheeks.

David Jennings

AFTER GLIDING PAST dark-green headlands for most of an hour, the Norwegian freighter *Knute Nelson* dropped anchor in the broad waters of Galway Bay on Ireland's west coast. A mid-morning breeze feathered the crests of the ocean's choppy swells, while leaden skies held back the sun's warmth.

In spite of the dreary scene, a sense of well-being filled David as he stood with his friends at the ship's railing. He felt certain the worst of their ordeal was over. Since leaving the scene of their rescue yesterday morning, David, Tony, and John had relaxed, napped, and enjoyed the occasional company of the three young women from the University of Michigan. Joan had kept busy helping a doctor care for injured survivors, while Barbara and Alberta had volunteered to distribute food and hot drinks.

The previous night, all six of them joined nearly a hundred other passengers to sleep in a temporary dormitory set up with mattresses and straw mats in one of the ship's empty holds. They had found a corner away from the crowd and entertained themselves singing songs from their universities until it was time to turn out the lights.

Now they were all crowded at the ship's railing to await their disembarkation. A mile across the water lay Galway, a sweeping carpet of whitewashed low stone buildings interrupted by gray church spires and the green copper domes of a few large buildings. Several hundred yards from their ship, a broad-beamed passenger tender made its way toward them.

"David, I enjoyed your singing last night," Joan said. "You have a lovely voice. Do you sing in a choir?"

"Thank you," he said, pleased that she seemed to have shaken off the sadness from their first night aboard the rescue ship. "I don't sing in a choir—just at parties or at home with my family."

"Well, I'm sure any choir would love to have you," she said. Encouraged by her warmth, David sought to make a more personal connection.

"I'll let you in on a little secret," he said. "When I was younger, I had a stammer."

"Really," Joan said. "You would never know it now."

"Maybe so, but growing up, I was so self-conscious I didn't say much. Lucky for me, my family enjoyed evenings standing around our piano and singing. I discovered that whenever I sang, my stammer disappeared. When I finally grew out of my stammer, I found I really just loved singing."

"Well, it shows," Joan said. "We had so much fun last night I lost track of the time. I should have gone to sleep much earlier."

"Gee, I'm sorry."

"Silly, it wasn't your fault," she said.

"What time did you get up this morning to help the doctor?"

"It was about three o'clock."

"How do you keep going on so little sleep?"

Before Joan could answer, a cheer from their fellow passengers announced that the tender had come alongside *Knute Nelson*. David looked down on the large party waiting to come up the stairway once again deployed along the ship's hull. The group included several official-looking men in dark homburgs and overcoats, doctors holding medical valises, nurses in starched white hats and gray capes, and uniformed soldiers carrying furled canvas stretchers. A man with a notepad and pencil looked up at David and his friends.

"How are you faring?" the man called out over the tender's chuffing engine.

Before David could respond, Alberta waved at the man and leaned out over the railing. "I've lost everything except my sense of humor," she yelled.

☆ ☆ ☆

IT TOOK NEARLY a half hour before the disembarkation began. David understood priority was being given to injured survivors first, followed by women and children, then families before he, Tony, and John would board the tender. He watched the soldiers carefully descend the stairway with their stretchers carrying the seriously wounded. Other soldiers gingerly cradled small children wrapped in blankets. They were followed by a seemingly endless stream of women and children. Joan, Barbara, and Alberta waved up at the boys as they went down the stairs.

Viewing the passing parade, David was struck by the realization that in spite of all the brave talk he had heard about the might of Britain's army and navy, the first victims of this war had not been soldiers or sailors, but defenseless civilians.

Barbara Cass-Beggs

THOUSANDS OF PEOPLE lined the shores of Galway's inner harbor and cheered loudly as the tender carrying survivors from *Athenia* made its way to the city's main passenger dock. On board the tender, Barbara was oblivious to the heartfelt cheers. She and her husband, David, had just been given the name of a Galway hotel by a city official with a snowy moustache and wire-rim glasses, who told them there would be no charge for the room.

"That's most generous of you," David said, "but we're desperate for any information about our daughter. She's only three."

"We put her in one of the first lifeboats off the ship and there was no room for us," Barbara explained. "Do you have a list of survivors?"

"I haven't seen much information about individual survivors," the official said. "I can tell you two English warships picked up survivors, and I believe they're arriving in Belfast this morning. There's a ship from Sweden that picked up survivors, but I don't know where they're going. Then, of course, there is the business about the two lifeboats."

"I'm sorry," David said, "what business is that?

"The two lifeboats that were lost. Have you not heard?"

"Oh God," Barbara gasped. "Two lifeboats?"

"Yes, ma'am. They sank during rescue operations."

"Were there survivors?"

"I'm afraid I don't know."

"But how do we find out?" Barbara pleaded.

"Bar, let's not jump to conclusions. Chances are she wasn't on one of the boats that sank."

Barbara nodded, but she felt a new edge to her anxiety. Until now, she had only worried how they would find Rosemary. Suddenly the question was *if* they would find their daughter.

"How soon can we leave for Belfast?" she asked.

"Well, ma'am, first we have to process you into Ireland. Do you have your travel documents?"

"Everything went down with the ship," David said. "We have nothing. Not even money."

"I see. I'm certain the authorities are prepared for that eventuality, given the circumstances and all. Once you're through immigration, there is the Red Cross in town. You might see what they can do regarding travel arrangements."

"Thank you. We'll look into that." David put his arm around Barbara. "We'll find her, Bar. I promise you."

Barbara reproached herself again for not keeping Rosemary with them. The sight of so many mothers and children in the crowd only added to her sense of guilt. Contemplating her shortcomings, Barbara numbly watched David repeat their story to a well-dressed young man who listened intently. The man nodded several times then held up his hand and turned to disappear into the crowd on the tender's open deck.

"He says he's with the Church of Ireland," David told Barbara. "He's gone to find the provost to see if he can help."

Several minutes later, the young man returned in the company of a silver-haired gentleman in a black suit with a clerical collar. The second man's round, open face broke into a warm smile as he introduced himself to the Cass-Beggses.

"I'm Reverend Nash," he said, shaking David's hand. "Young James here has told me of your situation and your hopes of being reunited with your little daughter. I think we can help. Come, follow me and I will get you straight off the ship when we land."

☆ ☆ ☆

SEVERAL HOURS AFTER stepping off the tender in Galway, Barbara and David found themselves in the crowded passenger lounge of the Midland Great Western Railway station at Athlone, in central Ireland, halfway to Dublin. The hardwood and carved stone surfaces of the Italianate lounge echoed with the conversations of the waiting passengers and announcements of arriving and departing trains.

Barbara's spirits had lifted temporarily after they departed the tender in the company of Reverend Nash, who took them to a nearby church schoolhouse where they received a hot meal, new clothes, and money to pay for their travel to Belfast. The headmaster of the school had driven them to the station in time to catch the train to Athlone, where they could transfer on to Dublin. In Dublin, they were to board a train to Belfast in hopes of finding Rosemary among the *Athenia* survivors who had landed there. Unfortunately, their train to Dublin was scheduled to arrive after the train to Belfast departed.

Waiting to board the Dublin train, Barbara fretted at the delay and paced off her impatience. David had gone to see the stationmaster to ask if the Belfast train's departure might be held up so he and Barbara could make the connection.

"Bad news, I'm afraid," David said, returning to the lounge. "They won't hold the train in Dublin for us tonight, but they'll put us on the first train to Belfast tomorrow morning and they're giving us a room tonight at a hotel near the Dublin station."

"Were you able to check on Rosemary?"

"I went to the Garda office and they're contacting the authorities in Belfast. They might know something before we leave here, otherwise they'll cable us in Dublin."

"I can't bear not knowing where she is or if she's safe," Barbara said. "My spirits have been up and down so often, I feel totally exhausted."

"I know." David put his arm around her shoulders. "We just have to keep moving forward."

When their train to Dublin was announced, they boarded and took their seats. As it began slowly rolling out of the ornate, gray stone station, the conductor handed David an envelope, which he tore open and quickly scanned. Barbara read the disappointment in his eyes.

"The *Athenia* survivors were taken to Glasgow, not Belfast. The authorities in Belfast are contacting Glasgow and will have a list of survivors for us by the time we arrive tomorrow. They are also going to make the connection for us on the overnight ferry to Glasgow." David offered an apologetic smile and squeezed her hand. "Everything seems at sixes and sevens right now. I wish I had better news for us, darling."

When they had placed Rosemary safely aboard the departing lifeboat, Barbara thought she and David would not survive the sinking. At the time, the thought of death had not scared her. Now she realized that without Rosemary, the thought of surviving was a more frightening prospect.

THURSDAY, SEPTEMBER 7, 1939

Oberleutnant Lemp

"YOU MAY CEASE firing, Mr. Hinsch." *Oberleutnant* Lemp lowered his binoculars and turned to his first watch officer with a smile. "She has stopped running and raised a white flag." Hinsch, who stood next to Lemp on *U-30*'s bridge, relayed his captain's orders to the gun crew on the deck below them.

The object of Lemp's interest, a small British cargo ship he estimated to be about five thousand tons, had come to a halt in the pale morning light, after initially ignoring the submarine's order to stop and be boarded. After a brief chase and several salvos from *U-30*'s deck gun, three shots had hit home and convinced the English captain he could not escape.

"Take the boarding party across," Lemp told Hinsch. "You have my authority to load the captain and crew into lifeboats if you find anything—and I mean *anything*—in her holds that would help the English war effort. Let's make sure we follow the protocol."

A few minutes later, *U-30* sat with its bow pointed at the cargo vessel, close enough for Lemp to read the merchant ship's name, *Blairlogie*, painted along the side of her bow. So far, at least, everything was taking place in accordance with the rules that had seemed so problematic when he attacked *Athenia*. He scanned the gray skies, wary of the conditions that made it difficult to spot aircraft.

"Mr. Hinsch," he called down to the deck, "don't take too long with your inspection." Hinsch nodded as crewmen slid a rubber raft into the blustery seas and held it taut against the U-boat's hull. The lanky first watch officer climbed into the raft along with an armed party of four men and they began rowing the short distance to the *Blairlogie*, where nearly two dozen sailors stood silently at the ship's railing.

He watched the raft negotiate the large swells as it doggedly made its way to the other ship. The protocol seemed even more impractical to Lemp now that he was following its strictures to the letter, but he was determined not to deviate from them. He shook his head and once again searched the sky for enemy planes.

☆ ☆ ☆

LESS THAN THIRTY minutes later, *Oberleutnant* Lemp watched the rubber raft return to *U-30* and its boarding party climb back aboard the submarine. He already knew he was about to sink *Blairlogie*, having seen Hinsch put the ship's crew off in their lifeboats, but he waited for his first watch officer to make his report.

"She's carrying steel and scrap iron from America," Hinsch said, after reporting to the U-boat's bridge.

"Not much question about sending that cargo to the bottom," Lemp said. "You may clear the decks, Mr. Hinsch. We'll make a surface attack. But first go down to the locker and bring up a couple of bottles of gin and two cartons of cigarettes. We'll make a delivery to *Blairlogie*'s captain and crew after we sink their ship. I wouldn't want the day to be a total loss for them."

Barbara Cass-Beggs

A DAMP MORNING mist shrouded the buildings and glistened on the footpaths of central Glasgow as Barbara and David waited for the Donaldson Atlantic offices to open at nine o'clock. Barbara hoped this morning's meeting with a company official would resolve the question of their missing daughter's whereabouts. It had been a fitful forty-eight hours since she learned two of *Athenia*'s lifeboats had been lost during rescue operations.

After arriving in Dublin Tuesday evening, Barbara and David had continued on to Belfast yesterday, where they were told the partial list of survivors landed in Glasgow did not include Rosemary's name. They were given space on the overnight ferry to Scotland, where Barbara managed only a few hours of sleep. She was hoping for some answers this morning.

George Fleming, a Donaldson manager, met them in the outer office and ushered the Cass-Beggses into a small room, where he quickly and apologetically told them their three-year-old daughter's name was not on the completed list of survivors.

"There is one more possibility," Fleming said, brushing his fingers over his thinning red hair. "An American freighter, *City of Flint*, took on more than two hundred survivors and is proceeding to Halifax, Canada. A list of those passengers is being compiled on the ship."

"Can you tell us anything about the accidents with the lifeboats?" Barbara asked. "Do you have the names of those passengers?"

"We don't compile passenger names for specific lifeboats. I'm sorry it's taking us so long to come up with a master list of survivors. I wish there were something more to be done in the meantime." Fleming sat back in his chair, steepled his fingers, and gazed intently at the gray water droplets forming outside on the room's only window. After a moment, he raised a forefinger.

"You might try going around to the Board of Trade offices," he said. "*Athenia*'s crew are being paid this morning. Perhaps a member of the crew might have some information about the lifeboat that took your daughter off the ship. It isn't much, but it's something to pursue while we wait for the list from *City of Flint*."

"Thank you, Mr. Fleming." David stood and put a hand on Barbara's shoulder. "How soon do you expect to have those names?"

"I'm afraid it might not be until tomorrow. It all depends on how quickly the Americans can put a list together."

☆ ☆ ☆

BARBARA AND DAVID made their way along the damp streets to the Board of Trade offices on the ground floor of a russet-colored stone building. Inside, men in work clothes stood talking in small groups, while a line of two dozen other men snaked its way around the edge of the lobby to a teller's cage at the far end of a long wooden counter. David introduced himself to a clerk at a desk marked "Enquiries" and was told a gentleman was waiting to see them. The clerk signaled to a dark-haired man in a double-breasted navy-blue coat with three gold braids around the cuffs. The man introduced himself as Barnet Copland, *Athenia*'s chief officer, and he directed Barbara and David to three chairs in a corner away from the bustle at the main counter.

"Mr. Fleming rang and asked if I might be able to help you," Copland said after the three of them were seated. "He mentioned something about a lifeboat with your daughter on board."

"There's been no word of her among the survivors reported so far, and we're concerned she might have been on one of the lifeboats that sank," Barbara said.

"I see," the officer said. "The lifeboat that took your daughter off the ship, can you tell me where it was located?"

"I haven't a clue. Everything was happening so fast." Barbara felt frustrated that she could not recall any of the details, but David seemed to sense her distress and reached over to take her hand.

"It was on the port side," David said. "Near the stern."

"Are you certain it wasn't on the top deck where most of the lifeboats were located?"

"No, it was the last station on the port side."

"If that's the case, then I think I can put your minds at ease. I've spoken with both the sailors who were in charge of the boats that sank," Copland said. "Both those lifeboats were launched from the boat deck, so I doubt very much that your daughter was in either of them."

"Oh, thank God," Barbara said. "Some welcome news at last." She squeezed David's hand.

"This process must appear terribly disjointed to you, but it's just as frustrating for us. *Athenia* embarked passengers from three different ports, and after she was torpedoed, five different ships were involved in rescue operations.

Now we have survivors landed at two separate ports and an American freighter with more survivors is on its way to Canada. I apologize for the delays, but at least now you see what's taking so long."

"Oh, please don't apologize," Barbara said. "Your news is most welcome. I feel I can breathe again."

Rhoda Thomas

SEATED IN A small storeroom aboard *City of Flint*, Rhoda watched Dr. Richard Jenkins finish wrapping a gauze bandage around her right hand after treating her superficial burns.

"You're fortunate your hand didn't become infected, Mrs. Thomas. You really should have seen me sooner."

"I suppose so," Rhoda said, "but I thought you would be busy with more serious cases."

"You should let me make that decision."

"Yes, of course." Rhoda looked at the bandage and flexed her fingers. The salve applied by the doctor had already eased some of the discomfort on the back of her hand. "This feels quite good. Were you the ship's doctor for the *Athenia*?"

"Me? Oh, no." Jenkins smiled as he removed his wire-rimmed glasses to massage the bridge of his long, straight nose. "I wasn't on the *Athenia*. I'm a passenger on this ship."

"Really? How many other passengers are there?"

"There are thirty of us."

"Thirty! I had no idea a ship like this carried that many passengers."

"They don't usually. But so many Americans were desperate to leave England, the consulate made arrangements for thirty of us to sail home on this ship. So we were very crowded even before we took on all of you folks."

"No wonder you have such a small office space."

"This?" Jenkins looked around the cramped space, its shelves filled with boxes, folded stacks of linens, and wire bins containing a variety of fixtures. "It's just a storeroom. The ship's sick bay is next door. I moved in here so a mother could have a quiet private space in my office to care for her daughter who was wounded when the torpedo exploded."

"Oh my goodness, I believe I was in the same lifeboat with them. The poor mother was beside herself. She was worried about her daughter's injury and about her youngest child she had to leave behind on the *Athenia*. How is her daughter doing?"

"It's hard to say, but she seems to be holding her own."

Rhoda recalled how she had tried to reassure the girl's mother that night before they witnessed the terrible accident with the lifeboat. Though still haunted by the tragedy, Rhoda's heart ached for the mother next door and the wounded child that reminded her of her granddaughter.

"Thank you, doctor." She stood to go, but hesitated with her hand on the door handle. "It may be a small comfort, but would you please let the mother next door know that I'm praying for her and her daughters." Even if her prayers lacked conviction, Rhoda hoped the mother might find them somehow reassuring.

Judith Evelyn

THE EVENING MEETING in a lounge off the lobby of Glasgow's Beresford Hotel had been set aside for American survivors of the *Athenia* sinking. Judith made her entrance as low-key as possible, although no one seemed to care or ask for proof that she was a US citizen when she appeared a few minutes before the scheduled meeting time.

Judith found out about the meeting when she and Andrew Allan had transferred earlier in the day from the Central Hotel to the Beresford, which now housed nearly all *Athenia* survivors in the city. The clerk at the Beresford told them about a meeting with the US Ambassador's personal envoy—his second oldest son, John Kennedy—to discuss arrangements for the Americans' return.

"You should go," Andrew had told her. "After all, you were born in America, and maybe you'll find out some useful information to help us get back to Canada."

Judith took a seat near the back of the room, which had filled with almost thirty people, mostly women of varying ages, along with older children and a few men. They sat in a variety of comfortable chairs that appeared to have been moved by their occupants so that friends could sit in groups. The arrangement gave the entire setting a haphazard look. At the front of the room, three men conferred quietly among themselves, seated at a table covered with a white cloth.

She immediately recognized the silvery mane of Patrick Dollan, Glasgow's Lord Provost. His picture had been in all the papers for the past two days, greeting survivors who had landed in Glasgow and starting a disaster fund to pay for their food, lodging, and clothing needs. She wasn't sure of the second man, who had short gray hair and wore a dark three-piece suit, but recalled some American official in Glasgow was supposed to make a few remarks. The third man at the table, seemingly in his early twenties, had to be the US Ambassador's son. He had an open, lean face, with a shock of cinnamon-brown hair, and appeared keenly interested as he tracked the conversation between the two older men.

"I wonder what young Prince Valiant will have to tell us?" an athletically trim woman asked as she settled into the seat next to Judith. "I can't believe that after all we've been through, we're having an audience with a teenager."

The woman, who didn't look much older than young Kennedy, introduced herself as Barbara Rodman and said she was a secretary for the Rockefeller Foundation in New York City. Judith reciprocated and revealed she was Canadian.

"You can say I'm here as an observer, although I was born in South Dakota, for what it's worth."

"That's good enough for me," Barbara said.

"I gather you don't think much of the ambassador's son."

"I suppose I can't blame him for being young. It's his father. My parents can't stand him. They think old Joe Kennedy is always looking to feather his own nest. I wonder how our American counsel feels about playing second fiddle to a man whose primary qualification for the job was the amount of money he gave to the Roosevelt campaign?"

"Isn't that how it always works?"

"Yes, but I'd like to think any politician might be a bit concerned about how the money was earned in the first place," Barbara said. "But maybe I'm giving them too much credit."

The Lord Provost cleared his throat and asked for everyone's attention. He began the meeting by telling the survivors they would continue to be guests of the city until permanent arrangements could be made for them. He introduced the American Consul-General for Glasgow, Leslie Davies, who thanked Mr. Dollan and the citizens of Glasgow for their generosity.

"Before we move on to the rest of the meeting, I do have an announcement," Davies said. "The State Department wants to know exactly what American citizens saw and experienced aboard *Athenia* when the explosion occurred. I invite each of you to come down to the consulate to give us a deposition. Your statements will be instrumental in helping us determine the exact cause of the emergency. Now, I'm pleased to introduce the Ambassador's representative, Mr. John Kennedy."

Judith noted that Kennedy seemed at ease in front of the room. His tenor voice sounded confident, but it took her a few sentences to fall into the cadence of his broad New England accent.

"My father sent me here to see if I could be of some help to you," he said. "I spoke with him this morning, and he asked me to tell you the government has plenty of money to meet all your immediate needs." Kennedy continued by telling them a ship was on its way to take them back home.

"The ship should be here in six or seven days. Mr. Davies will tell you where the ship will dock and when you can board it. Although it is primarily for United States citizens, if any English or Canadian citizens are traveling with Americans, we'll endeavor to accommodate them." He then opened the meeting to questions, and a woman in the front row with a bandage on her head asked if there would be a navy escort for their passenger ship.

"There are no plans for an escort," Kennedy said. "The President issued a statement explaining that American ships do not require escorts. It's safer to be under an American flag, because we are a neutral country and won't be attacked, so—"

"That's what you think, sonny," a man interrupted from the third row. Kennedy appeared startled by the comment. Before he could recover, there were more shouts from the audience.

"You can't trust the German Navy," the woman said.

"We don't want to spend another eleven hours in a lifeboat," cried a mid-dle-aged woman two rows in front of Judith. Her remark was met with general agreement from the assembled group.

"What about mines?" asked another woman.

Kennedy raised his hands, asking for calm.

"The American ship will be clearly marked with our flags and will be brightly lit at night, so that no ship can mistake its nationality," he said.

"No, sir," a woman called out. "I'm not going unless we have an escort. Until then, I'll sit right here."

"When Amelia Earhart went down in the Pacific," an older man observed, "half the US fleet went to look for her. Surely the government can spare a destroyer or two for us?"

"I'll tell my father about your concerns," Kennedy finally said. "I'm certain he will relay them to President Roosevelt."

The meeting ended with two minutes of silence to honor those who were lost in the *Athenia* tragedy. The Ambassador's son then stepped into the audience to talk with small groups of people. As others began to file out of the lounge, Judith turned to her neighbor.

"It sounds like your countrymen aren't going to leave England unless America sends a battleship to collect you."

"And if they don't," the young woman said, "there might be room for a few Canadians on whatever ship they do send. It might be your lucky day."

David Jennings

"DAVID, MAYBE WE could get a little fresh air." Joan Outhwaite leaned close to David to be heard over the applause of everyone on the dance floor of the Salthill ballroom on Galway Bay. The band had just completed a reasonable rendition of "Begin the Beguine" and the dancers enthusiastically rewarded the effort.

"An excellent idea," David responded. He took Joan by the hand and led her off the parquet floor, through a scattering of mostly unoccupied chairs, and out a side door to a small garden area. They walked along a pebbled pathway toward a vacant bench past a couple embracing discreetly in the garden's evening shadows.

"What do you think of all this?" Joan asked as they settled onto the stone bench.

"You mean the dance?"

"Yes, the 'Free Dance for *Athenia* Survivors,' and all the rest of it. The free hotel rooms, the meals, the clothes . . . I feel like a first-class mooch." There was sadness in Joan's voice that David had not heard since she described seeing a woman washed out to sea.

"I don't think you're a mooch. We're not asking for any of this. It's the Irish; they can't seem to do enough for us. I don't mind if they want to treat us like we're special."

"Yes, but you actually are special. You and Tony and John helped a lot of people get off the ship. You even helped the crew launch some of the boats. And you were the last ones off. That certainly seems worthy of recognition, if you ask me."

"We weren't the only ones—"

"But what did I do?" she continued, cutting him off. "I climbed into a lifeboat, floated on the ocean for a few hours, was picked up by the Norwegians, and delivered here. I could have been a sack of mail for all it mattered."

Two days ago, Joan had been so warm and friendly when they had sailed into Galway Bay. Sitting next to her now, David felt none of that warmth. Joan seemed lost in a cloud of despair, a cloud he wanted to disperse as quickly as possible.

"Aren't you the girl who worked so hard to help the doctor on our rescue ship? Seems to me you put in some very long hours." He took her hand in his. "Really, I don't think it's about what any of us did. It's about the fact that we were attacked and survived. Maybe becasue we survived, others believe they can survive this war, too."

"Or maybe they're just happy because they weren't torpedoed," Joan said.

"Maybe, but what does it matter? This isn't going to last forever. We'll be going home soon. For now, everyone seems happy to show us a good time. Can't you just relax and enjoy it while it lasts?"

"I don't know. Some things I can't get out of my head, like that poor woman who was swept away in the ocean. I'll never forget her terrified look when she passed by our boat, beyond the reach of our oars. That could have been me."

"But it *wasn't* you, and that's what matters," David said. "At least it matters to me." She smiled at him and put her hand on his cheek. The warmth of her touch reached deep inside him and he wondered for a moment if she had shaken off her sadness.

"Sweet David. You're so encouraging. I must be trying your patience." He started to say that wasn't so, but she laid her finger across his lips. "Before you say anything, please hear me out.

"It's not simply that I survived when someone else did not. The question is why? What can I do to justify my survival? This silly movie-star treatment isn't helping. And everything is happening so fast. My world has been turned on its head, and there's no time to think about it . . . to think about us."

"Us?" David said. The fact that Joan thought of them together brought him up short. He was attracted to her and enjoyed her company, but this was the first inkling that she had any feelings toward him. His mind raced. Could two people fall in love under such a confusion of circumstances?

How do I know if this is love . . . really love . . . and not just the elation we share because we are survivors?

When Joan spoke again, it seemed she was reading his thoughts.

"We only met last Sunday," she said, "then the torpedo hit, and we've been caught up in all this craziness ever since. If we hadn't been torpedoed and continued to Montreal, we would have had five days to get to know each other. Would we have ended up sweethearts, or just friends, or going our separate ways and never seeing each other again? We'll never know, will we?" Joan drew her hands into her lap and stared at them.

David longed to find a way to address Joan's struggles. Though uncertain of the depth and source of his affection for her, he plunged ahead anyway, trusting his intuition.

"Maybe we could start over," he said, "just try to get to know each other. What do you think?"

"How can we ignore everything going on around us?" Joan said. She looked out beyond the garden to the moonlight shimmering on the expanse of the bay. "What I really need is some time to sort this out."

David squeezed Joan's hand, seeking to reassure her. "Okay, let's take it easy for a few days and see what happens. Would that help?"

"Maybe." Joan stood, but was careful to keep her hand in his. "We should probably go back inside," she said.

Had he just marooned himself on the far bank of a river running between them, or joined her on her own lonely shore? Feeling quite unsure, David stood, and they walked hand in hand back toward the sound of the music.

SEPTEMBER 8–17, 1939

Barbara Cass-Beggs

WHEN BARBARA AND David returned to the Donaldson building Friday morning, a clerk met them in the lobby and escorted them down a hallway lined with color lithographs of ships bearing a variety of Donaldson logos from the Age of Sail to the present day. Near the end of the hall, the clerk ushered them into an office. George Fleming stood as they entered and asked them to please take a seat as the clerk left and closed the door behind him. In the formality of the moment, Barbara felt her stomach turn over.

"We have received the list from *City of Flint*," Fleming said, holding several sheets of paper with two columns of typed names. He paused. "I'm afraid there is no Cass-Beggs on the list."

Barbara struggled to understand the full implication of the words she had just heard. She fought against a sense of emptiness and let her thoughts race through the reasons why Rosemary's name might be missing.

She's only a child. It's possible the person recording survivors' names assumed she had the same surname as the adult next to her. Perhaps she wasn't present at the muster when names were taken, or her name was recorded incorrectly.

Somewhere beyond her desperate thoughts, Barbara heard David ask to see the list of names. "Let's look at every name on the list, just to make sure," David said, holding the pages between them.

She forced herself to focus on the names, which were arranged alphabetically. When they began scanning the names under the letter "C," they both immediately noted the third name was "Jack Caspieks," followed on the next line by "Rose Marie Chanler."

"Cass-Beggs might sound like Caspieks," Barbara said. "And the next name is close to Rosemary. They might have confused the two names."

"Maybe. Let's keep looking."

They continued down the list methodically. Under the letter "O" one particular entry caught their attention: "Rose Marie Oxford, Eng."

"Mr. Fleming," David said, "how many passengers on *Athenia* listed Oxford as their residence?"

"Let me check that for you," Fleming said. He picked up the phone and told a clerk at the other end of the line to review *Athenia*'s passenger manifest and identify all individuals who came from Oxford, England.

Barbara and David continued to look at the names on the paper in front of them, until they came to "Gabriella Wolleonde" without finding any other possibilities for their daughter. The phone jangled to life, and Fleming scooped up the handset mid-ring.

"Yes?" He listened for a moment, then said, "Very good. Thank you, Charles." He laid the black handset back in its cradle.

"You were the only family on board from Oxford, England."

"I think we have found our daughter—Miss Rose Marie Oxford," David said, wrapping his arm around Barbara's shoulder.

"Oh, my God," Barbara cried, covering her mouth and blinking back tears. For a moment, she could not move for fear of destroying the joyous spell that held her. The world filled with possibilities where none had existed seconds before. She leaned into David's hug and kissed him on the cheek.

"Darling, we must get to Canada as soon as possible," Barbara said, wiping the tears from her cheeks with the palm of her hand. Details began to multiply in her mind. "We should call our parents and let them know Rosemary is safe. And we need to cable Jim and Caroline in Ottawa and ask them to meet Rosemary when the ship arrives in Halifax. They'll have to take care of her until we can get there."

David smiled at her sudden enthusiasm. "Should I be taking notes?"

Barbara laughed and kissed him again. "Thank you," she said, "for being my Rock of Gibraltar."

Remembering her surroundings, she turned to Fleming, who sat at his desk with an amused expression.

"I'm so sorry, Mr. Fleming. We seem to have taken over your office, and just when you have so much to do."

"Not at all, Mrs. Cass-Beggs. I enjoy a story with a happy ending and you've given me a terrific tale to tell Mrs. Fleming tonight."

"Nevertheless, we should go," David said.

"Very good," Fleming said. "While you take care of your details, I will cable *City of Flint* and ask them for a description of 'Rose Marie Oxford' and tell them that you are both safe here in Glasgow."

"Thank you, Mr. Fleming," Barbara said. "It has truly been a pleasure."

Rhoda Thomas

ON *CITY OF Flint*'s sunlit, blustery open deck, scores of people huddled in blankets, shawls, and coats to witness the afternoon's diversion, a combination fashion and talent show organized by the passengers. Rhoda sat up against a bulkhead in her heavy wool coat and a crocheted cap, enjoying the festivities as several *Athenia* survivors modeled their mismatched outfits cobbled together from the generosity of crew members and the ingenious use of surplus materials. Adding to the occasion, a passenger had made himself into "Monsieur Schiaparelli," after the Paris fashion house, to offer commentary on the "styles" parading across the deck's broad, canvas-topped hatch cover.

"Now here is the latest in coordinated fashion for mother and daughter," the commentator gushed. A young mother dressed in a work shirt and towel for a skirt smiled as she stepped onto the canvas "runway" carrying her toddler in a nightgown with towel strips wrapped around the child's legs for warmth. "You're never at a loss for drying off at the seaside or poolside when you show up in this elegantly tailored dungaree shirt and towel skirt combination.

Meanwhile, your babe is ready for bed or bath in this precious flannel night-dress with non-matching towel stockings." Rhoda laughed and applauded with the rest of the audience.

She enjoyed the creativity of the clothing made from canvas, burlap, blankets, and even pieces of carpet worn by the "models," all of which taxed "Mr. Schiaparelli's" powers of description. The fashion parade was followed by a talent show that featured magic tricks by the ship's first officer, who managed to make playing cards change suits in spite of the windy conditions on deck. A dance instructor from Boston performed the hula, wearing a "grass skirt" made from unbraided rope and a lei composed of colorful pages crumpled from a magazine. She swayed to the beat of drums created by stretching canvas across empty garbage cans. Toward the end of the festivities, a precocious little girl with light-brown curls announced she was going to sing "Daisy, Daisy" loud enough for her mummy to hear on the big white boat.

As the child began to sing, Rhoda noticed Dr. Jenkins standing at the rear of the audience and looking downcast. She got to her feet and made her way toward him.

"Surely the show can't be that bad," Rhoda said as she joined him at the back of the crowd.

"Hello, Mrs. Thomas," he said. "Actually, I was all right until she started singing." Jenkins gestured toward the little girl who sang with a self-assuredness that seemed to captivate the audience.

"I'm sorry to tell you . . . Margaret Hayworth, the little girl who was in your lifeboat? She died early this morning."

"Oh, how terrible." The news stunned Rhoda. She had thought the child was recovering when she spoke to the doctor two days earlier.

Another child gone, with so much life to live.

"How is her mother doing?" Rhoda asked.

"Not well, I'm afraid. None of us are."

The little girl finished her song, and the audience applauded.

"If only I had more experience with brain injuries the outcome might have been different."

"It seems so unfair," Rhoda said, "having to deal with such awful injuries in the middle of the ocean. I'm sure you did everything you could."

"Yes, but that doesn't make the outcome any easier." Dr. Jenkins offered her a sad-eyed smile. "Do me a favor, Mrs. Thomas. Please don't mention this to anyone. I think we should let people enjoy themselves for now. There'll be time enough tonight to tell the other passengers."

Spirydon Kucharczuk

"MR. KUCHARCZUK, I have a visitor for you." The voice accompanied a gentle knock on the door of Spirydon's Glasgow hotel room. He recognized the voice of Mykola Zelenko, the Ukrainian-speaking Red Cross worker he met during the two days he had spent in the Western Infirmary recovering from his exposure to the cold ocean. He opened the door to admit Zelenko and gasped when he looked past the slender gentleman to see a dark young man standing in the hall behind him.

"Jan," Spirydon cried in surprise and reached out to embrace his son. "They told me you were in Ireland. When did you arrive here?" He stood back and put his hands on Jan's shoulders. "You look well. Have you eaten any supper?"

"I ate at the train terminal."

"You two have a lot to discuss," Zelenko said, backing down the hallway. "We'll talk tomorrow."

"Yes. Thank you, Mykola." Spirydon waved then turned to usher Jan into the small room with its twin beds, wooden dresser, and single chair. He offered the chair to his son while he sat on the nearest bed.

"I'm sorry Nela is not here," Spirydon said. "We will see your sister tomorrow morning at the hospital. You must tell me, how did we miss each other on the ship after you went for your brother?"

"Yes, but first, how is Nela?"

"She's getting stronger every day. The doctors say she was exhausted from the exposure of being in the water and on the raft for so many hours. It was very cold, and she seemed confused right from the start. But she is getting better."

Before Spirydon could get the boy to tell his story, Jan made him go through the entire account of being in the lifeboat that was caught in the propeller of the rescue ship, his struggles in the water to save himself and Neonela, and their miraculous rescue by the British destroyer. He told Jan he had been discharged from the hospital two days ago, but spent the days since then at Neonela's bedside, leaving only after she had eaten supper.

"And now, let's hear about you," Spirydon insisted.

"This is nothing like your story, Papa," Jan said, sounding apologetic. "I went back to our cabin, like you said. It took a while to find it in the dark. When I got there, it was empty and all the life jackets were gone. So I ran up to the meeting place by the stairs but no one was there."

"Yes, Stefan waited in the wrong place," Spirydon said.

"When I couldn't find anybody, I went to look for you at the lifeboats, but you weren't there. I thought you had left the ship already. I helped to load two or three boats, and then a sailor pointed for me to get into one of the last boats on the top deck.

"We were picked up by the Norwegian ship, and they took us to Galway. After two or three days in the hotel, I saw a list of survivors in Glasgow. I found the names 'N. Kucharczuk' and 'S. Kucharczuk.' You know, Stefan is such a good swimmer I thought it was my brother and sister on the list. When I arrived here, I checked with the Red Cross to see where I could find you. I was surprised when they told me it was you and not Stefan who was with Nela."

"No one told me you were coming," Spirydon said. "What a wonderful surprise when I opened the door." He smiled, but Jan did not smile back. Spirydon sensed he had more to say.

"Papa, I asked the Red Cross people if there was any new information about other survivors, and they said there was nothing. Mama, Stefan, Leksi, and Jakeb—their names are not on any of the survivor lists."

"I know." Spirydon had realized the moment he saw Jan at the door that his son's presence would force him to deal with the obvious implication of the missing names, and yet he was not ready to give up hope.

"This American ship will arrive in Canada in a few days," he said. "They could be on it even though their names aren't on the list. Maybe they didn't understand they were supposed to give their names, or somebody copied them down wrong. When they arrive in Canada and all the passengers leave the ship, the Canadian government will register everyone. They will be on that list."

Jan looked worried, so Spirydon reached across and patted his son's knee.

"You are here tonight. You'll see. We will have more good news this week."

Chief Officer Copland

A WEEK AFTER his rescue at sea, Chief Officer Barnet Copland strolled through Glasgow's George Square in the center of the city. Jimmy Turnbull, the young cadet who had sailed with him on *Athenia*'s last voyage, accompanied Copland. They had lunched at a nearby oyster bar and walked the two blocks to stretch their legs and spend a half hour in the sunny square before heading to the Board of Trade offices for a meeting with a representative of the Wrecks Commission.

"Should I be worried about this meeting, Mr. Copland?" Jimmy asked as they settled on a bench beneath the marble likeness of Sir Walter Scott in the center of the square.

"Why would you be worried?"

"It's an official record of the sinking. Everyone says we were torpedoed by a German submarine but I didn't see anything. I'm afraid I'll sound a bit simple."

"First of all, you're not going to sound simple. And second, this inquiry isn't just about the cause of the sinking. The commission also wants to know what each of us did after the torpedo hit. Did we follow procedures? Did they work well? Were there any complications? That sort of thing. They'll take everyone's testimony and try to reconstruct what happened and when. If anything needs to be corrected, they'll make recommendations in the final report.

"All you need to do, Jimmy, is tell them what you saw and what you did. And if they ask if anything could have been done better, tell them what you think."

"But I'm just a cadet."

"That doesn't matter. Because you're new at this, you might question something that the rest of have always taken for granted."

"If you say so, Mr. Copland."

They sat for a moment, noticing the steady stream of people passing through the open square. It occurred to Copland that aside from a few signs pointing to air raid shelters, Glasgow didn't feel like a city at war. Most shops were open for business, and people didn't seem anxious even though they all carried gas masks wherever they went. He noted it had only taken a week for some enterprising souls to make and sell much smarter looking containers for the masks than the government-issue cardboard boxes they came in. Copland began to wonder if his countrymen were taking this war seriously when Jimmy spoke up again.

"Sir, I wonder if I might ask a more personal question?"

"Go ahead, but we have to get moving in a few minutes."

Jimmy frowned as he seemed to wrestle with the best way to approach his subject. "Yes, well, ah, how do you . . . I mean how do I keep a certain lass interested in me when I'm spending so much time away at sea? I write a letter every day, but I can't mail them until we come to a port, and sometimes they don't arrive until after I'm home. She thinks . . . well, I don't know what she thinks. That's part of the problem."

"It's alright, Jimmy." Copland interrupted. "I get the picture."

"I guess I'm wondering, when I pass my certification, can I expect to have more time? I mean, time for personal matters?"

Now it was Copland's turn to frown. "No. If anything, you'll be even busier on your first assignments as a third mate. I can only tell you what's worked for me, and that is to put off any serious personal entanglements and concentrate on your duties. The more you do, the quicker you'll advance and eventually become the master of a ship. As a captain, you'd be able to bring your wife on those long sea voyages."

"But that will be years from now," Jimmy pleaded.

"It'll be sooner rather than later if you tend to your duties," Copland said, glancing at his watch. "We better go. Don't want to keep the commission waiting."

They started walking to the Board of Trade offices, and Jimmy fell silent. Copland wondered if he had discouraged the young man. Or was Jimmy simply considering what he would say to the Wrecks Commission?

His Spartan advice to Jimmy drew Copland's thoughts back to the Crow's Nest pub and his conversation with fellow Merchant Navy Officer Gordon Dunbar, two months before the war. Gordon told him war would scramble all his plans for the future. He hadn't thought much about the comment at the time, but it came back to him now in stark relief. Regardless of the protocol for conducting submarine warfare, Copland had no doubt Germany's U-boats were going to wage an unrestricted campaign to choke off Britain's supplies. That strategy would make targets of every merchant seaman and officer. Had he been right to put off his personal life to pursue his goal of becoming the captain of his own ship? The thought gave him pause. Still, the only thing he could think to do now was to continue tirelessly working toward his goal. But he was left with one troubling question.

How long can I trust my luck to last?

Rhoda Thomas

LIKE MANY OF her fellow passengers aboard *City of Flint*, on September thirteenth, Rhoda stood at the ship's railing as it entered the broad harbor of Halifax, Nova Scotia, sailed past a large, low-lying island, and slowly made its way to the city's main passenger dock. Hundreds of people lined the harbor under a hazy midmorning sun. While the rest of the passengers answered the crowd's warm welcome with waves and cheers of their own, Rhoda was indifferent to the gaiety. She told herself she was too exhausted to muster up any show of enthusiasm.

Twenty minutes after the ship docked at the city's Ocean Terminal, *Athenia* survivors began going ashore. At the bottom of the gangway, Rhoda welcomed the sensation of being on land for the first time in eleven days. Reporters and photographers stood on either side of two rope lines that defined a passage into the terminal. As she walked toward the building, Rhoda heard reporters calling out to various passengers, asking for comments or details of their experiences. They seemed keenly interested in the most disheveled survivors. A few of the women still wore oil-stained evening dresses and other survivors sported mismatched articles of clothing. Although she had worn the same clothes for more than a week and was embarrassed by the matted silver hair she kept hidden beneath her crocheted cap, Rhoda was relieved she didn't appear distressed enough to attract the reporters' attention.

Inside the terminal a Boy Scout directed her to a large room reserved for women and children. There she waited in line for nearly half an hour before her turn came to meet with a large woman seated at a long table with several other men and women. Dressed in civilian clothes, the woman wore a white armband with a bright red cross and a name tag over her right breast that read "Mrs. Campbell."

"Do you have any medical needs, ma'am?" the woman asked with a welcoming smile.

"No," Rhoda said, "I was seen by a doctor on the ship."

"Very good. If you need fresh clothes, we have blouses, skirts, sweaters, and dresses in the next room. They've been donated for the *Athenia* survivors," she said, handing a small paper bag to Rhoda. "Here are a few necessities for you, dear; a toothbrush, comb, and some toiletries. If you would like a hot shower or bath, there is a dressing room and bathing facilities through the door on the right."

"Thank you."

Mrs. Campbell ran down her checklist to review the immigration process, explain the procedure for sending a free telegram, and describe where to find the free cafeteria. After a week of living with the careful rationing of food, water, and living space aboard *City of Flint*, Rhoda was momentarily paralyzed by the breadth of choices offered by the Canadians' generosity.

"Is anyone meeting you here in Halifax?" Mrs. Campbell asked.

"What?" Rhoda said. "Oh, no, I don't think so."

"Then you'll probably want to take the train to Montreal. It's been arranged by your shipping line so there is no charge. In Montreal, you'll be able to make travel arrangements to get home. Should I put you down for the train?"

"Yes, please."

"Any questions, dear?"

"No, Mrs. Campbell, you've thought of everything. Thank you again."

As she began to consider what she should do first—cable her husband or enjoy a nice hot bath—Rhoda noticed several women in the room craning their necks to see out the window in the direction of the ship, where four soldiers carried a plain wooden coffin down the gangway. The soldiers were followed by a man and woman with their arms around each other, walking slowly and staring blankly at the coffin in front of them.

Rhoda recognized the woman as the mother whose daughter had died on the ship four nights earlier and remembered trying to comfort her in their lifeboat. She had told the mother someone surely would be looking after her missing daughter and that she believed there was a reason why the mother was there with her wounded daughter.

What would I tell her now about God's purpose?

Sadness weighed on Rhoda again as she considered the children killed by the submarine attack and her failure to see any purpose in the taking of such innocent lives. In a few days, she would be home with her family—her loving husband, two happily married daughters, and two precious grandchildren. How would she deal with her doubts then? Thinking of her family, Rhoda felt the first stirrings of hope since the *Athenia* tragedy had challenged her faith. She would draw on the strength of her family, and their support might help her eventually come to terms with these terrible events.

As the sad little cortège passed the window, Rhoda sensed the anguish in the mother's fixed gaze, almost as if she couldn't believe her little girl lay inside the coffin ahead of her. In that moment, she understood that while the passage of time might bring Rhoda understanding, no amount of time would bring back the mother's child. The realization moved her to say a prayer—her first in a week—that the war would end before too many more children died.

Oberleutnant Lemp

U-30 SAT WITH her bow pointed at the long black hull of Lemp's latest prize, the British freighter *Fanad Head*. A rubber raft with four sailors led by First

Watch Officer Hans-Peter Hinsch had nearly reached the abandoned freighter, which lay less than a hundred meters away under the midafternoon sun. At the moment, however, *U-30*'s commander was more concerned with the distant horizon than his submarine's boarding party. It had taken too long to reach this climax, and Lemp worried that enemy destroyers were racing to his position.

U-30 had chased *Fanad Head* through pounding seas for nearly ninety minutes before finally getting the freighter to stop. In the remaining minutes it took *U-30* to come alongside her prize, the freighter's crew had boarded two lifeboats and were lowering themselves into the water. Mindful of the submarine protocol, Lemp had taken the time to tow the lifeboats far enough away to be out of danger when he sank the freighter. He also had told *Fanad Head*'s captain a cargo ship from a neutral country had answered their distress signal and was coming to their rescue. The Royal Navy had almost certainly picked up the same signals and dispatched ships to come to *Fanad Head*'s aid. But how close were they?

He watched Hinsch and his men climb onto the freighter's deck, knowing that the operation would take the better part of a half hour before they could leave. The boarding party planned to scour the galley for any useful provisions, especially fresh bread and water, before setting explosive charges and opening valves to sink the ship. Lemp wanted to save his remaining torpedoes for the final week of his patrol.

He allowed himself a sigh of relief when he saw the boarding party come back on the freighter's deck carrying boxes and cans, which they tossed to a seaman in the rubber raft. When they signaled their scavenging had been completed, sailors on *U-30*'s deck hauled on a line attached to the raft and brought it back alongside the submarine. The men began unloading the provisions and stacking them on the deck.

"*AIRCRAFT!* Enemy aircraft dead ahead," shouted a lookout on the U-boat's bridge.

Lemp looked up to see the small, single-wing plane approaching them from just above the freighter's superstructure. Four small bombs were visible under its wings and one under the fuselage.

"Clear the deck," he shouted. The six sailors unloading supplies dropped their boxes and ran for the conning tower. They scrambled up the tower and through the hatch just as the plane roared over them, its British blue, white, and red roundels unmistakable on the underside of both wings. Lemp smiled at his luck that the plane's approach from over the freighter and *U-30*'s proximity to the ship had hidden his boat from the pilot until the last moment.

"Alarm!" he called out, signaling an emergency dive as he pulled the hatch closed above him and dropped down the ladder to the control room.

"All engines full astern," Lemp ordered, aware *U-30* could not submerge while going forward without hitting the freighter. The British pilot would need to adjust his angle of attack. Could they get under the water before he made his bomb run?

Seconds crawled by as the boat built enough speed to begin its dive. Moments later, two muffled explosions shook *U-30*, staggering everyone in the control room and sending loose objects clattering to the deck.

"Take us down to thirty meters, Chief," Lemp told his chief engineer, *Leutnant* Meckbach. At the appointed depth, he called for the boat to begin moving slowly forward in a wide circle and asked for a damage assessment. Reports from fore and aft told him *U-30* had suffered no serious harm. Lemp began to consider how and when he might recover his boarding party from *Fanad Head*.

He still has bombs, and the longer he stays up there, the closer the English warships come.

A minute later, just as he began to consider coming to periscope depth, another explosion in the water above them shook the boat, causing the lights to flicker.

"Down to fifty meters," Lemp ordered. As soon as the chief reported they reached the desired depth, another explosion pounded *U-30*. After diving another ten meters a fifth blast in the water above them rattled the submarine. Somehow the English pilot knew his exact location even though *U-30* was too far underwater to be seen from the air. He asked Meckbach if they could be leaking fuel, leaving a trail on the ocean's surface for the pilot to follow. The chief checked his gauges and reported no indication of a significant leak.

Five explosions meant the English plane had no bombs left. Lemp decided to come to periscope depth to determine what was going on. When the boat leveled off, he called for the wide-angle periscope to be raised, stepped to the rubber eyepiece, and began a circular sweep.

"Shit. We've snagged the line for the raft, and it's following us around on the surface like a Goddamned marker buoy."

Lemp called for a volunteer, handed the young sailor a saw-toothed knife, and outlined a split-second operation.

"The line runs right over the top of the bridge. As soon as we break the surface, open the hatch, cut the line, and get back down. As soon as he sees us, the English pilot will strafe the boat."

"Yes, sir." Lemp sent him up the conning tower ladder and called for Meckbach to bring the boat to the surface just enough to clear the tower.

Nearing the surface, *U-30* began rocking in the waves and the chief signaled the tower was free of the water. Lemp told the sailor to go. Moments later, the man dropped back down the ladder to the control room and the boat again submerged. Back at periscope depth, Lemp confirmed the raft had been cut free, but he also saw another plane approaching and noted it carried at least five bombs.

"Take us down to fifty meters," he ordered. "Where the hell are these planes coming from?"

☆ ☆ ☆

FOR AN HOUR more, *U-30* continued to slowly circle *Fanad Head* with more bombs detonating in the water, though not nearly as close to the submarine as before. Twice, when he came to periscope depth, he saw a plane strafing *Fanad Head*, apparently shooting at his boarding party, and he began to worry there might not be anyone left alive to rescue. With sunset approaching, Lemp calculated he could wait no longer. He planned to surface as close to the British freighter as possible to give Hinsch and the others the shortest possible distance to swim back to *U-30*.

Just before reaching the surface, *U-30*'s bow slammed into *Fanad Head*'s hull with a grinding crunch. The blow sent Lemp and several others reeling into the bulkhead. Not waiting for a damage report, he hurried onto the bridge, intent on recovering his boarding party.

"Three English destroyers are heading for us from the other side of the ship," Hinsch shouted to Lemp from *Fanad Head*'s railing. "We haven't been able to set the charges because of the planes."

"Never mind the charges," Lemp said. "Can you swim back here?"

Hinsch told him the other three members of the boarding party had been wounded, but only one seriously. Adolf Schmidt, a diesel mechanic, had been shot in the arm and they were having trouble stopping the bleeding. He thought they could probably swim the short distance to *U-30*, but he warned the destroyers would be on them in ten minutes.

"You should go now, before they get here," Hinsch said.

"I'm not leaving anyone behind," Lemp answered. "Get in the water." Hinsch nodded, but then he added a surprise.

"We have two English pilots here," he said. "Their planes crashed and they swam to the ship. We fished them out. One of them is burned."

Without waiting for any more details, Lemp ordered his first watch officer to get himself and his men back on *U-30*. It took a few minutes for the men to swim to the U-boat and be pulled from the water. The two pilots now stood at *Fanad Head*'s railing and refused to get in the water.

"Look here, we appreciate the help from your boys," one of the pilots shouted to Lemp in English. "But our chaps will be here soon, and we'd rather wait for them than become your prisoners."

"I am going to sink that ship," Lemp answered in English. "You can stay on board and die, or you can come with us. You must decide now." The two pilots looked at each other, then jumped into the water and dogpaddled to *U-30*, where they were helped on board and taken below to the petty officers' quarters.

After *U-30* submerged again, Lemp gave the helmsman a course moving away at a perpendicular angle from the freighter. He brought *U-30* to periscope depth and climbed to the combat center in the conning tower. Unsure of the extent of damage to the bow, he had decided to use the torpedo in the stern tube to sink *Fanad Head*. Lemp ordered the stern tube doors opened. He read off the targeting information and waited a few seconds for the data to be entered.

"Stern tube fire," he called, and pulled the firing lever as *U-30* passed five hundred meters beyond the motionless freighter.

"Eel running," the radio operator reported from his listening post.

As he watched through the attack scope, Lemp saw *Fanad Head* buckle, then disappear in a dense, charcoal-gray cloud that erupted amidships and sent fiery tendrils of smoke arching into the sky. Moments later, a deep booming sound resounded through the U-boat's hull.

"Direct hit," Lemp called out, still pressed against the periscope's rubber eyepiece. "She's broken in two and going down fast." The men in the control room below began cheering, but a shout from Lemp cut them short.

"*Alarm!*" he cried and slid down the ladder into the control room. "All available hands forward," he ordered.

"The English destroyers were just beyond the freighter when she went down," Lemp told Hinsch. They leaned back against the bulkhead, making room for several sailors who raced forward through the control room to add their weight to the bow and create a steeper downward dive angle. A minute later, the men filed back through the control room, returning to their battle stations as *U-30* trimmed its descent, continuing down in a more controlled dive.

"Stand by for depth charges," Lemp called out. Waiting in the boat's dimmed, red interior lighting, he realized no one on board, including himself, had ever endured an enemy depth charge attack. Before he could consider how his crew would react, the radio officer interrupted his thoughts.

"Charges in the water."

Lemp braced himself against the chart table. The depth gauge told him they were passing through fifty meters when a distant muffled boom astern of the boat gently rocked *U-30*. Another closer, louder explosion shook the submarine more violently, and Lemp called for the helmsman to steer sharply to starboard, hoping to take them away from the pattern of falling charges.

A clanging hammer blow from a massive shockwave slammed the boat sideways. The roar of its exploding charge enveloped *U-30*. The lights blinked twice but stayed on. Glass shattered. A hissing sound came from the engine room. Chips of paint and shards of glass littered the deck. Lemp heard water leaking somewhere in the boat. *U-30* creaked and rocked as it absorbed the blow from another explosion, this one farther off her port beam.

"Secure those leaks," Lemp called out, keeping his voice calm. "Chief, take us to a hundred meters."

"Aye, captain. We're passing though eighty meters now." Lemp was pleased to hear the calm cadence of Meckbach's words.

They'll take their cue from me. Be deliberate and don't panic. All we can do now is stay quiet and wait it out.

"More charges in the water," the radio officer called out. Lemp gave the helmsman a new heading to steer and the boat continued to dive.

The initial detonations sounded muffled and distant, causing the boat to roll sluggishly. Lemp imagined an approaching giant, his footfalls growing louder and more violent as they neared *U-30*. He saw Hinsch shut his eyes and hunch his shoulders in anticipation of the next blast.

Again, a sharp metallic clang and angry shockwave shook the boat and threw Lemp forward. The lights went out. The roar of an explosion filled his ears, and he thought the devil had come for him at last.

On the deck with his legs splayed out behind him, Lemp felt a dull pain in his forehead where he had struck the chart table when he fell. The ringing in his ears subsided, and Lemp heard shouts coming from the stern compartments. The crew began switching on flashlights, piercing the darkness with their narrow beams and illuminating a fine mist in the control room. Officers and men began picking themselves up from the debris scattered around them. He noticed the helmsman and the navigator did not seem to realize they were bleeding. Lemp gathered his wits and struggled to his feet, amazed that *U-30* still held together.

"Mr. Hinsch, see what's going on back there," Lemp called to his first watch officer. "And see how our English guests are doing."

The dim red lighting winked on again. From somewhere above in the conning tower, a thin stream of water began pouring into the control room. The faces of several more gauges were cracked, and Lemp wondered how many of them still worked.

"One hundred meters, captain," Meckbach announced.

"Take us down another forty," Lemp said. He knew he was nearing U-30's operational depth limit, but he wanted to try to get well below the damned charges to wait out the English assault. A few minutes later, Hinsch delivered his report.

"Water is leaking through the packing of both propeller shafts," he said. "The men are trying to stop it, but we'll need a bucket brigade to bring the water to the bilges amidships."

"If that's the worst, we should be able to deal with it. What about our guests?"

Hinsch smiled. "One of them told me if he'd known it was going to be like this, he would have stayed on the freighter."

Lemp nodded. "I might have joined him."

"They're coming back," the radio officer announced.

Ruth Etherington

THE SOUR EXPRESSION on Harold's face told Ruth her husband was not happy with the results of his visit to the temporary Red Cross office where he had gone to seek assistance to pay for their return to the United States. The office had been set up just off the main dining area in Halifax's Ocean Terminal, where Ruth and her son Geoffrey were enjoying a late lunch.

"I can't believe this," Harold said, approaching them in the busy dining hall. "The Red Cross will loan us money for the tickets. Loan us the money!"

He made no attempt to hide his agitation and Ruth noticed several people glancing in their direction. She sensed his distress was the result of a long day. They had been late in disembarking from *City of Flint* and found long lines in the terminal building as they processed through the various stations for *Athenia* survivors. By the time they had met with officials, taken hot showers, changed into new clothes, and gathered in the dining hall, it was midafternoon.

Harold had insisted Ruth and Geoffrey get something to eat while he went to the Red Cross office to complete their travel arrangements. Ruth thought her husband probably was tired and hungry, and she moved to diffuse the situation.

"It's all right, darling," she soothed. "We have money in the bank in Milwaukee, don't we?"

"That's not the point. We're the victims of an act of war. We shouldn't have to pay for our travel."

"But didn't they say the train trip to Montreal is free?"

"That's because it's being paid for by the steamship line, not the Red Cross."

"Hey, Dad, they have fish and chips." Geoffrey held up his plate for his father's inspection.

"Geoff's right, you should get something to eat. You'll feel better."

"Don't change the subject." Harold sat next to his son, glanced at the crispy yellow fries, then leveled his gaze at Ruth, sitting across the table from them. "I told the man at the front desk I wanted to talk to his boss. Do you know what he said? There was no point in talking to his boss because it was standard policy and his boss couldn't change it." Hal's voice rose in indignation.

"Can you imagine? People contribute to the Red Cross every day, thinking their money is going to help out the poor souls who are the victims of a disaster. But it seems they only loan the money out and expect to be repaid. It's a wonder they don't want to charge me interest on the loan."

"Really, dear, it is shocking, but there's nothing we can do about it here. We have so much to be thankful for. We're all together and none of us is injured. We've made it safely to land, and we'll be sleeping in our own beds in a few nights."

Hal scowled at his wife. "I know what you're doing. I don't need to be placated. I'm not a child, you know." Ruth glanced at Geoffrey and was pleased to see the boy enjoying his fish and chips like a little gentleman and seeming to ignore the scene being played out by his parents.

"No, of course not, and nobody's placating you," Ruth said. Given the contrast between her husband and her son, she found it difficult to keep a smile from the corners of her mouth. Harold shook his head at his wife and sighed.

"Dad, why don't you tell one of the newspaper reporters about the Red Cross?"

After a moment's hesitation, Harold's expression brightened. "Now there's an excellent idea, Geoff," he said. "I'll go one better. I'll write a letter to the *Toronto Star* about this curious Red Cross policy. Thank you, son." He leaned over and helped himself to a French fry. "Yes, sir, a very good idea."

Oberleutnant Lemp

SIX HOURS HAD passed since the English destroyers began bombarding *U-30*. The boat had descended to one hundred forty meters where Lemp had decided to wait out the attack while maintaining absolute silence. They had taken a hellish pounding, but the men had managed to quietly stop most of the leaks except those in the stern, and to mount a bucket brigade to move water to the bilges amidships to keep the boat level.

For the past hour, there had been no more explosions. The air inside *U-30* was stale and smelled of sweat, oil, and urine. Adding to the unpleasant conditions, moisture from the crew's breath condensed on the boat's cold metal surfaces and made everything clammy to the touch.

Lemp stood poised outside the listening station next to the radio room and watched radioman Georg Högel manipulate the directional listening device, hoping to pick any sounds of activity on the surface above them.

"Are you getting anything?"

Högel shook his head.

"You think they are waiting for us?"

"I don't know, sir. There's been no activity since they dropped the last salvo."

Lemp looked into the control room and signaled to First Watch Officer Hinsch and the chief engineer that he wanted to talk.

"How are the men holding up?" he asked Hinsch when they gathered in the alcove that served as Lemp's quarters.

"Well enough, I think."

"Good. And the leaks in the propeller shaft packings?" he asked Meckbach.

"The water is still coming in," the chief said. "There isn't much we can do until we get to port." Lemp nodded and considered his options.

"We have six hours before sunrise. Either we surface now and use the dark to escape or stay down another twenty hours until the sun goes down again. If we go now, the English will probably be waiting for us up top. If we wait, who knows? They could still be there." Even as he summarized their situation, the thought of remaining inactive for another day made him anxious.

"Chief, take us up to periscope depth. I want to have a look around. Take your time and be as quiet as possible. Number one," he said, turning to Hinsch, "pass the word we are still running silent."

When *U-30* finally reached the appointed depth, Lemp raised the wide-angle periscope and slowly swept the horizon all the way around looking for the running lights of any ships. He made two complete circles before he stepped back and retracted the scope.

"Prepare to surface," he ordered.

Moments later, the familiar rocking motion told Lemp they were on the surface. He scrambled up the ladder, opened the hatch, and climbed out into the black night, filling his lungs with fresh sea air. The watch crew climbed onto the bridge behind him, and First Watch Officer Hinsch followed. Clouds covered the moon, and the ocean rolled with large, wind-driven swells. If the English were waiting for them, he needed to know where they were before trying to make his escape. *U-30*'s portside diesel coughed to life.

A brilliant white spotlight stabbed the darkness a thousand meters off the starboard beam and began sweeping across the ocean.

"He's too far away to see us in these waves," Hinsch said.

"Let's hope he's the only one," Lemp said.

He waited several more minutes before finally relaxing when no more spotlights appeared. He called down to the control room to give the helmsman a course perpendicular to the spotlight's position.

Presenting the slimmest possible silhouette, *U-30* crept away into the darkness.

David Jennings

STANDING WITH HIS friend Tony Cassels in Glasgow's cavernous Central Station, David searched the departure board for the train about to leave for

Liverpool. He and Tony had come to say goodbye to several fellow Canadian *Athenia* survivors who were leaving for Liverpool to sail home tomorrow on the passenger ship *Duchess of Atholl*. David's name hadn't been on the travel manifest posted that morning at the Beresford Hotel where he was staying with Tony and John. Their names had been missing from the list as well. John reacted by going back to bed, but David chose to go for a long walk, have lunch, and see the train off in the early afternoon. Tony decided to join him.

The fact that they were not on the manifest also gave David and his friends a little more time to spend with the University of Michigan girls they had met on *Athenia*. Joan, Barbara, and Alberta managed to convince the American Consul in Galway to let them travel with the boys when all the Canadian survivors had moved to Glasgow three days ago.

"There it is," Tony said. "Platform eight." They hurried through the station and reached the train a few minutes before its scheduled departure. The first familiar face David saw was their former roommate, Alfie Snow, the one-armed "Mad Miner of Timmons." He was startled to see Alfie's right arm in a sling.

"Hello lads," Alfie beamed.

"What happened to you?" Tony asked.

"Can you believe it?" Alfie offered a tepid handshake with the fingertips that protruded from his cast. "Slipped on the wet pavement right after we arrived in Glasgow."

"That's terrible," David said.

"You haven't heard the worst of it. I'm drinking my pints through a straw now." The Mad Miner shuddered at the thought. "By the way, where's John? You boys are awfully casual, showing up here at the last minute. You almost missed the train."

"It's okay," David said. "We're not on the list, so we aren't going today. We just came to say goodbye."

"But you *are* on the list. They put up a second one with your names on it. Didn't you see it?"

"It must have been after we left," David said. Despite Alfie's revelation, David felt no misgivings. He was certain that he, Tony, and John would work out some arrangement to return home in the next several days.

A shrill whistle announced the train was ready to depart.

"You better get aboard," Alfie said. With the conductor's help, he climbed onto the bottom step in the doorway of the last passenger car.

"We're not packed," Tony explained

"And we can't leave John behind," David added. With a lurch, the train began moving slowly down the track. Alfie turned in the doorway and shouted over the rattle of the train cars.

"Suit yourselves, boys. See you in Canada."

☆ ☆ ☆

ENCOURAGED BY A recent break in the hot weather, David and Tony shouldered their gas mask boxes as they stepped out of the train station and started walking the mile back to the Beresford Hotel. Lost in thought about the fate of his relationship with Joan, David hardly noticed the street's stately blond sandstone buildings, dusted with decades of soot from Glasgow's industrial glory days.

"I suppose we'll be saying goodbye to our American friends fairly soon," Tony said as they waited for the traffic signal to cross Regent Street.

"I was thinking the same thing," David replied.

"What's happening with you and Joan?"

"I wish I knew," David said as the signal changed and they crossed the street. "We haven't talked much since that night in Galway when I agreed to give her some time to work things out."

"Sorry to hear that," Tony said. "I thought you two liked each other."

"I like her. But ever since we were rescued, she seems a little distant. She doesn't like talking about anything that happened after the ship was torpedoed." They reached Sauchiehall Street and turned to head for the hotel.

"I think she likes me, but I don't know for sure." David stopped in the middle of the sidewalk. "Part of me wants to get to know her better and part of me wonders if I should just walk away. I've never been so confused about a girl before."

Tony steered him to a nearby storefront out of the flow of pedestrian traffic.

"Davey, in my experience, not being able to make up your mind means you probably should take a pass. Do you want to get involved in a cross-border romance at this point in your life? You have a year to go for your degree and then what? Canada's at war now, in case you hadn't noticed. "

"Yes, but she's the most intriguing girl I've met in the last three years. She's smart and considerate and pretty. What if she's the one, and I don't say anything?"

"And what do you plan to say?"

"I don't know," David said, turning his palms skyward. "When the time comes, I'll think of something."

"That's reassuring," Tony said. He took a step closer and put his arm over David's shoulder. "Look, it's your decision. But hoping for inspiration doesn't strike me as a good strategy."

David smiled and nodded. "Thanks, maybe that's what I needed to hear."

When they walked into the Beresford's lobby minutes later, David saw John seated in a chocolate-brown leather chair. Three suitcases sat on the carpet between John and a sofa settee where Barbara and Alberta sat.

"Well, home at last," John said.

"Before you start," Tony interrupted, "we know they put our names on the list after we left. We went to the train station to see everyone off and Alfie told us."

"He also tried to get us to climb aboard," David said, "but we couldn't leave you behind."

"Although we did give it some serious consideration," Tony added.

"Very funny," John said.

"I'm sure there'll be another opportunity to sail for Canada," David said. Pointing to the suitcases, he asked, "What's all this?"

"It's all of our belongings," John said. "I packed our three cases and had them brought to the lobby on the chance you two might return in time for us to catch the train to Liverpool."

"What a friend," Tony said. "I'm sorry we weren't here."

"Now they're sorry," John said, looking at Barbara and Alberta. David noticed both girls trying to suppress smiles.

"Okay, what's going on?" he asked.

John sat back in his chair, wearing a lopsided grin. "It turns out we're not going to miss the ship," he said. "When it was obvious you two weren't going to make it back in time, I called the shipping office. They said if we could be in Liverpool by noon tomorrow, we would be okay. So I went to the consulate, and they issued me our ship and train tickets. We're leaving for Liverpool tonight at nine thirty."

John's revelation hit David like a splash of cold water. The moment he had hoped to put off for another day was suddenly at hand. He had only a few hours to decide what to do about Joan: talk to her about their relationship or keep her at arm's length? As his attention returned to the moment, David heard Tony speaking to Barbara and Alberta.

"I'm sorry, ladies. We talked you into coming with us to Glasgow, and now we're going to leave you behind."

"Oh, don't worry about that," Alberta said. "It's a big city, and there's a lot to keep us busy."

"We knew this wasn't going to last forever," Barbara said. "We've been lucky to stay together this long."

Sounding more in control than he felt, David suggested the six of them should enjoy a farewell dinner that evening. Everyone agreed, and he went to the hotel dining room to make arrangements while the others headed upstairs. On his way back through the lobby, he heard a familiar voice.

"David, do you have a minute?" Joan sat on the sofa settee and beckoned him over.

"Hello," he said, feeling quite unprepared for the moment.

"Come, join me," she said, patting the empty cushion on the settee. "Alberta told me you're going to Liverpool tonight, and we're planning a farewell dinner. I wanted to see you before then so I could apologize."

"You don't have to apologize," he said, sitting down next to her.

"I know I haven't been much fun lately," Joan said. "Ever since we talked that night in Galway, I thought about what you said. You know, about relaxing and enjoying all the attention."

"Maybe that wasn't the best advice."

"But then you sweetly gave me time to think all these things over. That's what I've been doing these past several days."

"Did you think about us?" David hoped he didn't sound anxious.

"Yes, and that's why I wanted to see you before we're all together." Her words gave him a sinking feeling. "I really care for you, David. You're sweet and very sincere. If only we'd met under different circumstances, with more time to get to know each other . . ." Joan's voice trailed off, but he knew she wasn't done.

"I realized I've never told you about my plans. After my senior year, I want to enroll for a masters in English at Michigan. After that I plan to teach. I don't really see myself moving to Canada."

"Gee, I—"

"I know I'm being presumptuous," Joan continued. "I'm not even sure how you feel about me. But with everything blowing up here in Europe, and now that Canada is in the war, the world seems a very uncertain place. What I'm saying is I think it's best if we don't get serious about each other."

David took a deep breath. He knew she was right, yet a part of him didn't want to let go. He realized Joan was waiting for a response.

"Just so you know how I feel, I think you're terrific—beautiful and smart and very sensible." Now it was his turn to pause, looking across the nearly deserted hotel lobby, hoping he was about to say the right thing.

"But I agree with you. This isn't the right time to start something so important." In the silence that followed, David tried to find something more hopeful between them.

"Maybe we could write each other," he finally said.

"Of course," she said, "and I promise to be more fun tonight."

Joan leaned over and kissed him on the cheek, catching David by surprise. They stood and smiled at each other for another awkward moment before she turned and headed toward the stairway. Though he felt they had made the right decision, David knew it would still be difficult to say goodbye.

☆ ☆ ☆

AFTER DINNER THAT night, they all crowded into a taxi with its masked headlights and rode slowly through a blacked-out city down to Central Station. They spent the half hour before the train's departure standing on the platform, reprising songs they had sung aboard *Knute Nelson*. When they concluded with "Auld Lang Syne," they laughed at the tears in their eyes.

The final call came for passengers to board the train, and David realized this would mean the end of their association. It had begun ten days earlier with a chance shipboard meeting on a sunny Sunday afternoon and continued through their shared experiences as "*Athenia* survivors." He understood now, despite the intensity of those experiences, they were not enough to provide the foundation for a lifelong relationship.

"I guess this really is it," he said, putting his arms around Joan's shoulders and pulling her toward him. "I wouldn't want to do it all again, but I will never forget you and all that we've been through together."

"Me neither." She looked up at him, tilting her head slightly, and their lips met in a long, sweet kiss. David surrendered completely to the moment, knowing it would never come again.

Barbara Cass-Beggs

FOR THE SECOND time in two weeks, Barbara stood at the railing of a passenger liner and watched Liverpool's iconic Royal Liver Building recede on the banks of the Mersey River as the ship headed out to the Irish Sea. This time, however, her three-year-old daughter, Rosemary, was not sailing with her and the name of the ship was *Duchess of York* instead of *Athenia*. And unlike two weeks ago, Barbara was leaving England with an anxious heart.

"I don't understand why we haven't heard a thing," she said to David, who stood with her at the railing, his arm around her waist. "That American ship reached Halifax two days ago. Why haven't they given us a list of everyone who disembarked? Even Mr. Fleming wasn't able to find out anything, and we've heard nothing from the Gibsons."

They had cabled Jim and Caroline Gibson, their friends in Ottawa, asking them to meet the American ship when it landed in Halifax and take charge of Rosemary. "It's not like Jim to ignore our request," she added. Along the Mersey River's northern shoreline, the city's office buildings gave way to low-lying wharves and warehouses.

"Fleming said priority was being given to wartime communication, and Canada joined the war last weekend," David pointed out.

"But Jim is with the foreign affairs office," she said. "You'd think he could send us a simple two-word cable saying, 'She's safe.'"

"Bar, we know she has to be safe in Canada," David insisted. "Even if Jim and Caroline weren't able to meet the ship, the Canadian authorities will take good care of her. You have to try to relax or you'll give yourself apoplexy."

"I know she must be safe," Barbara said. "I tell myself that a hundred times a day, but there's a little thread of uncertainty that always seems to unravel. It's so hard not knowing for certain."

"I'm afraid it'll be a week before we know anything for certain. I hope you can last that long."

"Don't worry, dear," she said, looking up at him and slipping her arm around his waist. "You won't have to nurse me across the Atlantic. I may be small, but I'm tougher than I look."

"Don't I know that," he declared. David leaned over and kissed her forehead.

"Not so fast," she said and pulled his lapel toward her with her free hand. "At a time like this, I need a proper kiss." In the warmth of David's familiar embrace, she told herself again that Rosemary was safe with friends in Canada.

They watched *Duchess of York* slowly overtake another liner, *Duchess of Atholl*, which had been waiting at anchor beyond the mouth of the river. Dull gray paint covered every inch of both ships, helping them blend in with the horizon, and both sported a large deck gun mounted on their raised after-decks. Two Royal Navy destroyers took up positions on either side of the liners as they formed a small convoy of four ships heading north into the Irish Sea.

Unlike their departure two weeks ago, Barbara noted, they would not be so vulnerable a target for the U-boats.

Spirydon Kucharczuk

SPIRYDON SAT ON the edge of the bed in his Glasgow hotel room trying to understand what Mykola Zelenko, the Red Cross worker, had just said to him. Instead, Spirydon began to notice several vivid details in the small room: the six drawers of the brown wooden dresser, with a broken knob on the lower right-hand drawer; the white porcelain basin sitting atop the dresser; the half-drawn window shade, the color of honey in the morning sun; the lilac floral pattern repeated on the room's faded wallpaper; his son Jan looking at him with a worried expression from beyond the room's second bed. What was it that Mykola had just told him?

The American freighter, *City of Flint,* had arrived four days ago in Halifax on September thirteenth. The final list of disembarking survivors did not include the names of the missing Kucharczuk family members. He had not given up hope then because *City of Flint* had sailed from Halifax with six *Athenia* survivors still aboard. Yesterday, the ship had arrived in New York City and all remaining passengers went ashore. This morning, Mykola had come to tell him that Ewdokia, Stefan, Aleksandra, and little Jakeb had not been on the ship.

The awful words came back to him. His wife and three youngest children were now presumed dead.

"But it is not official that they are dead," Spirydon suddenly protested. He felt weak and short of breath. As long as there was a rescue ship at sea, he had told himself, they might be on it. Now that the last ship had landed, he was unable to let go of his hope.

"Another ship might have picked them up," he protested. "It could still be at sea. Or maybe it has gone to some village in Norway or somewhere where there is no telegraph."

"Papa, don't do this to yourself," Jan said. "I don't want to believe it any more than you, but you have to be realistic."

"Why? Why do I have to be realistic?" Spirydon shouted. "They can't be dead. They can't . . ." His words dissolved into sobs as he rocked back and forth on the bed. Tears streamed down his cheeks, the pent-up fears of nearly two weeks pouring forth. He could not stop, not even when Jan sat next to him with his arm around Spirydon's shoulder. He cried until he was totally spent.

When Spirydon finally looked up, Jan sat next to him and Mykola stood at the foot of the bed. Both men had tears in their eyes. Now, for the first time, Spirydon realized he would have to face the future without his wife of two decades and without seeing his three youngest children grow into adulthood. Some part of him was missing, and he felt certain it could never be recovered. He would wake up every morning to that realization for the rest of his life. And yet, here was Jan, seated next to him. His daughter, Neonela, soon would be out of the hospital. They would be a family for a little while longer, he thought, but both his children would build lives of their own soon enough. What would become of him then? Spirydon felt tired and confused. How would he go on?

"Should we go to Canada?" he asked Jan.

"Yes, Papa, we should go. There is nothing for us here, and we can't go back to Poland. Besides, we have family in Canada."

"I don't know if I am strong enough to continue."

"You must continue. We need you."

Jan's words cut through Spirydon's despair. He was needed. He could not think only of himself. Even if his life was over, Jan and Neonela would need his help to establish themselves in a new country.

"I'm sorry, son." He looked at Jan and shook his head. "I am a selfish old man, not thinking of the family I have left. You're right. We must go to Canada."

"We should go tell Nela, Papa."

☆ ☆ ☆

SPIRYDON AND JAN found Neonela propped up against three pillows as she sat in bed glancing at a magazine in her lap. Sunshine spilled into the first-floor ward through the tall windows of Glasgow's Western Infirmary. Neonela's dark eyes brightened, and she smiled when she saw her father and oldest brother walking toward her. Spirydon saw her expression change to one of concern and realized she must be reading the emotions he could not keep from his face.

He and Jan pulled up chairs next to her bed, and Spirydon asked how she was feeling.

"Much better, Papa," she said, glancing at Jan. "What's happened?"

There was no delaying the dreaded news any longer.

"My darling, I'm so sorry to tell you this," Spirydon said. "Your mother, and Jakeb, and Stefan, and Leksi are . . ." He paused. "They are with God. They did not survive the accident."

Neonela absorbed the news in silence. She looked down and Jan reached over to take her hand.

"After all this time, I knew this was coming," she said quietly, without looking up. "I've thought about it a lot. I didn't tell you this, Papa, but Leksi was sitting on my lap when it happened. The boat jumped out of the water, and I grabbed for the railing to keep from falling. Then I was under the water. Everything was black. I realized I didn't have Leksi anymore. She was in my arms when the boat jumped and I let go of her. If I hadn't let go . . ."

Neonela shut her eyes. Tears slid down her cheeks and fell into her lap where Jan held her hand. Through his own tears, Spirydon watched his son and daughter comfort each other.

Oh, Ewdokia, help me find a way to be strong, like you.

SEPTEMBER 19–27, 1939

Oberleutnant Lemp

FROM THE BACK seat of the black German consulate sedan, Lemp spotted his chief engineer and first watch officer conferring on the dock next to *U-30*'s gangway. He jumped from the car as it came to a stop next to his submarine's berth, eager to hear their damage assessment. *U-30* had limped into Reykjavik, Iceland, only a few hours earlier, five days after the attack by the Royal Navy destroyers. A neutral country, Iceland provided a refuge for his crew to make temporary repairs to the boat. If he stayed in port too long, however, he risked being trapped by the British.

"How bad is it?" Lemp asked, responding to the salutes from both men.

"Number three torpedo tube is unusable," *Oberleutnant* Hinsch said without any preamble. He glanced at a small notepad and continued his report. "The diving tank is damaged, but we can submerge. There is seawater in the lubricating oil, and we haven't found its source. Water is leaking into the stern torpedo tube and the exhaust valve, but we can manage it. And, of course, the navigation systems cannot be fixed."

"We can use the stars," Lemp said. "Chief, what about the propeller shaft leaks?"

"Sir, we'll have the leaks stopped by this evening," Chief Engineer Meckbach said.

"That's good. It could have been worse," Lemp observed. "At least we can get home."

"It will probably take us a week," Hinsch observed. "Sir, were you able to make arrangements for Schmidt?"

"The council is organizing an ambulance to take him to the hospital. I'm going to tell him the good news right now."

"Too bad we can't find a hospital for our boat."

Lemp smiled at the thought. "Repair what you can. Work through the night if you have to, but I want to be out of here before sunrise tomorrow."

☆ ☆ ☆

"I NEED TO talk to Schmidt alone," Lemp told the small group of men gathered in *U-30*'s petty officers' quarters just aft of the boat's control room. The wounded sailor lay in a lower bunk, his right arm heavily bandaged from the shoulder to the elbow. Schmidt looked uncomfortable and pale from loss of blood, but he was awake and appeared alert. Lemp sat down next to him and waited until all the men left before he spoke.

"Good news, Schmidt. You're going ashore to the hospital where they can give you proper medical attention."

"Sir, will I be back in time to leave with you?" The sailor's voice was weak and breathy.

"I'm afraid not. We leave tomorrow morning at first light."

"But I want to stay with my crewmates."

Lemp nodded his understanding. "I know, but the boat is heavily damaged, and it will take a week or more for us to return to Wilhelmshaven, if we make it at all. We can't manage your loss of blood for that long. Besides, there's the risk of infection. You will stay here in Iceland. That's an order." Lemp saw the disappointment in the young man's eyes.

"Now, I have one more requirement for you," Lemp said. He pulled a single sheet of paper from his shirt pocket and unfolded it. "This is a declaration under oath. I'll read it to you, and you will sign it." He tilted the paper to better capture the light and began reading.

"I, the undersigned, swear hereby that I shall keep secret all happenings of third September, 1939, on board the *U-30* from either friend or foe and that I shall erase from my memory all happenings of this day." Lemp handed a pencil to Schmidt, placed the paper on top of a book, and held it steady in front of the young man.

"Sir, I'm right-handed."

"Do the best you can."

Schmidt scribbled his signature with his left hand, and Lemp refolded the paper and put it in his pocket. He sat for a moment, holding Schmidt's gaze with his own cold-eyed stare before nodding and patting the young sailor on his knee.

"This will be our secret," Lemp said.

Judith Evelyn

TWO WEEKS AFTER arriving back in Glasgow, Scotland, Judith stood in a dockside crowd with her one-time fiancé, Andrew Allan, slowly shuffling up the gangway to board the American passenger liner *Orizaba*. Although the ship had been chartered to bring *Athenia*'s American survivors home, space became available for others when several Americans decided not to go because the ship was sailing without naval escort. To strengthen her case for accommodations, Judith had emphasized her birth in South Dakota, and to help assure Andrew's passage, they decided to pose as a married couple.

Coming aboard under such pretenses normally wouldn't have bothered Judith, especially as several of their countrymen were boarding with no more connection to America other than Canada's proximity. Nor would they be sleeping together; men and women were to be separated aboard *Orizaba* in order to maximize space. Yet she felt guilty walking hand in hand with Andrew because she no longer saw a future in which she could be married to her former lover. Judith fretted about finding the right opportunity to tell him, particularly while he grieved for his father, whose death was now official.

"What do you think of a book?" Andrew asked as they stepped onto the *Orizaba*'s promenade deck.

"What do you mean?"

"A book," he said. "I'm thinking of putting a collection of Dad's radio talks into a memorial volume to honor him."

"That's a wonderful idea."

"Good, that settles it. I have most of his scripts from the last few years. Perhaps you could help me edit them while you decide what you're going to do."

Was this the right time, Judith wondered? With so many people streaming on board, it wasn't the quiet, private moment she imagined. Yet Andrew had extended an invitation and he was waiting for a response.

"Actually, I've been thinking a lot about my career lately."

"Good. It's time you started thinking of the future."

"Yes, but I'm not sure you're going to like my decision."

"Oh?" Andrew stopped walking and turned to her with an appraising eye.

"After I go home and see Mother," Judith said, "I'm going back to New York to look for work on any stage that will hire me."

"You'll be starting over," he said. "It would be easier to reestablish yourself in Toronto. I'll be there, and we both have connections in the theater that could help you."

She shook her head. "Toronto is a step back from London. I want to move forward. I know I'll be starting over in New York, but after London I feel certain I can do it."

"New York's hard on actors. I'd hate to see you come back home with your tail between your legs."

Andrew's lack of faith in her talent wounded her, but his words stiffened her resolve to succeed.

"Don't worry about me," she said. "Nothing I ever face will be as terrifying as clinging to the hull of that lifeboat in the middle of the ocean."

Andrew placed his hands on the railing and watched the passengers coming up the gangway. "So it's you in New York and me in Toronto," he said. "That's not likely to help a long-term relationship, is it?"

"No, it's not," she said. The words felt liberating.

"I gather you've come to terms with it, then?"

Judith nodded. "And you?" she asked.

Andrew took a moment before responding. "I suppose I have. Putting our professional lives together inevitably would require one of us to sacrifice. I couldn't ask that of you, and I wouldn't want you to ask it of me. So there you are."

"You're not bitter?"

He leaned his elbows on the railing and appeared to weigh her question carefully. Judith appreciated the performance, but she believed he had long since insulated his emotions in preparation for this moment. When he finally spoke, she was surprised the wistful note in his voice sounded so convincing.

"I'm more sad than anything. Like coming to the end of a good novel and realizing there are no more chapters to be read." He smiled at her. "But it was a wonderful story while it lasted. Truly, I wish you all the success in the world."

Judith was pleased his comments did not trigger any doubts in her mind.

"Thank you," she said. "That's what I hoped to hear."

It seemed ages ago when she and Reverend Allan spoke at breakfast aboard *Athenia*. Judith wondered if the good reverend had known all along what she finally would discover in her heart. She smiled at the thought and felt certain she had made the right decision.

Barbara Cass-Beggs

BARBARA COULD BARELY contain her anticipation. She and David watched the rural Ontario landscape give way to neighborhoods and then to crowded city streets as their train slowly covered the last several miles into downtown Ottawa's Union Station. In a few more minutes, she would be holding their three-year-old daughter for the first time in three weeks.

Two days earlier, Barbara had been unable to shake her worst fears. The Cass-Beggses arrived in Quebec City without knowing whether Rosemary had been met by their friends Jim and Caroline Gibson when the child arrived in Canada. Unable to find an available public phone in the dockside terminal, they had jumped in a taxi and headed for the main Bell Telephone office. Barbara was in no state to admire the old stone buildings and picturesque charm of the city as the taxi sped along, particularly as they were driving on the opposite side of the road. When they finally secured a phone, David had made the call.

"Jim, it's David Cass-Beggs." Barbara ached for any clue in her husband's expression. "No, we're in Quebec . . . listen, we're beside ourselves. We've received no word. Is Rosemary with you?"

David listened for a moment, then turned to Barbara with a wide smile.

"They have her."

Barbara had nearly fainted with relief. The specter of her worst fear loosened its grip on her heart and vanished. Rosemary was with Caroline and Jim and nothing else mattered.

☆ ☆ ☆

BARBARA AND DAVID hurried off the train as soon as it came to a stop in Union Station. They walked quickly past meandering passengers toward the main terminal, looking for Jim's or Caroline's familiar face in the milling crowd. Barbara spotted Jim first and waved as she and David moved in his direction. Caroline was walking next to Jim and there, hand-in-hand between the two of them, was Rosemary, wearing a blue dress and looking curiously at the people walking past them. When she saw Barbara, her face lit up.

"*Mummy!*" she shrieked and ran the last several steps into Barbara's arms.

"Darling, you look wonderful in your pretty blue dress," Barbara said as she knelt to welcome Rosemary's embrace and kiss her cheeks. Feeling her daughter's little body in her arms once again filled Barbara with a host of memories, and she felt tears welling up in her eyes. She heard David thanking the Gibsons for taking care of Rosemary.

"Mummy, why are you crying?"

"Because I'm so happy to see you at last," Barbara answered. Rosemary threw her arms around her mother's neck and hugged her again tightly. The smell of the little girl's hair, the smoothness of her skin, and sweetness of her kisses filled Barbara with a determination that she would never again leave her daughter. When Barbara finally stood, David lifted Rosemary into his arms and kissed her.

"Oh, how we missed you, sweetheart," he told his daughter.

"I missed you, too, Daddy." Even as she said it, however, Rosemary twisted her body to get a better view of Barbara, who was talking to Caroline. Clearly, she was more interested in her mummy, and David reluctantly put her down again. Within minutes, Rosemary was walking with her parents, regaling them with her adventures as they all headed for the exit.

"Auntie Davidson stayed with me on the big ship," Rosemary told them. "She was so nice to me, and brushed my hair and gave me clothes because I only had my pajamas. And we had a party for all the children. There was a big cake, and they made cookies, too. And I sang 'Daisy, Daisy.' And guess what? A nice man met us when we came to Canada, and he had another Panthy for me."

When at last Rosemary slowed down, Caroline explained that the woman Rosemary called Auntie Davidson had looked after their daughter on the rescue ships and stayed with her on the train to Montreal, where the Gibsons met her. Auntie Davidson had given Caroline a letter she wrote for Barbara, recounting everything that happened while she was caring for Rosemary. Barbara also learned from Caroline that the man the Gibsons asked to greet Rosemary in Halifax had, quite by coincidence, purchased a toy panda bear at a shop as gift to the little girl.

"Well," Caroline continued, "we learned from Auntie Davidson that Rosemary had lost her panda bear when the *Athenia* sank, and she talked about it quite a bit. Our friend couldn't have chosen a more appropriate gift."

"Quite amazing," Barbara said.

"Mummy!"

"Yes, what is it, Rosemary?"

"Did you have the bottom part of your pajamas in your lifeboat? Because I didn't!"

The earnest tone of the question made it clear Rosemary expected a serious answer.

"Oh, dear," Barbara said, struggling to keep from smiling. "I'm sure no one noticed you in the dark."

Oberleutnant Lemp

THE BAND MUSIC carried across the water as *U-30* slowly made its way toward the submarine docks at Wilhelmshaven, nearly five weeks after departing on her first war patrol. *Oberleutnant* Fritz-Julius Lemp watched from atop the submarine's conning tower as a small welcoming crowd came into view on the shore alongside *U-30*'s berth. The midmorning sunlight glinted off the band's brass instruments. Several young women in traditional-print dresses stood in the crowd holding bouquets of flowers. In front of the assembly at the head of the gangway, with his arms folded across his chest, was the unmistakable ramrod figure of *Kommodore* Karl Dönitz, the U-boat fleet commander. Facing Dönitz would be the final trial of his star-crossed war patrol.

At the top of the gangway, Lemp gave a stiff-armed Nazi salute to his commander and accepted a bouquet and a kiss from a pretty young girl. As a few members of his crew began coming ashore to the accompaniment of band music and the crowd's applause, Lemp asked Dönitz if they could meet in private.

On the way to a nearby building, Dönitz asked him about *U-30*'s return trip, and Lemp was glad to focus for the moment on the details of their harrowing voyage home from Reykjavik.

"We had heavy seas all the way back home," Lemp said. "Our navigation instruments were knocked out during the English attack, and after we left Iceland, our radio detection finder stopped working. Then we lost our echo-sounding equipment and finally the portside diesel engine failed. But we were able to navigate by the stars and only had to dive twice to avoid English aircraft."

They reached the building and stepped into a small room just off the entryway, where Lemp finally addressed his most burdensome action.

"Sir, I believe I sank *Athenia*."

Dönitz's dark eyes bored into Lemp, and the young captain knew there was no way around his responsibility for attacking the passenger ship. He had resigned himself to a court martial and the likely end of his career. For the moment, however, Dönitz's look of disapproval hurt worse than any possible trial verdict.

"I suspected *U-30*," Dönitz said, "but in the absence of any communication from you, I kept my suspicions to myself. How in God's name could you have made such a mistake?"

"It was dusk, sir, difficult to see. *Athenia* was sailing an evasive course, and she was blacked out. I thought she was an armed merchant cruiser. When I came to the surface after it was dark, I discovered she was a passenger ship. We left immediately, and I decided to maintain radio silence."

"That was your second mistake," Dönitz said. "*Athenia* was sending a distress call, so you wouldn't have given away your position if you'd reported, and we wouldn't have been surprised by the news the next morning. But without any word from you, I told Admiral Raeder none of our boats had reported an attack at those coordinates. He told the *Führer* and our government has been denying any responsibility for the past three weeks."

"I apologize, sir."

"There is more. Herr Goebbels blames Churchill, says he planted a bomb on *Athenia* to sink the ship, kill Americans, and bring America into the war on the side of the English. Nobody believes this fantasy, but Goebbels won't let up. Do you see what an embarrassment you have caused our National Socialist government?"

Lemp had chosen not to think of this reckoning for the past three weeks. Now that it was here, he decided to attack the moment as aggressively as he would an enemy ship.

"Sir, I take full responsibility for my actions. I did what I thought was right at the time. I should have made a positive identification, and I did not. I offer no excuses."

Dönitz leaned on the side of a small desk, folded his arms, and stared at the floor. The ensuing silence grew increasingly awkward for Lemp, until Dönitz finally looked up at him.

"This afternoon, you are going to fly to Berlin and tell your story to the High Command. I suggest you get your facts in order and don't leave anything out. You can say that on my orders you were concerned about armed merchant cruisers, but the decision to fire on the passenger ship was yours alone. Do you understand?"

"Yes, sir." Lemp knew his naval career would depend on the next twenty-four hours, but he sensed the *Kommodore*'s tone had moderated, and that gave him some hope.

"Before you leave, I want you to call your crew together and tell them to keep your attack on *Athenia* confidential for now. They must tell no one . . . *no one*. Is that clear?"

"Very clear, sir. I informed the crew when we left Reykjavik and swore them to secrecy. And when I put my wounded crewman ashore in Iceland, he signed an oath before he left the boat that he would not reveal to anyone what happened September third."

Dönitz's dark eyes once again skewered Lemp.

"And where is this signed oath?"

"In my safe, aboard *U-30*."

"Keep it there. I hope to God you put nothing in writing when you talked to your crew."

"No, sir."

Dönitz straightened and walked to the room's single window with its view of the dock where *U-30* was being secured after its long voyage. He stood looking out the window with his hands clasped behind his back. When he spoke again, the brittle tone of command was missing.

"I don't have enough boats to strangle the English. Abandoning the protocol and going back to unrestricted warfare is the only course that makes any sense." He turned away from the window, once again fixing Lemp in his hawk-like gaze.

"I was aware of your seamanship and bravery when you took command of *U-30*. The Reich needs men with these qualities. It would be a shame to lose you because of one rash act."

"Yes, sir." Lemp shifted uncomfortably.

"A curious situation, is it not? Your blunder creates the opportunity for our U-boats to strike real fear in the hearts of the English. But we are too concerned about the Americans to seize the initiative. God help us."

MAY 9, 1941

Chief Officer Copland

AS THE SUN neared its zenith in a cloudless sky over the North Atlantic, Chief Officer Barnett Copland tapped a cigarette from this pack of Woodbines and lit it with a match artfully cupped in his hands. He rested his forearms on the portside railing of the Donaldson Line freighter *Esmond*, one of forty cargo ships and tankers that made up a westbound convoy headed for Sydney, Nova Scotia. With the decline of passenger traffic, Copland now worked exclusively on cargo ships.

His latest watch had ended nearly four hours earlier, and he had spent the morning conducting firefighting exercises with the ship's deck crew. Taking time to relax before the midday meal, Copland drew on his cigarette and exhaled a thin wisp of gray smoke. Although lookouts stood watch in the fore and aft crow's nests and more than a dozen Royal Navy escorts patrolled the convoy's perimeter, he watched the distant whitecaps for the feathery track of a periscope. Two nights earlier, a submarine had sunk two ships in the convoy, raising unpleasant memories of his ordeal on *Athenia* nearly two years ago.

"Looking for U-boats, Mr. Copland?" Second Officer Jimmy Turnbull joined Copland at the railing, his watch due to start in half an hour.

"Force of habit," Copland responded. "Good morning, Mr. Turnbull."

"Now our air cover is gone, do you think Jerry will hit us in the daytime?"

"The Germans certainly know our location," Copland observed. "And with a full moon, it probably doesn't make a difference whether they attack day or night."

Copland and Jimmy were sailing together for the first time since the young man's turn as a cadet aboard *Athenia*. Jimmy's slender frame had filled out somewhat during the ensuing twenty months, but his red hair still seemed to defy the comb and brush. Copland was glad to see the young man had applied himself and advanced quickly to the rank of second officer.

"Smoke?" Copland offered a cigarette from his half-used pack.

"Thank you, sir, but I don't smoke."

"Good for you," Copland said. "Although I don't know how you'll get through convoy duty without some sort of crutch." He glanced at the Woodbine in his hand. "This seems more harmless than whiskey, I suppose."

"I don't drink either."

"Good lord, Mr. Turnbull. If I'd known you had no vices when you were a cadet, I wouldn't have given you such a glowing evaluation."

"Now I'm an officer, I expect it's safe to let you in on one last secret."

"I'm afraid to ask."

"This time next month, I'll be a married man."

Copland looked down, made a show of examining his fingernails, and let out a long sigh. "You didn't listen to a thing I said, did you?"

"I took most of it to heart, sir."

"You'll both regret it every time you ship out, but I suppose your homecomings will be warmer than mine." He clapped Jimmy on the shoulder and shook his hand. "Congratulations."

They grew silent, looking out at the array of ships stretching toward the horizon. *Esmond* sailed in the northernmost of the convoy's five parallel lines of ships. The five rows spanned more than two miles of the ocean's surface.

"It's quite a sight, isn't it?" Copland took a long pull on his cigarette.

"Yes, sir. Seeing all these ships together, it's hard to believe the U-boats have any hope of success."

"They're sinking our ships faster than we can build them. Unless our boys can turn the tables . . ." Copland fixed Jimmy in a sideways glance. "Much as it pains me to ask, have you thought about transferring to the fighting service? They're always looking for bright young officers."

"Thanks, but I doubt they'd take me on account of my hearing. I had a high fever when I was young, and it cost me almost all my hearing in my left ear."

"So you found another way to risk your neck for king and country."

"How about you, Mr. Copland? Have you thought of the Royal Navy?"

"It wouldn't be very practical for me. I'd be far down the navy's command structure. But here, I'm a promotion away from my own ship. The Merchant Navy needs good officers, too."

Jimmy glanced at the time and stood up from the rail. "I should be on my way."

"Your watch doesn't start for another twenty minutes." Copland also straightened and flicked the stub of his Woodbine over the railing.

"I want to walk the ship before I go on duty," Jimmy said. "It's a habit I picked up from an old officer when I was a cadet aboard *Athenia*."

"Now you're pressing your luck, laddie," Copland said, raising a hand as if to cuff the young officer on his ear. Jimmy backed away with a smile, then turned and headed toward the bow.

Kapitanleutnant Lemp

STANDING MOTIONLESS IN the control room of *U-110*, *Kapitanleutnant* Fritz-Julius Lemp listened to the high-speed propellers of the Royal Navy escorts pass over his submerged submarine and fade away. His U-boat moved quietly one hundred meters below the surface of the North Atlantic. After spotting the westbound convoy in the moonlight the night before, Lemp had rendezvoused with a second submarine to arrange a plan of attack, then taken up a position ahead of the convoy and waited to be overtaken. The fading sounds meant the lead escorts had not detected him.

A new, lower-pitched rumble began to penetrate the boat's hull from the slower-turning propellers of dozens of freighters and tankers in the approaching convoy.

"Sounds like better hunting this time around," Lemp said under his breath to his first watch officer, *Oberleutnant* Dietrich Loewe, who stood next to him in the control room. Loewe nodded and smiled. On Lemp's first combat patrol in *U-110*, he had failed to sink a single ship.

He would have preferred to attack at night, but a bright moon the next few nights precluded such a tactic and waiting for better conditions risked losing contact with the convoy. Lemp's plan called for attacking without delay, and as senior officer, he would strike first.

"Chief, bring us to periscope depth," he said softly. "All hands continue silent running." His order was repeated quietly up and down the boat.

Fifteen minutes later, *U-110* was in position twelve meters below the ocean's surface. Lemp had climbed into the boat's combat center inside the conning tower above the control room. He raised the attack periscope and made a quick survey to confirm his position and speed. Targets filled the surrounding horizon.

"Control room," he said softly, using the speaking tube, "steer heading two eight zero. All ahead two-thirds. Torpedo room, flood all tubes."

After waiting a minute for the boat to come to its new heading, Lemp raised and lowered the attack scope for another brief observation. "Open all forward tube doors," he called into the speaking tube. Moments later, confirmation came from *Oberleutnant* Loewe in the control room below that the doors were open and all four tubes were ready to fire.

Once again, Lemp raised and lowered the attack periscope in quick succession, deciding which four ships to target with his four torpedoes. Finally, he raised the scope and read off the data for the first three eels he would launch, calculating the distance, speed, and bow angle of the three ships he targeted, all approximately the same distance from his U-boat. His fourth target, a large oil tanker, was closer. Lemp planned to delay this fourth shot by several seconds so the detonations would be nearly simultaneous and prevent evasive maneuvers by the ships he targeted.

"Tubes one, two, and three, fire," Lemp said, toggling the firing lever and swiveling the scope to find his fourth target. The whoosh of compressed air bubbles signaled the eels were on their way. In the control room, Loewe confirmed all three torpedoes had been launched and began counting off five-second intervals.

Lemp waited twenty seconds. "Tube four, fire," he said, again pulling on the lever.

"Malfunction in tube four," Loewe called out. "The eel didn't launch."

"Damn it, man, get it fixed," Lemp called down to his first watch officer. "I want a shot at that tanker." He lowered the periscope to avoid detection. Thirty more seconds ticked off before the muffled boom of a distant explosion penetrated the boat's hull. A torpedo had found its target, announcing his presence. He could not afford to wait much longer at this depth.

Chief Officer Copland

ESMOND'S OFFICERS' MESS was a modest affair, a small room with a table fixed to the deck, four straight-back wooden chairs, and a sideboard. Two overhead light bulbs and a pair of portholes filled the room with a bright noonday glow as Copland and the ship's chief engineer sat down to eat. Copland had sailed twice before with the chief, an older man who had served as an engineer aboard cargo ships in the Great War. The table held two bowls of "mystery" stew, so called because the cook never revealed the contents of his stew. Mugs of steaming coffee and a plate of sliced bread rounded out the midday meal.

Copland stirred his spoon through the watery stew, having learned from experience to search for foreign objects before taking his first mouthful. The chief followed suit, and they ate the first few spoonfuls in silence.

"So tell me, Barty, are the rumors true?" Whether it was his seniority or his well-known aversion to ceremony, the chief preferred informality when addressing his fellow officers. The lone exception was the ship's captain.

"What rumors?"

"That the King awarded you the OBE for your actions when *Athenia* was sunk."

"Yes, it's true.

"Did you meet the King?"

"Sorry to disappoint you, Chief, but I was at sea when I got the word."

"I'm not disappointed. I never met an OBE before. What did you do to get it?"

Copland paused. It wasn't that he minded anyone knowing about his honor; he simply didn't want any fuss over it. "The truth is, I just did my job. I saw to it that all our lifeboats got away safely, but it helped that *Athenia* stayed afloat for so long. The next morning, I found out we'd left an unconscious woman aboard. So I want back with two other crewmembers, and we rescued the woman about twenty minutes before *Athenia* finally sank."

"Sounds like you were one lucky bastard."

"I'll drink to that." Copland saluted the chief with his coffee cup and took a sip. "It hasn't been two years since *Athenia* went down, but it seems like a lifetime ago. Looking back, I can't believe some of the chances I took inspecting the damage after the torpedo hit. I'm not sure I'd do it again if—"

A powerful blast ripped the air and sent *Esmond* reeling to starboard as if broadsided by a speeding locomotive. The blow knocked the chief off his chair and splashed coffee over the tabletop. Copland grabbed the table to brace himself as the ship rolled back to her port side, slowing to a stop with a pronounced tilt off center.

"You all right?"

"I think so," the chief said, climbing to his feet. "Goddamn Germans." He snatched his cap off the table and put it on, oblivious to its coffee stains

Copland stumbled to his feet. His mouth had gone dry and chills crept up his back.

This can't be happening again.

Fighting to regain his wits, Copland followed the chief. Outside on deck, he saw wisps of gray smoke and smelled the same acrid odor he had smelled aboard *Athenia* after she was torpedoed. Instinct told him to see if the ship could be saved, and he began moving in the direction of the explosion.

Kapitanleutnant Lemp

LESS THAN A minute after the mishap with tube four, Loewe relayed word from *U-110*'s forward torpedo room that tube four was ready to fire. Lemp raised the attack scope to find the tanker and recalculate his shot. When he swung the scope around in the tanker's direction, he saw the splashing bow wave of an enemy destroyer heading straight for him.

"Alarm!" Lemp shouted. "Prepare for depth charges."

He felt *U-110*'s bow begin to sink as he slid down the ladder into the control room. Seconds ticked by as the boat slowly responded. With the arrow on the depth gauge approaching forty meters, an explosion slammed the boat, rattling fixtures and causing the lights to flicker, but otherwise doing no serious damage as far as Lemp could tell. Before he could thank his luck for the Englishman's poor aim, the radioman called out from his listening post.

"More charges in the water . . ."

A series of deafening explosions shut out the world.

Chief Officer Copland

ESMOND WALLOWED IN the long intervals between the ocean's six-foot swells, her engines dead and listing to port. Copland saw no signs of a fire as he hurried aft along the debris-strewn main deck. Approaching the stern, he found water washing over the deck's planking. The torpedo had blown the cover off *Esmond*'s stern hatch, an eerie echo of *Athenia*'s damage. Short of breath, Copland staggered to a stop, his vision narrowed, his throat constricted.

The frantic shouts of women and children filled his ears. The air suddenly held the sickening odor of cooked flesh and the sour smell of burned hair. Twisted, blackened bodies lay scattered near a hatch opening and floated in its green water.

Copland gagged and vomited into the hold. He wiped his mouth with the back of his hand and stared at the seawater lapping several feet below the top of the hatch opening. The sensations faded and his mind cleared. As he watched, the sea continued slowly rising up the blackened sides of the hold. There was no question *Esmond*, like *Athenia*, was doomed, and he hurried back to the bridge to report his findings.

☆☆☆

FOLLOWING THE ALARM to abandon ship, Copland waited while crewmen brought the two portside lifeboats level with the deck. Still shaken by the vividness of his earlier memories, he worked to keep his focus on the tasks before him. When he took an informal survey of the men at his muster station, Copland realized someone was missing.

"Has anyone seen Mr. Turnbull?"

"I saw him on deck near the stern just before we were hit," one of the deckhands said. "Haven't seen him since."

"Anyone see Mr. Turnbull after we were torpedoed?" Copland called out. He felt a stab of anxiety when no one reported having seen the young officer. He wanted to make a quick search of the stern, but his duties called for putting his men into the lifeboats and seeing the boats safely launched. When he spotted the chief in his coffee-stained cap, he made a snap decision.

"Chief, are all your men accounted for?"

"Aye, the torpedo hit well astern of the engine room."

"Do me a favor. When the boat reaches the water, hold your falls for a few minutes. I'm going to make a quick inspection to be sure no one is left behind."

"She's leaning pretty far, Barty. You're cutting it awfully close again."

"I know. Just a few minutes, then pull away, whether I'm there or not. If you need to leave sooner, I'll understand."

"All right. And Barty," Chief said as Copland turned to go, "below decks is clear. My donkeyman checked our quarters."

Copland nodded and headed aft again, moving quickly and fighting for his balance on the sloping deck. He considered the possibilities. If Jimmy had been near the torpedo strike, the concussion might have knocked him out or blown him overboard. He scanned the ocean and noted bits of debris in the water, but nothing large enough to be a person.

Refocusing his efforts, Copland concentrated on the deck that remained above the advancing water. He looked behind pieces of equipment, next to the large ventilation cowls, around the far edges of the hatch opening, hoping to find Jimmy's inert figure. He stepped over a fallen boom next to the stern mast to search the starboard side of the ship, but found no sign of the young officer.

With time running out, Copland hesitated before started back toward the lifeboats, haunted by the specter of leaving Jimmy behind. Had he overlooked anything? Should he go back one more time to make sure? Looking forward, he saw the lifeboats had been launched and no one was left on deck. His hesitation threatened to take him down with the ship. The realization galvanized him, and Copland raced to the empty portside muster station. The sight of lifeboat 4 waiting in the water greeted him when he reached the railing. He grabbed the stern fall, slid down into the boat, and took command.

"Pull for all you're worth!" he shouted. "She's going under any minute." Within minutes, the men at the oars had pulled a quarter of a mile from *Esmond*, and Copland looked back to see her bow slowly lift skyward. When it reached halfway to perpendicular, muffled explosions announced the meeting of cold seawater with *Esmond*'s red-hot boilers. She began sliding backward into the sea, accompanied by the hiss of air forced up and out every opening in the ship above the water. A moment later, the bow disappeared, leaving only the same cauldron of bubbles in the sea that had marked *Athenia*'s demise.

Copland assessed their situation. A clear sky meant good visibility for their rescue, although the other ships in the convoy had taken evasive action and turned to the south in unison. Rescue would have to come from one of the Royal Navy ships—two destroyers and a corvette—dropping depth charges about a mile due south of their lifeboats.

"You men can stop rowing for now," he said. "We'll keep our distance until our lads finish their operation. I hope they're giving Jerry holy hell."

Kapitanleutant Lemp

A FOUL MIST hung in the air as Lemp picked himself up off the deck of *U-110*'s control room and tried to make sense of what had happened. He brushed his hand across his forehead, then noticed his fingers were smeared with blood. In the boat's dim emergency lighting, he saw the control room littered with shards of broken glass, chips of paint, fragments of piping insulation, and other debris. The glass of several gauges had cracked and broken.

Lemp noticed two of the wheels that controlled the flow of high-pressure air had been sheared off and lay on the deck. Loosened conduits looped down from overhead.

He called for a damage assessment and the chief engineer reported the electric motors were out—no propulsion. More reports were shouted into the control room. An aft fuel tank had ruptured. Seawater seeping into the boat's cracked batteries began generating chlorine gas below the forward torpedo room. Flooding in an aft compartment threatened to sink the boat if it could not be stopped.

"Good Christ," the chief muttered. "The diving planes and rudder are not responding."

Lemp began to register the extent of the catastrophe. A depth gauge read just beyond one hundred meters, but could it be trusted?

"Prepare for emergency blow," Lemp told the chief. Without propulsion or steering, this last desperate measure was his only chance to reach the surface and save his men. But before the chief could execute the blow, the boat began to rock. The motion could only mean *U-110* had somehow surfaced on its own. He rushed up the conning tower ladder and opened the hatch to a circle of blue sky.

Emerging onto the bridge, Lemp saw three enemy ships closing fast with every forward gun firing at him. One of the ships appeared headed directly at his boat. He knew the English often rammed U-boats to disable them, and realized his men would have no more than a minute to escape.

"All hands abandon ship!" he shouted down the ladder. "Hurry, they're going to ram us." A few bullets clanged against the side of the conning tower's armor plating. "Forget setting the charges. Chief, open all ballast vents," he yelled. "She's going down. Save yourselves."

As the men scrambled up the ladder and began jumping overboard, the firing from the English ships let up but did not stop entirely. Lemp counted each man, wanting to make sure everyone escaped. When the radio operator reached the top of the conning tower, Lemp noticed he did not have the Enigma encryption device used for all communications.

"Where's the Enigma machine?"

"In the radio room."

"Did you destroy it? What about the codebooks?"

"Sir, they said there was no time."

"Shit," Lemp said, anxious about leaving the device and its codebooks behind. But there was no question of going back for it with the tide of men still coming up. "Never mind," he said. "Go, go!"

When the forty-fourth man jumped into the water, Lemp knew the boat was empty. He told Loewe to vacate the bridge. Was there still time to return to the radio room? He looked over the side and saw the ocean was nearly a meter above the conning tower base. *U-110* was sinking and would take all her secrets with her. Satisfied he had done all he could, Lemp climbed over the side and jumped.

The icy water hit him like a slab of concrete, and for a moment Lemp thought his arms and legs might stop working. Treading water, he looked around and saw the heads of several other crewmen bobbing in the ocean. Nearby, Loewe flailed at the water but seemed able to keep his head up. Lemp located the three English warships. The smallest one, a corvette, appeared to be making a wide circle around them. The destroyer set to ram his boat had altered course, and the second ship had also veered off.

Glancing again at his boat, Lemp was shocked to see the bow and conning tower now above the water. *U-110* was not sinking. Did the chief open the valves? Could they have been damaged? He looked back to the nearest destroyer, which had slowed its approach. Fighting against the weight of his clothes, Lemp barely kept his head above water. His breath came in short gasps.

The destroyer had stopped within twenty meters of *U-110*'s bow. Several sailors in a small rubber boat paddled away from the ship. Lemp thought the boat looked too crowded to rescue very many of his men. With a start, he realized they weren't going to rescue anybody; they were going to board his boat.

Oh my God. If they find the Enigma machine and code books, all our operations will be compromised.

"Loewe," he called to his first watch officer in the water nearby, "we have to get back to our boat before the English. Come on." Lemp pulled his arms through the water in an attempt to swim toward *U-110*, but struggled in his wet clothes and heavy boots. He felt uncoordinated, detached from his body. His boat was drifting away from him.

"Come back, Goddamn it," he screamed at *U-110*, desperate to reach the boat and throw the Enigma device overboard. Frigid, salty water filled his mouth and nose as he slipped beneath a wave. He clawed his way back to the surface and saw the English sailors climbing aboard his boat. He was powerless to stop them now. With no chance to prevent the impending catastrophe, he understood only one action could atone for his colossal mistake.

I must go down with my boat. It is my duty . . .

Lemp stopped swimming. He clasped his hands over his head and kept them tightly clamped as he slipped under the water, down into the deep that would hide him one last time.

Chief Officer Copland

LIEUTENANT GORDON DUNBAR pulled a bottle of Macallan single malt from the drawer of the desk in his small quarters aboard the Royal Navy corvette H.M.S. *Aubretia.*

"I think you've earned this," Gordon said, pouring two fingers of the dark-amber scotch into a glass tumbler and handing it to Copland. "Cheers, my friend."

"Aren't you going to join me?"

"I'd love to, but I go on duty in half an hour."

Copland sipped, closed his eyes, and let the scotch warm its way down his throat and slowly radiate throughout his tired body. *Aubretia* had rescued forty-nine members of *Esmond*'s crew, and it turned out to be Copland's great good fortune that his friend and former Merchant Navy officer was now the executive officer of the corvette that had plucked them from the sea.

"I may not have earned this, but I certainly appreciate it," he said, lifting his glass in salute to Gordon. "You've done well for yourself, Lieutenant-Commander

Dunbar. An executive officer in less than two years since mobilizing. Very impressive."

"I'm still a lieutenant, Barty. No promotion yet. I owe my good fortune to all those old Lend-Lease destroyers from America. The Admiralty needed a lot of officers for those ships." Gordon sat on his bunk and indicated Copland should sit in the desk chair. "And what about you, Barty? I should think you'd have your own ship by now."

"We're losing too many. We seem to have more captains than ships." Copland took another sip and set his drink on the desk, careful not to let go of the glass with *Aubretia* rolling thirty degrees from starboard to port.

"Wish we could do a better job for you," Gordon said. "At least Hitler has one less sub to work with after today. Our boys picked up about thirty of the U-boat crew in the water. No sign of their captain, though."

"With any luck, Lucifer is welcoming him through the gates of hell about now."

"I'd drink to that," Gordon said, "if I weren't going on duty." In the silence that followed, Copland listened to the unfamiliar creaks and shudders of the corvette as she sailed through the North Atlantic's moderate seas.

"I was wondering, Barty, have you given any more thought to coming over to the Royal Navy?"

Copland swirled the scotch in the bottom of his glass. "Whenever it crosses my mind, I think, well, the Merchant Navy needs experienced men, too."

"For what it's worth, you have my admiration. My regular Royal Navy mates have no idea what it's like to go to sea in a slow, fat target that can't get out of its own way. For my money, you lads have it all over us in the bravery department, but don't tell any of my men I said so."

Copland lifted his glass in response to the compliment.

"In truth, Gordy, I think I'm completely drained in the bravery department. This war has turned me into an old man." He sat back in the chair and stared into the glass of liquor.

"Today, onboard *Esmond*, after she was hit, I went to check the extent of the damage. The next thing I knew, I was back on *Athenia*, seeing the burned bodies scattered over the deck and smelling the death. I don't know where it came from, but it made me sick, physically sick. I don't know how much longer I can do this."

"Every man has his limit, Barty. There's no shame in reaching it."

"I've been thinking a lot about what you said the last time we met before the war. You remember? You told me I was working too hard—not paying attention to the other parts of my life. You said there was no guarantee my life would turn out as I planned.

"It came back to me today because of our Second Officer Jimmy Turnbull. He's the only one of our crew who didn't make it. I trained him when he was a cadet on our last voyage in *Athenia*, but I hadn't sailed with him again until this crossing. He'd turned out to be a very capable young officer. Told me he was going to be married next month."

"That's rough."

"He just disappeared, Gordy. Gone off the face of the earth in an instant." Copland shook his head in disbelief. "How many more times can I survive a torpedo before my luck runs out? And if I die tomorrow, what would I have experienced beside the satisfaction of doing my job? Is that enough for a man's life? You were right. I should have asked these questions a long time ago."

The two men sat in silence while *Aubretia* continued her rhythmic conversation with the ocean's swells.

"Listen, I shouldn't tell you this," Gordon finally said, "but maybe it'll buck up your spirits to know your lad's sacrifice had a purpose. You've got to keep this under your hat, but our flagship put a boarding party on that U-boat we forced to the surface today. Without giving away any details, let me say our boys recovered some material that might help us save a lot of our convoys in the future."

"If only it would shorten this bloody war," Copland said. He swallowed the remainder of his scotch and set the glass on the desk.

"Thanks for the drink. Don't worry about me, Gordy. Maybe things will look a little brighter in the morning."

AFTERWORD

ATHENIA WAS THE first British ship sunk in World War II. Despite this distinction, few British citizens and even fewer Americans are aware of the ship and its place in history. This may be due to the relatively low casualty rate (ninety percent of the passengers and crew survived) and to the fact that the attack did not draw the United States into the war. Though the Nazis denied responsibility for the sinking throughout the war, hardly anyone outside of Germany doubted that a U-boat was the cause. Even so, it wasn't until the Nuremberg trials in 1946 that Grand Admiral Karl Dönitz admitted under oath that *U-30* had sunk *Athenia* seven years earlier.

Athenia sailed from Liverpool with 1,102 passengers and a crew of three hundred sixteen. Of these, ninety-three passengers and nineteen crew members died as a result of *U-30*'s attack. Passengers holding British passports (including Canadian citizens) accounted for fifty fatalities, followed by thirty Americans. Of the one hundred twelve people killed, seventy-six percent were women and children.

In spite of the loss of American lives, US public opinion remained strongly opposed to entering the war. However, the *Athenia* incident, coupled with other events in the weeks following (including *City of Flint*'s capture by the German Navy), served notice that the United States could not avoid being entangled in the war. These events gave President Franklin Roosevelt the support he needed to convince Congress to amend the American Neutrality Acts and allow the sale of arms to combatant nations. The new "cash and carry" policy permitted the combatants to pay cash for war materiel from the US and carry it home in their own ships, greatly benefiting the British cause.

☆ ☆ ☆

OTHER THAN FRITZ-JULIUS Lemp, the principal characters in *Without Warning* survived World War II and went on to lead lives of varying accomplishment and notoriety. Lemp's death, following his attack on the British freighter *Esmond*, became part of the seventy-five percent casualty rate suffered by the U-boat service, the highest such rate of all the German forces in World War II.

The *Athenia* story quickly faded from the headlines as the war grew in scope and intensity, leaving its survivors largely forgotten. Following are brief accounts of each of their lives following their rescue.

Barbara Cass-Beggs and her husband, David, remained in Canada until 1952, finding the country welcoming and less class-conscious than England. In 1941, Barbara gave birth to twins, Michael and Ruth. During the war years, Barbara organized music programs for employees at an aircraft factory, while David created control systems for a human centrifuge that aided in designing flight suits for Canada's fighter pilots. Barbara and David also became active in social democratic politics, volunteering their time and efforts to the Co-operative Commonwealth Federation (CCF) (now known as the New Democratic Party), the Canadian equivalent to Britain's Labour Party.

Barbara's love of music remained a central element of her life. After the war, she taught music and worked with youth as director of the University Settlement Music School in Toronto. During this period, she began collecting Canadian folksongs to use in her teaching. Meanwhile, David began consulting with the Saskatchewan Power Corporation (SPC) and the provincial CCF to study the feasibility of bringing electricity to farms in rural areas.

In 1952, the family returned to the British Isles for David to lead the electrical engineering department of a university in Wales. Three years later, the couple returned to Canada when the Saskatchewan government asked David to be general manager of the SPC. Not long after, the twins joined them in Regina, while their oldest daughter, Rosemary, began her university studies at Oxford, England, which culminated in a degree in philosophy and psychology.

Beginning in 1955, Barbara taught music at the Regina Conservatory for nine years and founded the Saskatchewan Junior Concert Society. She began writing down her teaching philosophy regarding music and young children. In 1969, she initiated music courses at Algonquin College, Ottawa, for teachers of preschool children. Her devotion to teaching musical awareness and development in very young children coalesced into a program Barbara called *Listen Like Learn*. She presented papers at conferences and started training programs that introduced her techniques to other cities in Canada, then internationally at conferences in Tel Aviv and Vienna. She published several books on her *Listen Like Learn* program and was widely recognized and honored for her innovative efforts.

David was subsequently hired to lead the state-owned power utilities in Manitoba and later British Columbia, before retiring in 1975. He died in 1986, leaving Barbara a widow after fifty-four years of marriage. She died in Ottawa four years later in September of 1990, at age eighty-five. Rosemary continues to live in England, and Ruth in Canada. Michael died in Canada in 2007.

Barnet Copland received the OBE (Most Excellent Order of the British Empire—Civilian Division) when the King's honors were announced in January 1940. The appointment cited Copland's leadership in safely evacuating *Athenia*'s passengers and his heroism in returning to the ship hours later to rescue Rose Griffin, who had been left aboard while unconscious in the ship's sick bay. (Sadly, Mrs. Griffin never regained consciousness and died a few days later in a Glasgow hospital.)

Two months after *Esmond* sank, Copland secured an appointment as a Clyde River pilot, where he worked until his retirement. In 1951, at age forty-three, he married Margaret Aitken Hogg, thirty-one, in Dundee, and they initially settled in the town of Gourock on the Firth of Clyde. The couple had no children.

Later in life, they moved to Milngavie, a town on the northern outskirts of Glasgow, where they lived quietly in retirement. In 1973, at age sixty-five, Copland died of a heart attack and neighbors were surprised to learn upon reading his obituary that he had been awarded an OBE for his heroism during *Athenia*'s sinking. Margaret passed away in 1992 in Kinghorn, a seaside resort on Scotland's east coast. She was seventy-three.

Ruth Etherington returned with her husband, Harold, and son, Geoff, to their home in Milwaukee following their rescue from *Athenia*. When the United States entered World War II in 1941, Ruth put her university studies in mathematics and chemistry to work as a hydraulic engineer for Allis-Chalmers Company, a position she resigned from on the day the war ended. She was an avid amateur photographer and artist and often found civic causes to support in the many communities in which the Etheringtons lived.

Ruth was a vivacious complement to her husband's important engineering career, which included pioneering work in nuclear energy. Harold Etherington helped to develop the US Navy's first nuclear submarine power plant and was instrumental in designing reactors for commercial nuclear power plants. He was a major contributor to, and editor of, the *Handbook for Nuclear Engineers,* an indispensable reference work. Seen as one of the fathers of nuclear power, he received the US Atomic Energy Commission's Gold Medal in 1974 for his contributions to the nation's nuclear energy program and was elected to the National Academy of Engineering in 1978.

Geoff, the Etheringtons' only child, earned a mechanical engineering degree from Purdue University, a master's degree in business administration from the Kellogg School at Northwestern University, a law degree from Loyola University of Chicago, and a medical degree from Yale University. He went on to found his own successful corporation, Etherington Industries, headquartered in Madison, Connecticut. The business acquires struggling companies and turns them into profitable enterprises to be resold or retained by the parent company.

Ruth died in 1994 at age ninety. Harold, ninety-four, died that same year. Geoff is retired but continues to own an aerospace machine shop. He and he and his wife, Marie, live in Connecticut and Florida.

Judith Evelyn moved to New York City in 1940 to pursue her acting career. She landed a featured role in *Angel Street*, which ran on Broadway from 1941 to 1944. Other successes followed, most notably leading roles in *Craig's Wife* in 1947 and two productions of *The Shrike*, in 1952 and 1953. From Broadway, Judith moved on to movies, receiving featured roles as Miss Lonelyhearts in Alfred Hitchcock's *Rear Window* and as Queen Taia in Darryl F. Zanuck's production of *The Egyptian*, both in 1954. In 1959 she appeared with Vincent Price in the horror film *The Tingler*. Throughout the 1950s and early 1960s, she appeared in numerous American television series. Judith was never seen as a star in movies or television, but she enjoyed steady work as a character actor in more than fifty productions.

Judith's friend, Andrew Allan, compiled a distinguished career as a pioneer producer and director of radio drama. He was the head of radio drama for the Canadian Broadcasting Corporation from 1943 to 1955. A prolific and talented writer as well, Andrew was credited with helping to develop a Canadian "voice" in North American drama. Andrew published a memorial volume of his father's radio talks, titled *Memories of Blinkbonnie*, in 1939.

Judith and Andrew remained friends. She never married and died at age fifty-eight in New York City. Andrew, who was married twice briefly, died in Toronto in 1974. He was sixty-seven.

David Jennings completed his senior year at the University of Toronto in 1940, earning his degree in engineering. He worked briefly as a quality control officer at a local de Havilland Aircraft Company plant before joining a Royal Canadian Navy officer-preparation course at the newly opened Royal Roads facility in Vancouver. While training at Royal Roads, David went on a blind double date with an officer at the school and the two agreed to switch dates in the middle of the evening. That is how David met Mary Helen Patricia Drexel, whom he married a few months later in February of 1942. Beginning in 1941, he served in the navy as an engineering officer aboard minesweepers, first accompanying convoys in the Pacific and later in the Atlantic. He retired as a lieutenant colonel at the end of the war in 1945.

When David came home after the war, his mother advised him that family obligations would mean he could never be his own man if he stayed in Toronto. David's wife, Mary, had roots in western Canada, so the young couple moved to Vancouver, BC. David worked as an engineer with companies that built boilers, before he and his partners established the Columbia Engineering Company, which focused on serving the forestry-related industries so prevalent in the west. He helped to develop control systems for the process used to make particle board. The firm was very successful and David traveled the world helping to establish particle board factories.

David and Mary were married thirty-eight years until her death in 1980 at age sixty. David died in 1995 at age seventy-seven. They had two children, Davidson and Deborah, both of whom live in British Columbia.

David's university friends who traveled with him in Great Britain, Tony Cassels and John Woods, also received their degrees from the University of Toronto. Tony earned a law degree and practiced in the Toronto area until his death at age sixty-four in 1981. David, Tony, and John apparently had no further contact with the three young women from the University of Michigan whom they met aboard *Athenia*. All three women married and went on to successful careers. Barbara Bradfield Taft earned a PhD in history from Bryn Mawr College in 1942 and had a long, successful career as a historian. She died in 2007. Joan Outhwaite Sillin received bachelor's and master's degrees in English from the University of Michigan, taught English, and was involved in community organizations in and around Greenwich, Connecticut. She died in 2010. Alberta Wood Allen graduated from the University of Michigan Phi Beta Kappa and was the first woman to graduate with honors in the history department. She was a beloved civic leader in her hometown of Louisville, Kentucky, and traced her commitment to community service to her experiences aboard *Athenia*. She died in 2011.

Spirydon Kucharczuk mourned the loss of his wife and three youngest children for the rest of his life, though he remarried several years later. In the immediate aftermath of the family's tragedy, Spirydon obtained new travel documents for him and his son and daughter. They boarded the steamship *Cameronia* in Glasgow later in 1939 and made their way to Canada. There they changed the spelling of their last name to Kucharchuk, dropping the *z*, and anglicized their first names: Spirydon to Steve, Jan to John, and Neonela to Nina. They spent the first winter in Whitemouth, Manitoba, living with Nikola and Julianna Zachary, Ewdokia's sister and brother-in-law, who had come to Canada a year earlier. That first year the Kucharchuks helped the Zacharys work their farm.

The next year, Steve traveled west to Alberta Province to stay with his stepbrother and look for suitable land for a farm. With loans from relatives and generous terms from the seller, Steve was able to buy a parcel of land that had been homesteaded in 1912. Slowly, over several years, they began to make the farm pay, but life wasn't easy. Money was always tight, and the Kucharchuks had to adjust to a new climate, new crops, new culture, and a new language.

Nina married in 1941 and had two children, but tragedy struck their family in 1946 when Nina's husband was killed in a truck accident. In January of 1948, Nina married Walter Chwedoruk, and their marriage lasted until his death in 1998.

John Kucharchuk worked the family's farm until 1946, when he purchased a sawmill that became the foundation of his successful business. When logging played out in one area, John moved the mill to another center of logging activity. In 1953, John married Sophie Kasianiuk and moved to Edmonton, where the couple had two children.

Steve also moved to Edmonton in 1953, sold his farm, and married Marie Hababa. He loved visiting his grandchildren and often helped out on Nina and Walter's farm. After Marie died in 1975, Steve lived alone until he became ill with cancer. Nina took him to her house, where he passed away in 1977. John died in 2008, and Nina died two years later.

Rhoda Thomas returned home to her family in Rochester, New York, and made good on her promise to buy an Electrolux vacuum cleaner to honor the company's owner, Axel Wenner-Gren, who rescued her along with three hundred seventy-five other survivors the morning after *Athenia* was torpedoed.

Following the war and the confirmation that a German U-boat was responsible for sinking *Athenia*, Rhoda, like many other American passengers, pursued a claim against the German government to recover compensation for the property she lost at sea, which she valued at nine hundred dollars. In order to pursue such reparations, Congress needed to establish a body to adjudicate claims against the German government. The process dragged on for many years, and in the end, neither Rhoda nor her family members received any compensation for her losses.

After Rhoda's husband, Frank, retired, the couple moved from Rochester to Southern California in the mid-1950s, where they lived near their daughter, Stella, son-in-law, Robert Sanger, and grandsons, Thomas and Richard. Rhoda died in September 1957 at age seventy-two. Her written account of her experiences related to the *Athenia* tragedy was the initial inspiration for *Without Warning*.

ACKNOWLEDGMENTS

I AM DEEPLY indebted to the many people who graciously shared their time, memories, and mementoes of the events that make up *Without Warning*. My greatest debt, however, is owed to my wife, Kay, who not only encouraged and supported me every step of the long journey to bring this book to fruition but also spent countless hours researching the story's details in archives and libraries and reading and critiquing every draft of the manuscript.

I was privileged to meet with five *Athenia* survivors who shared their personal insights of those long ago events: Rosemary Cass-Beggs Burstall, Geoffrey Etherington, Heather Donald Watts, Donald Wilcox, and Helen Rodman Wilson. Several descendants of the people featured in the book corresponded with me to provide family stories and details that greatly helped to bring their relatives to life. My deepest thanks to Donna Biscotti, Steffany Chwedoruk, Jonathan Copland, Davidson Jennings, Deborah Jennings, Ruth Valentine Kasianiuk, and Lisa Park for entrusting the memories of their loved ones to me.

Others assisted in researching, reading, and/or critiquing *Without Warning*. They include Steve Andres, Kristen Barrett, Linda Bernstein, Mark A. Clements, Robert M. Connell, Larry Hasswell, Emily Malcolm, George Malcolmson, Joan Mangan, Peter Monte, Silvie Prewo, Wilfried Prewo, Bob Skelton, Judy Skelton, Terry Snyder, Babette Sparr, and Richard Wolf. I am also indebted to Daniel H. Spiegelberg for translation services and to Barbra Drizin, Scott Gordon, and the wonderful people at Monkey C Media for helping to develop and maintain my presence on social media and the Internet.

Many excellent websites deal with the history of World War II, the exploits and lore of U-boats involved in the Battle of the Atlantic, and the operations of the world's merchant marine fleets. The most indispensable site for me, however, was "Ahoy—Mac's Web Log," which devotes a significant portion of its many pages to the *Athenia* tragedy. The site was started by the late Mackenzie J. Gregory, whose twenty-year career as an officer in the Royal Australian Navy began, like my book, at the start of World War II.

Finally, I also wish to offer my profound thanks to the men and women who work so anonymously in national archives and research libraries. These stewards of history were extremely helpful in locating valuable original accounts of the events depicted in this book. Among these institutions were the British Library, in London and Colindale, UK; British Maritime Museum Archive, Greenwich, UK; British National Archives, Kew, UK; Deutsches Marine Museum, Wilhelmshaven, Germany; Deutsches U-Boat Museum, Cruxhaven-Altenbruch, Germany; Glasgow Museum of Transport (located in the Riverside Museum), Glasgow, UK; Imperial War Museum Archive, London, UK; Metropolitan London Archives, London, UK; Mitchell Library, Glasgow, Scotland, UK; National Archives, College Park, Maryland; New York Public Library, New York City, New York; Royal Navy Submarine Museum Archive, Gosport, UK; and U-boat Museum U-995, Laboe, Germany.

ABOUT THE AUTHOR

THOMAS C. SANGER is a San Diego–based author who has written for a variety of publications and audiences during a thirty-year career in journalism and public relations. He worked as a reporter for the Associated Press and KABC radio in Los Angeles, researched and wrote television documentary scripts, and directed corporate communications for a major Southern California energy company. Sanger is the author of numerous articles and nonfiction books. *Without Warning* is his first novel.